THE BLACK LOTUS

FATAL FLORALS DUET
BOOK TWO

K. CARDELLA

Editing by Inked Edits Developmental
Cover Design & Interior Formatting by Disturbed Valkyrie Designs

SCENE - DO NOT CROSS · CRIME
SCENE - DO NOT CROSS · CRIME SCEN
CRIME SCENE - DO NOT CROSS · CRIME S

CONTENT WARNINGS

THIS BOOK IS AN ADULT ONLY DARK ROMANCE. THE CONTENT IS INTENDED FOR PEOPLE OVER THE AGE OF 18. THIS BOOK HAS CONTENT WARNINGS THAT ARE, BUT NOT LIMITED TO.

- Murder
- Knife Play
- Primal Play
- Blood Play
- Dub-Con
- Stalking
- Burning Alive
- Stabbing
- Talks of Forced Cannibalism
- Forced Autocannibalism
- Talks of Child Abuse
- Tattoo Play
- Use of Sex Toys
- Cutting up a Body
- Emotional Abuse
- Mental Torture
- Knife Violence
- Axe Violence
- Gun Violence
- Blowing up body parts
- Sword Violence

- Kidnapping
- Talks of rape, but not the actual act
- Talks of bathing in blood
- Mention of drinking blood
- Eye torture
- Penetration of inanimate object

CRIME SCENE - DO NOT CROSS

THE BLACK LOTUS

SPECIAL EDITION   *   Daily O...   ...RDELLA   10 APRIL 2025

A DARK ROMANCE

VOL. 10, NO. 5

EXCLUSIVE
EXCLUSIVE
EXCLUSIVE

In these quiet moments, you engage with your thoughts and emotions, gaining clarity on your true desires and values. Embracing solitude helps you recharge, enhances mental clarity, and fosters emotional well-being. This introspection nurtures personal growth and cultivates a more balanced and fulfilling life.

SOLITUDE   *   SOLITUDE

CRIME SCENE - DO

DO NOT CRO...

PLAYLIST

Lock Me Up - Marisa Maino
Animals - Nickelback
Mayday - Three Days Grace
Darkside - Neoni
Madhouse - Nessa Barrett
In Bed With A Psycho - Layto
Who's A Good Girl - Manic Kazzy
Sweet But Psycho - Ava Max
Monster - Layto
Paint The Town Red - Doja Cat
On Your Knees - Ex Habit
No Mercy - Austin Giorgio
Five4Three2One - Layto
Sleepwalker - The Pretty Wild
Button Eyes - The Pretty Wild
Crazy - Patsy Cline
If It Doesn't Hurt As Well - Nothing More
Fool and The Beggar - Melrose Avenue
The Things I Do For Love - Bludnymph
Tyrant - Dre Tamashi
Coming Home - Falling In Reverse

I'm Your Fool - Katie Hargrove
One For The Money - Escape The Fate
Stuck In Your Head - Iprevail
You Want A Battle? Here's A War - Bullet For My Valentine
Trigger Warning - Falling In Reverse
Retribution - Anna Pena
Him & I - Halsey
Lethal Woman - Dove Cameron
A Grave Mistake - Ice Nine Kills
Bad Things - Summer Kennedy

CRIME SCENE - DO NOT CROSS
CRIME SCENE - DO NOT
THE BLACK LOTUS
SPECIAL EDITION
Daily
ARDELLA
10 APRIL 2025
A DARK ROMANCE
VOL. 10, NO. 5
THE BLACK LOTUS
EXCLUSIVE
EXCLUSIVE
EXCLUSIVE
SOLITUDE
SOLITUDE
CRIME SCENE - DO
DO NOT CRO

This book is for the ones who cheer for the fictional serial killers to get their happily ever after.

SS. CRIME SCENE - DO NOT

THE BLACK LOTUS

EXCLUSIVE
EXCLUSIVE
EXCLUSIVE

SERENA

SOLITUDE

T. CROSS

CRIME

ONE
SERENA

It's been a month since Zephira came, and I moved into Aster's home. It's weird not falling asleep in my own bed, but he's made the transition feel like a breeze. *Like I'm right where I was always meant to be.* By his side. Sleeping and waking up next to him every day. Even though it's only been a few weeks, it feels like years; maybe because I've been dreaming of him for so long, obsessed with who he is secretly. I'm in love with the monster he hides from the world. I feel incredibly lucky I get to know the real *him.*

The last month has been a whirlwind, but Aster was there for me. With my world being completely turned upside down and my life changing in the blink of an eye, he made sure everything went smoothly. The move, getting me settled in, even giving me more than half of his closet for my clothes. The small gestures really made me forget the chaos around me and quieted my dark thoughts.

At first, I didn't know how to process the fact that his parents were alive, and some of the world's most notorious serial killers. The Patchwork Killers. That was a hard pill to swallow, but after I quickly got over that fact, I had a little fangirl moment.

What are the odds that not only did I fall in love with my

favorite serial killer of all time, but his parents are legends. The true crime junkie in me was ecstatic at that thought. But the more rational side, one that, let's be honest, isn't as mindful as it should be, was actually afraid. Was it just his mom, or did both of his parents want me dead? Will Aster truly protect me from the two people who raised him? Or will he choose them in the end and I once again become one of his little lambs? I shiver at that haunting thought, and try to shake off the unease of the unknown.

Aster has doubled all the security, upgraded his locks, and holds me close at night when we sleep, just so he knows I'm safe. It is honestly comforting having him protect me every night. Asters smell alone calms my nerves.

Aster has been teaching me everything he knows from fighting, to most importantly, not getting caught. He hasn't taught me how to dispose of a body properly yet, but that is something he said needs to be taught when it happens. I'm assuming that will be when we kill the first assassin, if they ever come that is.

I'm exhausted and my muscles ache from the amount of training Aster has me doing, waking up parts of my body I have neglected for so long. Drinking more coffee than I have ever consumed just to stay awake, but the stress of it all is slowly making me go more insane than I already am. *I still can't believe she views me being with her son as a threat.* She doesn't even know me, or what I'm capable of. But if she wants a fight, then a war is what she will receive. My teeth grate at the thought of her disturbing the life me and Aster are trying to create. If she thinks sending serial killers after me is going to extinguish my existence, then I'll show her that her son fell in love with the killer forged from nightmares.

Aster stands in front of me, shirtless, in the gray sweatpants he knows drive me wild. My eyes travel his body as he points to the newest suspect. We go over potential killers three times, to get them engraved in my brain. The way they kill, how they operate, what to do if either of us gets caught. This is the first lesson I'm hearing about this killer, but the way his abs constrict everytime he lifts his arm higher distracts me from his teachings, and I mindlessly bite my bottom lip, a quiet groan escaping me. The sound of the marker I hear, even in my sleep, stops.

"Serena," he warns, eyes never leaving the board. *He only calls me by my name when it's serious and not paying attention to the people who want me dead is a punishable offense.* My body heats at the thought. I reluctantly tear my gaze away meeting his heated stare, my breath catching in my throat.

I cross my arms, moving restlessly against the island countertop I'm sitting on, calming the heat rising in me. "It's not my fault you decided to look like a snack during our lessons knowing damn well I'm hungry." He turns to face me, and I look down at Asters growing erection, his appetite as evident as mine.

Aster smirks. "If you're a good girl and can tell me what you learned proving you were in fact paying attention, I might be inclined to… reward you. If you're bad, then I will tie your hands behind your naked back, stroke my cock inches from your face, and come all over your chest. Never letting you feel or taste what your greedy cunt craves."

My mouth clamps shut, a whimper falls from my throat, and I pull my legs underneath me. Aster's eyes dip to my chest, my cut up shirt distracting him from continuing. His throat bobs, body leaning towards mine before he tears his gaze from his favorite stress reliever. Reluctantly turning back to the board to finish the lesson.

He's currently tracking a female killer, who uses a katana as her preferred weapon. The media calls her the Dishonored Bushi. I scan the crime scene photos Aster placed up. Each victim's body was hunched over, their hands holding the katana that they used to end their own lives. Under the motive section Aster writes in big red letters, *seppuku,* a ritual suicide. She only attacks in the dead of night, and the body of her victims is found a week after they go missing at the exact time she took them.

Dishonored Bushi's body count is only five, the strikes she makes with the blade are precise, meant to torture and cause maximum pain but not kill. How she gets them to end themselves is a big mystery. One thing is for certain, she is one of the killers I don't want to cross paths with. My body erupts with goosebumps, a shiver racking up my spine with the thought of being caught by her crosses my mind. I rub my arms, wrapping them around myself in a protective way, as I read over all of Aster's notes.

"Can my little vixen tell me what she has learned?" Aster turns around, tucking his thumbs into the waistband of his sweats, pulling them down slightly, waiting for my answer.

"I could, but then I wouldn't be getting the punishment I love," I tease, jumping off the island and taking slow, sultry steps toward him.

He doesn't move a muscle, seemingly unaffected at my attempts to taunt him. I bite my lip, ignoring Aster's feeble attempt to hide his want for me. My fingers walk slowly up his chest, his heart beating steadily. Once I reach his chin, I pull his lower lip, feeling his breath ghosting over my finger. I shiver with anticipation, knowing I got him right where I want him, I lean my body against his chest, his gaze dipping to the opening of my shirt.

"Careful, little vixen, if you don't behave, I might not be inclined to show you the surprise I've been working on."

"Surprise?" I step back, a Cheshire like smile creeping across my lips.

He steps to the side, the cards being turned against me, and I follow Aster out of the kitchen then up the stairs.

Staying on his trail, I pester him about the surprise. "Did you get me a flamethrower?" Silence greets me, "Is it a new toy to test on my victims?" I poke at his back, my steps in sync with his. "Hmm, I know!" I say tapping my finger against my lip, "A new toy for the bedroom." Still nothing, knowing he has this round, I give into what he wants and tell him what I learned.

"You were teaching me about the Dishonored Bushi." I say, stopping him in his tracks at our bedroom door. His foot begins to hover over the step and the words fly out of me. "She always attacks at night and kills within a week." His foot hits the step in front of him and I spew the rest of what was splayed on the board. "She somehow has them kill themselves and is a bad ass bitch I don't want to come after me. But if she ever did come after me there is no way she would ever get me to kill myself, or you for that matter, no matter the type of torture she puts me throu-"

His finger silences my ramble. "Very good, little vixen." He locks his arms around my legs and throws me over his shoulder. I lift my head slightly, Aster side eying me as I ask excitedly, "Are you taking me to my surprise?"

He doesn't answer, simply turning forward and proceeding to walk back down the stairs, my body bouncing with each step. He doesn't pause or lose his grip as he slips his boots on, striding through our yard towards the direction of the kill shed, a place neither of us have been since I killed Bradley. Excitement courses through me from the memory of that fateful evening, the night everything changed.

The night I finally accepted the darkness and became who I was always meant to be.

As we walk, my mind races with what my surprise could be.

"Have you finally decided to dispose of your little lamb?" I tease, despite knowing I won't get an answer.

It's funny, how the one person who meant to kill me is the one who showed me I am just like him. I was upset when Aster told me the truth, showing me who he really is. But I didn't have much time to process it before the truth of who I really am was revealed to me. The memories of what I did consumed me entirely. I accepted it. Embraced it. Reveled in it. That's what makes moving on easy. There was a monster dormant inside me for so long, being set free wasn't difficult. It was welcomed. Wanted. A part of me finally became whole, the darkness lurking beneath the surface fully exposed to the harsh light of reality. Now my beast is awake, and it'll never be put back to sleep.

I don't want it to.

For so long I have been fascinated by serial killers. Their methods. Their kills. Their desires. What are the odds I fall in love with my favorite killer?

"Do you want your surprise or not, little vixen?" Aster asks, stopping to look back at me. I give him a sheepish smile, bringing my hand to my lips, zipping my mouth shut, pretending to lock it and then place the imaginary key in Aster's back pocket, smacking his ass for emphasis. He shakes his head and smirks, continuing down the path.

"Close your eyes," Aster demands as his steps slow.

Instead of listening, I lift my head and peek at what he wants to shield me from seeing. I yelp, as his grip loosens, my body plummeting to the ground. My eyes slam shut, and just as my head is about to slam into the grass, his arms tighten around my ankles, stopping my fall.

"Now, are you going to be a good girl and listen to your fox, or am I going to have to let your face meet the earth?"

I shake my head, my eyes pinched shut. "I'm a good vixen; my eyes are closed. I promise!"

"I'm going to place you on the ground, so put your hands out in front of you, and don't look, or so help me Serena, I will burn your surprise to the ground."

Extending my arms in front of me, I collapse into an inelegant heap, feeling the dirt beneath my fingers. I crawl towards where I think the shed is, feeling Aster's hands wrap around my arms, helping me up.

"Can I trust you to keep your eyes closed, or do I have to cover them for you?"

I turn towards his voice, biting my lips at his threat. "I promise, as your little vixen, I will *try* to behave."

He hums his approval, grabbing my hands and guiding me to where my gift awaits. We stop. I hear keys jingle and a door creaking open. *It doesn't sound like Aster's kill space.* It's a quieter, groaning sound. Almost sensual in how it caresses my ears, my core liquifies. The urge to peek is strong, and as much as I love watching flames shine bright and flicker, I don't want my present to be engulfed by them. So, like the good girl I'm not, I keep myself in the dark.

Aster's hands grab my waist, preventing me from moving forward. His breath fans my neck, as he whispers in my ear, "On the count of three…"

"One."

The excitement from anticipation of what awaits starts in my stomach, wings flapping wildly around.

"Two."

The urge to peek is getting stronger with each shadow of a number leaving his lips.

"Three." His hands release my waist, and my eyes spring open, my fingers cover my mouth, as tears threaten to fall.

I turn towards him, unable to form the words I desperately wish to say. He just smiles, answering my unspoken question with a dip of his head.

The room we are standing in is covered head to toe with shelves upon shelves of bookcases full of books, mostly dark romance. There is a giant chaise in the corner of the room with a big fluffy blanket. My feet must be ahead of my brain because before I can register what is happening, my ass is planted in the seat, and I swear it is the comfiest place my ass has ever been. My body melds into the cushion, and if there wasn't so much to look at, I would be getting under that blanket, ready to drift to sleep.

"What do you think?" Aster asks, crossing his arms over his chest, leaning on the doorframe watching me with an amused look.

I pull the blanket up and nuzzle my face into it. "When did you have the time to do this?"

He pushes off the wall and sits on the arm of the sofa. "I

finally had a reason to spend the money I've made from Graves, and what's the point of being rich if I can't spend it on the woman I love?"

"You could have put the money back into Graves."

"Graves can survive even if I built you ten more of these." My eyes widen at his confession.

"While that sounds like a dream, I really hope you don't spend that much money on me, ever."

"Serena." He sits down by my legs. "I would give you my last dollar if it meant I could see your eyes light up the way they did when you saw your personal library."

I grab his hand and squeeze it, tears threatening to fall, "How did you get this done without me seeing? Or hearing for that matter."

"You were too busy screaming when the crew was working." My mouth falls open.

"That's why you were keeping me so satisfied so often?"

He quirks an eyebrow. "You think the only reason I fucked you until we were both raw was because I wanted to distract you?"

I shrug. "You kind of just said that."

"Serena, I fuck you because that is what I want to do. Not as some distraction, you are far from that. You are the one person who consumes me completely. Do you know how hard I have to fight the urge to destroy you when we're training?" He lifts my chin, heated eyes meeting my own. "It kills me every time we are near one another and I'm not inside you. But your safety is my number one priority even over fucking you. That's where your final surprise comes in." He extends his hand out silently asking for mine.

Eyeing him suspiciously, I take his hand. If there is anything I've learned, it is that there is always more than meets the eye with Aster.

"Do I have to close my eyes for this?" I ask, dragging myself from my new favorite place.

He shakes his head and walks me over to a shelf I hadn't noticed, filled with my Stephen King books and other horror novels I haven't had the pleasure of reading. I may be a girl who loves her dark and twisted romances, but I was a lover of horror way before that. Stephen King was my introduction into adult novels.

In the middle there is a huge rebound version of Stephen King's *It*. It's black with red foiling on the side and the words 'You'll Float Too', under the title name. I reach for the book, entranced by the red letters, desperate to trace my fingers over them. Pulling the book from the top, I try to ease it off the shelf to get a better look, but it stops halfway.

Then I hear a little click.

Whirling to look at Aster, hand still on the book that won't budge, I tilt my head. He smiles, a smugness curving his lips "What's your favorite horror novel besides *It*?"

Glancing back at the shelf, I find *Salem's Lot*. This one isn't bound, but it is a hardcover copy. With *It* still hanging halfway off the shelf, I pull the spine, frustrated this one also does not come off, but another whisper of a click sounds.

How did he know that was another one of my favorites?

Frustrated, I stick my bottom lip out in a pout. Aster brushes the delicate flesh with his finger. "One more to go, then that frown will be turned upside down."

I turn back to scan the shelf for my third favorite novel written by King, but try as I might, I can't locate it. "It's not here," I grumble, running my finger along each book to make sure I didn't miss it.

"It's there."

"It *isn't*. Also how do you know which books of his are my favorite? I never told you." I murmur, my pursuit to find the book never stopping.

His arms wrap around my waist, head resting on my shoulder. "If I told you, then I'd have to kill you," he teases.

"Ha, ha; very funny. We both know you had your chance and

chose to keep me instead." I turn my head, our breaths mingling with one another.

He looks at my lips and whispers, "You're right. And not killing you was the best decision I've ever made." I look down at his lips, a moment away from planting mine on his, when I feel him reach over my head and hear a door open.

I whip my head back and see the third book, *Misery* hanging halfway off the shelf. *I swear that wasn't there before.* The bookshelf swings open, and Aster reaches above my head to pull the door on silent hinges. My breath catches. Laying behind is a surprise even better than my own personal library.

CRIME SCENE - DO NOT
CRIME SCENE - DO NOT
THE BLACK LOTUS
THE BLACK LOTUS
SPECIAL EDITION
Daily
10 APRIL 2025
A DARK ROMANCE
VOL. 10, NO. 5
THE BLACK LOTUS
EXCLUSIVE
EXCLUSIVE
EXCLUSIVE
EXCLUSIVE
EXCLUSIVE
EXCLUSIVE
CRIME SCENE - DO
DO NOT CR
SOLITUDE
SOLITUDE
SOLITU

CRIME SCENE - DO NOT
THE BLACK LOTUS
EXCLUSIVE
EXCLUSIVE
EXCLUSIVE
SERENA
SOLITUDE
T. CROSS
CRIME
Regular solitude fosters deeper self-discovery
and personal growth. In these quiet moments
you build resilience, gain new
and strengthen your inner
solitude as a tool for
body, and soul
and purpose

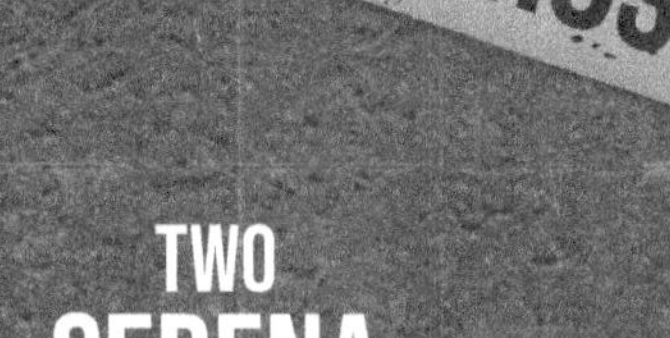

TWO
SERENA

My hands cover my mouth, tears threatening to fall once again and stealing the breath from my lungs, as I gaze upon the room before me. Behind the bookshelf door is my very own kill space. The walls are painted a deep red, with splashes of blues, greens, oranges, and yellow splattered around random spots. The artist in me is in awe of the abstract design, while the killer in me is excited to explore the rest of the room. In the corner, bolted to the ceiling, are hooks similar to the ones I used on Bradley.

Walking over, I reach up to touch the tip of the pointed metal, hissing at the bite of steel. Before I can place my finger in my mouth to stop the bleeding, Aster's hand wraps around mine, his tongue lapping at the bead of blood before his lips curl around my wound. The action alone makes me moan, my panties becoming damp.

He takes my finger out of his mouth with a popping noise, his eyes locked on mine, he says, "Your blood still tastes as addicting as I remember, but I prefer it mixed with your essence instead."

A blush rises up my neck, and before he has the chance to entice me further, I spin around and go explore. As much as I

would love to have him taste me, my curiosity is stronger. I want to continue looking around my new space, my domain.

Playtime can come later.

Gliding my fingers across the metal table sitting in the middle of the room, feeling the cool surface, I head towards the drawers on the far wall of the building not far from his. *I wonder if the structures are connected or how far my space is from his?* Opening them one by one, I find an array of weapons of every kind.

Aster must be more concerned about his mom putting a hit on me than he has been letting on. With all the lessons, and now my very own kill room, he says we have nothing to worry about, that he will protect me. Yet, when push comes to shove his actions are speaking louder than his words, like they always do. I glide my hand over the handle of the blade, noting how they're stacked shortest to longest. He can say he's not scared, that he is ready for whatever is thrown our way, but this level of preparation in such a short amount of time shows me otherwise. He feels the same way I do, he is afraid, but he is more rational than me, and when the time comes I know he will have my back. I know he would eliminate everyone in his path to keep me safe. That thought alone has a stray tear falling from my eye.

I wipe it away, and slowly shut the drawer, my hands shaking. I am met with green eyes of remorse, a feeling I know he's never felt before. Tears threaten to fall once more and I look away. Not ready to face the feelings we share, to face the truth of the situation. I want to live in denial a little longer.

Being a serial killer, he usually doesn't have those emotions. I've learned myself that I don't feel any regret for the lives I take.

Giving into my need to touch him, feel him, I cup my hand to his cheek, his eyes shuttering closed as he nuzzles into my palm. "Everything is going to be okay, Aster." The lie rolls off my tongue as easily as the truth does. Part of me believes we will make it out of this, the other part fears we both will meet our maker, and part ways forever.

His eyes slowly open. "We don't know what my mother is capable of."

"No, we don't, but she's behind bars. Her reach can only go so far."

He takes my hand off his cheek, and grips my fingers with his, looking at me with eyes that tell me to shut up and listen, without ever saying those words.

"She may be behind bars, but we don't know who her connections are. Or how many serial killers she sent after you. We know Zephira is keeping tabs on us, but we don't know if she is going to try to kill you. I don't want to kill my sister I just found out about. But I will. To protect you."

Zephira is ten years younger than Aster, but you'd never guess she was so young because of how she holds herself. After we found out who she was, we researched Salem's Man Eater. Salem may be where she got her start, but she hasn't locked herself to one city. She has killed all over Massachusetts, and her number is high despite being so young. She has mutilated fifteen men and counting. Although she's never killed a woman, I wouldn't put it past her. To gain more love from a mother she never knew, she wouldn't hesitate to gut me where I stand.

Aster's hands squeeze mine. "My own flesh and blood could never stop me from loving you, or being with you." His thumb brushes over my skin, sending a trail of goosebumps in its wake. "I would kill them all, to know you were safe."

Squeezing his hands back, I look up at him with softened eyes. "I know you would, Aster, but I'm not scared of anyone coming after me. Your mother's never getting out; she's in a high security prison, like the one Hannibal Lecter was in."

He brings my hands to his lips, breathing onto them as he whispers, "I know, but I just got you. I won't lose you. For the first time in my life, I am scared. I love you, my little vixen." He kisses my knuckles, closing his eyes and leaving his lips planted.

"I love you too, my fox," I whisper back. His eyes open at my words, a feral look darkening his face as he walks me over to an incinerator in the far corner of the room, one I didn't notice before.

"I know how much you love fire, so I thought, when it is necessary, you can watch your victims burn."

Releasing his hand, I bend down to caress the machine. "I do love watching flames lick away at bubbling flesh."

"For the ones dumb enough to attack in the open, I thought we could come up with a calling card. Something to let everyone know, we are ready, and they are next."

Standing back up, a grin plasters my face. *I already know what I want my calling card to be.* I wanted a flower, like Aster, but I needed it to embody my story. My truth. My strength. Something that showed the beauty of darkness, rebirth, and transformation.

"Black lotus. That is what I want as my calling card," I say, leaving no room for argument.

A smile twists his features, a look of approval passing over his face. "My little vixen, we really are one in the same. I was hoping you would choose that flower. It describes you perfectly."

"Oh, yeah? Why is that?" I say teasingly, jabbing a finger into his chest. Instead of answering, he grabs me and drags me out of the kill room. He picks me up and throws me back on the comfy chaise and walks away.

"What are you doing?" I ask, wanting to get up but knowing if I try, he will push me back down.

He walks over to my killer bookshelf and grabs a box hidden on top. *Even if I wanted to, I'm too short to even reach up there. I didn't even think to look on top of the shelf. What's in the box?* I sit up on my knees, peering up at what I can only assume to be another surprise, but before I can get a good look at it, he hides it behind his back, I fall back into the position he left me in as he kneels right in front of me. *Oh god, I hope he isn't going to propose.* I back further into the chaise, away from the crazy man on his knees. Before I have a chance to escape, he stops me, his calloused hand digging into my knee. I look down, my breath caught in my lungs. Unable to move, unable to speak, I'm stuck, suspended in time with Aster.

"Serena-"

He takes a big breath preparing himself for his proposal. *He only says my name when it's serious, but this isn't a romcom, for fucks sake.* We are both killers; ones who are just starting to get to know one another. It is too soon. I haven't even thought about marriage. Sure, I'd risk my life for him, kill for him, even die for him, but *marriage*? I am not ready for that.

"-I need to ask you a serious question, one I don't know if you're going to say yes to." He rakes his fingers through his hair. *Fuck, he's nervous.* "You are the most important woman in my life, and I can't see myself doing this with anyone else. I will go to war for you, *with* you. I would give my last breath to save yours."

I lift my hand to silence him, my heart pounding so hard I swear he can hear it. *I don't want to hear those four words. I'm not ready.* He grabs my hand and places the box in my palm. I pinch my eyes closed. "Aster, I'm not-"

All I hear is his deep laugh. I slowly peek one eye open. This mother fucker is full on belly laughing *on the floor.* Shock spirals through me, my fingers shaking around the box I debate throwing across the room. *I didn't know marrying me would be so funny.* Before I can get mad at him for something I didn't even want to begin with, I look down and realize the box is way too big to be holding a ring. This box is long and sleek; a ring would be too small to fit in a box this big. I wouldn't put it past him to put the ring in a box, inside another one, like one of those Russian dolls.

I glare at him, opening the box with a stilted yank. My body freezes. Inside is a shiny, serrated hunting knife with a blue handle. I chuck the box at his head, and he dodges it, like I knew he would. *Fucker is always in my head, knowing what I'm going to do before I do it.*

"I thought-"

"You thought I was going to propose?"

I look at him wide eyed, nodding in shock.

He sits back on his heels. "Of course I knew."

"Why did you let me think you were doing something so crazy?" I wave the knife between us, and he captures my wrist.

"First, let's not swing that around. Second, messing with you is the highlight of my day. The way your nose crinkles, panic swirling in those blue eyes of yours." He sniffs the air by my face. "I can smell the fear radiating from your pores, vixen. I've never smelled a more intoxicating ambrosia."

Pushing him away, I point the tip of the blade a mere centimeter from his nose. "One day I'm going to be the one making you sweat."

He swats my hand, the knife still gripped tight in my palm. "I'd love to see you try. Plus, when I propose, it would be after we kill everyone coming after us."

Shoving him onto his back, I crawl over his lap, straddling him with a vicious grin. "Those killers are not ready for the fox and his vixen." I lean down, a hair's breadth away from kissing him. He closes his eyes, and I nip at his lip before pressing the blade against his throat. He tries to move, but I hold his chest down.

"Careful, vixen, you're going to start something I will have to finish."

I shake my head slowly, a small smile lifting my cheeks. "Not this time, fox, any small movement, and your blood will be glistening on my new gift."

He chuckles, dark and menacing. My stomach drops, but I'm his vixen for a reason, and that haunting sound won't scare me from trying to put fear into him.

"I didn't get you that to use on me, although, I wouldn't be opposed. I know how much you love watching us bleed."

Leaning down, my blade still tight against his throat, I whisper in his ear, feeling his growing erection with every move

I make. "I do love watching the red seep out of you." I lean back up, bringing my knife with me and admiring my reflection in the steel. "Why did you gift me this beautiful blade then? If not for us to play together."

He surges up, leaning on his hands and invading my space. "I wanted to turn a bad memory into a good one." My eyebrows pinch together, my mouth parting slightly, the playful energy surrounding us dissipating with those words.

"What do you mean? What happened?"

Aster scoops me into his arms and places us on the chaise. He looks down at his hands, bracing to relive a memory I can tell he'd rather forget.

"The day my parents were taken was the day they got me a knife. A knife, to this day, I use to end all my little lambs'. I was supposed to use it for the first time that night, on my victim that got away, the one, I have since realized, I base all my lambs on."

My hands cover my mouth, the realization of why all of his victims look similar to me sinks in. *Has he been looking for her this whole time, and settled on look-a-likes until he finds her? Does he still want to finish what he started so long ago? If he does find her, will our time together end?* My heart aches at the thought, and his voice brings me out of my downward spiral of what ifs.

He tells me of the night everything changed, of the parting words his mother left him. Words that shaped the rest of his future. Words that brought us together. In a way, I should be thanking his mother for the role she played in our story, but I won't. She doesn't deserve the air she breathes for risking our lives over something so petty.

I drop the knife, grabbing his face with both hands and planting a kiss softly on his trembling lips. "Thank you," I whisper, "I love it, and I promise to bathe the blade red with the blood of our enemies."

He kisses me back. "I can't wait to see what you're really capable of."

"You think you're a monster? You haven't seen anything yet."

I get off the chaise, leaning down to peck his lips, and head out the door, towards our house, hoping to be chased and punished. Before my foot passes the threshold, I'm yanked back, pulled into Aster's chest with his strong arms banding around me.

He breathes in my scent. "I'm not done with you yet, little vixen."

My heart pounds as I look up, meeting his darkened gaze and feeling his erection against me. I squirm against his hold, but it's no use. I'm his captive and he is my captor.

"What else do you have planned?" I whisper.

He spins me around, my chest colliding with his, our breathing picking up. "I want to hear you scream. I need to see you bleed."

I try to run out of his arms, I try to hide my excited grin, but he watches the gears turning in my head as soon as the words leave his mouth. He picks me up, ignoring my punches, kicks and jabs, throwing me over his shoulder and clamping a heavy arm across my thighs before swatting my ass. Hard. All plans of escape vanish in a second. I try to wiggle out of his arms, but his hold is tight. We walk back into my new torture chamber, and he places me on the table, my core clenching around nothing knowing I'm truly his little lamb. My eyes trace his path across my space, watching him close us in as darkness threatens to overtake us.

Knowing I can't escape, because he has yet to teach me how to open it from the inside, I am truly trapped. I make myself comfy on the cold steel as I await my punishment. Excitement thrumming through my veins. Even though I didn't get the chase I wanted, I know he's going to make me scream, and that thought alone has my pussy aching.

He grabs a belt hanging on a row of hooks by the door,

dangling it in the air as he saunters back, teasing me and placing the worn leather next to me.

He walks over to the workbench, opening the top drawer I know is filled with all different types of knives and selects his favorite. I stay still, awaiting my fate with eager anticipation. I don't even try to run, knowing damn well he would catch me.

"Time to bleed, little vixen," he says, closing the drawer.

Fuck me.

CRIME SCENE - DO NOT
THE BLACK LOTUS
EXCLUSIVE
SERENA
T. CROSS
CRIME

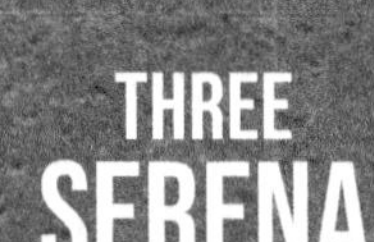

THREE
SERENA

The last, and first, time he brought me pleasure with a knife, I was blindfolded. This time I'm not. I can see him stare down at my fully clothed body, deciding what he wants to do. My nipples pebble at his hungry eyes. The way he's staring at me feels like I'm a deer caught in the middle of a field and he's a ferocious lion waiting to devour me. I wish he would just rip my clothes off already, instead of standing there waiting for the perfect moment. Stalling the inevitable is making me crave him even more. But this game of cat and mouse is too fun to end. So I slowly close my legs, giving him no access to what he craves.

He clicks his tongue, shaking his head with a near manic look in his eyes, and pries them back open, stepping between them to prevent my denial of him.

He pushes me down until my back hits the table, then takes the knife and places the tip of the blade under the button of my jeans. My eyes meet his, and before I can object what he's about to do, the button goes flying.

"You really love destroying my clothing, don't you?" I almost growl. *These were my favorite jeans.*

"I love destroying something else more."

I gasp, my mouth instantly dry as my core weeps for his cock. Any smart comeback I might have had floats away. I need him inside me, wrecking me. Filling me. Breaking me.

He trades the knife for his belt beside me and saunters around the table, my eyes tracking his every movement. "What are you going to do with that?" I ask, my head tipping up to watch as he grabs both of my hands and places them flat against the table. "You really have a kink with that belt of yours, huh?"

He ignores my question, looping the belt around my wrists and securing it tightly. His face annoyingly neutral, he reaches under the table and grabs a rope of some kind, wrapping it around the makeshift restraint. I try to tug my hands away, but they aren't moving a muscle, heightening my arousal.

Walking back down to the end of the table, I strain to see what he's doing, but I feel his hands grip my legs, grabbing one at a time and locking them in some type of restraint. I attempt to kick out, but they aren't going anywhere.

He really thought all of this through. There is no way anyone could escape once captured. Just when I think he's done, he picks up the knife and slices the middle of my shirt revealing my breasts to him. Asters pupils dilate, and his breathing picks up as he traces the flat of the blade around my hardened nipples, my breath catching in my throat. Instead of scolding him for ruining yet another piece of clothing, I simply lay there. Waiting. Watching. Anxious to see what he will do next. He places the knife in his mouth and grabs a strap under the table, placing it on my stomach before walking to the other side and grabbing the other end, securing it over me and leaving me entirely immobile.

"Aster-"

He places the blade against my lips, silencing me. "Little vixen, the fun is coming, but first you need to be punished."

"Punished?" I mumble against the knife. "But I was paying attention to your lesson. I even told you what it was about!"

He removes the weapon from my lips, crouching beside me.

"You did, yes, but before I reprimanded you, you were paying attention to my body, not the board."

I scoff, "I'm not the one who decided to wear gray sweatpants that outline everything." I look down and see the shadow of his erection through the thin material of his pants, glancing back up through my lashes with a satisfied smile.

He grips my leg, a deep growl emanating from his throat. One I can't tell if it's from warning, arousal, or both. "That was a test, one you failed, and for that, you must bleed." With the last words, he takes the knife and slowly, shallowly, slices across my upper thigh. I suppress a whimper, biting my lip to cancel out the sting the blade left behind. I strain my neck to look down, seeing red soak into the denim.

Laying my head back down, I pinch my eyes closed as I wait for the next cut. *Why is he actually hurting me?* He said he loves me. He said he would never hurt me. Yet, he's slicing me with his knife? I crack one eye open, glancing at his face, his eyes have darkened, lip jutting out, as he watches the spot on my denim become larger. It looks like he's enjoying it, but the way his hand has a slight tremor gives me all the assurance I need. He doesn't actually want to cause me pain. I shut my eyes once more, thinking of all the ways I'll get him back for this. It doesn't necessarily hurt, but I like to be the one to make myself bleed. I don't want anyone to do it for me. *He has to have a reason for this.* He wouldn't just hurt me to see me squirm. No, Aster is meticulous; he has a reason for all of his actions.

I look at him and see him watching me now, not the blood his eyes were zoned in on a minute ago. "What... What are you doing?"

He tilts his head, like I should already know the answer with his actions. We stare at one another and, finally, he huffs a breath.

"We need to see how much pain you can handle."

"What?" I ask, my mouth agape. *I knew he had a reason.*

"If..." He closes his eyes and takes a deep breath, opening them only when he speaks again, the sadness in his eyes evident.

"If you ever get caught, if you ever end up in the hands of one of the people my mother sent… If I'm not there to protect you, or you're unable to protect yourself, you need to be strong. To not give up. To take the pain and channel it into something else. Something stronger than the agony they're inflicting."

"Something else?" I ask, my heart dropping to my stomach at the thought of being captured by anyone. But I get a ping of excitement at the thought of escaping and sending a more bloody message to anyone else.

He cups my pussy hard through my jeans, eliciting a whimper from my lips. That's what he means; find pleasure in the pain, so it won't be as painful as the torment truly is. I close my eyes, concentrating on how his hand feels against my cunt, wishing he'd just discard the barriers between us as well.

As if reading my mind, Aster lifts the top on my pants and slashes all the way down, my panties falling away with the jeans, the blade mere centimeters from nicking my skin. The hairs on my legs instantly rise from the sheer excitement and fear this lesson is bringing.

"Do you trust me?"

I open my eyes, lifting my head as high as it can go. My breath hitches when my eyes lock onto his swirling green ones. They're the darkest I've seen, an animalistic feeling seeping from them. All I can manage is a nod, my throat dry and unable to form words.

He braces both hands on the table, jumping up to cradle me with his legs. My pussy tingles when I feel his hardened cock graze it through his sweats. I shimmy my hips for some friction, desperate to release some of the pressure, but the ache is still there. And growing.

This is torture in itself.

He reaches into his pocket and grabs a blindfold I didn't know he had, a sudden pit in my stomach growing from not being able to watch. I was enjoying the parts of the lesson I could manage to see, and now I'll only be able to feel. It will heighten that sense and he told me to trust him. Aster motions for me to lift my head, being the obedient student he likes to see, I do as he asks, and then my world goes dark. My heart races with the light suddenly gone, and laying in the unknown waiting for the torture to begin. My chest tightens, and I stiffen when I feel Aster's hand touch my erratic chest.

"You're safe."

My breathing returns to normal remembering it is Aster who is in control, I begin to calm, anxiously waiting for the lesson to continue.

We haven't done a lesson that involved pain and pleasure yet. He taught me basic fighting and self defense moves, but they never ended in sex no matter how horny I got seeing his arms flex while he was teaching me. The way his veins would bulge when he had his hand wrapped around my throat and told me to flip him, or when I would come at him and he captured me with unnerving ease, my panties soaked instantly. And he knew, the smug bastard. He would scold me afterwards about paying attention, claiming our lessons were serious and could save my life. *How is a girl supposed to focus when her man is looking so delectable?* I wanted to lick the sweat glistening off his abs, and I almost did, but he stopped me. *Fucking asshole.* Eventually I learned to pay attention and stop thinking about his dick inside me the whole time, I couldn't handle the punishments of no dick for a couple days, so, for him to bring pleasure into this lesson, I am feeling all kinds of emotions right now. My nipples ache to have his mouth wrapped around them. My pussy is weeping, begging to be fucked. Worst of all, my stomach is in knots, awaiting the impending pain. Never knowing when the lesson will resume is worse than waiting to be pleasured.

"Fuck!" I seethe, feeling the sting of the blade against my inner thigh. A second later Aster's tongue glides across the cut, instantly soothing the burn and making my insides churn.

"Aster. Please. I need to see you." I beg, the urge to rip this blindfold off my eyes increasing with the silence. But with my arms strapped down, I'm unable to move. The last time he drew blood and licked my essence off the knife, I made myself bleed.

Looking back, I think that's when the darkness sleeping in me began to awaken. The memories that laid dormant for so long were starting to stir and that's why I was seeing less and less of Jessica.

Aster's body moves up mine, his breath on my chest, his mouth hovering just above my nipple. The moment his lips make contact, I feel another slice on top of my chest. I don't react to the pain of the knife, too distracted by his tongue flicking my hardened nipple, a small moan rumbling in my throat.

Good thing I'm not gagged.

His mouth moves, making me gasp from the loss of his heat. I feel his head move to the other side of my chest, his tongue gliding over the cut.

"Aster..." I moan, pulling against my bindings, "*please*, I need more."

"Ever the impatient one," he says, kissing down my body, inching closer and closer to my aching cunt.

His breath hovers over my waiting pussy, his fingers spreading me open as he blows a breath onto my clit, goosebumps erupting across my flesh.

He did say he was going to punish me.

His mouth wraps around the sensitive bud, and I wait for the pain to accompany the pleasure, but all I feel is the satisfaction of the release I've been holding in. He moans his approval against my pulsing pussy, my head tipping back, hips gyrating against his face. Two of his fingers enter me, my back bowing off the table as he curls them upward, hitting that sensitive spot he never seems to miss, and with his mouth on me, his fingers working in and out, I feel myself slipping further and further into ecstasy.

I feel his fingers quickening their pace, no pain breaking through my hazy pleasure, but I feel something warm trickle down the side of my leg. *Did he cut me?*

I don't get a chance to question his actions, my stomach tightening as the euphoria I've been begging for finally courses through me. Aster groans, the rumble heightening my pleasure while he laps at all the juices, my body spasming under him. His mouth leaves me and I feel his hand reach around my head, taking the blindfold off of me. My eyes squint against the dimmed lights above me, slowly adjusting to my surroundings as I come down from my impossible high.

Aster is sitting above me, staring at my body with a different kind of admiration than I usually see from him.

"Your blood coating your skin, with your cuts scarring it, almost makes me want you as my little lamb."

"Too bad your heart got in the way of your addiction."

"Too bad indeed."

A blush paints my cheeks as I look up, straining to see what he's seeing, but before I can ask him to help me see his marks, he undoes the strap around my stomach. Then moves onto the bindings on my legs, and finally the one keeping my arms above my head. The relief I feel moving my aching joints and waking them back up, is almost as good as the orgasms were. Almost.

He reaches his hand out to me. "You look beautiful with your blood covering you."

Covering me?

I look down, my breath hitching, sure enough, my body is covered in fresh and drying blood. I run my finger through the red, tracing my finger against his lips like a macabre balm.

"If you tease me with your essence, you'll make me want to bleed you every time I bring you pleasure," he warns.

I stick my finger in his mouth, ignoring his threat. His eyes flare as he moans around the intrusion, sucking it clean.

Taking the finger out of his mouth his pupils dilate, I try to get off the table, hesitant to look at myself, my back slamming onto the table with an echoing crash as Aster's mouth devours my own.

My hands tangle in his hair, nails digging into his scalp to deepen the kiss as my tongue dances with his. *My turn to make him bleed a little.*

His hips grind against my pussy, wet and dripping and begging to be filled. His hands slip to the waistband of his sweats, pulling out his dick and surging into me without warning. I gasp from the hard intrusion, pressing my chest against his as waves radiate through me.

"Fuck, Serena," Aster groans. "Your pussy is squeezing the life out of my dick. If you keep gripping me like that, we'll both come before we're ready to."

Ignoring his words I constrict around him, making him moan. I wrap my legs around him, dragging him deeper into me. He leans down, slamming his hands down around my head, pounding deeper and deeper. I reach between us and circle my clit, bringing myself to another orgasm, losing count of how many I've been given.

"That's it, vixen, coat my cock in your blood and cum." He pumps faster, stilling above me as his orgasm rips through him. "Fuck!" He roars, breathless, his head dropping against my own.

He slowly pulls out, breathing hard and helping me sit up, my legs shaking. He gets off the table first, and I follow nearly collapsing to the concrete floor. Before he has a chance to tempt me with his dick for round two, I walk to the door and wait for him to open it.

He laughs, "Oh, you want out?"

"That would be nice," I say, arms crossed, waiting for him to show me how to escape.

He walks over and reaches above my head, my eyes watching as he pulls a latch you wouldn't know is there from looking at it. I duck under his arm and head for the mirror in the corner to see the results of my training.

I gasp, looking at my reflection. *One, two…* I start counting the cuts he made, my eyes growing wider with each one I find. Twelve; there are twelve cuts across my entire body, blood still trickling from the deeper ones.

He comes over, wrapping his arms around my body, resting his chin on my shoulder and kissing my neck softly.

We stand together, staring at my reflection. "I thought you cut me five times, not twelve." Our eyes lock in the mirror. "How come I didn't feel them?"

A small smile plays on his lips. "See what adding pleasure does for pain? You didn't feel the other cuts, only the sting of bliss they created."

I shake my head, laughing at his crazy methods.

He kisses the back of my head. "I'll be right back."

Before I can ask where he's going, he walks back into my kill space and comes back later holding a rag and first aid kit. He walks over and sits on my chaise, tapping the spot beside him. I stand there, my upper lip curling in disgust, refusing to move. *I don't want to get blood on my furniture.*

"Serena," he warns.

"Are you going to clean up the blood that stains my new favorite spot?"

He moves to the floor and spreads his legs. "Better?"

I smile. "Much."

"Good, now sit in front of me, on your knees." Before I have a chance for a dirty remark, he adds, "You will suck my dick later, vixen. Now we need to get you cleaned up."

I plop down in front of him, on my knees like he asked, not wanting to be punished any further, and he begins cleaning my wounds.

"Shit, that stings." I wince.

"Did you think it'd tickle?"

I stare at him, open mouth, surprised he's being a smart ass. Well, not surprised, more taken aback. It's not like he hasn't been a smart ass before, I just haven't seen this side of him in awhile. Ever since he got the letter from his mom, he's been more worked up than I realized.

We never really talked about his parents, but after the bomb of Zephira, Aster dove into a spiral, making sure I knew everything and still teaching me more every day.

"Hey, Aster?" I ask, placing my hand around his, stopping him from cleaning the last cut.

He hums, focusing on my wounds with an eye for detail I'd only seen when he was the Morbid Monet.

"How come you told me your parents were dead?"

He stills, looking up at me with the rag still resting over my chest. "They were dead to me."

"I get that, but… why?"

He takes a deep breath and places the rag down. "When I was eighteen, I learned which prison they were housed in, and the first thing I did was go to their cage to see them." He pauses, looking away. I'm silent, waiting for him to continue. Bringing my hands to my lap, I pick at my nails, a million of why's crossing my mind as the silence weighs us down. "When I got there, I was turned away. They told me my name was on the restricted access list." He bunches his hands into fists, the memory replaying in his mind as he repeats it to me. "I fought with the guard, saying it has to be a mistake. I'm their *son*; surely, they would want to see me after being taken away." Tears well in my eyes, my nose burning at the pain coursing through him. Reaching out, desperate to offer any comfort I can, Aster rips his arm from my grasp, his brow furrowing as his hands slice through the air. "I demanded to speak to the person in charge, insisted I be allowed to speak to them. Instead of kicking me out, which I thought they would, they told me to sit. So I did. Five minutes later, the warden of the prison was kneeling before me explaining how he went to speak to them, but they refused to see me. I couldn't believe it, but I couldn't punch the face of the man in front of me with so many witnesses, so I shook my head, silent tears falling down my face, and left." His hands fall limply into his lap and I grab them, rubbing my thumb over his shaking palms, my jaw tightening as he continues. "I left and wrote them each a letter. I sent it but got no response. For five years, I tried.

I'd go back, I'd write more letters, but eventually… I gave up. They clearly didn't want to see me." He looks up, sad eyes meeting my own. "After that, I decided they were dead. I was already carrying on their legacy, so I made my rules, vowing to never make the same mistakes they did. The very rules I broke with you." He laughs, squeezing my hands. "Serena, even though my mother is after you, she died a long time ago. If she ever dared show her face in front of me, I would snap her neck without a second thought. She is trying to kill the woman I love, and for that, she has to die."

He pulls me into his arms, my shoulders relaxing as he holds me tight. "I will protect you, Serena; I won't let anyone hurt you or come between us. I will kill her. I vow it on the blood spilled between us."

I snuggle into his chest, placing my hand over his racing heart and letting his words sink in.

If his mother ever appeared before me, I would slit her throat and bathe in her blood, dancing while her screams rang out. She hurt the man I love in irreparable ways, and she will never be forgiven.

She will pay. She will burn. She will regret the day she locked out her precious fox.

CRIME SCENE - DO NOT CROSS   CRIME SCEN
BLACK LOTUS
EXCLUSIVE
ASTER
SOLITUDE * SOLITUDE
SOLITUDE * SOLITU
CROSS
SCENE - DO NOT CROS

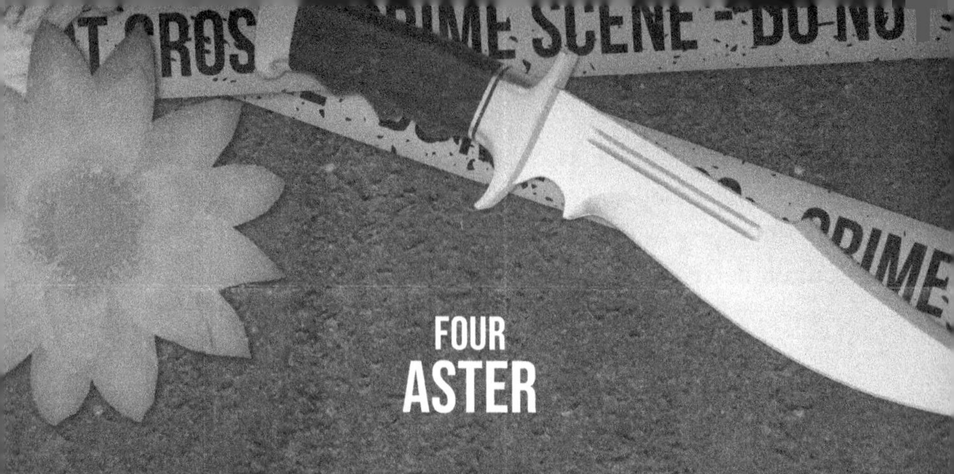

FOUR
ASTER

I carry Serena back to the house bridal style, and we lay in bed, silently wrapped around one another. She was processing everything I told her, what I went through. After I left the orphanage, I sought out my parents, desperate to gain advice about what to do next, how to continue their legacy. We'd already lost so much time, I wanted to rekindle our relationship, be the son they always wanted me to be, and being ignored each time left me gutted.

Like any good son who had been waiting a lifetime to see his parents, I tried again. And again. And again. After the fifth time, I was thirsty for blood, and the next thing I remember is finding myself in the darker, more depraved parts of a town near their prison. Some hooker walked up to me, trying to get money from a lost kid who seemed down on his luck, and I let her take me away. I remember walking down an alley. I remember her kissing my neck. I remember being repulsed by it, disgust roiling in my veins. I shoved her off and just as she turned to walk away, I snatched her by her hair, hissing I wasn't done with her yet. She was shorter than me, but that wasn't unusual. I've always been tall, and when her back slammed against my chest,

I didn't hesitate. I gutted her, leaving evidence of how I felt behind, her blood and entrails staining my shoes.

All I saw was red, all I felt was piping hot anger, and I took it out on her. Some helpless, nameless whore. I felt no remorse or empathy for what I'd just done. It was my first kill and the only emotion I felt was hunger. I needed to kill again. I needed to see crimson splayed everywhere.

I left her body for the police to find and I walked away, taking the knife my parents gifted with me. The weapon I kept close by as a reminder of what could have been.

The police never found who killed her, but it was all over the news. Turns out she was a runaway from a prestigious family and they wanted to find her murderer. I didn't know, or care, if I left behind any evidence. I didn't, but I knew I needed more. More blood. More destruction. More carnage. No matter how pissed I was, I knew my parents' legacy would live on. I had a taste for blood, one that needed to be quenched, but it wouldn't be careless hookers. No, I needed *more*. I wanted to learn from my parents, but after being treated like I was never born, I created my own legacy. And the Morbid Monet was born.

Since meeting my vixen I haven't thought once about another little lamb. I haven't been the Monet for several months. If I'd never met Serena I would have hunted my next victim, killed, and displayed her by now. My hands would be red with lamb blood not contaminated by all the other lives I've taken. I've strayed so far from who I was, but who I am becoming with Serena is the man I should have always been. Knowing what it is making my mother go through to not have her little boy be who she wants makes falling in love that much sweeter. I may not be the Morbid Monet right now. May not become him ever again. Now I have a partner in crime and together we will create a new legacy. One that will have everyone always looking over their shoulder.

I stay quiet, letting Serena think about the important parts I told her, wrapping her in my arms. If she wanted to know more about how I became who I am, I would tell her, but only if she asks. Until then, I'll just teach her what I know. Her cold hand rests on my naked chest, and I wrap my hand around hers to warm her. She smiles slightly, eyes closed, falling asleep with the comfort from one another and our shared pasts.

When we woke up she was her cheerful self, and said she wanted to go out for breakfast. I was grateful the events of last night didn't dampen her appetite. I teased her, telling her I had something she could eat, but her stomach rumbled and we both laughed. We pulled on our clothes and drove into the city to the diner.

The weather outside is much colder, all the trees are dead, and with Christmas approaching, every store and restaurant is playing the same songs and making my ears bleed. Serena sits across from me, hands clasped around her mug, blowing on her coffee and mouthing every word to the song. I don't know what is playing, something about jingle bells? They all sound the same to me.

Growing up, Christmas wasn't a holiday I looked forward to. The children rarely got anything, and when we did, it would be socks or scarves, sometimes even mittens, to keep us warm from the harsh winter weather. The other kids would fight over whose was whose even though they all looked the same. Black socks. Black scarves. Black mittens. All as dark as the hell we lived in. I didn't care for any of it. The only reason I participated in the frivolous holiday at all was because it was a rule, and if the rules weren't followed you would be punished. The punishments were far worse than they sounded, and I was given them more than the other children because of who my parents were. The people who ran the orphanage called me evil and treated me like the devil's maker. They didn't know how right they were, and the day I turned eighteen I ran, trying not to slit the throats of every single person who made my life a living hell. My fingers shake around my mug, rage surging through me. *One day I will get my revenge, hopefully with my little vixen by my side.*

Taking a sip of coffee, I watch Serena, now humming to herself and smiling at me, the blood lust dissipating, making this month a little more bearable.

The waitress returns to our table, food in her hand, and slowly places my plate in front of me, attempting to brush her hand with mine. I move it away, and she straightens her back, clearing her throat. Serena glares daggers at the unsuspecting woman, clutching the butter knife in her hand, pointed up and ready to strike. I bite the inside of my cheek, suppressing a moan at the thought of watching *my vixen* kill this woman.

"Can I get you anything else?" the waitress asks, addressing only me.

The waitress jumps back at the sound of the knife Serena was holding as it hits the floor. Serena says nothing, just bends down, picks up her cutlery, and returns to eating her food, her eyes never leaving the spooked woman. I bite the back of my knuckles to keep from laughing at the whole ordeal.

The waitresses face pales, her eyes looking like they're about to pop out of her skull, and instead of apologizing, she huffs and stomps away. Serena tracks her through the busy restaurant, mindlessly twisting the knife in her hand.

"I'm going to kill her," she whispers, her leg bouncing up and down.

I reach over and grab her hand, her leg stilling. "You can't kill her," I say in a soothing voice.

She whips her head in my direction, her daggers now pointed towards me. She tries, and fails, to take her hand from mine. "Why the fuck not? She was blatantly flirting with you, ignoring my presence. I'm surprised she even took my order at all."

I run my thumb across the back of her hand. "She probably already told her co-workers about your little stunt, so if she were to go missing, we would be the first suspects, and we have enough heat right now with Tyler because I let my anger get the best of me."

She manages to pull her hands from mine, crossing her arms over her chest. "Oh, so you can let your anger get the better of you, but I can't?"

I sit back, taking a deep breath and smothering the beast for a moment. As much as I love how jealous my little vixen is right now, we can't have her getting us caught. Pushing away from the table, I walk over to her side of the booth and trap her in her seat. Before she can look away, I catch her chin and force her to look at me. Lowering my voice, making sure no one can overhear me, I loom over her. "Soon, little vixen, you will have someone on *your* table and you can pretend it's that waitress, slicing them beautifully and making the floor pool red."

Her eyes, finally meeting my own, show the depths her beast is aching to go. "Promise?"

"I promise, Serena. Once this is all over, and we are free to do as we please again, we can come back here and slaughter the bitch."

Her eyes light up with that promise, and she kisses me. "I'm sorry I snapped like that; this thing with your mom has me on edge, and trying to keep it together, while also trying not to get killed has been, a lot."

I kiss her forehead. "Hey, it's okay. I know this is a lot, and we are in the unknown and have to keep our wits about us, but I am right beside you. You are not alone; you will never be alone. It's me and you until the end." I lean back, looking down at her as heat floods me. "If you need to get your stress out, use my body." I run my finger up her covered thigh, caressing the cuts I know lay just underneath the fabric "Maybe I'll let you make me bleed next time."

She hums, turning to her plate and shaking hot sauce over her food before taking a big bite. I shake my head, amazed at how fast my vixen's mood can change with the promise of revenge and playtime, pulling my plate over and eating in silence, my arm slung possessively over her shoulder.

A different waitress returns to give us our check, and we leave the diner, stuffed, and satisfied.

The cool air hits us as soon as the doors open, and Serena lifts her head to enjoy the cold. She's just like me, we both thrive in the colder weather. She closes her eyes and breathes in the fresh air. Lacing her fingers with mine, she smiles as we walk back to the car. "Smells like it's going to rain."

"Oh yeah? Why do you think that."

She smiles at the darkening sky. "When it's about to rain, the air has a wet smell to it. Fresh. Like how it smells after it rains." She stops walking, "Can't you smell it?" I close my eyes, and inhale. *She's right; the scent is different.*

"You never cease to amaze me, little vixen."

"Keep me around and you'll never stop being impressed."

"Oh, I know-" I stop talking, every instinct in my body on high alert.

"Aster, what's wrong?" Serena asks, her hand tightening around my own.

I lean down to whisper in her ear, looking behind her in the process. "Someone is watching us." Her spine straightens. "Don't react. Take a breath and relax your body" She takes a breath, and I kiss her cheek. I change our course of action, leading us into a store packed with people. I take note of every single face as we walk in. Glancing at Serena, I see she is also observing everything. I smile proudly. *My vixen has been paying attention and learning.*

Serena walks over to a rack of clothes, not interested in any of them, and proceeds to say, "I think we should go. Let's try the next store."

I nod, and we stroll out. As soon as we hit the sidewalk, we quickly walk into the next store, again noting everyone who comes in and out.

We do that four more times, and only one person we both notice who has gone in and out of every store we've been in.

We can't see if they are male or female, their big winter coat and blue scarf obscuring their face and body. We can tell they're short, but can't pinpoint their height as they walk with a slouch. Possibly Caucasian from the brief flash of skin we did see as they never take their hands out of their pockets.

I lean down, and whisper in Serena's ear, "We're going to walk to the back of the store and make eye contact with the person following us. When they look away, we'll make a break for it and run. Do not stop running until you get to the car."

"Okay," Serena whispers.

Walking to the back of the store, our pursuer hot on our tails, my heart races. Serena walks to one side of the long rack of clothes and I amble to the other. Once I feel eyes watching us, I look up to give Serena the signal, but I see she's already looking at me smiling. My eyes flash, impressed at my vixen's instincts, and we both turn at the same time, confronting the first of many of my mother's assassins.

We make eye contact, and just as I hoped, they look away, making the mistake of turning their back to us. We make a run for it. Bursting out of the door. I grab Serena's hand and we sprint across the holiday traffic. I unlock the car and we both dive in. Out of breath, we screech out of town, just as the perpetrator hits the sidewalk. I catch a glimpse in the rearview mirror, pleased their hood fell down, and revealing who they are. I'm too busy getting us the hell out of there, so I didn't get a good enough look, but Serena is staring back, cataloging every feature she can.

WE SKID TO A STOP IN THE DRIVEWAY, LOCKING DOWN THE OUTSIDE fence, and running into the house. We walk around together, searching and securing the home, making sure no one got in or is waiting for us. Once I'm sure the house is clear, I sit Serena on the couch in the living room. I open up the secure app showing every inch of property, but I don't notice anything out of place.

The feeling of being hunted is not the same feeling as being the hunter. Anxiety, I didn't even know I had, courses through me as I pace back and forth raking my fingers through my hair. I was prepared to take out my mothers killers on my terms, but knowing they don't care to go after us while we're out in the open has me frazzled. My mind is reeling, more worried about making sure Serena is safe, than finding out who that guy was, and hunting him down to kill him. If he's as skilled as I think he is, since my mother hired him, I know he will be coming here soon. That thought has me stopping my downward spiral.

"Did you see what the person looked like?" I ask, sitting next to Serena.

"It was a guy. I didn't get a good enough look as we were driving away since they turned their back and walked away," she says, twiddling her fingers.

I grab her hands, and she looks up at me. "You did good, little vixen."

"What if they followed us?"

"Then we deal with it."

She laughs, her eyes sparkling. "I think you jinxed us when you mentioned killing someone your mom sent after us in the diner."

I chuckle. "Yeah, I think I did."

Pulling her into my arms, we sink into the couch, enjoying the silence until my phone blares the alarm we both know means someone entered the property uninvited. After Zephira got in undetected, I put up extra security breaches all over my property. Cameras in every spot, recording every little thing. Motion detectors. Hidden tripwires.

Nothing was going to get past me. Nothing.

Serena sits up as I dig my phone from my pocket, seeing the person from earlier stalking our land. Retrieving my hunting knife from a shelf by the stairs, and three karambit knives, I hand two to Serena. She takes the blades, excitement shining in her eager eyes.

It's too bright to hide in the shadows, but I know this land like the back of my hand, and I've shown Serena everything, so she knows it well enough to become the predator she was born to be. I place my finger over my lips, silently shushing her and checking to see where the guy is at.

After clicking through the feed, I see him lurking around the back of the house, weighing his options on where to enter.

Nowhere is safe. There's nowhere to run and no way of achieving your goal. His death warrant was signed the moment he accepted my mother's hit.

I motion to Serena to go to the front door, bending down to whisper in her ear, "If anything goes wrong, promise me you will run to your kill room."

She looks up at me, eyes wide and lips slightly parted, her brows dipping in an angry vee. "I won't leave you." she harshly whispers.

"Serena." I say sternly, gripping my hand around hers, the handle of the blade digging into her palm, "You will not put yourself in any danger. If you can't get the jump on this guy, or I falter, you will run. I won't let anything happen to you."

She narrows her eyes, and juts her bottom lip out. "Okay," she says quietly.

I kiss those pouty lips I can't get enough of. "I love you."

"I love you too."

Her words say she'll obey, but if I've learned anything about Serena, I know her eyes hold the truth.

Right now her eyes are screaming disobedience.

This girl is going to be my ruin.

CRIME SCENE - DO NOT CROSS · CRIME SCENE

VOL. 10, NO.

BLACK LOTUS

EXCLUSIVE
EXCLUSIVE
EXCLUSIVE

ASTER

SOLITUDE * SOLITUDE

SOLITUDE * SOLITUDE

CROSS

CRIME SCENE - DO NOT CROSS

FIVE
ASTER

Being stealthy with Serena wasn't as difficult as I thought it would be. During our training sessions that often turned into me fucking her when I found her, she would often give her location away by snapping on a twig or crushing the leaves beneath her. Her small mistakes led to me catching her rather quickly, but the more I hunted the better she became. Still, this level of furtiveness is impressive.

Her hand is gripped in mine as I pull us quickly and quietly through the woods. She is a fast learner, and that is something I was grateful for when we started the lessons.

I wonder who the first killer assassin is, chancing their luck with taking us out. I know their primary target is my vixen, but my mother has another thing coming if she thinks I'd let that go down without a fight. That I wouldn't give my life to save Serena's. She could no longer hurt the little boy she abandoned. *Too bad that little boy grew up to be a serial killer who wouldn't think twice about marking his own mother's lips with my special shade of red lipstick and laying her to rest forever.* I started painting the lips of my victims red as a testament to her and everything I came from; even when she was dead to me, she was still my mother and a small part of me hoped she would be watching. Hoped she'd be proud of me. Now I know she is, but it's too late. She wouldn't be a Jane Doe. She would be the first, and only, victim with a name and face.

I'd leave my signature so everyone who knows our connection knows I killed my mother.

Sure, the cops could question me, but I'm her son, one she hasn't ever had contact with since being arrested, and I'll have an airtight alibi. They would never connect the dots.

I pull us behind a tree, the trunk big enough to hide us both. Turning and pushing Serena's back up against the bark. "Ast-" I clamp my hand over her mouth and peer around her to see if our pursuer is done searching the house and level a glare at her. She bites her lip and instant regret fills me. She mouths the word sorry, making my eyes soften. I take my hand away from her mouth and signal her to be quiet. She nods once, I kiss her forehead and look back at the house.

The spot I chose for us to wait in has the perfect view point of the house. When he comes out I can see him, but if he searches where we're at, the tree will conceal us. A wicked smile stretches my lips, Serena's fingers flexing around my biceps as she peers over my shoulder.

The hunted become the hunters, and our prey was stupid enough to try and strike on land he knows nothing about. I could have bear traps set up all over these woods, just waiting to snap and snare. I don't, but now that I think of it, maybe I should lay traps down. With Serena, so she knows where to avoid. Granted, if she was running from two or three killers, then if we had to split up, and she wasn't paying attention; what if she ended up caught in a trap, I would never forgive myself. The trap could hurt her, but it could also lead to her death. That is something I don't ever want to think about. *Yep, it's decided; no to the bear traps.*

I hear Serena blowing into her hands and rubbing them

together, her body shaking against mine. Looking down, I see the tip of her button nose turning red, as are her cheeks. *Shit.* I know we both love the cold but today was forecast to be one of the coldest, and although we both have winter coats on, neither of us had time to grab gloves before we were out the door. I grab her hands, rubbing them between mine and blowing against them. She sighs quietly, her hands warming.

"I like the cold, but not when it's nipple painful cold."

"Nipple painful?" I ask, quirking an eyebrow.

She giggles at my confusion. "Yes, I don't know about other women but when it's really cold my nipples harden to the point of pain." She brings our hands and rubs her sensitive nubs. "Not the kind of pain I welcome either."

I laugh, bringing our hands to my mouth and kissing the delicate skin over her knuckles.

The door to the house slams open, banging against the wall and cracking through the trees. I peer over to see the man standing at the edge of the stairs looking around with a long rifle in hand. *Bastard.* No serial killer worth their reputation kills with a gun, and if he thinks his name will be praised for using one on us, then this sad fuck has another thing coming.

"He has a gun," I whisper, my eyes not leaving our prey. Her body stiffens, her hands tightening in mine. "We need to make it to the shed before he does." Her spine straightens, ready to move on my word. We hear a creak of the worn wood and our heads snap to watch as the guy takes slow, measured steps down, stopping at the edge of the porch.

He's shorter than me from the looks of it, and on the skinnier side now that the giant winter coat he was wearing is replaced with a tight black jacket. He may be more skilled than I give him credit for, and I'd be foolish to think I could take him just based on his looks. I have no idea who he is, how he kills, or what he is capable of, just that his choice of weapon is a rifle. *The best thing for us to do is to catch him by surprise and get him into Serena's kill room.*

We could always kill him in mine, but I want every person who comes after her to perish by her hands, in her space. To unleash her darkness in the place she will soon be most familiar with.

He finally starts walking towards our shared killing rooms, and once he's out of view, my shoulders and hands relax, my knuckles returning from white to their normal color.

"Aster?" Serena whispers, placing her still cold hand gently on my cheek and making me flinch.

I look down and see her brow dipped in concern. Placing my hand over hers, I close my eyes, feeling my heart slow at the contact. "It's okay, little vixen; he walked to the sheds." He may think he's a cat hunting the mice, but he'll soon find out we're the foxes hunting him.

Her eyes close as she tilts her head towards the sky, her body stilling against mine.

"We should start moving." *Leave it to my vixen to bring me back into the moment.*

Instead of responding, I start stalking towards the sheds, careful to be quiet and stay out of sight.

"Aster?" she whispers.

I hum in response, not bothering to look at her, too determined to get us to our destination.

She tugs on my hand, stopping me in my tracks. "I wanted to play with him before we ended him, maybe get some information." She drops her head, disappointment evident in the way her body slouches a little. "How are we supposed to get the jump on him when he has a gun bigger than your dick?"

I nearly trip over the root sticking up from the ground, missing it just in time. "Fuck, Serena, warn a guy before you compare his dick to anything."

She shrugs, unaffected. "What? I was expecting a gun the size of your hand, not one almost half your height. That thing looks like he's compensating for something."

"I get that, but-"

"But why compare it to your cock?" I nod and she steps into me, her finger trailing ice up my chest. "Because, even in a situation like this, all I can think about is your dick pounding into me, preferably bathed in that poor sap's blood."

Fuck. Me.

My hand grips her ass, my cock pressed firmly against her. "After we get this over with, I'm going to make you scream my name, begging me to stop so loud your voice never recovers. I won't. Not until your tears have soaked the ground below you as I make you come over and over and over again."

She shivers in my arms, her chest arching into mine. *"You'll be the one screaming."*

I lift a brow. "Oh? Is that a challenge?"

She steps out of my embrace. "One I intend to win. But we have someone to kill first, and as much as I love teasing you, I *need* to watch that asshole's life leave his eyes while he begs to keep it."

I groan, reaching into my coat pocket. *Now is not the time.* "I grabbed this before we left the house." Her eyes widen as she admires the syringe I'm holding in front of her.

She grabs my hand, her finger brushing against the cover of the needle. "Is that what I think it is?"

I laugh, delighted at how well my vixen knows my M.O. "And what do you think this is?"

Her hands still wrapped around mine, a wicked gleam in her eyes she says, "The drug you use to capture your victims."

My cock jumps. "That's right, vixen"

She jumps up and down, joy radiating from every inch of her. Seeing her like this makes me grateful the first killer came for us at our home; now the fun she craves can begin.

"Can I do the honors?"

As much as I would love to see my vixen take down her first assassin, I haven't taught her how to properly place the needle to get the fastest and most potent results. She looks up at me, making her eyes bigger and sticking her bottom lip out as her fingers once more wrap around the syringe.

"Please?"

Fuck, this girl. I reach down to adjust my growing erection, grateful I put on sweats.

No, I have to be strong; if I let her do this, something could go wrong, which could lead to her death. *I can't.*

"I'm sorry, vixen, not this time."

She bites her lip, her nose running the length of mine. "I'll let you fuck me in the ass."

"Serena…" I groan as her fingers dance up my chest. "As much as I would love to feel your tight hole grip every inch of me, *no*. You haven't had the lessons to know how to do it."

Her fingers stop, her brows dipping as she steps away and crosses her arms. "And whose fault is that?" She mocks, turning her head away.

I pull her head back, tugging her hair enough and her glare locks on my face. "Once *I* take care of the man, I will let you do whatever you want to him. Cut him. Skewer him. Even burn him." Her eyes light up. "But, if you want to get him to talk, then send him to his grave, you have to listen and be patient with me. Okay?"

She huffs, but her shoulders relax. "Okay."

I bring my lips to softly kiss her own, a promise that her time will come.

I look around the tree, making sure the coast is clear and that our loud whispers didn't attract any unwanted attention from our uninvited guest. Seeing nothing but trees and snow, I place my finger in front of my mouth, miming to Serena to be quiet. She rolls her eyes, but walks quietly behind me.

Walking closer to the sheds, it's eerily quiet. It doesn't sound, or look like either door has been pried open. The sound opening my shed could be heard from where we wait, and neither me nor Serena heard that familiar sound. I look back at my vixen, her eyes wide and chewing mindlessly on her bottom lip, nerves radiating off her. I can't tell from fear or excitement. *Maybe both?* I tug on her arm, and her eyes lift to mine, breaking the spell between her and the buildings. She shrugs, clearly more unbothered than I first assumed. Realizing my energy was the nervous one, and I was projecting that onto her, a thin laugh slips from my lips, the stress exiting with it. *I need to get my shit together.* If my vixen isn't worried, then I sure as hell shouldn't be either. We are in this together and we won't go down without a fight.

She squeezes my hand softly, mouthing the words, "It'll be okay." I squeeze her hand back, letting her know I trust her. *More than myself at the moment.*

Standing here in the unknown, waiting for anything to happen, hearing nothing but the wind blowing and our cold breaths sets my teeth on edge.

Snap!

Our heads whip towards the sound, and we duck out of sight, crouching behind a bush that has somehow not died with the rest. It sounds like our attacker hadn't made it to the sheds yet, instead looking in the woods. My fingers tighten around the syringe, getting ready to strike. The guy's getting closer, him being far less quiet than we are. *Makes for an easy target.* It's safe to assume he's a newer killer playing his hand at getting his name, and who he is, out by fulfilling the hit on Serena.

When we hear him only feet away, we quietly maneuver around the brush and watch as this kid- *Shit.* Now that we are closer, I can make out his features, and he doesn't look older than twenty at the absolute most. Serena notices too, and her face morphs from excitement to worry. Guess we both weren't expecting our first victim to be a kid. *How did my mother get her claws into this piece of shit? What is she promising everyone to make them come after my girl?* They have to know they'd be going up against the Morbid Monet, a feared name even among other killers. Sure, none of us know who the others are, but when my name is whispered, you can see the fear in their eyes. Yes, I have my prime victims, my little lambs, but soon the whole world will know that I placed my brush down for a new set of prey. If they aren't scared yet, I will make them fear me and my vixen. Anyone who comes after us will know how their story ends.

With a blue rose and black lotus.

Even before Serena told me her signature, I went ahead and ordered a bundle of black lotuses to a P.O box that has a different name, hoping it was what she would choose. A part of me knowing that would be her choice.

The loud squeak of my shed shatters the silence, and I look up in time to see the bastard flinch and look around. After a minute of waiting he scoffs and enters my space. My muscles tighten. "Stay here," I whisper to Serena. Her mouth opens, but before she can protest, I place my hand over her mouth, and her nostrils flare. "*Please*, Serena. Once I take him out, you can come help me move his body into your space. Then the fun can begin."

A muffled, and sarcastic, "Thanks" fills the air, and I chuckle. *There's my bloodthirsty girl.* All this waiting has made her more bratty and defiant than usual, and her simple remark has me hoping she's going to listen so I can keep her alive.

I lean down and kiss her forehead before making my way to the shed.

Watching my steps, I avoid the spots that would make any noise. Before entering my kill space, I take out my phone and turn the camera on to see if I can see where the guy is and what he is doing.

He's looking through my drawers, touching my weapons. My hand tightens around the smooth glass, my jaw clenching when he picks up the knife I use to end my little lambs. One I haven't touched in quite a while.

My feet are moving, my hand raised high overhead, before I register what I'm doing, my anger taking over. "That's mine," I growl.

The kid turns around, the knife falling from his hands and clattering to the ground. He fumbles for his gun, but before he can grab the rifle, my needle is in his neck. His hand wraps around the injection site. He coughs, falling backwards and knocking down my table of instruments in the process.

Leaning down, I remove the cover from his face, my nose scrunching in disgust at his cowardly ways. *It's as if he doesn't take any pride in his kills. He doesn't crave the fear and dread the rest of us do.*

I hear pants from my vixen, her steps becoming louder as she gets closer to the shed. Closing my eyes, I stand, my hand snaps out and closes around her neck, squeezing just enough for her to feel the frustration.

"I thought I told you to *wait* until I called for you?"

"I thought you were in trouble," she gasps through my hold, clawing at my hand for the air she so desperately needs.

I force her against the wall, my hold tightening as my body begs for hers. "If you thought I was in trouble, you should've run."

She lifts her chin, challenging me despite our power imbalance. "I will never run," she strains, face turning red.

Exasperated, I release her, watching as she falls to the floor in a coughing fit, her eyes flaming. She steps up to me, jabbing her finger into my chest. "I would rather die than watch you fall."

I wrap my hand around her finger, silence all around us. We stay there, eyes locked, neither one of us backing down.

Her chest heaves, the anger coursing through her unable to be contained. *I should've known my vixen wouldn't obey me.* I should have known she would run in here ready to die for me.

I bring her finger to my mouth, slowly wrapping my lips around it, her eyes watching the movement with rapt attention as she mindlessly licks her own lip. A small smile tugs at my cheeks, her hand jerking back when my teeth bite into her sensitive flesh. She cradles her hand to her chest, her forehead wrinkling in shock.

"Next time, it'll be your clit."

Her mouth falls open, and before she can respond, I walk away. "We have an assassin to question; I suggest you close that pretty mouth of yours unless you want me to shove my cock down your throat before slitting his."

I look over my shoulder to see her mouth snap closed, an arrogant smirk breaking through my haze of anger.

Her shoulder bumps mine as she bends down to grab the sleeping fool's feet.

"Aren't you going to help me?" she grumpily asks, his feet suspended in the air.

I lean back on the table. "I don't know; are you going to be a good girl and listen when I tell you to stay put?"

"I'm not a fucking dog."

Pushing off the table, I bend down to help lift him. "No, but you are *my* vixen. Even foxes run from danger."

She grunts, as we walk him to her shed. "I'm not like the other vixens. When I see danger, I walk right up to it, look it in the eye, and say, 'you chose the wrong girl to fuck with; time to die.' Then, I'll slit their throat or something."

I laugh at how nonchalant she says the last part, almost dropping the fucker. "I don't pity anyone who dares go against my vixen."

She smiles. "It's why you love me."

I shake my head, chuckling. "Bold of you to assume that."

"Hey!" She bolts upright, shock and pain painting her face.

"Shit! Serena, don't drop him!"

She grips his legs tighter. "Don't say stupid things."

Sighing, I suck my teeth before giving into her demands. "Yes, it's one of the many reasons I love you."

She smiles triumphantly. "That's better."

I'm going to have to teach her a lesson later.

We reach Serena's shed and I carefully toss him over my shoulder. "You're telling me you could have carried him yourself this whole time?"

Tightening my grip with one arm around his legs she opens the door. "Yep."

"Then why the hell did you have me help you?" She throws her hands in the air.

"I like watching you struggle." I shrug.

Her jaw drops. "Asshole," she mumbles, making me chuckle.

She stomps into the room and I watch as she pulls her favorite three books in order to get into her kill space. Three clicks later, the door opens and we bring the idiot into the room, towards his demise.

CRIME SCENE - DO NOT CROSS - CRIME SCENE

BLACK LOTUS

EAGLE EXCLUSIVE

ASTER

SOLITUDE   *   SOLITUDE

SOLITUDE   *   SOLITUDE

SIX
ASTER

"Put that down," I tell Serena, the guy's gun clutched in her hands. After we got him secured, she left and came back holding the rifle. I told her we didn't have time to play; we needed to wake him up and get him talking, but my vixen isn't known for her listening skills. I tighten the straps holding him down with a grunt, my frustration evident in the unnecessary way I overly secure him. She is acting too carefree for someone who could've been a victim. I move down to his legs repeating the same process wishing she'd just be a good girl and obey, but that isn't the woman I fell in love with. I need to start trusting her, she can take care of herself, and I need to let her, even if it kills me in doing so.

"I think it's a musket." She tips the barrel down, examining the weapon.

Spinning around, I snatch the gun to examine it myself and, sure enough, it is a musket.

"Shit."

"What's wrong?" Serena asks, coming up behind me.

Instead of answering, I walk over to the sleeping guy and reach into his pockets, pulling out a musket ball. I turn the rusted ball over in my hand, seeing the initials CK on them. My hand tightens around the ball like a snake constricting around its prey. Anger seeping from every crevice in my body at the thought that this waste of space would dare attempt a shot at Serena, my vixen's life.

"Aster?"

"It's the Concord Killer," I mumble, lifting the ball into the light. She takes the cool steel from my hand, squinting at it.

"He makes these himself, doesn't he?"

"I do."

Coughing echoes behind us, and we spin around to see the Concord Killer is awake. *How is he awake already?* In all the years I've used ketamine, no one has woken up that fast. It usually takes me doing something to my victims to begin the fun. Squinting at the man before me, I examine his state without touching him, trying and failing to understand how he is speaking right now.

"You've heard of me." His eyebrows dance in an arrogant way, his nose turned up at us like the pompous ass I expected him to be.

I stalk over to him, a snarl ripping from my throat, peering down into his unbothered eyes, his black hair falling across his face. "What I *know* is you're cocky, arrogant without cause, and shunned in our world."

He rolls his eyes. "Just because I use a gun doesn't mean I'm not a better serial killer than any of you assholes."

"It means you're a coward. Someone looking for prestige without earning it." Serena sneers, walking into his line of sight.

He lets out a low whistle. "You are a sight for sore eyes, beautiful. Heaven sent. Too bad you have to die."

My knuckles connect with his face, spit and teeth scattering across the floor. "Shut the fuck up."

He laughs, blood dribbling out of his mouth and coating his teeth. "I could have her screaming around my coc-"

A pop echoes around the room and my thumb digs into his eye, blood cascades down when I pull it out. I drop it, letting it dangle off the side of his face. He screams as his body lurches off of the table, his hand desperately trying to break free to cover the pain. My fists slam into him over and over again even after his one eye closes and his screams cease. The red I see isn't just his blood, it's the rage I feel realizing how little Mother, and everyone else in our world, cares about Serena. *Who the fuck does he think he is speaking about my girl that way?* I wanted to get answers, but I crave his death more. It isn't until I feel Serena's hand touch my shoulder, my name a whisper through the angry fog, for my rage to fade and my wrath to cool. My hands are bloody, but I'm not sure if it's mine or his.

"We need him alive," Serena says, pulling me away from CK's unconscious body.

"I know, but-" Her hand caresses my cheek, my breath catching at her softness.

"But you let your emotions get the better of you."

"Yeah." I hang my head in shame. How am I supposed to expect Serena to keep her emotions in check when I lose all control.

"Sounds like we both need to work on that."

I kiss the inside of her palm, my heart slowing. "When it comes to you, I lose all sense of rationality."

She brings her lips to mine, effortlessly erasing the high I was in. "Want to talk about what just happened while we wait for him to come to? If he comes to…"

I hold onto her hand like a lifeline, keeping me from tipping over the edge again and place my fingers on his neck. "He has a pulse."

She smiles softly. "That's good."

She opens a couple drawers, searching for something until she finds and pulls out a rag, tossing it at me. "Clean yourself up and meet me in the library."

With that she opens the kill room door and leaves. Her eyes showed understanding and her touch felt compassionate, but I can't help and feel like I'm a child who is about to get scolded for his behavior.

After I clean myself off, taking my time to get every speck of blood, I join her.

She pats the spot next to her, and I climb onto the chaise. I lay my head on her lap, her fingers brushing my hair, bringing me a sense of calmness I have never experienced. My mother never showed the kind of love Serena shows me, she showed it through food and lessons.

I wonder if this is how Serena would be like with our child? The thought of being parents to our own little monster warms my heart, but also brings a sense of dread. *What kind of parents would we be?* Would we raise our child as mine did me and make them into a killer? Or would we be like Tiffany and Chucky and abstain from murder? I would leave that up to Serena, but I couldn't imagine not being able to get a little stabby to the ones who deserve it. *Could I stop being who I've always been to create a family I don't deserve?* I never thought I was the type of killer to ever want a family, but I've found anything with Serena is a possibility.

Serena's calming voice pulls me from my thoughts. "You know, as hot as that was watching you lose control, we don't know how many killers are coming or how many we could actually get information from."

"I don't regret it." I sit up.

"Me either," Serena says softly, and we both start laughing.

We sit back, letting the silence surround us as our thoughts consume us. The Concord Killer has a high kill count. He's cocky; the headlines for his kills emphasize how he doesn't care about the shot heard around the world. He's precise as a sniper, which is begrudgingly impressive given his choice of weapon. Running my fingers through Serena's hair, I realize I know more about CK than I thought I did. He's not quick, but he's unnervingly deadly. No one knows where he got his musket from, and they can't trace who he is because he makes his own ammo.

What are the chances he's the one landing in our laps? He seems arrogant and smug, but his eyes hold the truth. He is scared, even though he says he isn't. *I can work with that.* After all, fear is what I feed off of, and any man or woman who says anything to my girl is the best meal a killer could have.

Serena stands up, reaching her hand out to me. "Are you ready to make this poser squeal?"

Placing my hand in hers, we walk back into her kill room.

"Where do you keep the smelling salts?" Serena asks, bouncing on her heels. I retrieve the salts from a drawer, dropping them in Serena's grabby hands.

She runs over to the table and snaps the bag, his swollen eyes springing open.

"Rise and shine, CK," Serena singsongs.

"It's Nate." The idiot spits, pulling against his restraints.

Serena grabs a knife and touches the tip to her finger, hissing and sucking her finger into her mouth. *This woman is going to be my undoing.* The fabric of my pants stretching uncomfortably with my growing erection. I adjust myself as Serena brings the blade inches from the one eye still intact, his throat bobbing the closer she gets.

"Did I ask for your name?" She stabs the blade on the table beside his head, making the coward flinch. "I don't give a shit about learning the name of the person sent to kill me. What I want to know is what you get for my head."

A serpentine smile spreads across his face "What do I get if I answer your question, beautiful?"

Restraining myself from killing him, refusing to take away Serena's fun, I press my back into the wall, my knuckles white.

Serena brings the blade to his neck and his breath hitches. She looks up at me and smiles as the knife nicks his pale skin, his teeth grinding from the pain. I cross my arms, digging my nails into them to keep myself from ripping the clothes off my vixen. The way her monster is coming out to play is making mine restless.

Her eyes widen as she watches the blood form from the cut, her gloved hand pressing on the wound opening the cut further and making him hiss. A satisfied grin lifting her cheeks. She removes her fingers and walks around the table, his wide eyes following her every movement. The knife swings back and forth as it loosely hangs upside down like a clock ticking. His gaze tracks the movement waiting for the moment she strikes again.

She tosses the knife in the air, time stops as I will my body not to lunge forward to push her out of the way. Nate's eyes pinch closed just before she catches the blade next to his ribs with a cackle escaping her lips. I let go of the breath I was holding, watching in amazement at the knife skills I didn't know my vixen held. The knife pierces his skin as she walks up the table, his jeans staining red.

He's trying to hide it, but it seems like the cocky facade is slipping with each bite of the steel she cuts into his skin.

My hand twitches as I will myself to stay put. I feel like a fish out of water with the urge to take the knife from Serena to finish the job. The last time I cut into flesh was my birthday kill, and even then I wasn't fully satisfied. Will I ever be able to satiate the hunger that came with the hunt and kill of my lambs? Will these hunters be enough for me to kill? Or will I revert back to the monster I was before Serena? Only time and killing will tell.

"You, Nate, will get nothing except the satisfaction of your death delivering my message to everyone waiting to come next. So, if I were you, I'd start talking, or the torture will be worse than anything the demons in hell will throw at you when you get there."

Nate's throat bobs and sweat begins to glisten across his forehead. He turns away, probably thinking she won't hold true to her threat. *Oh, how little he knows about my venomous vixen.* At his snub, Serena jabs the knife under his kneecap, the small bone nearly dislodged from the force of her ire, and an ear shattering scream rips from Nate's throat. "Fuck! You fucking bitc-"

She rips the blade out, blood seeping into his pants as she

slams it into the other side, "That isn't what I asked." She slowly drags the knife across his skin, lifting it to watch the blood drip down the tapered end.

"Fame…" Nate wheezes.

"Fame?"

"The most notorious serial killer to ever live. Taking you out is the first step"

"Is that it?" Serena asks, annoyed.

"Yes!"

She steps closer, ripping his shirt open and sending the buttons flying. "Now, why don't I believe you?" she asks, dragging the knife over his chest.

"I swear it's the truth."

His nipple goes flying, and I make a mental note to find that to dispose of later. "Money!" he squeals like the pig he is.

"See; was that so hard?" She slices the other nipple off with a delicate flick of her wrist.

"What the fuck, cunt! I answered your question!"

"You did, but I couldn't leave you uneven. Next question, and if you answer with no backtalk I might not use this on…" She points the blade down his body, and his eyes get so big they would pop out of his head if I didn't remove one earlier.

"How does this kill list work?"

He coughs, but answers without a retort. "Cynthia sent untraceable letters to serial killers around the states. There was a number to place your bid, and coded details for an offshore account to get your spot after you submitted money." His voice becomes raspy, the more he speaks. "I was the lowest bidder, so I got first dibs. Whoever kills you gets all the money in the account, minus Cynthia's normal cut, and the money stays in the pot until someone succeeds. It's a lot. It would even tempt lover boy over there."

Serena stares impassively at Nate. "See? Was that so hard? I guess you get to keep your balls. For now." Nate tries to cover himself, but his hands don't reach. "Next question. Do you know why she's doing this?" My head tilts at the question we know the answer to. *She's a distraction according to my mother, is she trying to see if he's telling the truth or searching for something else?*

He barks a laugh, blood dripping down his chin "You think a woman like Cynthia would tell us why she wants you dead?" He scoffs, relaxing against the table. "We're just servants doing her bidding. She's powerful. She has eyes everywhere." His eye meet Serena's, his cockiness creeping back in. "You'll never escape."

Her fingers shift around the handle. "Last question. Who won the next bid?"

Nate's eye darkens, a bloody smile twisting his bloated features. "The Twisted Trickster." A maniacal laugh echoes around the room as my spine stiffens. Serena slices the knife across his throat, silencing Nate and watching the life drain from his eye.

CRIME SCENE - DO NOT CROSS
CRIME SCENE - DO NOT
THE BLACK LOTUS
SPECIAL EDITION
Daily
ARDELLA
10 APRIL 2025
A DARK ROMANCE
VOL. 10, NO. 5
THE BLACK LOTUS
EXCLUSIVE
EXCLUSIVE
EXCLUSIVE
EXCLUSIVE
EXCLUSIVE
EXCLUSIVE
CRIME SCENE - DO
DO NOT CRO
SOLITUDE
SOLITUDE
SOLITUDE

THE BLACK LOTUS

SERENA

CROSS

SEVEN
SERENA

It's the witching hour as we drive to the dump location Aster has yet to disclose to me. He says the destination is a part of the journey and, just like when he disposed of his little lambs, every location is different but secluded.

I wanted nothing more than to lay down curled up next to Aster and fall asleep after we killed him, but Nate's body needed to be dealt with. My needs were not as important as completing what we started. If we waited too long the body would start to decompose, making it harder to relocate. It had to be at night when no one could see what we were doing.

Unlike his little lambs, he did not paint Nate's body, so the world will know the true face of the Concord Killer. When I asked Aster why he didn't want to paint Nate, he said since the Morbid Monet has a partner in crime now, he wanted to recreate his signature with me. When I asked why he painted them to begin with he said that he wanted his lambs to remain his, no one was to ever know who they were after they laid on his table. The thought that I was almost his lamb has me grateful I'm now his vixen, the match to his crazy. My crazy is different from his since I was seeing a person who wasn't actually there, but we both crave power. Taking a life, watching the blood splatter is the kind of chaos our love was made in. He may have been bred to be a serial killer, but he was always meant to be mine, and together we will paint the world crimson.

During my interrogation to find out more about Cynthia's plans, I expected Aster to join in, to give me hands-on learning experience, and for us to kill Nate together. But, just like Bradley, he stood off to the side watching. I understand that he loves watching the beast within me break free and run amuck, but I want his darkness to join mine. I want to create a bloody master-piece of *our* victims. Together.

The car slows to a stop in front of an old, abandoned ware-house. There is a chain link fence blocking our entry, so Aster reaches behind him and grabs the bolt cutters he had laying on the floor. "Stay here," he demands, his voice almost unrecogniz-able. Without waiting for a response, he leaves the car, his door left open as he cuts the lock and pushes the gate all the way open. You would think with how old this place looks the hinges would squeak, but nothing except the sound of the harsh wind hits my ears, the cold bite and my killing high slowly fading has me shivering, even in a long sleeved shirt.

He gets back in the car and we pull around to the back of the building. "Have you been here before?" I ask, placing my hand against the window.

"I have several places picked for dump sites I have scoped, but not used yet."

My breath fogs the window. "For your little lambs?" I turn to look at him. "Or for our victims."

He smirks leaving my question unanswered and hands me a black bonnet. "What's this for?" I ask, wrapping my hair up and placing the cap over it.

Aster reaches over, tucking a fallen strand of hair into the cover. "This is your first time disposing of a body; we don't want any chance of your DNA being left behind. Here." He hands me a pair of matching black gloves.

"No fingerprints." I smile, pulling them on.

"Exactly."

He gets out of the car, and walks to my side holding small boots in front of me. My mouth drops open, my nose scrunching in disbelief. "My feet will be squashed in those."

"We need to make them fit." He bends down and takes a cloth out of his pocket. "If we leave any kind of footprint behind, they need to never track it to us." I hiss as he wraps my feet, kissing the top of them after each one is secure. No wonder he hasn't been caught or has never been a suspect; he goes to extensive lengths to make sure no trace of him is left behind. Just evidence of someone that doesn't match his well, *anything*.

"After we're done here, I promise to give you a foot massage."

He slips on the boots, each one entering without resistance. "It better be a toe curling, orgasmic foot rub." I wink.

He chuckles, getting off his knees and holding his hand out for me. "Look at you being all gentlemanly," I tease, wrapping my fingers around his.

"Even monsters are taught manners. How else do you think the lambs fall at my feet?" My eyes travel down his body. *Your dick.*

His hand captures my wrist as I try to smack his chest. *Asshole is goading me on purpose.* The fog from our breathing clouds the air between us, his eyes taking on a predatory look through the mist, one that has every instinct in my body screaming at me to run as my core begs for him to fill it, but we still have a body to dispose of. Reluctantly, I pull my hand from his, breaking the spell, and walk to the trunk. "This body isn't going to take care of itself," I tell a still frozen Aster. "You can chase me and live up to the promise in your eyes later, fox." He shakes his head, clearing his shock before sauntering over to me.

"Grab that bag." He points to a black duffel he must've put in here when I was getting ready.

I huff, dragging the bag out of the trunk. "Why is it so heavy?"

"You'll see," Aster chuckles, a deadly smirk stretching across his lips.

He effortlessly hefts Nate's body over his shoulder, grabbing his musket in the other hand, and I follow, taking note of my surroundings as we walk to the building. We drove for quite some time, and this warehouse, along with several more flanking either side, are all abandoned. Broken and boarded up windows make up most of the building's features now. We walk towards the door and I flinch when I step on a piece of broken glass. A loud bang has me dropping the duffel in my hand, my wide eyes locking on Aster's laughing ones. "What the fuck, Aster!" I whisper shout, picking up the heavy bag with a growl.

He shrugs. "Had to open the door somehow." *And alert everyone to our presence.*

Storming through the door, no longer caring about being quiet. *If he doesn't care about being loud, then neither will I.* "What'd you do? Kick it down?" I ask sarcastically, already knowing the answer.

He gives me a cheeky grin. "Exactly."

I roll my eyes while striding past him into the dark pit of Nate's new resting place. "Welcome home *poser*," he says, laying Nate's body down on the cement floor. Dropping the bag, I sit beside the body, out of breath from our trek into the building. Plus, my feet are killing me. Sitting criss-cross, I massage one foot through my boot, trying to relieve some of the ache. *I really hope I won't have to do this every time we kill someone; I'd rather just burn them. No body, no evidence.* Glancing around the gloomy space, my nose curls at the damp smell I can't escape. *Easier than all of this.* But Aster said we need to send a message to the others coming after us, to let them know what will happen if they try their hand for my head. And I agree. We know it won't deter all of them, but some have to be smart enough not to go up against us. My lips thin at the thought. Only time will tell.

"Hand me the bag," Aster says, reaching behind his back and waiting for me to place the bag in his hand.

"Get it yourself."

He grabs the bag, effortlessly and walks back to Nate. "Come here," he demands.

I crawl over to him, a second failed attempt at easing some of the pain from my feet. *Man, I wish I could rip these boots off.* I sit quietly on my knees watching Aster sit Nate's body up against a pile of rubble.

When I was in my killing space, taunting and torturing my first assassin, it felt like an out of body experience. Looking at a different version of me, someone darker and more twisted, I was the monster who had finally been set free. I just know when Aster finally joins me it'll be euphoric and end with us naked and fucking next to our victim. I bite my lip at the thought as I rub my thighs together, failing to ease the ache between my legs.

After he places him how he wants him, he pulls out a blue rose and black lotus from his back pocket. *When did he grab those?* My eyes zero in on the beauty of them both, thorns protruding from the rose and barely visible on the lotus. Both flowers are lovely, but one wrong move and they both can make you bleed.

Aster tries to hand the lotus to me but I stop him before he can, a devious idea crossing my mind.

"What are you doing?" he asks as I stand on wobbly legs offering me his arm. I grab it and pull myself up. Once I'm steady I walk over to grab the musket.

Checking to see that there is still ammo in the gun, I point the barrel at Nate's chest, motioning with my head for Aster to move.

His eyes widen as he steps behind me, covering his ears, watching as I blow Nate's chest cavity wide open with his own weapon. *Shot heard around the world.* I chuckle as my ears ring, somehow having not dropped the gun in the process, my bright idea biting me in the ass. After the buzzing in my head stops, I wipe the sweat mixed with gunpowder and guts off my face, and lay the gun back down. "All done, you can continue."

Aster closes his mouth, shaking his head in disbelief and

places the rose where Nate's chest had been. He looks back at me, features softening as he hands me the black lotus. "You choose where you want to leave your signature, vixen."

My heart swells as I contemplate where to leave my mark. This is a big decision. What I choose today is where I will need to leave my flower every time. I need it to mean something. Something only Aster and I will know the true meaning behind. My eyes scan Nate's body, moving from each part until finally landing on the one. *I can't believe it took me this long to figure out where I wanted it.* It's so obvious that if I'd waited any longer deciding, the dead body would have come back to life and bitten me.

Leaning down, I place my lotus right next to Aster's rose, answering him before he has the chance to ask why. "Your signature was about the heart you didn't have. Mine is to show who owns it." He leans down and kisses the top of my head before we both sit back and admire our work.

He reaches into the bag to grab a different rose, taking two petals off, but I stop him. Shaking my head, I limp over to where the bag lays, my feet screaming to be set free. *I am going to burn these shoes when we get home.*

I kneel down to examine the contents in the duffel. *No wonder it was so heavy.* This is a kill bag, most likely Nate's since there are extra balls and what looks like gunpowder in it. I grab what I'm looking for, a mischievous smile splitting my cheeks. Placing the items over the eyes, I look down at our handiwork.

Aster pulls me to my feet and spins me around. "You have quite the sense of humor."

I laugh along with him. "You have a partner now, my fox, and I'm just getting started."

"My, my what do we have here?" A familiar voice sounds from the doorway startling us both. We turn around to find Zephira standing with her arms crossed. "When I heard the gun go off I thought that the Concord Killer might have won the bid after all." She pushes off the wall and steps closer. "But then I thought no way could that wannabe killer get the jump on my big brother or his lamb."

"Vixen," Aster growls, correcting his sister.

"For now," she says, placing her hands behind her back as she stands next to Nate's body looking down at him. "Quite the number you did on him. I'm assuming this is your finishing touch, brother?" She turns around at the last word.

I answer before Aster has a chance to. "Actually, this was my idea *and* my work."

Her eyebrows shoot up and the corner of her lip lifts. "Impressive. Who would have thought that a killer was lurking inside you. Very poetic, killing him with his own weapon."

"There is a lot about me that you and-" I spit the next word, "-your mother will never know."

"Indeed." She walks past me, her shoulder brushing mine, sending a skitter of goosebumps trailing up my arm. "It's going to be hard to let you go."

"She's not yours to let go!" Aster yells after her, but she has already left the building, leaving us standing there in the silence. "Even in death I would never let you go."

"And I you."

He kisses me, lifting me into his arms bridal style, my feet *finally* getting the break they needed. I smile up at him as I relax into his hold and we go back to the car, leaving all the evidence of who Nate is behind, ready and waiting for anyone to find.

CRIME SCENE - DO NOT CROSS

BLACK LOTUS

EXCLUSIVE

ASTER

SOLITUDE   *   SOLITUDE

SOLITUDE   *   SOLITUDE

EIGHT
ASTER

"Breaking news at eleven! We come to you live on the scene with Deputy Wiley to tell us what was found at an abandoned warehouse." The news reporter points the microphone at a cop that looks vaguely familiar. Sitting up straighter I look at the young deputy who is being interviewed, taking in all of his facial features. I feel I have seen him somewhere before, but the mustache covering his upper lip reminds me of a hairy caterpillar and it is throwing off my memory.

Serena and I sit on the couch, a blanket thrown over our legs and her head resting on my chest as we watch our work being investigated. It took only a day for the body to be discovered by a homeless person who was looking for a warm place to sleep. Poor old guy got more than he bargained for.

"What can you tell us about what happened here? People are speculating it was the Morbid Monet, some claiming he now has a partner, or worried it is a copycat? Can you elaborate anything on this matter?" the reporter asks.

"Evidence points to the Monet's signature, but we have to evaluate everything before we can come to any conclusions," says the deputy, looking right into the camera.

"Can you tell us who the victim is?"

"Without DNA evidence we won't know for sure, but based on the items left behind, we believe the victim is the Concord Killer." The reporter's mouth falls open at the shocking news, but she quickly composes herself. *"That is all I can tell you for now."* Deputy Wiley walks away before she can ask anything else, the camera following his frame as he heads back into the warehouse.

The reporter appears back on the screen. *"You heard it here first, folks. Has the Morbid Monet changed his victim profile? Has Salem's most notorious killer gained a partner in crime? Or is it someone else entirely?"* She places her gloved hand to her ear. *"What? Okay,"* she gulps into her ear piece *"Ladies and gentlemen, we have pictures from the crime scene that an anonymous party has sent in; we will show it to you now but as a warning, viewer digression is advised."*

Serena looks at me, her eyebrows dipped as she sits up and stares at the scene intently. "Do you think it was Zephira?" she asks, her body vibrating from anticipation.

"Who else would it be but my annoying little sister?"

"She's not that bad."

I quirk a questioning brow at my sweet, naive girlfriend. "She's keeping tabs on you for my mother, the woman who wants you dead."

She shrugs her shoulders. "For now." Turning her head to look back at me, a devious smile that has me fearing the ideas churning in her head. "I think we can get her on our side."

"Sure if my mother didn't have her claws embedded into her." Serena rolls her eyes and focuses her attention back to the tv, relaxing back into my arms.

The frame switches to the picture of Nate laying there with his gun beside him, flowers in his hand over his open chest, and his musket balls over his one eye and the socket of the hanging one. Serena starts laughing, and I chuckle at her cleverness.

"You have to admit that is fucking funny," she cries, swiping a tear from her eye.

Kissing the top of her head, I agree. "Yes. Yes, it is, my little vixen."

The screen switches back to the reporter with her gloved hands covering her mouth, the microphone now hanging upside down in her grasp. Someone whispers her name, breaking her shock. She shakes her head and composes herself.

"As you can see, it looks like Monet's signature, but we can't be sure until the police release more information. Thank you for joining us, and we will report back when we have any updates."

Serena clicks off the tv, stretching her arms above her head and yawning. "I could go for some coffee; want a cup?"

Pushing her back down onto the couch, I get up. "I'll make it; lay down and rest your eyes. It will take a while to brew."

She nods, eyes fluttering closed as she lays back down. I grab the blanket she discarded and place it back over her, walking to the kitchen to make us coffee.

The events of last night were weird, but welcoming. *I've never prepared a body with anyone before.* I've always been alone, doing things my way. Getting to do them with Serena, having her special touch added, paying homage to me in her own way, swelled my heart.

I make a whole pot because I know my sleeping caffeine addict has to have more than one cup a day. She usually goes to her favorite coffee place in the morning, but I told her to switch up her routine. *If I already learned her routine, there is no telling who else is learning it, too.* So now she makes coffee at home, complains it isn't the same, but she agrees with my thought process and only goes to the shop randomly.

"You seriously need to slow down on your coffee intake, it isn't good for your heart."

"You need to learn to mind your own business when it comes to my favorite thing," Serena teases, sucking loudly through the straw.

Scooting closer to my brave woman, my eyes travel to her lips as I whisper my next words. "I know the vice you prefer over that poison."

Her sipping ceases, her gaze traveling down my body as her teeth chew on the plastic. I sit back on the couch. "But if you'd rather have caffeine filling you over me..."

She grabs my bicep, the drink placed in her hands stopping me from leaving her side. "Can't I have both?" she muses.

Shaking my head I lean in, my voice caressing her ear. "I'm the only poison that can wreck you." Her face turns a light pink shade as I go to grab her cup. My hands wrap around it and she grabs my wrist, a warning growl slipping past her lips. Did she just growl at me?

"If you want to keep those fingers you better let go of my cup."

My hands retract and I wiggle my digits in front of her face. "You need these fingers to please you."

She scoffs, showing me her own hands. "I have my own to use."

She gets off the couch after placing her cup down. Before I can say anything, she saunters up the steps. I stalk behind her like a leopard waiting for the right moment to pounce. Her steps slow as she makes her way to our bedroom, her breath being the only sound I can hear. Her hand stalls turning the knob of our door, my breath tickling the back of her neck as she waits for the punishment she knows is coming.

"Go ahead. Open the door," I taunt.

She takes a deep breath as the knob turns and I take that moment to wrap my arms around her legs, tossing her over my shoulder and laying a hard smack on her ass. She squeals, but doesn't fight me, just lets her body hang.

I toss her onto our bed, her body bouncing when she lands, her hair a beautiful halo around her. Her mouth drops slightly open as I undo my belt and take it off. "Turn around."

She licks her lips and obeys, laying on her stomach.

Placing my hands under her, I pull her into the position I need her in. "On your knees."

She turns her head to look at me over her shoulder, her hair falling down in waves covering her beautiful face. I tuck a strand behind her ear, pressing the middle of her back down. Her head dips as my hands travel down to her ass to take off her jeans.

I growl my approval as my hand brushes her plump ass. Folding my belt in half I swing it down over my head, her skin turning a bright red from where it struck.

She moans her approval. "More."

A dark chuckle slips out, my lips turning up. "You're going to regret saying that."

Harder, the belt lashes against her flesh, her teeth sucking in from the pain. "How many times do I have to whip you for you to learn your lesson?" I ask.

"One," she breathes.

The sound of her ass being smacked by the black leather mixes with her panting, the erection in my pants growing. "Try again. This time you better be honest with yourself."

"Seven."

I place my finger on my lip, contemplating her answer. "Double it."

A small gasp escapes her as her eyes pinch shut. She nods her head in defeat as I begin my assault on her skin. Small grunts of pain accompany the sound like a melody of my own creation. Her cries of torment will end in pleasure as her moans create a symphony of bliss.

After the seventh smack, I drop the belt, tearing my jeans down as I slam into her and her screams become my desire while my hand lays the final seven blows.

Her pussy constricts around my cock at the final strike, my cock emptying inside her, filling her with my volition.

Our breaths soon match one another as I slide out of her and kiss the marks of my fervor.

THE MACHINE BEEPS, AND I TAKE THE WHOLE POT AND PUT IT IN THE fridge. Serena likes iced coffee after a nap, hot right when she wakes up in the morning, and whatever sounds good in the evening. Putting it in the fridge gives her the option for either and keeps the coffee good for twenty-four hours, although with her, it never lasts that long.

I join my sleeping girl on the couch, placing her legs on my lap. Tipping my head back, thoughts of who might be coming next briefly crossing my mind before exhaustion takes over and I drift to sleep.

I wake to the sound of liquid hitting ice. Sitting up, groaning at my aching muscles, I look over and see Serena drinking her iced coffee with a mischievous look in her eyes.

Walking over to her, I grab the pot from her and make myself a cup. "What's that look for?" I ask, placing the mug in the microwave.

"I was just thinking," she hums, a calculating smile lifting her cheeks.

"About?" I ask, putting my vanilla cream and sugar in the steaming cup. I may be a dude but that doesn't mean I don't like my coffee sweet. I actually prefer it that way. There's nothing worse than bitter bean water.

She hops up on the island, and I stand between her legs, waiting for her to answer me. "About the tattoo you're going to give me today."

I raise one eyebrow. "Oh? Am I now?"

She nods enthusiastically, her hair swaying behind her. She looks up at me, her eyes big as her lower lips pouts, her hand reaching toward my already growing erection. "I'll make it worth your while," she teases, squeezing my cock.

Closing my eyes, I bask in the way her fingers work me up and down, my body humming and begging for more. Then her hand is gone, a soft growl filling the air. When I open my eyes in protest, hers are pinned on mine. I grip the sides of her hips, making her yelp and her coffee slosh. "Only if I get to make you scream."

Her eyes light up at my answer, the wheels already turning,

trying to figure out if her screams will come from pain, pleasure, or both. I take her cup out of her hand, and lift her off the counter.

"So, is that a yes?"

"What do you think?"

She squeals. "I already know what I want!" She wiggles out of my arms and runs towards the stairs. "Well, I have an idea."

"I can't wait to hear it," I say, threading my fingers with hers as I lead us up the stairs to the room that holds all of my tattoo supplies.

We stop in the middle of the hall, her eyes scanning the room. "Why did we stop here?"

A wicked smile stretches my lips as I lift a framed picture of a fox sitting next to a hidden Grim Reaper with ominous woods in the background and a full moon shining high in the sky.

"Has that always been there?" she asks, tilting her head.

"I thought you were more observant than that," I tease, pressing the button behind it that drops the stairs to the attic down.

Serena nearly jumps out of her skin, her hand clutching her heart as she falls back into my arms, my laughter shaking us both. She removes herself from my arms and tries to shove me. "That wasn't funny. And you have a secret attic?"

Intertwining my fingers with hers, I lead us up the wooden steps. "You didn't think I killed where I marked my own skin, did you?" I ask, lifting a brow, stopping to look behind me.

"It was either in your kill shed or one of the four other rooms, I'm sorry five rooms you have in your house."

"Our house." I correct her.

She smiles sheepishly. "Our house." I turn back around and continue our journey up. "Don't think that sweet comment will make me forget you had a secret part of your house. Any other secret rooms like a basement you're hiding more things in?"

"Nope. Just this." I motion as we step into the room and she takes in all the art I've drawn over the years. They cover every wall, except the one that has a circle window where a tattoo bed and all my supplies sit under.

"Wow." Her hand glides across a drawing of a faceless man with his chest blown open and a swirl of words coming out. "You drew these?"

"I did."

She looks at the others and then jumps onto the tattoo bed. "Who knew your drawings were even more breathtaking than your body art. You could give me a run for my money."

I sit on the stool and wheel towards her, stopping between her legs. "No one, not even me, comes close to your art. Your nightmares in particular." Kissing the inside of her covered thigh I push back. "Now are you ready to be marked by me forever?"

A DARK ROMANCE
SPECIAL EDITION
Daily O...
...RDELLA
10 APRIL 2025
VOL. 10, NO. 5

THE BLACK LOTUS

EXCLUSIVE
EXCLUSIVE
EXCLUSIVE

In these quiet moments, you ... with thoughts and emotions, gaining clarity on your true desires and values. Embracing solitude helps you recharge, enhances mental clarity, and fosters emotional well-being. This introspection nurtures personal growth and cultivates a more balanced and fulfilling life.

... about isolation ... personal space where ... your own needs and ... for introspection ...

CRIME SCENE - DO NOT CROSS

SOLITUDE

CRIME SCENE - DO NO

THE BLACK LOTUS

EXCLUSIVE
EXCLUSIVE
EXCLUSIVE

SERENA

T.CROSS

CRIME

SOLITUDE

NINE
SERENA

After my nap I feel like a new woman, one who is officially a serial killer in her own right with three bodies to my name, not counting my mother's. Although the detectives and news anchors haven't figured out we are a team yet, I'm sure with the next body, whoever that may be, will point them to a killer duo. For now, they can think it's a copycat, but once they further examine the kills, they'll see Aster's signature can't be replicated. My touch is what will throw them off. I'm not worried if they figure out we're a team; unlike Aster's parents, they won't catch us.

I wonder what serial killer name they'll end up giving me. A carefree giggle fills my chest. *Will they even realize I'm a girl?* A couple more kills and I'm sure they'll give us a new name. One I'll wear secretly with pride. Sure, it'd be nice to be my own killer, but I couldn't have gotten this far or awoken the monster inside of me without him.

My ass is planted on the table, my legs swinging as I lean back watching Aster prepare to give me my tattoo. I can't believe he had a secret room hidden in our home. Honestly, I'm hurt that this was kept a secret for so long, but I also understand how it easily slipped his mind with all the stress of training and making sure I am safe. Glancing around the room, my body thrums with anticipation. His art is definitely in a league of its own, abstract and dark but screaming for someone to notice there is more to them than meets the eye. It makes me want to unveil the skeletons they hide, searching for the hidden picture lurking within.

Looking at his art makes me miss the feel of a brush in my hand as it swipes across the canvas. The feeling of creating something that makes people stop and stare. Since everything we are facing has happened so fast, I've closed the shop and haven't been to a market. We can't be sure who might be watching… waiting. Aster said it would be the perfect time for someone to strike. All it would take is one second of lowering our guards down. Maybe he'll paint with me again like we did when I first showed him my paintings. Or maybe we can go take a sip and paint class. There are so many people who go to those and in such an intimate environment, surely no one would be stupid enough to strike.

Before we went up to the attic, I ran to our room to grab my sketch because I didn't want to draw it again. When Aster first saw my idea, he didn't say anything, making my heart drop thinking I'd lost my touch. But then I saw his lip twitch with amusement and I knew he liked it. I left my drawing in black and white and told him to add whatever colors he wanted, but now I regret telling him because the array he brought out has me picking at my nails anxiously as I wait. I only thought a small part would be in color, but now I'm not so sure.

"Is this going to be full color?" I ask, peering over his shoulder.

"Color brings the most pain," he teases.

"Pain doesn't make me scream."

He sits on a rolling stool and reaches into the same drawer of the display cabinet he was just in, lifting a hidden compartment and pulling out a tray with a black vibrator and watch next to it. "No, but pleasure does."

My eyes widen, my hand twitching to grab them, but I have a feeling if I try, my colorful pleasure tray will be ripped from me.

"You remembered our first conversation?"

He places the metal sheet over his head away from my reach, my eyes desperate to follow the movement, but unable to look away from Aster's penetrating stare. "I remember every moment. Good and bad." I swallow, shifting as he grabs the platter of fun to hold right in front of me. "Grab the vibrator; leave the watch."

"What if I want both?" I breathe, clutching the toy and turning it over in my hand, wondering how it works. It is shaped like a curve; the little bud would cover my clit, and the end would reach just before my butt. I'm intrigued, my pussy aching and getting wetter waiting for the vibration to begin and I'm tempted to use it before he gives me permission. Since meeting Aster, he is all the pleasure I have needed. I haven't had the urge to touch myself. In fact, I haven't thought once about the box of toys under my bed, but this toy has me second guessing my decision. *They're collecting dust now.*

"Too bad," Aster teases, placing the tray behind him. "Lay down."

I obey without hesitation, clutching the little curve to my chest.

He stands, placing his cool hands on the bottom of my shirt, slowly lifting it over my head. Tracing his fingers over my lacey black bra, goosebumps erupt across my skin as he strips me naked from the waist up, my nipples pebbling from the cold air hitting them. He has me lay down, his hands sliding to the top of my jeans, and I lift my ass without him having to ask, letting him slip them off with a gentle tug. He grabs the little black bundle of joy and places it in my panties over my clit as I mindlessly bite my lip, watching his seductive action. His fingers wrap around the black fabric, snapping the thin band and causing me to twitch as my core greedily clenches around nothing.

"Do you know where you want this?" he asks, holding up the transfer paper.

"Where is a place you can tattoo and not mess up if I move?"

He lifts an eyebrow, picking up the tattoo gun and holding it in the air to look at. "You underestimate my skills?"

"Never," I promise, shaking my head softly as he grabs my hands and places them above my head. "What are you doing?" I ask, nervously.

"It's a part of my process. *Trust* the process."

I relax against the cool leather table as he secures each of my wrists, and then does the same to my legs, tying me spread eagle and at his mercy. Bringing me back to the memory of the first time he bound me at his haunted house. Instead of a knife, this time he'll mark my skin with a tattoo gun.

"Good girl." He secures the bracelet around his wrist, then turns on the machine, the unfamiliar buzzing echoes through the room. The hairs on my arm rise, my body anticipating the sting. I close my eyes, waiting for the pain, but feel nothing. As soon as I peek an eye open, Aster brings the needle to the skin of my leg. My first reaction is to twitch, but I bite down on my bottom lip and endure the shock of his first line.

"I can't tattoo a moving canvas, no more than you can paint one."

"Sorry," I whisper as I stop my wiggling, letting go of the breath I'm holding and hiss through the pain, my body feeling like it's being stung over and over again. *This feels nothing like the slice from his knife.* This pain is foreign, and I'm not sure if I like it.

Soon the pain dulls, and as Aster continues to work my leg, I begin to feel almost nothing. Every now and again I'll feel a little prickle, but it's like my body has adjusted to the pain. The thing that hurts the most is when he cleans the tattoo; every time he wipes I have the urge to punch him in the throat, but these restraints keep me from doing so.

People say getting tattoos are painful, but what they don't prepare you for is the cleaning part.

Aster turns the gun off and sits back, brushing his forearm along his forehead. I go to sit up, wanting to look at it but forgetting I'm strapped down, disappointed it's over so quickly. *He didn't even use my toy.* He takes his gloves off, tossing them in the bin behind him, while his finger hovers over a button on the band.

"I thought we were done."

"That was just the linework and shading; now the real fun begins." He switches guns then switches around his inks, bringing the tray of colors next to him and puts on new gloves. I watch with bated breath, eager for the color to begin so this can be over.

He turns his tattoo gun back on, immediately pressing a button on his watch which has the toy buzzing to life in my panties. My hips shift, begging to find the missing friction. I groan, pulling against my restraints. *The vibration alone won't bring me to my climax.*

The mixture of the color, which is way more painful than the linework, matches the vibrations of the toy, setting my body on fire in a delicious way. My hips find a pace, hitting just the right spot and my back arches slightly, matching the motion of the gun against my skin.

"Look at you, trembling underneath my needle," he says as the tattoo gun continues to penetrate my skin over and over. "Tell me, are you trembling from the pain or the pleasure I bring you?" He asks, his eyes never leaving the spot he's coloring on my leg.

My teeth chatter as I answer, "Both."

I don't know what to concentrate on, but the pleasure from the vibrator overpowers the sting of the needle. My toes curl as Aster works on my leg, turning the pressure up a notch, *but it's too much!* My body convulses as Aster turns off the toy, my orgasm ripped away from me.

"Aster! What the fu-" My words are stolen, my panties

ripped away as something fills me completely. My entire being focuses on the pleasure pouring through me, my orgasm blasting through me the moment his hand moves, a stronger vibration torturing my clit. "Oh, fuck! Aster," I pant. "That feels so fucking good."

"Come all over this toy, vixen. Imagine it's my cock filling you. Scream for me; I want your voice."

He pumps the toy in and out, the needle picking up its pace at the same time, and I do as he commands. My legs shake and my breathing turns erratic as my vision blurs and he pulls the vibrator out of me.

"Is this even sanitary?" My teeth chatter from the cold sensation that envelops me, my body not knowing how to react to what it's being put through.

"I'm wearing gloves and the hand I'm tattooing with isn't anywhere near the mess you're making," he reassures me.

"How are you even doing both at once?"

"You let me worry about the skills you didn't know I had and focus on coming all over me."

Swipe!

"Fuck!" I grunt, the pain tearing my high from me. "Please tell me we're almost done."

"Halfway there, baby; you're doing so good. But I will have you screaming for me again before we're finished."

Before I have a chance to ask what he means, he thrusts the toy back into me and I buck off the table, too sensitive to handle anymore. "Aster," I gasp, "I can't." Tears flood my eyes.

He places his hand on my lower abdomen, my pussy tightening around the toy. "You can. And you will."

In. Out. The toy goes tortiously slow, pleasure melding into pain, my cunt sore, unable to go on, desperate for a break. But, true to his word, just as the needle presses against my skin once more, he quickens his pace with the toy.

Sending shock wave after shock wave of pleasure through

my system. This pain isn't as delicious as the other times he's sent my body into another world, lighting every nerve on fire. The sensation from the rubber cock wars with the now pleasurable needle, confusing my body and blending the two sensations into one. I don't think my body will be able to get off without some type of pain accompanying it. Which worries me since I really enjoy sex with Aster, but adding knife or blood play into it every time, I don't think my body could handle that kind of scarring.

"Your blood glistens so beautifully against your tortured skin."

I glance at Aster's beautifully concentrated face. His eyes are dark with unhinged desire, his brows pinched in concentration and pain. I can tell he wants to taste me, his eyes glancing at my glistening cunt as his tongue slowly traces his bottom lip. Blood and cum, his favorite combination, but he's restraining himself. Trying to quickly finish the tattoo without compromising his vision.

I'm on the verge of finishing again myself.

The needle stops buzzing just as I explode. My body spasms, euphoria consuming me, locking my body in place. I want to look at my tattoo, I want to see what magic Aster has created, but my body trembles, stuck in the position I've been in for hours.

"Hold my hand," he says, unlocking my restraints as I wrap my fingers around his, slowly sitting up while his other hand rests on my back.

I look down at my leg, seeing splashes of colors that blend seamlessly together. *I'm surprised all the movements I was making didn't make it look like a blob.* I lift my leg ever so slightly to get a better look, almost getting a charley horse from bending my body in ways it rejects after being tied up across Aster's table, so I stop and impatiently wait.

The design I chose embodies our journey together, and

although it hasn't been long, it has been memorable and traumatic. Having it tattooed on me forever shows the commitment I am making to not only Aster, but to myself. *We are partners in crime now, and even if we are taken from one another in this life, we will find each other in the next.* Nothing and no one can separate us from each other. He is my fox, and I am his vixen. We will eliminate anyone in our path, forging our own way through this world.

Helping me off the table, Aster walks me to the full length mirror in the corner of the attic. I nearly collapse seeing his beautiful artwork on my leg, my hands covering my mouth as tears threaten to fall.

"Oh, Aster..." I whisper, turning around to face him. "It's perfect."

He swipes a tear from my cheek, kissing the spot gently, turning me back to face the mirror as he wraps his arms around my waist so we look at the piece together. It's a blue rose next to a black lotus with spots of purple bridging the middle. The rose is wrapped in barbed wire all the way down to the stem, an outline of a black and white sheep with spots of watercolor red resting at the bottom, and the lotus appears pristine, except for a few bruised petals, with a sitting fox in a wash of reds, oranges, and yellows at the base.

"I wanted to add some red on the lamb to show how you've always had a taste for blood," Aster says, booping the tip of my nose.

"Just took a blood thirsty fox to awaken it," I purr, turning around to place my hand on his chest.

He leans down, placing a soft kiss against my lips. "Now I crave something else." He grips my waist, and lifts me effortlessly, walking us back to the table to place me back on it as I wrap my legs around his waist.

He tears off his shirt, primal hunger tensing every muscle. Ripping his pants down, he jams his cock into me hard and deep.

I scream out his name while my fingers rake down his back,

leaving red marks in their wake. My tattooed leg hangs freely as he lifts the other and thrusts deeper, stronger, careful not to hit it.

"No toy can satisfy you the way I can," he grunts.

"No toy is as big as you," I gasp, "or can go as deep."

His hands grip my hips with bruising force, tugging me closer to the edge until my ass hangs off, going further in than he ever has before, making my whole body lift off the table and my hands wrap around his neck. Up and down I bounce, his hands gripping my ass to keep me suspended on him. He walks us to the wall under the window, my back slamming against it. My moans and his grunts combine to create a hauntingly beautiful symphony. Over and over he pounds into me, my desire rising higher and higher until we explode together, bathing the room in our cries of pleasure.

Panting and breathless, he slowly lowers me to the ground, holding on to make sure I don't fall over. I lean my head on his sweaty chest, and he presses his lips against the top of my head.

Our bliss is interrupted by Aster's phone going off, the alert telling us someone has entered the property. My breath locks in my chest. Both of us start panicking, grabbing our clothes and putting them back on as quickly as we can. I'm careful not to touch my tattoo as I peer over his shoulder and see someone with cinnamon hair enter our house. Their mouth is hidden under a mask, the curves outlined in the tight black clothing they're wearing. My shock quickly morphs to rage. *A girl is in our home. Who the fuck does she think she is and how did she get in?*

She makes her way into our living room and steals Aster's old and ratty stocking he got when he was at the orphanage. He hasn't told me much about his time there, but I know it was bad and that his stocking is important to him. It's well past Christmas, but with everything going on, we haven't had the time or energy to take down our stockings, even though they were the only things we managed to put up.

She grabs an envelope out of her jacket and places it on the mantle before turning around and looking right at the camera, waving Aster's stocking in the air, then tucking it into her leather jacket.

Aster's hand tightens into fist as she leaves the house, he clicks a button behind another picture and the stairs begin to fall. He storms down the steps to chase after the culprit, leaving me to follow behind my raging boyfriend.

THE BLACK LOTUS

SPECIAL EDITION   **Daily**   ARDELLA   10 APRIL 2025

A DARK ROMANCE

VOL. 10, NO. 5

EXCLUSIVE
EXCLUSIVE
EXCLUSIVE

In these quiet moments, you connect with your thoughts and emotions, gaining clarity on your true desires and values. Embracing solitude helps you recharge, enhances mental clarity, and fosters profound well-being. This introspection nurtures personal growth and cultivates a more balanced and fulfilling life.

SOLITUDE

ASTER

SOLITUDE * SOLITUDE

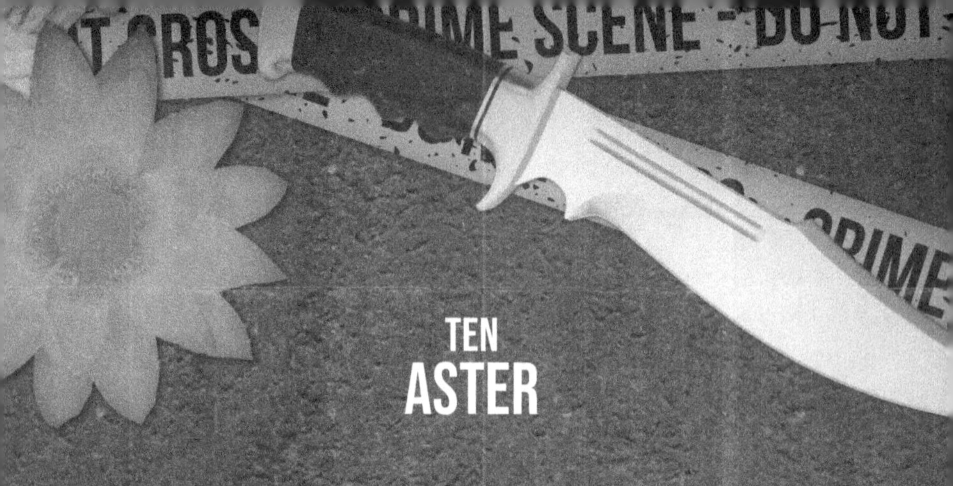

TEN
ASTER

Rage consumes me as I stride furiously down the stairs, my stomps rattling the house. *Who the fuck does that bitch think she is, taking my stocking.* Serena is huffing behind me, trying to keep up. I reach my hand behind me, never slowing my pace and feel her hand clasp around mine, calming some of the storm raging inside me.

"Aster," Serena pants. "What if it's a trap?"

"Then it's one they'll find themselves caught in. She'll be dead before she has a chance to try anything."

I feel Serena tug on my arm, trying and failing to plant her feet to stop me, but nothing and no one, not even my worried vixen, will stop me from finding out who that girl was and what she'd left behind.

We get to the living room and I snatch the note and crush it in my hand after reading the words.

If you want your stocking back, then you'll have to find me. Follow the clues that will lead you home. Deliver the girl into my hands.

First clue: A place you've been only once, where your touch was gentle and left no haunts.

My body jolts from Serena's cold fingers wrapping around my hand that's still gripping the note. My chest rises and falls as she takes the crumpled paper from me, silently reading it to herself. Her brow dips, her lips mouthing the words as she scans the riddle over and over.

If this cunt thinks I am going to hand over Serena to get my stocking back, she is sorely mistaken. I will kill her before her fingers even have a chance to touch a hair on Serena's head. I will leave with my girl and my stocking and I'll leave a body behind for Deputy Wiley to find.

There are not many places I haven't been in Salem, though there are many I avoid. I stick to what I know. I have a routine. Places I go. People I hunt. Rules that no longer matter since meeting Serena. The stocking she took was the only thing I kept when I left the orphanage. I didn't have many belongings when I first arrived and everything I did have was thrown away. Regardless of who you are or where you came from, on your first Christmas each child was given a stocking to put whatever they wanted on it. That stocking was the one thing that was solely *mine*. When it was first placed in front of me, I stared at it, drowning out the voices surrounding me intent on telling me what to do with it. Only when the paints and crafts were placed on the table I sat at with the other newcomers did my hands move to grab and create. I ended up painting a fox watching a little lamb munching on grass. The sky was dark and ominous in the background. The caretakers thought the whole thing was innocent, complimenting me on my talents. All except one; the one who punished me the most saw right through my art. She didn't throw it away, but she did whisper angrily in my ear that I am a devil just like my creators. That comment warmed me at the time; someone more evil than my parents saw through my innocent tortured broken boy act. One day I will kill her for the things she did to me and the other children, but today I need to murder the one who stole my stocking.

Serena's voice brings me back from the past. "Where is the one place you didn't kill?" Her fingers mindlessly tracing the note, searching for the answers in my eyes. Answers I don't have.

I pace back and forth, my mind whirling through the memories of the places the riddle might be pointing. There aren't many places I've been to once without killing, but I grab a paper and pencil and start writing down the ones I can think of. Serena watches from over my shoulder, her breath tickling the back of my neck. If it were anyone else, I would have snapped their neck already, but because it is Serena doing it I feel more at peace. A sense of zen one would feel after meditating. After I finish jotting down the possible locations, we stare at the words together.

Serena's hand reaches from behind me. "There." She points at the word *zoo*. And I smack myself for not realizing it sooner. *It was staring me in the face the whole time.* The one place my hands didn't hurt anything. The one place the orphanage took us to from my childhood. An effort to make them not seem like a bad place; like they weren't abusing the children who lived there.

Turning around to kiss Serena, I grab my burner phone, both of our jackets, and just as I'm slipping on my boots to go to the one place that had been a light in my dark childhood, Serena tugs at my arm.

"Aster, the zoo is closed."

I look up to see the night sky greeting me. If I wasn't so worried about Serena and drawing too much attention to us, I would break into the damn place.

Of course, she had to steal my stocking when I couldn't even get to the next clue until morning. I angrily kick my shoes off, watching them bang against the wall hard enough to dent the sheetrock. "Fuck!" I roar, my blood boiling. I stomp up the stairs, Serena hot on my tail.

"It'll be oka-"

"How? How will it be okay?" I scream at the one lifeline I have left. I wince, instantly regretting my rage, knowing I messed up when Serena's eyes darken a shade, her jaw clenching and her hands fisting. *Probably to stop herself from hitting me.* My shoulders slump. *Fuck.*

My face softens, and I reach out to touch her. "Serena, I'm-"

She flinches away. "Don't," she warns. She shoulder checks me walking up the stairs to our room before slamming the door shut.

Standing on the stairs, I gather myself, calming the fire inside. I should not have lashed out at her; she was only trying to help calm me down, but when strangers touch my things, take what belongs to me, I lose all sense of control. I inhale a deep breath and rasp my knuckles against the door, the only warning I give her before stepping in. *I'm surprised she didn't lock the door.*

"Serena. I'm sorry." She looks up, eyes glassy, anger still brewing within them. "If you know what's good for you, you'll stay right there."

Leaning up against the doorframe, my head tilted to the side, I give the best puppy dog eyes a ruthless killer like me can muster. She giggles a little but quickly covers it up and her scowl returns.

"Come on, Serena. You know you can't stay mad at me." I move towards her.

She crosses her arms and looks away. "Watch me."

I stride towards her and sit next to her on the bed. "I shouldn't have yelled at you."

"No. You shouldn't have." She looks up at me and cups my cheek, her delicate fingers resting lightly against the small stubble of my beard. "I know you're upset. I promise we will get your stocking back and kill whoever that girl is." Her nails dig into my face. "But if you ever lash out at me like that again, you will be the next one to bleed." She drags burning lines across my cheek, her fingertips red. "And it won't end with your dick shoved inside me. It will only be pain."

I shiver at the thought of Serena in control, picturing her making red seep out of my body. My dick hardens against her ass, my body desperate for the release I know only she can provide. She tries to get up, but I pull her onto my lap and tighten my hold.

"If it earns me your forgiveness, you can cut me until nothing but your anger coats my body."

She shifts her weight, accidentally grinding against my erection. *The last thing she needs is my cock buried in her tight cunt.* What she needs is my reassurance, my apologies, and my arms holding her until dawn breaks.

Pulling her off my lap, I tuck her in under the covers and then join her in bed. Wrapping my arms around her waist, she places her hand over my bicep, tugging it tighter into her. The one thing we need is sleep, to wake with a clear mind in the morning and start on our revenge.

No one threatens me. No one will get my vixen. Everyone will die. Blood will rain and peace will follow.

CRIME SCENE - DO NOT CROSS
BLACK LOTUS
EXCLUSIVE
ASTER
SOLITUDE
SOLITUDE
SOLITUDE

ELEVEN
ASTER

The zoo doesn't open until nine, but I woke Serena up at seven. I had to dodge a pillow being thrown at me, but since it was almost an hour away from us, she got up. The sun is high in the sky, beginning to melt yesterday's snow, and I'm grateful. The zoo doesn't open if there's any snow, and I probably should have called before we made the drive, but all rational thoughts went out the window. I just want my damn stocking back. I grip the steering wheel tighter as my foot presses on the accelerator.

Serena is drinking her iced coffee and researching the park itself, seeing what animals are there, where the exits are, and the different places one could hide for a sneak attack. I am over-whelmed with pride as I reach over and grab her hand, brushing my thumb over her warm skin. She looks over at me and smiles, squeezing my fingers before going back to her research. She's hopeful this is where we will find the girl and my belonging, but I know better. This is just the first stop to get us to our bloody destination. Call it killer's intuition, but I have a sinking feeling that this killer likes to play games.

We both sit up straighter when the signs for the zoo come into view, heading towards the parking near the giraffes since it has the most opportunities for a quick getaway. Seeing the parking lot empty makes my stomach drop. Even before the zoo opens, there are usually people waiting to get in before the rush.

"This was a mistake," I say, hand on the gearshift, ready to reverse out of the parking lot.

"Aster, wait!" Serena yells, placing her hand over the wheel and pointing at a man walking out from under the awning, holding a sign and waving at us with a haunting smile.

Gritting my teeth, I find the closest parking spot, and as much as I want Serena to stay in the car, I know she won't. I reach over and grab her hand to help ground me. "Are you ready for whatever trap we're about to walk into?" I ask, squeezing her hand tighter.

"I'd walk into the flames of hell for you." she says, kissing my knuckles as she gets out of the car, and I meet her on the other side.

We walk up to the guy and I shield Serena from his eyes and reach, doing everything in my power to keep her safe. He's wearing a zoo uniform with no name tag and a hat pulled low over his face, holding an envelope that says *Open Me*. Never dropping his creepy smile and without fully showing his face, the guy hands me the piece of paper and walks away. Serena and I look at each other, both confused, but she urges me into opening the paper.

We both read the words with bated breaths.

Congratulations! You found the next clue and are one step closer to getting your stocking back, and I'm one step closer to killing your pretty girlfriend. The zoo is deserted, you can thank my friend for that. I told him I'd give him a cut of the money from your girl's head, and well, he agreed. People will do anything for money! It's time you and I took this little game seriously! Here's your next clue:

This creature is your favorite, cuddly but deadly. A face of innocence with claws ready and willing to rip your throat out.

Happy hunting, Aster!

"It's a fox, right?" Serena asks as I shove the paper into my pocket.

"That would be too obvious." I shake my head, clenching my jaw, pissed. "Plus, that wasn't my favorite, that's just what my mother called me." I stride into the zoo, Serena next to me nearly jogging to keep up.

"What is your favorite animal?"

"Was. And you'll see when we get there."

She slows her pace, a dazed look crossing her features, but she stays silent. After my parents were taken, nothing was the same. I would rather forget my childhood than be forced to relive it like this. *I will tell her everything in due time, just not when her life is on the line.* Walking through the zoo takes me back to the only time I came here and the day I also vowed to never come back again.

"ASTER BALCOM, GET BACK HERE RIGHT THIS INSTANT!" I HEAR Ms. Crumbwell yell after me as I dart away from the group. She's a scary lady who I would much rather avoid crossing and I'm not one to usually disobey orders, especially from Crumbwell, but since they announced we were going to the zoo, I couldn't contain my excitement. Consequences be damned.

I've been in this hell hole, this joke of a home, for a year now. I was bullied for a while, but after I stabbed another kid in the leg with a pencil for knocking over my milk at lunch, the others stayed away and left me alone. I was severely punished, locked in the basement for two weeks with only bread and water for my actions. I felt no remorse; the asshole had it coming.

Although I didn't mind the solitary, I was a growing boy and needed more food to sustain me, so I behaved after that. Running away from the one who likes to punish me the most is not going to be pretty. *I should be scared, but I'm not. This is my first taste of real freedom since being sent here and I am going to soak up every moment. I don't know when I will get the chance again.*

She inflicts pain on us, but never leaves scars, ensuring there's no proof of abuse if we were to ever be examined. But I couldn't care less as wind whips my hair, temporarily blinding me.

I wish I could run away, find my Mommy and Daddy, but I know if I run, they'll catch me. *The fear of the punishment that would come from trying to escape is what keeps me there. I long to see my parents again, to have them teach me how to be a good killer, to be their little prodigy, but they're locked someplace I don't know how to get into. I miss them everyday and one day I will see them again.*

I haven't tried to escape, but one kid did and when they brought him back, his screams were heard throughout the halls. Then he was never seen again. I hope running doesn't get me killed like him. *The thought alone has me stopping dead in my tracks and running to the nearest bathroom I can find. Saying I really had to go is a good excuse to not be killed, but it won't stop me from being punished.*

I wash my hands and run back to find the group. I see them standing in front of the rhino exhibit, and Ms. Crumbwell looks less than happy. I knew this was coming.

She snatches the hood of my hoodie, no witnesses in sight. "You are going to get it when we get back home," she seethes into my ear.

"I had to use the bathroom, and that place isn't my home," I say back, my tongue tainted with disgust.

"Why you!" I close my eyes when I see her hand raise, bracing for the sting of her slap, but my butt hits the ground instead. When I open

my eyes to see why I hadn't received her act of rage, I realize it's because a family of four are walking up to the exhibit. I let out a breath of relief.

"Aster, are you okay?" she fakes sympathy, reaching for me and I smack her hand away.

"I'm fine."

She rustles my hair and looks over at the family. "Boys are always getting hurt, I swear."

The family looks down at me, pity filling their eyes, but instead of saying anything, they politely smile and usher their kids away. I plead with my eyes, begging with my mind for them to come back and help me, to help us all. But nothing works. No one helps. No one will ever rescue us. We will either die here or grow up to be our worst selves. I will grow up to be exactly what my parents wanted me to be, and one day, I will kill Crumbwell.

Crumbwell goes back to the group and walks us all around the zoo, and as much as I want to enjoy the experience, knowing what is waiting for me once we get back, makes it hard for me to focus on this experience.

The sounds of oohs and ahhs break through the gloom. Curiosity gets the better of me as I walk up to the glass to see a fluffy creature I've never seen before. I see three in the enclosure next to one another, huddled together like a family, before I notice one off to the side, sitting by itself and enjoying the seclusion from the others. I walk over while the others stay and watch the other three, placing my hand against the glass and watch in awe as the fluffy creature's paw mimics my action. My heart begins to race, excitement and curiosity at the forefront of my mind. It's like it is telling me everything will be okay, to not give up. It's like it sees me, like I'm not alone. I stand there watching the creature for what feels like forever until I hear my name yelled from a distance and reluctantly walk away, glancing back to see it's still watching me.

We stop in front of what was once my favorite animal, the red panda, and see not only the beautiful creatures but the creepy guy from the entrance holding yet another clue.

"I wasn't expecting this to be your favorite," Serena wonders, walking up to the guy taking the envelope then handing it to me. I don't open it until he walks away.

"They were a long time ago. They were the only creatures who ever saw me."

"Oh, Aster," Serena wraps her hands around my own, her hands shaking with how hard she's gripping mine. "I see you."

Bringing her hands to my lips, I kiss the back of her palms. "And I see you."

She releases our hands and wraps her arms around my neck pulling me down for a kiss full of reassurance.

"Shall we see where we're going next?" she asks, breaking our kiss.

Nodding my head, I open the paper for us to read together. Hesitating for a moment to get myself in the right headspace and not let my anger get the best of me.

You didn't forget! That makes me so happy. I wonder if it is still your favorite animal or if that has since changed... Well, I guess I'll just ask you when you find me. Don't worry! This game has just started, and I can't wait to get my hands on the target, so it won't be long until I'll be blowing her up and you'll get to watch. Here is your next clue; good luck!

Night or day, this place was a safe haven; not many knew except two.

-TT

I have my suspicions about who this could be. There is only one person from my childhood who I considered a friend, but why would she do anything to hurt me? Is money truly more important than the bond we'd formed? Is she a serial killer now, too? Or is it someone my mother just sent to keep tabs on me, hidden in the shadows.

"Oh look, she signed it this time," Serena points out. *I don't know anyone with those initials.* Maybe she signed it with her real name instead of her killer name. The only way to know is to go to the next place.

"I know where we need to go next."

"Are you going to tell me this time?"

"A park; it was the one place growing up I could hide from the teachers."

"Hide?" Serena asks, concern wrinkling her beautiful face. I bend down to kiss her forehead, my attempt to help ease her concerns.

"Yes. Before you ask, I will tell you everything, just-"

"Just not now," she finishes for me, arms crossing against her chest.

Smiling sadly, I nod, taking her back to the car, back to yet another childhood place.

And one step closer to killing whoever the fuck TT is.

CRIME SCENE - DO NOT
THE BLACK LOTUS
EXCLUSIVE
EXCLUSIVE
EXCLUSIVE
SERENA
SOLITUDE
CROSS
CRIME

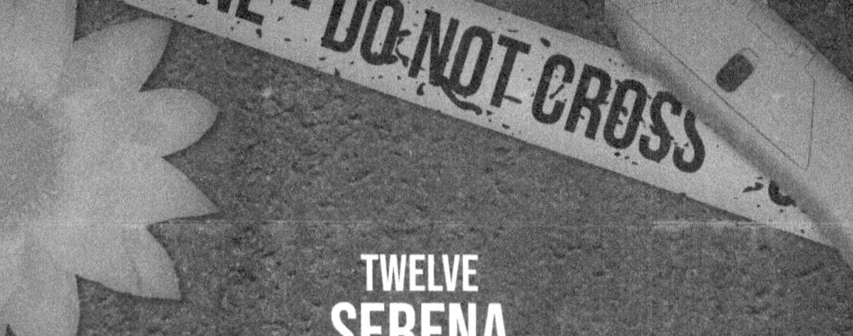

TWELVE
SERENA

I'm pretty sure the girl who took Aster's stocking is the Twisted Trickster. I wanted to bring it up, I wanted to let Aster know she is the one connected to his past somehow, but the distress he is in… I look over at him, his face scrunched and the need to reach over to release some of his tension is strong, but I keep my hands to myself. I think he needs to discover who it is for himself. If he's going to keep me in the dark about his past, I'm going to keep the truth from him for as long as I can. Let him get a taste of his own medicine. It's not like concealing what I know will get us killed. *At least… I hope not.*

The afternoon sun is being shielded by the gray sky. A testament to how this day is going with Aster in charge, which I don't mind in the bedroom, but this has to do with *my life*. My very existence on earth. *If he just tells me what he keeps putting off, then maybe we could find the Twisted Trickster faster.* Get his stocking back, get more answers, and then kill her.

Only to wait for the next hit.

The feeling of constantly having to look over your shoulder, never knowing what is coming next has been utterly exhausting. I'm not scared of Cynthia or whoever else she sends. What I do

fear is the possibility of death and being ripped away from the one thing that makes sense in my life, Aster.

The car pulls to a stop in front of an abandoned park, one you would see in a scary movie. Two swings slowly sway one after the other, as if someone was actually on them being pushed. Every instinct in my body screams to turn around. But I can't. Cynthia took that choice away the moment she placed the hit. As we get out together, we hear the sound of the worn seesaw creaking eerily in the cool breeze. The wind picks up the closer we get, a silent warning to turn back from the run down and forgotten place that seems to hold more than old memories.

"Wait here," Aster says, walking up the rusted stairs toward the biggest slide I've ever seen. Even if he didn't tell me to wait, I wouldn't have gone. This place looks like one wrong step before falling into a world of pain.

No, thank you. I'm happy right where I am.

"Serena. Did you hear what I said?" he says with an accusatory tone. I know I don't have the best track record following his orders, but even if you paid me to enter that death trap, I'd turn my head at the offered money.

"Loud and clear. I won't move." The next words come out as a whispered mumble. "Don't want to fall to my death on the playground from hell."

He quirks an eyebrow, humming playfully, then continues his climb to the top.

I hope he's being careful and watching his step; as annoyed as I am right now, I don't want to see him get hurt. He scales the play set like it's engraved in his memory. I guess it is, but he's way bigger now than he was as a child. Maybe after this is all over, we can take a trip down memory lane, and he can show me some pictures. He can tell me why his parents are so evil, share about his time in the orphanage, and, maybe, just maybe, heal some of the scars it left.

Just as I'm sitting down on the cement ledge that dips into

the park, Aster appears in front of me, startling me with how quickly he retrieved the next clue that is now crumpled in his hand, with a worried look in his eyes.

Cautiously, I tug the envelope away and read the clue myself, causing him to jump and breaking whatever spell he was under.

"Serena?" he questions.

Aster! You found the final clue, and I'm so proud of you! Now, all you have to do is come to me. I'll wait for you, and my next victim, in the place holding all your nightmares. See you soon, Asty. It's been too long.

-Twisted Trickster

"I know who is behind this."

"Are you okay?" Handing back the clue, I wring my hands together as he puts it into his back pocket.

"Well, yeah, she signed her name instead of her initials this time."

We walk back to the car in hurried steps, both of us wanting to leave the skeletal equipment behind. Sitting down, I pick at my nails. Unease of confessing what I knew all along to Aster washing over me like a waterfall I don't want to be under. "I should let you know I knew it was the Twisted Trickster after the zoo. Nate said she was coming next, but you've been so secretive with your past, shrouding everything from me, I didn't want to tell you. Plus, I knew you would figur-"

"Serena," Aster cuts me off, placing his hands around mine to stop my fidgeting. He takes a shuddering breath, his eyes unfocused outside the windshield. "I'm sorry I haven't told you anything and kept you in the dark. I promise, once we deal with Kelsey-" *Her name is Kelsey?* "-we will sit down for however long we have, and I will tell you everything." He turns, leaving the ghost of his touch behind. *Why does it feel like his actions aren't going to match his words?* I'm tired of empty promises.

He turns the key, his car rumbling beneath us. "Do you trust me?" He asks the question he's asked me several times now, and my answer is always the same.

"Yes," I sigh, clenching my jaw, feeling defeated and irritated at his broken record speech. I trust him, but my patience for answers is wearing thin.

He smiles softly, but it doesn't reach his eyes, making my stomach drop slightly.

His sadness creeps its way into mine, up my arm, crawling slowly like a spider would, making me swat at the invisible force. Shaking the emotion away, I swallow back the sob that wants to break free. I take a deep, shuddering breath to keep my mind focused and my emotions in check for the reunion. This is literally life or death. *My life.* I can't afford any kind of distraction.

Staring out the window, the car slows in front of an abandoned building. A broken, burnt sign claims we've arrived at 'Angel's Mercy Orphanage'. Based on the little I've gotten from Aster about this place, I doubt any mercy was ever given. The sign makes me sick, the lies this place holds and the truth of the evil hidden behind the plastered on fake smiles I imagine the children were forced to wear. It makes my blood boil. If this place was still standing I would free all the children, then lock away the ones who were supposed to love and take care of them. Then I'd burn it to ash and watch the wretched souls be pulled below.

"Promise me, no matter what happens, or what I say, you trust me."

My brows furrow. "Say?"

He huffs out a breath, not one of annoyance, but one of regret. "I may have to say some things that are not true to distract Kelsey." My heart drops. "They are just empty words, Serena, meant to give a chance to take her down. When I give you an opening, you take it." He looks away, clenching his fists.

I place my hands over his, his fingers uncurling and wrapping around mine. "I trust you. I know you love me." His eyes meet my own. "Whatever you have to do, I know it's to protect me. I won't let what you say or do distract me from my own mission."

Bringing my hands to his mouth, he kisses the back of my palms. "Our mission."

My heart settles and I force a smile, my confidence growing knowing we're facing this together. "Our mission."

Getting out of the car, I study the building of broken, boarded up windows and a door hanging off its hinges. *If the building had steps, they would definitely be rusted and dissolved by now.* We step into Aster's childhood hell and the smell of mold and wet moss hit my nose, the rancid smell making me gag.

We walk into what I assume used to be the foyer and see a table with a game of scrabble sitting on it, caked in dust and dirt aside from the six letters that spelled out two words in the middle.

Find me.

Aster knocks the table over, grabbing my hand before storming up the stairs and down a series of hallways that keep rounding corners, never seeming to end. A maze that leads to Kelsey. Broken picture frames litter the walls and floor, so we watch our step, careful not to crush the glass below us. She may know that we are coming, but she doesn't need to know when. If she hears us, she can get the jump on us and that is a problem we don't need.

We stop in front of a door, the only one in the hallway we find ourselves in. It's brown and corroded but has a drawing taped to it of a little boy and girl holding hands with a heart around it, 'Aster and Kelsey' written above their heads.

My hands fist at my sides, my vision turning red as my heart pounds erratically. *Is she in love with* my *Aster?* I'll kill her before she has a chance to even say his name.

The glass beneath my feet crunches as my body responds before I can react; instead of walking over it, I reach down and grab a piece, the sharp edge piercing my skin and biting into my flesh.

"Serena!" Aster whisper yells, grabbing my weapon out of my hand and placing it in his pocket. "I'll take care of that later." His now bloody hand covers mine, and his words snap me out of my murder fueled haze. "Remember what I told you. I need you to use your head; don't let your emotions fog your mind."

He talks about my emotions distracting me, when his are written all over his face. His mouth is parted open and his thumbs are rubbing back and forth over my palms in a fidgeting sort of way. I may have wanted to stab her over and over again to get this over with, but the pleading look in his eyes has the fire inside me settling, regaining the composure I lost.

Shaking my head, I take a deep breath. "I'm sorry, that-" I point at the picture. "-surprised me."

His cold hand covers my cheek, glancing at the picture as he whispers, "You're not going to like what I have to do next." He hands me black gloves to put on and with trembling fingers I secure them. My hands aren't shaking from fear, they're aching to be wrapped around the throat of the one who dares to want what is mine. When I get the signal, she's going to wish she never got the list. I will make her regret ever accepting the hit.

I worry my bottom lip, the anger bubbling back up. Aster's thumb pulls it free before that, too, starts to bleed. His lips ghost over my own. "It's all an act." He softly kisses me again, breaking away too quickly, grabbing the picture and opening the door. Sheer determination set in his green orbs, the persona of the Monet settles on his features, sending goosebumps up my arm. I wouldn't want to be Kelsey right now. She may think she set a trap for us, but Aster is setting one for her. One I would rather not be a witness to, but beggars can't be choosers.

The scene before us is more gruesome and twisted than anything Aster or I could ever be capable of. What she has set up makes me wish I didn't eat today because it feels like I'm about to paint the floor with it. I swallow back the vomit, take a deep breath, and look at the scene from a killer's point of view, going numb to everything and admiring it instead of feeling disgusted by it.

They call Kelsey the Twisted Trickster for a reason and she definitely lives up to her name.

CRIME SCENE - DO NOT CROSS   CRIME SCENE

VOL. 10, NO.

BLACK LOTUS

EXCLUSIVE
EXCLUSIVE
EXCLUSIVE

ASTER

SOLITUDE   *   SOLITUDE   SOLITUDE   *   SOLITUDE

CROSS   CRIME SCENE - DO NOT CROSS

SCENE - DO NOT CROSS

THIRTEEN
ASTER

"Asty!" The nickname she had for me as a child makes me internally twitch, hating the way it sounds coming from her lips. Kelsey's chipmunk like voice echoes around the empty room as she waves around—*is that an intestine?* She's dressed fully in her killer costume. Her face is painted white, a pink smile slashed over her mouth, with black diamonds shaping her eyes. She's wearing a pink and black striped bodysuit and a frilly tutu to match. *She'd fit right in at Graves.* Every spot on her, from outfit to her face, is sprayed with blood from the victim she has hanging from hooks pierced into his back with a tube up his naked ass. I follow the line to the tanks that are stashed on the edge of the room, my face grim. *That could've been Serena.* Glancing back, his body is blown up, his eyes almost popping out of his head and his stomach slashed open, guts tumbling across the floor.

Fuck.

"Give me one minute; I'm almost done," Kelsey singsongs, twisting the intestines together. "Ta-da!" She beams, holding her creation proudly in front of her. "Do you like it?" I squint, my stomach churning as Serena fidgets behind me. It looks like she made a heart with something dangling in the middle.

She skips towards us with a childlike glee and I walk to meet her in the middle of the room to shield Serena standing at the door from her line of sight, every nerve on high alert. The Kelsey I knew is not the Kelsey in front of us now.

I knew this killer, before finding out it was Kelsey, had a childlike mind, desperate to be loved and admired. Kelsey had a hard life; she always believed her parents would come back for her. They never did. Just like mine, her parents were serial killers, but hers dressed as clowns and never got arrested. She was abandoned at nine, but when she was sixteen she found out the truth. Her parents never gave her up, they were killed in a standoff with the cops. The real story of what happened was concealed from her and she grew up believing a lie. The day she learned the truth, something inside her snapped.

Her deranged behavior has me not wanting her to see Serena even more, but the way my vixen loves to put herself in danger, I know she will make herself known. I just hope she listens long enough to let me give her an opening. I need to trust that she won't step foot into this room until the right moment. I need to concentrate on the psycho in front of me, make Kelsey believe in the same hopes she has dreamed of for so long. Create the illusion that is the Monet and trick her into my web of lies, entangling her in my words and actions until Serena bites off her head. I smirk at the thought of Serena as a spider, with eight legs and a dozen eyes always watching and waiting. A shiver racks my spine; *actually I don't like that image,* it is rather creepy, I'd rather Serena just cut her head off. That image relaxes me and brings me back to the woman closing in on me.

She jumps to a stop in front of me, arms outstretched with blood dripping down her arms. The body part stretches as far as it can go since it is still connected to the man behind her. "I made it for you! It's your favorite, see?" She points to what looks like a red panda, made from other body parts, dangling in the middle of the heart. I just stare at it, curling my lip with disgust. My body tense waiting for her to make her next move.

She pouts, tilting her head. "Do you not like it?" She kicks away a pebble, her eyes dipping as her mouth twists to the side. "I worked so hard on it."

Snap out of it Aster, you are the Morbid Monet, act like it. "That's not my favorite animal anymore," I state calmly, trying not to agitate the woman in front of me.

Her eyes light up, the pink smile growing across her cheeks. "Oh! Well, that's an easy fix. What's your favorite animal now?"

"I don't have one," I lie, not wanting to give her more than necessary, hoping that she can't see through the facade.

She scrunches her brow, rocking back on her heels. "You grew up." She looks me up and down, annoyance flashing across her features before she walks away. She throws the gift in the pile under her victim's body, her hands shaking. "I guess the police will get two gifts this time," she grumbles to herself.

Taking a hesitant step forward, glancing back to make sure Serena is still behind me; I can't tell if it is all an act or if that is how she truly is. It's all a little unnerving, causing my steps to slow. Not knowing what she will do next keeps me watching her every move. She is kneeling down and moving the intestines around, displaying them.

I know we didn't have a childhood growing up, and as we aged she never truly matured, but I thought once we both finally escaped that hell, she would finally act her age. I see now that is not the case. My shoulders slump as my mouth thins into a grim line.

She bolts up, startling both me and Serena by clasping her hands together, her eyes lighting up seeing my vixen behind me. "You brought me my gift!" she exclaims, grabbing her bloodied axe off the floor, tiptoeing toward Serena.

No way is she killing my vixen, especially with a weapon already used on her previous victim. Based on her little surprise taped on the door, she still has a crush on me, and for my plan to work, I need Serena to keep her emotions in check and trust me.

I look over my shoulder at Serena, determination and understanding shine in her eyes, giving me the reassurance I need. I step towards Kelsey and away from my future, sliding on the mask of the Morbid Monet with each step, the feeling of rightness settling over me.

Caressing her cheek, I lay on the charm as she nuzzles into my touch. "I love the gift, and I can't believe you remembered my favorite childhood animal."

She places her hand into mine and steps slowly into my chest as her other hand relaxes against my chest. "I don't know what changed from when you came in to now, but I don't care. I missed being held by you." She breathes in my scent. "You smell different, but I like it," she hums.

"I was just caught off guard after not seeing you for so long."

"That's all? You promise?"

"I promise." The words fall out of me easily, the lies being covered by a half-truth.

Her fingers dance up my chest, but before her touch can land on my face, I stop her pursuit, wrapping my hand over hers. I hope Serena doesn't kill me for flirting with someone in front of her, but I lay the charm on. *I hope she knows I am doing this for her.* I fight the urge to look back, keeping my gaze on Kelsey's. *This is the only way.*

"I remember everything about you, Asty. Do you remember my favorite animal?" She looks up, batting her eyelashes and leaning into me further.

"Red panda." I feel Serena's blood boil from how quickly I answer, the energy switching from cool curiosity to a blazing inferno of rage. "You liked everything I did." I quickly clarify, hoping that helps dim the fire swirling around us.

She twirls her skinny, blood-stained fingers around a lock of my hair. "I still do," she whispers, standing on her tiptoes and looking directly at my vixen. My spine stiffens as all the oxygen seems to be sucked from the room.

She steps out of arms, the emptiness bringing relief. "Too bad the one thing you seem to like has to die." She shrugs, swinging her axe towards Serena.

I grab her arm, stopping her pursuit. "I don't like her." Her head whips in my direction as her eyebrows dip in confusion. Keeping my focus off Serena I cup Kelsey's cheek. "You know you were the only one I ever liked," I lie, the words souring my mouth.

Her eyes close, her grip on her axe loosening. "You were always there for me; when I had no one, you hid with me when the teachers were in one of their punishing moods. You kept me safe, taking the beatings for me," she says, stepping back into my chest.

"You're the one who found the best spots."

"You're the one who discovered the park down the street." She looks up at me. "Remember how we would sneak out past curfew and watch the stars?" She interlaces her fingers between my own, my skin crawling at the intimacy between us. "How we would hold hands and time stood still." She turns our hands over, tracing a heart on the inside of my gloved palm. "You always said, 'One day, when we got out of here, we would meet at that park to reminisce'."

"I remember." The memory causes conflict inside me; save her or kill her. *Can she be saved?*

"I always hoped, when we reconnected, we would fall in love and be partners in crime. Just like both our parents were."

"Our parents were some of the best."

She shakes her head. "No, your parents were the best; mine didn't want me. I was in their way, wanting too much. They abandoned me and then got killed."

"Mine got caught," I retort.

"They only got caught because of jealousy."

Her words hit me in the chest and I push her away, gripping her arms as confusion and curiosity swirl inside me like a storm, creating a tornado of emotions.

"What do you mean? What jealousy?"

"I promised I wouldn't say," she whispers as her eyes dart around the room from fear someone could be listening.

I shake her, her cheeks turning red from the force. "Tell me!" I demand, anger slowly taking over me.

"I'm sorry, Asty. She'll kill me if I say anything."

"Who, Kelsey? I'll protect you."

Her eyes drop, the girl I grew up with finally poking through her mask. "Not from her. You can't protect me from her."

"I can keep you safe if you just let me in. I am here for you." The words leave my lips, desperate for answers about the day that changed the course of my life. *I need to know what happened.* I need to know who turned my parents in and why. Kelsey knows, and I'll do anything to find out.

I grip her chin, her eyes widening in disbelief as I tilt her head to look at me. Channeling my feelings, my love for the woman having to watch all this, I whisper, "I'll always be here for you, Kels." The childhood nickname slips out as she closes her eyes, curling into my touch, which gives me a chance to look at the doorway to check on Serena, but the spot is vacant. My heart races, fear Serena left thrumming through me.

"I'm sorry. Not this time." She places her hand on my chest, her pupils widening as a deranged look crosses her face. "It was nice, traveling down memory lane together. But I have a job to do, and I'd like to do that quickly. Then we can finally be together."

All thoughts of wanting and craving answers dissipate as panic takes over from the need to keep Serena safe. I want answers, but I *need* Serena. I will kill Kelsey before I let her touch a hair on her head.

Before I can search the room for my angry vixen, my body jerks and Kelsey spits blood as my name leaves her lips, her eyes wide as a manic Serena stands behind her, her knife sticking out of Kelsey's back. I let her fall and rush to Serena, but she steps away from me as my arms drop to my sides.

She stares daggers at the dying woman on the floor, then

looks up at me with a fire I haven't seen before. The need to hold her is strong, but the waves of anger I feel coming off her, keep me planted where I stand as I whisper the words. "It was all an act."

Her eyes finally meet mine, returning to their darker shade of blue. "You called her by her nickname, then she started saying things about your past, things I didn't know about you… My emotions took over." Her fists clench and unclench at her sides. "The whole time I kept repeating 'it's just an act' in my head, but when she was in your arms, my jealousy took over and my body reacted before my mind could catch up, and well, now she's dying." Serena looks toward the body still hanging from the ceiling, her brows low on her forehead. "I'm sorry. We could have gotten answers."

I step towards her, bringing her eyes back to mine and this time she lets me touch her as my hand rubs up and down her stiff arms. "If I saw you sweet talking another man, even if it did keep me safe, he would have been killed instantly. You held off longer than I would have. Don't be disappointed. She was never going to reveal the truth." My teeth clench at that realization. "I am so proud of you." Her eyes start to water, the final bits of hurt and rage dissipating as our lips softly meet.

We only break apart when we hear coughing near our feet. Realizing Kelsey is still alive, Serena kneels in front of her, her gloved finger tucking Kelsey's hair behind her ear. "Did you really think Aster would choose you over me?"

Kelsey's eyes well with tears as she looks up at me standing behind Serena, my hand on her shoulder. "Asty?" she croaks.

"Eyes on me," Serena demands. Kelsey glares at Serena. "You may have had him when you were children, but I have him as a man and you will never see him again." Serena rips the knife from her back and Kelsey screeches, the sound making both me and Serena flinch from the ear bleeding sound.

"It's not going to be me, but someone else will succeed. It's only a matter of time before you're here with me."

"They can try." Serena stabs the knife into her neck. "But they'll all meet the same fate."

We stand and watch as the life drains from Kelsey's eyes, hand in hand. The memory of who we were as kids dying right alongside her. A piece of me I will never get back.

"Well, that was anticlimactic." My hand squeezes around Serena's as I pull her behind me and turn towards Zephira, making my muscles tense. Her randomly showing up after every kill is starting to not only irritate me but it's making me nervous knowing she is reporting everything back to our mother.

Zephira jumps down from the broken windowsill she was sitting on. *How the hell did she even get up there?* Walking towards us, she lightly kicks Kelsey's side. "I was expecting more of a fight from the Twisted Trickster. Guess her love for you distracted her from Mom's goal. What a shame." She walks towards Serena, picking up a section of her hair and inhaling. "How did it feel to kill my brother's first love?"

Gripping Serena's hand, I drag her behind me and growl at my sister. "The only woman I have ever loved is Serena. This girl," I look down at Kelsey, "she was my friend, but I never loved her."

Zephira steps behind us, hands behind her back and whispers across our necks. I spin our bodies around, not liking my sister being out of view for even a second. "But you did *fuck* her."

I tense as the truth no one but Kelsey should know washes over me. Serena releases her hand from mine, a million questions swirling behind her eyes. She hugs her arms around her body, and I step into her, placing my hands firmly on her shoulders.

"Yes, it's true, but that was ages ago. She may have been my first-" Serena lets out a little gasp, her body curling in on itself as my hands move from her shoulders to grip both hands. "But you were the first to truly get my heart. You are the last woman who will ever have any part of me. I love you and only you, Serena."

Her eyes become glassy as she looks up at me and nods in

understanding. It was such a long time ago, a memory long since forgotten, but the thing people say about your first is true. I never forgot, but I never thought about her again after I escaped the orphanage. Seeing as Kelsey has only thought of me, I will have to explain everything to Serena to ease her beautiful mind. To keep her in an alert headspace, and not distracted. *I can't lose her.*

"Well, you two are no fun. I at least thought there would be a big fight so I could comfort poor, beautiful Serena." Zephira pouts as she walks towards the door. Before I can threaten her, again, to keep her eyes and hands off of what's *mine*, she continues, "Oh well! Have fun cleaning up the mess, and Serena?" Zephira turns to look at her. "Maybe next time I can be the one to make you scream." Zephira winks and walks away, leaving my vixen's cheeks turning a shade pink.

I step into her line of sight. "If you don't close that pretty mouth of yours, I'm going to shove my cock so deep down your throat you'll be crying for air." Her mouth clamps shut, her cheeks darkening. "Don't let my sister's flirting distract you from what's in front of you." I kiss her lips quickly, leaving her wanting more.

"Never. She just startled me."

"Tell that to your red face." I whisper.

She places her hands on her cheeks and looks up at me. "You're right. But I promise I don't want anyone other than you."

I spank her ass. "Good girl. Now help me clean this up."

We rid the place of any evidence that we were here and place Kelsey under her last victim's body on a chair Serena fetched from another room. We place a blue rose and black lotus in Kelsey's hands and leave.

CRIME SCENE - DO NO...

THE BLACK LOTUS

EXCLUSIVE
EXCLUSIVE
EXCLUSIVE

SERENA

CROSS

CRIME

SOLITUDE

FOURTEEN
SERENA

A million questions swirl around my head like angry hornets with nothing but vague answers to satiate the sting. My legs bounce up and down from the rush of killing Aster's first girlfriend. I know he said she wasn't that important to him, but I saw the love in her eyes, the pining she felt with her whole body, how she was too distracted by what is mine to feel the knife penetrate her… *She thought differently.* She thought they could kill me and live happily ever after hunting their victims together. *Sorry, Kelsey,* her name sours my thoughts, my legs stilling, *the spot of being a partner in crime with Aster is already taken, and you found out the hard way.*

I smile to myself, the thought of my hand once again wrapping around the handle of the knife as I plunged it into her neck, the look of betrayal crossing her features before her eyes died along with her, eases some of the rage bubbling within me.

"What are you smiling about?" Aster teases, reaching for my hand.

Flinching away, he frowns, his knuckles going white on the wheel "Killing your little clown girlfriend."

An exasperated sigh leaves his lips. "Serena, she isn't, and

never was, my girlfriend. When we get home, I'll tell you about my past and why she was so infatuated with me."

I turn my head, rolling my eyes and ignoring his excuses. Nothing but silence greets him until my stomach betrays me and pierces through my cloud of annoyance, hunger taking over.

Aster chuckles, grating my nerves further. "Let's get you washed up and fed. Maybe after I feed the beast, you'll be more inclined to listen."

Feed the beast? My head whips towards him, wanting to lash out further as I dig my nails into my palms. I've been working hard on getting a grip on my emotions. Instead of replying with a threat, which is what I really want to do, I take a calm, steadying breath and look out the window, staring at the top of the trees as they zip past us.

The tranquil scenery has my body relaxing and my eyes reluctantly fluttering closed, the soft music from the radio lulling me to sleep.

"Serena! Where are you my sweet girl?" An unfamiliar angelic voice calls out for me. The sound of her words sets my excited nerves at ease as my rapidly beating heart goes back to its steady pace. I don't know the woman looking for me, or why I'm hiding from her, but I do know she won't hurt me.

I love her so much.

I dash across the hall, giggling and find myself stopping at the large mirror hanging on the wall. Where am I? My tiny hand reaches out to touch the glass, staring at my five-year-old reflection. My hair is in pigtails, little red bows wrapped around each one and I'm wearing a velvet green and red checkered dress with black clicky-clack flats and white stockings.

Is this a dream, memory, or both? The actions prove I am

looking at child me from the eyes of my present me, but I don't recall this memory. I watch my head tilt in the mirror. Understanding shining in my eyes. I shouldn't be surprised; repressed memories seem to be a common thing with me, and dreams are how it starts when a memory resurfaces. What have I forgotten? Or rather, who have I forgotten?

Footsteps pound behind me, and I take off running as a smile stretches my cheeks from playing my favorite game; hide and seek. I collide with my mother in the kitchen and hide behind her legs, peeking out at the woman chasing me.

"Serena, are you playing hide and seek with-" my mother asks, but the woman's name is muffled, the word statics, making it impossible to decipher. I look up at my mother's grinning face, a younger, healthier version of her, and nod my head vigorously. My heart aches as my hands tremble, wanting to reach out and hold her and never let go. She is a memory I can't keep, and it pains me that I'll never hear her voice or see her face except for in my dreams. Dreams I wish could last forever.

My mother is in a beautiful red dress, her lips painted the same color, as Christmas tree earrings dangle from her ears and a reindeer apron is wrapped around her, protecting her outfit from getting covered in flour. Looking at her, I see how much I resemble my mother, and it warms my heart to know her habits didn't die with her, that I do what she did.

She drops to her knees and dabs my nose with a little flour. "Run to Mommy and Daddy's room and hide under the bed; she'll never find you there." She winks, nudging me with her elbow.

Kissing her cheek, I run to my hiding spot, leaving Mommy with her hand on her cheek and a warm smile on her face.

No! Don't go. Turn around and go back to Mom! *I yell at my child self, glancing back as the woman I miss everyday fades from my vision. I don't want to play hide and seek or find out who's voice that is; I just want my mom. Please don't go, Mom. I'm sorry.*

I feel myself sobbing, my body shaking as I crawl under the bed. I hear my name being yelled by the angelic voice, the playful tone echoing around the house, but soon the voice morphs into panic. I cover my mouth to stifle the giggle threatening to break free. That woman always tricks me into coming out of my spot with her scared voice. Not this time. This time I know better, and I will stay put.

Her feet come into view, the black, knock off Doc Martens pacing the room, the words she is saying blocked out by a different voice screaming my name, getting louder and louder each time. The woman drops to her knees and just as her face looks under the bed, I'm jostled awake.

"Fuck! Serena," Aster's words rush together as he caresses my face, swiping away the tears staining my cheeks. "You started whimpering in your sleep, then crying, but we were almost home, so I sped up, and I started screaming your name, but you stayed asleep. Then your body started to convulse, and I didn't know what was going on. Were you having a seizure or something else? Your body looked possessed." My hand covers his heart, the muscles panicking in his chest, and his breathing finally slows. "I had to wake you up, but you seemed trapped. I panicked. I didn't know what else to do. I was about to slap you awake, or pour water all over you but then your eyes burst open and-"

"I'm okay," I whisper, calming my freaked out fox. "I was dreaming of a memory, but my mom was there, and…" my voice cracks, "and I didn't want to let go again." Tears drip off my chin, and this time I'm awake to feel them. "She looked so healthy. I can't remember the last time my mom looked like that."

He pulls me into him. "I miss her so much." I cry into his arms, forgetting all about Kelsey. Forgetting all about Cynthia and her stupid vendetta against me. Forgetting everything but him.

He feels so warm, so comforting. *He feels like home, like how my mom used to feel.* I snuggle deeper into his arms, his silence bringing me solace.

"As much as I love holding you, I would rather do it in a

more comfortable position." My stomach growls, reminding us both I am starving. "And we need to get you fed."

I lift my head, sniffling quietly. "You also owe me some answers," I say, my voice no longer angry.

Getting out of the car and heading up the steps, Aster's face crumbles, his eyes guarded and scared. "Everything is yours, Serena, and that includes my past."

The wind whistles behind us as the door shuts, the air heavy as Aster's past surrounds us.

ENE - DO NOT CROSS · CRIME SCEN

BLACK LOTUS

EXCLUSIVE
EXCLUSIVE
EXCLUSIVE

ASTER

SOLITUDE * SOLITUDE
SOLITUDE * SOLITUDE

CROSS

FIFTEEN
ASTER

Anxiety. Is that what I'm feeling right now? It feels like I'm a piece of wood, stiff and unmoving, as emotion eats me alive like a termite buried deep within. I'm not familiar with this feeling, but there are a plethora of new emotions I continue to experience since Serena came into my life. My past with Kelsey needs to be told, but how will she react? We were just children; all we had was one another in a dark and lonely place. We were each other's solace, and even though she loved me, I never felt those feelings towards her. That should help dull the sting I know will accompany Serena's feelings.

Walking to the fridge after our shower, I grab a bottle of water and some leftovers, the kitchen feeling tense as they heat up in the microwave. I plate the food and hand it to her along with the bottle.

"Where do you want to talk?" Serena asks, walking up the stairs towards our bedroom already having made her own choice. Not letting her assumption upset me, I follow behind, because I know she needs to be in control right now.

"Our room," I respond, trying to grab her hand, but she snatches it away. My fingers shake as I curl them into fists. *Great; she's still upset.*

Serena plops on the bed, crumpling the black duvet and leaning back on her hands as she waits for me to begin my story, her food sitting behind her, cooling down.

"Are you ready for the truth?"

She levels me with an 'are you serious' look as she arches a brow. "I've been ready."

I sit beside her, wanting to reach out but knowing she'll refuse my touch anyway, so I keep my hands folded in my lap. "I already told you how I feel now. Everything back there was an act to get Kelsey to drop her guard." She winces. "The Twisted Trickster," I correct, trying to get Serena to lower her defenses, "can't hurt us anymore. So don't let her, or the past I shared with her, get in your head."

Her shoulders relax as she sits up. "I'm ready." She grabs her food and begins to eat.

ASTER, 10 YEARS OLD

It's so cold. *I stand shivering, rubbing my hands up and down my arms, as I wait outside with the rest of the children for the newest child to arrive. I heard the adults talking about who she is and where she comes from. Apparently, her parents were serial killers like mine, just not as skilled. I hope she doesn't expect us to be friends with one thing in common. I don't want to make friends, they'll only get in the way and cause more problems for me. Unwanted problems.*

*When her parents got caught, they fought back and were killed. At least mine were smart enough to surrender and are locked away some-*where safe. One day, I'll see them again.

The car pulls up and I feign annoyance through my curiosity as a little girl hops out, her hand held tightly in one of the teacher's, looking around with wide, terrified eyes. Her hair is in lopsided pigtails, her dress fit for a princess, and she wheels a unicorn suitcase behind her. I hope she's not attached to that. *We make brief eye contact as she passes, and I look away, uninterested in catching her attention. She can give it to someone else in this hell hole.*

Making friends with anyone is a death sentence that means more beatings and less of a chance of being taken away from here. Not that I want to be picked. I'd rather wait out the next eight years here than somewhere else that could try and change who I am. Becoming close to anyone can make you soft, and I've seen kids here protecting one another firsthand, it only led to them getting punished even more.

I am the monster they say I am. I learned to keep my beast at bay, but one day that woman will be repaid tenfold for what she has done to me. I swear, the bitch gets off on torturing me, and most of the time it's unprovoked. I glance at the end of the line of people where she stands, my jaw clenching as I fist my hands at my side.

I haven't even been here a year, but everyone knows who my parents are. Cynthia and Adam Balcom. Salem's feared Patchwork Killers. They treat me as if I was the one doing all of the killing. I was meant to be their prodigy, but now everything is ruined and I'm here slowly becoming the slayer they fear I am, in a place that wishes I were dead.

We walk back inside in a single file line like a trail of worker ants never straying from our course, until we cross the threshold, then the children split apart to their respective classes.

I walk in and take my normal seat in the back corner away from everyone and out of Crumbwell's view as much as I can get. Slouching in my chair, my peace is interrupted by her grating voice introducing the new girl. Kelsey. She tells her to take a seat and make it quick. I stare at the ceiling, already counting the seconds until our first break of the day, when I hear the seat next to mine creak. My jaw clenches. The tiny thing decided to sit right next to me. *She'll learn quickly that I'm someone to stay away from.*

I turn my attention to the front, but I can feel Kelsey staring at my face. I ignore it, I ignore her, and when the bell rings, I jump up to go back to my room.

Several days go by, and, to my surprise, Kelsey hasn't tried to talk to me. She's smarter than she looks. She seems content just watching me from the corner. She thinks I don't know, but I do. I feel her everywhere. Her stare causes irritation to rise in me and I want to confront her, but that would mean speaking to her and that is not happening. I wish she would just leave me alone. I don't want her obsession bringing unwanted attention from Crumbwell. It's weird though; I haven't felt her presence today.

Strolling down the hall munching on a granola bar, stale and tasteless, but a boy has to eat. I'm stopped by a huge circle of kids huddled around someone crying on the floor. It isn't until I hear the chant 'clown killer' that I stop and turn around to peer through the gaps and see a sobbing Kelsey with her face smeared in clown makeup that I care. Seeing her like that takes me back to when the kids teamed up and bullied me and I was just like Kelsey, until I grew a backbone and struck so much fear into them that they finally left me alone. Afraid of what I would do if they pursued me again. Now they have a new victim and as much as I don't want to get involved, I know exactly how she feels.

Something inside me snaps, and I push through the kids to get to her. Her tears become sniffles as I kneel beside her and wipe her face with the back of my sleeve. I glare at the mob surrounding us. "Unless you want me to show you how creative I can be with a fork, I suggest you all leave." A collective gasp echoes around the hall as feet scurry away in all directions.

"Thank you," she whispers, staring at me with a small smile.

I shrug and plop down next to her. "It was nothing. Want to tell me why they were all picking on you?" I turn my head, resting it on the wall behind us.

"They found out who my parents were." She sniffles, swiping her nose with her sleeve and avoiding my eyes. I guess not everyone here

eavesdrops on the teacher's conversations like me. I wonder how they found out.

Nodding in understanding, I look around the empty hallway. "You know my parents are like yours."

"I know who you are."

Of course she knows. *Standing up to leave, annoyed and not wanting to hear anymore of her pity, I feel her little hand grab my sleeve, stopping me. A single strand of her wavy brown hair has fallen in front of her face, and something compels me to move it behind her ear. My fingers tingle from where I brushed against her cheek, and I chalk up that feeling to my compulsion to make sure nothing is out of place.* I hope I grow out of that one day.

"What have you heard?" I growl.

She looks around, as if she's scared someone might overhear, and drags us to the girls' side of the house.

"Boys are not allowed on this side," I whisper, planting my feet and frantically looking around, hoping a teacher doesn't see.

She pulls me harder and I fall forward, catching myself before I run into Kelsey. "It's fine. No one will find out."

They will if they catch us. *When she finds out what they do to the naughty children, the ones who don't follow the rules she will be sorry. I should run away, but curiosity outweighs my fear of getting caught. Hesitantly, I follow behind her, curious about what she wants to tell me about myself that I don't already know.*

We stop in front of a white door, my brow furrowing. Strange; the girls side has white doors instead of black. Maybe it's to show one side is the girls and the other is the boys or maybe to show girls are more pure than boys. On her door is a plaque similar to what boys have, her name written in cursive across the worn brass. The one thing I like about this place is each child is given their own room. I think they separate us so we can't plot to escape, or in my case, team up and kill them all. What they're too stupid to realize is I don't need a partner to kill them. The only reason they're still breathing is because my actions could lock me away and then I'd never get to see my parents again.

She looks back and forth before shoving me in her room, popping her head out one more time, then quickly shutting it. Her room is bare, nothing but a bed and single dresser, the girls' uniforms laying on a stack at the end of her mattress.

"You're the Patchwork Killers' son."

No shit, Sherlock. *"Yeah,"* I mutter, *sitting down on her bed. Is* this seriously the reason why she brought me back to her room? To tell me what everyone else already knows? *I already know why I am labeled evil in their eyes.*

"My parents told me stories of the Patchwork Killers and how they had a little boy who was just like me." I sit up, intrigued to hear more. *"They said they were teaching their son to be just like them, to fulfill their legacy if they ever got caught and carry on the family name."*

My head dips, the memory of that day making my heart ache. "They did get caught though, and I'm not out there doing what I was meant to do. I'm stuck here pretending. *Pretending every day to be someone I'm not. Hiding the monster my parents created."*

She sits beside me, placing her hand on my thigh. I move from under her touch and she brings her palm back to her lap. We may have killer parents in common, but that doesn't mean she has the right to touch me. *Dragging me was different, plus she was gripping my sleeve, not my hand.*

"For now." She stands and places her arms behind her back, looking out the barred window. "When we get out of here, we can show everyone whose children we are'."

"Everyone already knows where we come from."

She ignores me, her cheeks turning red through the paint smudged across them. "Everyone who bullies us, every teacher who hurts us, they will all regret it. One day they will be the ones shaking in fear just from hearing our names."

I stand up, my eyes light up with excitement to imagine taking the lives of everyone in this god forsaken place. I guess Kelsey isn't so bad.

She excitedly walks over, careful not to touch me this time, her eyes sparkling "We could be partners in crime! Like our parents!"

Before I can respond, the door crashes open, an angry Crumbwell stands in the doorway with three children I don't recognize snickering behind her.

"Well, well, well, when I was told Aster went to the girls side with our newest recruit, I couldn't believe it. No way Aster would risk the basement. Not so soon after he just got out. But, low and behold, here you are." A sinister smile splits her face, sending chills racing down my spine, my hands becoming sweaty as I take a step back.

Crumbwell snatches the back of my collar with one hand, Kelsey in the other, and drags us out of the room.

"No!" I scream. "It was all me; Kelsey had nothing to do with it." What am I doing? I know very well what awaits me below, but after her little speech she sparked a fire of hope inside me and I can't let her be punished. If she experiences the basement; I don't think she would come out the same. Her fire would be extinguished and I would have no one to help me burn this place and these people to the ground.

"Very well," Crumbwell drops Kelsey, her butt hitting the ground, then continues down the hall. I look back and give her a small, reassuring smile. "To the basement then, Mr. Balcom."

Everything in me screams to fight back, but I know she will overpower me and my punishment will be worse, so I relent and follow behind, her grip still tight around me. My breaths come in ragged gulps, my hands becoming sweaty the closer we get to the torture chamber. My eyes widen as my breath is stolen from me when she shoves me through the door, my heart dropping when it creaks closed, locking me in the darkness with a truly evil woman. All feelings of hope dissipating as she stalks towards me.

THE BLACK LOTUS
CRIME SCENE
EXCLUSIVE
SERENA
CROSS
SOLITUDE

Hearing that makes me wish I could have tortured her longer, really prolonging her death, but I fear that would have hurt Aster. I could see he was really struggling with the decision to save her or end her. There was an internal battle I couldn't see raging inside him and the only thing I wanted, besides her death, was to free Aster from his inner turmoil. Free him from the guilt that would come from ending the life of his only childhood friend. From not being able to come to her rescue. Be the knight in shining armor she grew up admiring and fantasizing about.

To my surprise, I feel relieved hearing how his time with the Twisted Trickster started. I'm more secure in myself and who I have become. If past me went through this, I would have killed her the moment she touched Aster, but I held back because I trust him. My knuckles go white against my plate. Granted, when she started talking more and more about their past, I blacked out, so I will blame my killing her on that. I don't bother hiding the smirk stretching across my face. *Female rage is a scary, unpredictable thing.*

Placing my food down, I move in closer, Aster's gaze

piercing me, his eyes begging me to understand. I do, and yet…
"Thank you for telling me. But I have questions."

"I'll answer anything," he answers quickly, the words being said so fast they almost blend into one.

I nod my head once, contemplating what to ask first. "Your bond with her happened because of who your parents were?"

"Yes."

"What made you want to save her from the bullies?"

"Honestly, to this day, I don't know what made me jump in and save her. I could chalk it up to our similarities in how we grew up or maybe I saw myself as she cowered from their cruelty. Scared in an unknown place, judged because of where we came from, automatically labeled a monster and bullied not only from the kids, but from the adults too."

My mouth thins into a line, my heart breaking not only for Aster, but for Kelsey, too. *Even if she did try to kill me, she was a victim just like Aster.* They weren't born evil, the people who raised them made them that way. They are not monsters, they're misunderstood, only knowing one way of living. If anything, not killing in a place that deserved death shows they never were out of control. They are both products of their parents' creations.

"I understand," I whisper, smiling sympathetically. "Why did you break your promise to her?"

He sits in silence, his fingers covering his mouth as he ponders the question. "I didn't love her. I couldn't see myself becoming partners with someone I only saw as a friend. As we got older, I knew she was falling in love with me." He smiles sadly, his eyes unfocused on a past that finally caught up with him. "I didn't know I was capable of that emotion until I met you. So, when I got out of there, I never looked back. I never had any intention of finding her. I changed my last name, partly so she couldn't find me but also to separate myself from my parents abandoning me again."

"Looks like your plan worked."

He looks down, fiddling with his hands as a sad chuckle escapes his lips. "Yeah, it did."

"Do you regret it?" I ask breathlessly. Waiting for his answer feels like time has stopped and the world is falling off its axis. His answer can either make me drop right along with it or have me soaring above it. With everything we've been through, I would think it'd be an easy answer, but as the silence stretches on, that voice in the back of my mind, the one I thought I'd crushed, is waking from its slumber as it threatens to rear its ugly head. *Please say no.*

He sucks in a greedy breath, holding it for a beat before murmuring. "I just hoped better for her. I wanted her to be more than what her parents made her into."

"You followed in your parents' footsteps."

"That's different. Yes, I am a killer like them, but I was a monster before they made me into one; fascinated with death."

"That doesn't make you a monster."

"It does if you imagined every possible way to kill someone and looked forward to your first kill growing up." A sad, quiet chuckle slips past his lips as his fingers rake through his hair, unbelieving of the truth he is reliving.

I crawl into his lap and straddle his waist. "You didn't kill me."

"You were supposed to be my next lamb," he mutters, regret filling his eyes as his fingers dig into my hips, a forceful grip that feels like he's pouring all of his regret into his hold on me.

I lean in closer and my next words come out as a whisper across his lips. "Now I'm your vixen."

His lips crash against mine, his fingers digging into my sides as my hands grip his hair. He flips us, gripping my ass and lays me on the bed, trailing kisses up my body.

He straightens, ripping off his shirt, and I place my hand out to stop him from kissing me again. His eyebrows crease, and before he can ask why, I slip out from under him.

"Lay down," I demand. He turns to look at me, his brow

lifting in question as he scoots up the bed, his back hitting the headboard. He stares at me with a playful challenge in his gaze as I cross my arms over my chest daring him to challenge me. A smirk lifts his cheeks as he slinks down, his back finally resting against the bed. "Close your eyes."

His eyes disappear, my heart racing as my core clenches.

I walk over to the dresser and retrieve my gift, flipping it open quietly. "Keep your eyes closed," I order, stripping and walking back to the bed to straddle him. Taking the cuffs that hang behind the back of the bed, I grab each of Aster's hands and secure his wrists so he can't move.

"I guess you're done asking questions."

"I am," I muse.

"Can I open my eyes?"

I hold the blade in front of his face and hum my agreement. His eyes open, instantly finding the knife I'm holding.

"What are you planning to do with that?" he asks, his dick hardening beneath me.

Looking at my reflection in the silver blade, the beast within me lifts her head. "It's your turn to bleed."

He shifts under me as I trail the tip of the knife down his stomach, stopping at the top of his pants. Shimmying down so I'm sitting at the end of the bed, I tilt my head as a wicked smile sharpens my face. "You won't be needing these," I say, gripping the top and slicing the fabric all the way down to his cock. "Payback for all the clothes you've ruined," I tease.

"How long have you been waiting to do that?" he asks as he lifts his butt to help me take the pants the rest of the way off and I toss them to the floor.

Ignoring his question, I tap the flat part of the blade against my lips as my eyes trail his naked body. . "Where should I cut you first?"

Crawling back up his body, my mouth salivates thinking about my lips wrapped around his cock. I freeze, stuck with an impossible choice. *Feed the beast or satisfy the beauty?*

"You can always punish me later. I can see how badly you want to taste me."

I bite my lip, tempted to do just that. "You would like that, wouldn't you?"

"You would, too."

Draping myself across his chest, I flip my knife and bring the blade to his arm, slicing slowly across it. Not deep enough to scar, but hard enough that a line of blood forms and drips down his arm.

His eyebrows raise slightly as his mouth makes an upside-down, closed smile and before he can say anything, I lean down and trail my tongue up his arm, the warm copper coating my senses. We both moan as my lips wrap around his length and I suck. I do the same to the other, basking in the taste of pure *him*. I go back for more, our moans cocooning around us, but with some superhuman strength I didn't know Aster possessed, he rips free from his restraints and snatches the knife from my hand, nicking my fingers as he places it on the side table.

He flips us over, my hair drapes in waves over the pillow, his chest rising and falling as he looks down at me with a hungry gaze. "I wasn't done marking you," I say, breathlessly looking up at him.

"I was done waiting."

"Fuck!" I scream, as he shoves his cock hard inside me, my eyes pinching closed at the intrusion. My nails rake down his back hard enough he hisses, punishing me as he slams into my core over and over.

"Have to make you bleed somehow," I tease, smiling up at him.

His hand slides underneath me lifting my ass to pound deeper and my hands fall to the side, gripping the sheets.

"That didn't last long," he grunts, nipping at the delicate skin where my shoulder meets my neck.

"Neither will you," I say, reaching down to massage his balls, my blood marking his skin as I clench around him.

"Fuck, Serena," he moans, his eyes fluttering as I feel his balls constrict, emptying inside me.

"Told you." I lean up to kiss him, tracing bloody shapes across his chest.

"Your turn." He dips his head to my glistening cunt and laps at the juices, flicking his tongue over my throbbing bud.

Clenching my thighs against his head, one hand tangles in his hair, pushing his head deeper as the other grips our bedding. My hips gyrate against his face, chasing my release as I get closer and closer to exploding.

As much as I loved being in control, being the one to make him bleed for once, and hearing the pleasured hiss release from him, I'd much rather be the submissive one. There is just something about Aster taking control that gets me all giddy and excited for what's to come. His unpredictability heightens all my senses and I always crawl back begging for more.

His fingers slide into me, pumping in and out, teasing my sensitive walls with his cum, making the pleasure all the deeper.

"Come for me, Serena. Paint my face in your essence."

At his command, I explode. My legs shake as I cry out so loud my voice cracks. I try to push him away, the feeling too much, but he doesn't relent until he's had every last drop.

CRIME SCENE - DO NOT CROSS
THE BLACK LOTUS
A DARK ROMANCE
SPECIAL EDITION
Daily
10 APRIL 2025
VOL. 10, NO. 5
THE BLACK LOTUS
EXCLUSIVE
EXCLUSIVE
EXCLUSIVE
SOLITUDE
SOLITUDE

CRIME SCENE - DO NOT

THE BLACK LOTUS

EXCLUSIVE
EXCLUSIVE
EXCLUSIVE

SERENA

SOLITUDE

CROSS

CRIME

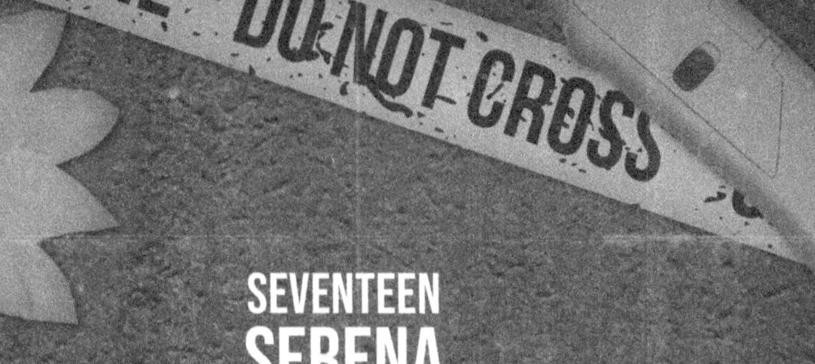

SEVENTEEN
SERENA

"Serena!" Lena exclaims from behind the counter, placing the new glass design she was working on down and rushing around to greet me. "I haven't seen you in *ages*! Where have you been?" She tackles me without slowing, hugging me tightly.

Sucking in a deep breath, I sink into Lena's embrace. I missed the smell and feel of Sinister Beans. Aster promised me last night, after his punishment, which he was enjoying way too much to truly be considered one, we would go out and get my favorite coffee instead of making it at home. We've been so distracted with everything, it's been a while since I've been in, so Lena must have some new designs ready for me to fill our cupboards with.

She releases me from her hold and pulls back, her fingers tightly wrapping around mine. Her breath catches, the words getting caught in her throat as she takes in the man behind me, her eyes nearly popping out of her head. Pulling me close, she whispers. "Don't look now, but there is a god-like man standing behind you."

Giggling lightly, I step back beside Aster and lock my arm with his. "Lena, this is Aster, my boyfriend." I blush, and pride shines over her features. "Aster, this is Lena, my friend who owns this amazing place." I gesture to the shop around us.

Aster reaches his hand out to greet her, but Lena goes in for a hug instead, making him tense up and me swallow my laugh. "I'm a hugger, and I refuse to apologize for it," she says, letting him go. "It's nice to meet you! Now I understand why I haven't seen you around." She winks and we all walk together towards the front to order. "Oh! Serena, I got some new designs and recipes for you to try."

My smile is instantaneous. "Really? I can't wait to try them."

"Here," Lena says, reaching over the counter to grab me a menu they didn't have before. "We're trying something different. Go sit down, look over what's new and I'll be over shortly to take your orders."

I stare at the options and glance around to see more tables clustered in the shop. *Almost all of them are filled.* I didn't notice when we first walked in, but Lena's little coffee shop seems to be more, waiters and waitresses walk around taking orders and bringing food out. *I think it's a diner now.*

The familiar smell of roasting beans is now overshadowed by the food as a sense of longing washes over me. Wishing for the comfort that this place once brought me as a feeling of discomfort takes its place, while I glance around the unfamiliar space, fidgeting with my fingers.

I grab Aster's hand, and we walk to an empty table for two. "Was it always like this?" Aster asks.

I shake my head as a frown replaces the excitement I first had walking in. "No, this is new." We sit in silence, each looking over our menus. The front of the menu has all the food options, one half boasting everything savory, the other sweet, and on the back of the menu are all of Lena's coffee's including the new ones she mentioned. I wasn't expecting to eat here, but now that I'm seeing and smelling all the food being brought out, I think I will try the new menu as well as a coffee.

"Do you know what you're getting?" I ask Aster.

He looks up. "These apple cinnamon pancakes sound good." *The man loves his sweets.* I smile. *Maybe I should learn to bake for him.* "What about you?"

"I'm feeling something savory since my coffee will be sweet."

"Let me guess," he says, glancing across the options once more. "You're going to get a breakfast burrito with the Chucky drink."

"You know me so well," I tease, just as Lena comes to our table.

Even though we haven't known each other long, the way he can just read my mind tugs at my heartstrings.

"So, what do you think of the new setup?" she asks, pen on her notepad.

"I love it! Your new coffees sound amazing and the food smells delicious. Whose idea was it?"

She blushes. "It was actually Jessie's; he's doing all the cooking."

"Jessie is her husband," I say to Aster, who nods once. "Who's watching the boys?"

"My mom is; she's been a saint through the whole transition, and even though it hasn't been long, we are hoping to gain more customers. Jessie loves getting to try new recipes."

"That's wonderful."

"Thanks. I'm really proud of how far we've come." Lena takes a deep breath, shaking away the emotion in her voice. "What can I get you two?"

"I'll take your breakfast burrito and the Chucky coffee, please."'

"I had a feeling you were going to choose that one," she teases, her pen scratching against the paper. "And for you, Aster?"

"Apple pancakes and a Ghostface coffee."

She smiles. "I'll be back with your drinks shortly, and the food will be out soon." She places her pen and pad into her apron and walks away after I say thank you.

I eye Aster warily, wondering if my boyfriend got body snatched while I wasn't looking. "I'm surprised you ordered the Ghostface coffee; I thought you'd want something not as sweet."

He shrugs, settling back into his chair. "I knew that would be your next choice, and we don't know when we will be able to visit again. If I don't like the drink, I'll order something else, but at least you'll get to have two new cups."

My heart swells. *He's always thinking of me.* Seeing him like this makes me giggle.

He raises an eyebrow. "What's so funny?"

"It's just knowing who you are, and how," I whisper the next word, leaning in close and cupping the side of my mouth, "blood thirsty you are, it's cute to see your soft side, especially with how on edge we both have been."

He reaches across the table, intertwining our fingers. "I've always been soft for you, little vixen."

Blushing as he kisses the back of my hand, we don't shy away from each other even as Lena returns, placing our cups in front of us. My mouth waters. Both have whip cream with red drizzle on top and a little knife sticking out.

"Enjoy!" Lena beams, walking into a set of doors I assume leads to the kitchen.

On my glass is a cartoon Chucky holding a bloody knife with the words 'Wanna Play' written in dripping letters with a bloody handprint and red splatter around him. *Perfect for my collection.* I take a sip of the drink, forgetting what was in it until my taste buds are consumed by caramel, mocha, and pecans. The flavors have me closing my eyes and moaning my approval.

Opening my eyes, I'm met with the hungry vision of Aster staring intently at me. My breath catches in my throat and I slowly swallow down the liquid as I lick my lips and push my glass towards him, taking his while he tries mine. He hasn't tasted his drink yet, most likely waiting for me to decide which I prefer.

His glass has a cartoon Ghostface in a bloody mask, holding a bloody knife with the words 'What's Your Favorite Scary Movie' around the image and blood splatter.

I wrap my lips around the straw and am hit with flavors of toasted marshmallow, cinnamon, and toffee. I groan again, my eyes fluttering closed at the taste. *I don't know which one I like more.*

Taking my cup back, I slide Aster's slowly across the table, not wanting to give it up.

He pushes his coffee back towards me with a smirk. "They're both good, not too sweet either."

"The perfect amount," I grin.

Lena returns, dropping the food in front of us with a wink and walks away. We eat in comfortable silence, the food too good to interrupt with talking. Everytime Aster cuts into his food, his sweater tightens around his chest. When he put it on this morning, I made a comment about it getting warmer, and he said he needed to hide the evidence of last night's escapades. Which made us both second guess even leaving the house, but my need for coffee won over my need to be ravished.

Once we're done, Lena comes back and pulls up a chair to sit with us.

"What did you guys think? Can we keep this up?"

"Lena, I say this as your friend…" I trail off and her eyes drop, her mouth tilting downward. I grab her hands, too excited to pretend anymore. "Everything was delicious; my only complaint is that you didn't do this sooner."

Her eyes light up. "I'm so happy you love it! I was hoping when I saw you again it would be a great surprise."

"It was."

Her knuckles go white as she looks out the window, a grim look darkening her features. Aster and I look where she is and see nothing. We turn back to look at one another, my brow dipping in concern as Aster shrugs just as confused. She looks at me, pursing her lips and mouths a word I can't make out. "I'll be right back." She bolts from the table, leaving me and Aster sitting there alone and confused.

I shrug, answering Aster's silent question. Lena has never acted like that before, but she looked like she saw a ghost with how her face paled and her energy alone made the feeling in the room chill. I rub my arms slowly, the feeling of dread washing over me like a phantom wrapping its hand around my throat and slowly taking away my oxygen. Aster tenses as he sits up straighter and pins me with a concerned look. His body twists to the side as if he is about to get up and come to my side, but I look at him and shake my head, mouthing the words, 'I'm okay,' which has him relaxing a little.

Lena runs back into the room, out of breath with a manic spark in her eyes, and places something into my hand. "Keep this with you. I don't know why, but I have this overwhelming feeling you are going to need it." Her eyes plead with mine to listen.

Confused, I look down, opening my hand to see a small box cutter that has a wrist attachment to it. She slides the cord around my arm, slipping the blade up my sleeve. "Keep it hidden."

Her words cause a dread of wary to skitter across my skin. *Does she know something I don't?* The only logical answer, I refuse to believe, is she knows about the hit list and what is coming. I look at her, trying to find any crack in her features, but she is truly scared for me.

Nodding my head, I whisper, "I promise." She smiles, relieved, squeezing my fingers briefly before walking away, and I look at a not too happy Aster. He is on edge, his knuckles white around his nearly empty coffee. Before I can assure him everything is okay, my phone goes off. *Only two people call me regularly, and one of them is sitting across from me.* I answer without looking, hearing a crying Sharon on the other end.

"Serena." Every cell in my body freezes, the feeling I had

multiplying tenfold as my breathing stutters in my lungs. I feel Aster's hand grip my arm as my vision blurs.

"Sharon, what's wrong?"

"It's your dad, he… he was in an accident."

A sob escapes my lips, my eyes meeting Aster's in fear. "Is he okay?" I ask, my lips trembling.

"No, he's in the hospital. I'm outside the coffee shop. Hurry."

Not thinking, I jump to my feet, toppling my chair in the process. My brain is thinking of all the horrible possibilities. *Does Dad's accident have to do with me? Did someone hurt him to get to me? Is he okay? Fuck. Please be okay.* I hear Aster screaming my name as I run out the door and jump into Sharon's car.

Clicking the seatbelt, I turn to Sharon, tears streaming down my face. "What happened to my dad?"

She's eerily calm for someone whose fiancée is in the hospital. Before I can process why her mascara isn't running down her face, I hear Aster banging on the back door trying to get into the car. I go to unlock it for him, but feel a cloth cover my face. I don't register what is happening as my vision darkens and my head hits the window. The last thing I see is an evil smile crossing Sharon's features as Aster screams my name, the tires screeching away.

ENE - DO NOT CROSS CRIME SCEN
BLACK LOTUS
EXCLUSIVE
ASTER
SOLITUDE * SOLITUDE
SOLITUDE * SOLITUD
CROSS
DO NOT CROS

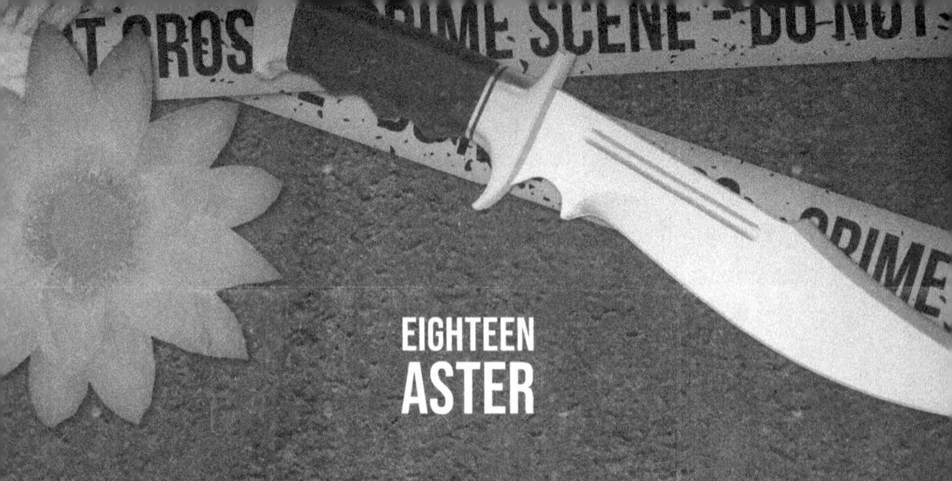

EIGHTEEN
ASTER

Unable to do anything, I stand breathless watching as some woman drives away with Serena. The feeling of defeat knowing I'm unable to chase after them crashes through me. The thoughts of what she has planned for Serena lock me in place. *I need to save Serena.* I saw her put something over her mouth and then she slumped over, so I can only assume it's chloroform and that the woman is the next assassin. I didn't get a good look at her face, all I saw was blonde hair and an evil smile before she sped away with my vixen. *I can't let her succeed.*

I turn around, rage colors my vision red like an inferno, and I see Lena with her hands over her mouth in shock. *Bullshit.* I storm towards her and grip her wrist without remorse, pulling her to the alley and trapping her against the wall. "Where is she?" I growl, my voice menacingly low.

"I don't know."

"Where is she!" I roar. She has to know something. Right before Serena got a call I could barely make out through the tiny whimpers she was making, Lena gave her a box cutter. It's too much of a coincidence for it to be anything else. "You told her she would need the box cutter, then she gets taken. Who. Took. Her."

Lena sobs. "I don't know! Sometimes I get an overwhelming feeling, almost like a vision, and they're never wrong."

I scoff. "Like a fucking witch," I say, more as a statement then a question.

She nods, trembling, her eyes wide as she stares up at me in fear.

"What did you see?" I demand, punching the brick wall above her head, my knuckles tint red as I make her flinch. *If I had my tools, I could carve her skin until I bleed out the answers I desperately need.*

"Serena. Tied up." My body tenses, but she continues as if she doesn't notice. "Then the words 'box cutter' and 'save her' kept repeating." I step back, finally allowing her room to breathe as I search her face for any lie, but find none. Raking my hands through my hair, I drop to my knees as I rock on my heels, fisting my hands to keep them from pounding into the ground. "I don't know why or how, but I hope by giving her what I was compelled to do will keep her safe. Is..." she gulps, her cheeks flushed. "Is she safe?"

I stay silent, not trusting this woman enough to say anything more.

She steps off the wall, her lower lip trembling. "We need to call the police."

I grab her arm, slamming her back against the wall and shake my head. "No."

"No? Your girlfriend was just kidnapped!"

"You don't understand. No cops."

She steels her features, eyeing me skeptically. "Why not?"

I search her face. *Serena trusts her... can I?* "Just trust me; I will get her back."

She worries her bottom lip, and reluctantly nods. "I will bring her home. We'll be back for our glasses."

I leave the alley in a rush, diving into my car and slamming my hands on the steering wheel, begging my mind to settle so I can concentrate on the conversation she had. My head whips up when I remember she said the name Sharon. *That's her dad's fiancé.* Thoughts of why she would take her cross my mind briefly, but quickly vanish when thoughts of what could happen to her take over. My anger bubbling to the surface, overpowering the fear of what could happen. If anything happens to her I'll show her the face of the Morbid Monet and have her begging for her pathetic life.

I take her phone out of my pocket, thankful she dropped it on the table when she ran out the door. I don't even think she realized, she looked so panicked.

My hands shake as I unlock her phone, going straight into her contacts to find her dad's number.

"Hey, honey, what's up?" her dad asks.

"Mr. Raven, it's Aster."

His voice becomes icy. "Why are you calling from my daughter's phone?" A beat passes, and when he speaks again, his voice takes on a worried, fatherly tone. "Is Serena okay?"

I breathe out the next word. "No." Even as I say it the word tastes sour on my tongue. I don't want it to be true. I *need* her to be okay, but from what I've learned about Thomas is he cares deeply for his daughter. If he thinks she's in danger there are no lengths that man wouldn't go for her. I went from hating him to respecting him and hoping I am half the man he is for our children one day. Children I hope come into play in the future, but if I don't get her back then any future with her is non-existent.

"What do you mean no?" Panic rises in his voice. "What happened to my daughter?"

"Your fiancé took her."

Silence stretches on as I wait for him to respond, my fingers tap against the steering wheel as my leg bounces up and down. Every second counts. I need to find Serena.

Finally, he breaks the quiet, surprising me with what he says. "I knew this would happen."

"What do you mean you knew? You knew your *fiancé* would kidnap your daughter and potentially try to kill her?" My jaw clenches, my fingers tightening around my phone and any type of respect I had for him vanishes as I wish it was my hand around his throat.

He takes a deep breath, as if the weight of the world rested entirely on his shoulders. "Not exactly that, but Sharon was showing signs of jealousy towards Serena, and with where she comes from... Something was telling me she didn't want to share me."

What the actual fuck? How could he stay with someone who could potentially hurt his daughter? Serena said their relationship was better, that she wanted me to meet them both after all of this was over, but if he knew this was going to happen... Someone is going to have to stop me from snapping his neck.

I place my hand over my leg to stop the shaking, digging my nails into my jeans, my body no longer able to contain my wrath. "How could you?" I grind out.

"I didn't actually think she would do anything that would risk losing me, but hearing she took her..." He sounds worried and distraught. *Good. He should; this is his fault.* "Aster, I need you to find them, and if my daughter hasn't already killed her, you need to."

My eyes widen. "You want me to *kill* your fiancé?"

"Yes. She took the one person I had left to remind me of my wife. The one person I truly care about in this world. She is the only one I would kill for and if anything happens to Serena, I will go to jail."

"So, you want me to go to jail instead?"

"We both know you won't get caught."

His words have my breath hitching, my movements ceasing as the world stops and crashes down on me.

"Just find my daughter; I'll take care of the rest."

Before I can respond, he hangs up leaving me confused and nervous about what he may know about me. *Does he know I'm the Morbid Monet? If he does, why would he let his daughter stay with me?* My heart races, my vision narrowing. *Why hasn't he turned me in?*

Serena's phone pings with coordinates I can only assume leads to my vixen. I click the picture and read the text accompanied by it.

DAD

Sharon's family owns this property.

She is the only one to ever tend to it.

This is probably where she took her.

I will meet you there.

My ETA says three hours.

Please save my daughter.

I take out my burner phone, punching in the coordinates with surprisingly steady fingers.

Hang on, Serena, I'm coming.

CRIME SCENE - DO NOT
THE BLACK LOTUS
EXCLUSIVE
EXCLUSIVE
EXCLUSIVE
SERENA
CROSS
CRIME
SOLITUDE

NINETEEN
SERENA

I groan, my body feeling as though it weighs a ton. *My head is killing me.* I try to rub the sensitive spot, desperate to relieve some of the ache, but my hands don't move. *What the fuck?* I can't panic, maybe this is some test from Aster. If I get caught, how would I free myself? Slowly blinking, my eyes adjusting to the bright light shining down on me, I look around. *Where… where am I?*

Tugging again, I realize my hands are strapped behind me and my legs tied to each of the chair legs. My shoulders burn and are begging for some type of release. I try to wiggle them, which just makes the soreness worse. "Hello?" I croak, my throat feeling like it's on fire. *I need water.* I try to swallow, but my tongue sticks to the roof of my mouth. *Now I know how Spongebob felt in that one episode where he was literally dying without it.*

Furrowing my brow, I try to remember how I got here. I was at Sinister Beans with Aster when I got a call from Sharon saying Dad was in an accident. My breath catches, the pain in my shoulders fading for a moment. *That's right, my dad is hurt.* Wiggling around, I try to loosen my restraints, but the harder I pull, the tighter they become. It's like that finger trap toy every kid

played with. The one where the harder you tried to free your fingers from the holes, the harder it would be to free them.

"You can try all you want, but you can't escape." I hear a familiar sickly sweet southern accent from somewhere from the shadows. My head whips up towards the direction of her voice as I squint my eyes to see where she hides. *It isn't Aster training me, but Sharon who has kidnapped me?*

"Sharon?"

I blink as her figure walks into the light and shields me from the incessant brightness. "I'm losing my touch; you woke up far quicker than expected."

I tug against the ropes until I feel the burns lining my wrists. "Where am I? Where is my dad? Is he okay?"

Sharons shakes her head, tsking with disappointment. "You stupid girl. Are you really naïve enough to think your dad was hurt?"

I cock my head to the side. "Yes. You're going to be his wife, why would I not believe you?"

She walks around me, like a shark circling its prey while waiting to strike. Her cold hand caresses my cheek, her touch leaving a clammy feeling. "Your naivety is going to get you killed."

She walks away, leaving a cold chill in her wake and sending shivers up my spine. "Why are you doing this?" I ask, dreading the answer.

"It's simple. I want your father to myself, and you, just like your whore of a mother, are in my way." Her hands flail in the air as she speaks, her eyes wide like a mad woman before she clears her throat and turns around.

Her words don't make any sense. From what they told me, my mom pushed them to be together. *How would my mother be in her way if she's the reason they're together?*

A cold plastic touches my wrist, my fingers feeling around for what it is, before I remember Lena's warning. *The box cutter!* She said to keep it out of sight so I wrapped it around my bicep, out of sight. Sharon is a lousy kidnapper considering she didn't even search my body; I still feel it. I rub the back of my arm on my back so the key to my freedom can be within reach while Sharon composes herself. My hand moves around to grab the blade just right, finding the lever that will free me so

I can escape. *Thank you, Lena.*

"I thought you loved my mother," I say, keeping her talking long enough to free myself.

"She thought that too, but in order to get to your father, I had to pretend. Which was hard because I'm a classy, southern lady who has never been with a woman, but when you come from the family I came from. Well…" she scoffs, "let's just say acting comes easy."

"You only wanted my father?" She wormed her way into their lives, tricked them both into believing she actually cared, when she only wanted my father. She was a snake in the grass just waiting for the perfect time to strike. Anger boils inside me building like a volcano the more she speaks.

Sharon grabs a pair of scissors from a tray I didn't notice behind her, swiftly turning around and pointing them in my face. "Are you even listening, you stupid girl," she spits.

"I am," I say, trying to calm my voice to not give her the reaction she wants. "I want to know why you think my father would ever leave my mother."

She sticks the blade of the scissor under her fingernail, treating it like a nail picker and making my lip curl. "I knew he wouldn't; that is why I decided your mother had to die."

"She was already dying." The anger swirls inside, blending with the sadness of remembering my mother slowly withering away and not being able to do anything to save her. *No. Concentrate Serena. You need to escape.*

She growls, her knuckles going white around the scissors. "Until she wasn't."

I stop fiddling with the box cutter, my breath catching in my throat. My mother had cancer. She was dying. The treatments were not working. I was by her side the whole time. She was never *not* dying. She had a moment where it looked like the treatments were working; she was brighter, more herself, but she relapsed. My heart breaks, my eyes burning as tears blur my vision. She got so sick, she couldn't even leave her bed. I was there when the doctor told us she didn't have much time left. My mind races, refusing to believe her lies. *They are lies… right?*

"What do you mean?" I whisper, my voice hoarse, resuming my cutting with a new sense of urgency.

"Now you're asking the right questions!" She taps my nose with the scissors, a manic glee in her eye. "But before I tell you the truth, don't you want to know why I'm killing you instead of turning you in for your crimes?" *No. I want to know your so-called truth.*

The first strap snaps, quietly enough Sharon doesn't hear it. A sigh of relief leaves me as I move the blade to my other hand to cut the other. Her question is irrelevant; she's obviously going to kill me in order to have my father all to herself. Turning me in would mean I was still a part of his life. But I'll play her little game, for now, until she tells me whatever truth she claims to know. Her incessant need to explain everything, like a villain would, is grating on my nerves, but the longer she talks the higher chance I have of getting free. Whatever she tells me will decide her fate; will I run or will I kill the woman who wears a mask?

"Why not turn me in?" I ask, my eyes piercing hers.

"Because," she sneers, "you would still be in your father's life. We both know he would visit you every chance he got. All turning you in would accomplish is you stealing my time with him. The only way to ensure we were truly there for each other is to kill you, and while I was devising a plan, I got the letter." A feral grin stretches her cheeks too wide. "I got the hit on your head from Cynthia." All my movements cease as her words hit me like a ton of bricks. *Sharon is one of the killers after me? It's kill or be killed—she has to die.* She said she came from a family that did things. Are they a family of serial killers like what Aster grew up with? She wears her mask, never slipping up to let her true colors show; a woman who others would fear. But I'm not like everyone else and she knows that, but she doesn't know my true face. She will cower away when she finds out who *I* truly am.

She turns around, fiddling with something I can't see on the tray in front of her. My hands are finally free, my fingers tingling from the returned blood flow. *Now I just need to figure out a way to cut my feet free while keeping her back to me.* I reach down, cutting the strap on one foot, never taking my eyes off my prey. Before she turns back around, my back snaps up, and my hands go back to where they should be. I hold my breath, scared that heavy breathing could alert her, and I wait for her to turn back around.

She squints, then shakes her head. *She should learn to trust her instincts.* "What luck! Not only could I kill you, but I'd be rewarded for it too. But here's the kicker, the one I was shocked about, she included another letter, one just for me."

She turns once more, returning to what she was doing and I bend down quickly, slicing my last leg free but keeping it locked against the leg chair after kicking the rope under me so nothing looks out of place. If she got close enough, she could see, but by then she'd be dead. I don't think she's smart enough to realize I've cut myself free since she was too stupid to check my body.

She holds up a letter, one I can only assume to be the hit on my head; the words that are tempting people to put the nail in my coffin. I want to read it to see if Nate had been telling us everything or if he'd left anything out. But I need to be patient, that can come later.

She clears her throat, reading aloud in a Massachusett accent. **"Sharon, as you can see, I have put a hit on your future step daughter's head, but my sources tell me you're already looking for ways to get rid of her. I think we can come to a mutually beneficial arrangement. If she is still alive, then the others have failed. I hope you won't fail me like they did. My foolish son has fallen for her, and she is distracting him from his** work. Be a dear and get rid of her for me; not only will you be compensated generously, minus my cut of course, but you will finally have her father all to yourself. Sounds like a win/win to me. If you agree, send in your bid to the untraceable account in the other letter. I hope you don't disappoint me. Cynthia."

Sharon drops the letter, I watch it slowly fall to the ground as if it were a feather floating in an invisible breeze. "Who would have thought Aster was the Patchwork Killers' son! I wonder if he takes after his parents..." Her finger taps her bottom lip, contemplating as she eyes me with unveiled disgust. "Since you're still alive, I doubt it."

"Wouldn't you like to know," I taunt, wanting to cause her the same curiosity she's awakened in me.

She clicks her tongue, her sneer answers enough. "Would you like to know the truth before I kill you?"

There she goes again. Gritting my teeth, my fingers flex around Lena's blade. I honestly couldn't care less, I just want to kill her, but I need an opening. *And if I'm honest with myself, a tiny part of me is curious as to what she is talking about.*

"Yes," I state simply, refusing to give her anything more.

"Pity." She pouts, pursuing her lips as she shakes her head. "I was hoping for more begging. Oh well." She shrugs, "maybe you'll beg for your life instead."

I bite my lip to keep back the snarky comeback on the tip of my tongue and losing my chance to distract her.

"The truth is... I killed your mother."

The room spins, the weight of her words washing over me like a wave trying to pull me under. It can't be true. My mother *begged* me to kill her. I suffocated her. I ended her life.

"You're lying," I breathe, shaking my head from the words trying to claw their way in.

"Technically, you delivered the final blow, I'll give you credit for that, but I was poisoning her, giving her the long, slow, painful death she deserved."

Everything stops; time itself freezes. My head sways as my

body fights the gravity from the need to tip over. My hand grips the box cutter so tight, my hand shakes as my thumb presses hard on the slider to slide open the blade. Running my finger along the edge to dim the anger rising in me, I welcome the pain, feeling the blood dripping down my hand. My beast peers through my eyes, stalking the pathetic excuse of a human before me. *When the moment is right, this blade is going right into her throat.*

"As her nurse, I had to give her the daily medicine she needed, but no one knew I was adding an extra ingredient. Granted, she wasn't my first victim, just the first to not die by my needle."

She turns around to grab an injection off the table, speaking while she loads it. "The thing about this particular drug, if you use too much at once, it will kill you. Good thing I perfected the dosage on your mother."

Red consumes my vision, all rational thoughts abandoning me as I leap out of the chair.

SCENE - DO NOT CROSS   CRIME SCENE

BLACK LOTUS

ASTER

SOLITUDE   *   SOLITUDE

SOLITUDE   *   SOLITUDE

CROSS

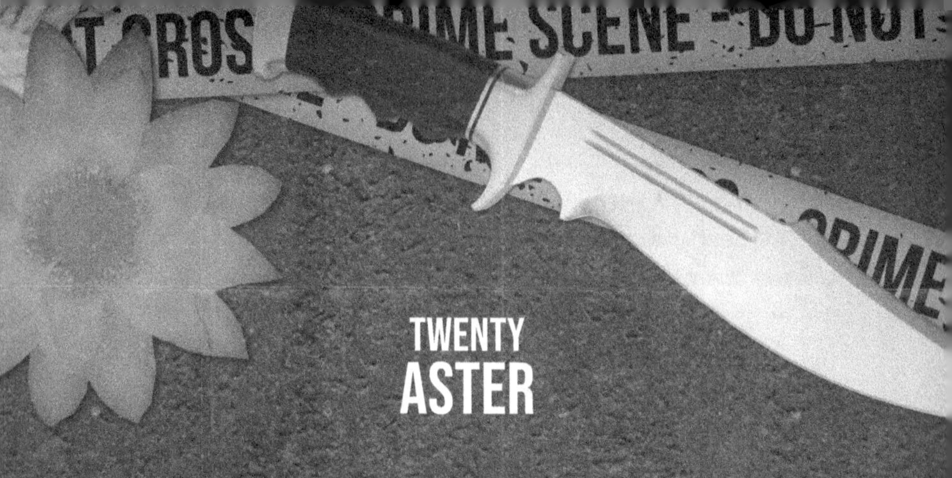

TWENTY
ASTER

Panic like a snake surges through me, slithering up my neck, and constricting my throat, stealing every drop of oxygen from my lungs. *Hold on.* My foot presses harder on the accelerator, the GPS loudly telling me how to get to my vixen. Luckily, Sharon's farm is out in the middle of nowhere, so all the roads are back roads that I can speed down without worrying about getting stopped. Plus, I have a scanner telling me where the cops are hiding.

When I get my hands on the stupid bitch who dared take my girl, I'm going to do exactly as I promised. My blood hums, the thrill of the hunt setting my body on fire. *That is, if Serena doesn't kill her first.*

I turn on the radio, needing to block out all the scenarios running rampant in my head, needing to distract myself from the what ifs. The leather steering wheel groans beneath my palms. Serena is smart, she is strong, and after everything I have taught her, she can handle herself. Lena gave her that box cutter; I only hope Sharon wasn't smart enough to search her and take it. The thought of her still having it is the only thing keeping me from losing control.

'Breaking news! We come to you with an announcement of another terrible kill. The Fatal Floral Killers have struck again.'

My heart races. *Serena is going to love hearing the name they came up with for us.* It's perfect, showcasing both our signatures seamlessly. The corner of my mouth lifts, some of the tension fading from my shoulders. *We've been named, vixen; that means we need to kill again and again and again.*

'Authorities have yet to disclose if the Morbid Monet is involved in any way or if the kills have been an overzealous copycat, but with the details we do know, we can guess the Morbid Monet has found a partner. It appears the Patchwork Killers have been reincarnated, though we can't officially say that.'

My jaw ticks despite the pride filling my chest. Guess the media is smarter than the authorities, unless they're hiding information to make sure I don't catch on. But I'm smarter than all of them; they'll never catch us. The news, however, will most likely get in trouble for saying that and spreading unofficial information.

'The newest victim of the Fatal Florals Killers is none other than the Twisted Trickster. She was found the same way she leaves her victims.'

I snicker, imagining the horror on the officers' faces when they discovered our masterpiece. Neither myself nor Serena are practiced with balloon animals, so we struggled to get the shape correct. But we are artists, through and through, figuring out what to shape her parts into once we got the hang of it was easy.

'Her intestines were shaped into a fox, the signature blue rose and black lotus resting in both hands, and she was placed under what we can only assume was her latest victim. The cuts and how the deceased was blown up are her signature, but the way she was showcased hadn't been seen before.'

What better way to leave our mark than to leave a fox. Granted, they'll never know the true meaning behind it; that's for me and Serena alone to know.

'The victim's name has yet to be disclosed, as we're waiting for permission from the family, but the Twisted Trickster has been identi-

fied as twenty-seven-year-old Kelsey Barrett; daughter of the infamous Killer Clown duo. Sad to see their daughter turned out just like them, even dressing as a clown while she went on her kills.'

It isn't sad that she followed their legacy. My hands squeeze the steering wheel, my frustration pouring off me. Kelsey was better than her parents who would book children's parties and later murder and dismember the family members of the children, leaving them orphaned. Kelsey's kills were cleaner and her trail is better hidden. It's not her fault she wanted what our parents had with me, and I wanted the same with someone else, deep in my blackened heart. I didn't think I'd ever have what my parents did until I met Serena. *But what we have is better than them all.* What we have, no one will take away, and I will protect her with my life.

I switch the channel, having heard enough and knowing all the details no one else is privy to. The song *If It Doesn't Hurt* by Nothing More blasts through the speakers. The lyrics thrum through me, the bass matching the speed of my thundering heart.

The sound of my phone ringing interrupts the song. Thomas's panicked, urgent voice comes through as soon as I answer. "Aster! I tried calling Sharon, but her phone goes straight to voicemail. Please tell me you're close."

"Still 30 minutes out." *I need to go faster. I need to get to Serena.* Sharon not answering isn't a good sign, but it could mean anything.

"Shit. Okay, I tracked her last location, and it was the farm. I'm still almost two hours out-" His voice cuts off, but before I ask if he's still there, his voice comes through again. "-Thank you, Aster."

"Anything for Serena."

The call clicks off and I press harder on the gas, hoping I reach her in time.

CRIME SCENE - DO NOT
SS CRIME SCENE
THE BLACK LOTUS
EXCLUSIVE
SERENA
SOLITUDE
CROSS
CRIME

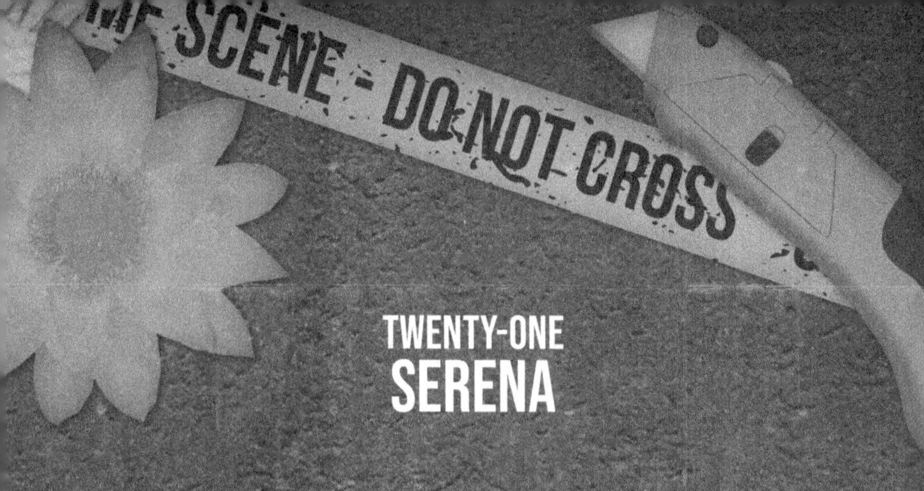

TWENTY-ONE
SERENA

Hefting Sharon's unconscious body onto a table she didn't use herself was a lot harder than Aster makes it look. *Thank God I have him as my partner in crime;* he does all the work I'd rather not do, *and* I get to have all the fun with him afterward.

After hearing what she did to my mother, I decided I wanted her to fear me. I didn't want to kill her, not yet. I wanted to torture her and have her begging for her pathetic life.

I found some duct tape in one of the drawers and wrapped that all over her so she can't move. Stepping back to admire my work, I can't help but giggle excitedly; she looks like a mummy. *Aster would be proud.*

Rummaging through her belongings, I slip on some gloves, something she was too stupid to think of. *Who's the stupid one now, Sharon?* Finding her phone, I take the SIM card out and snap it in half, placing it back on the tray to be disposed of later.

Hearing movement behind me, I turn around, a big smile plastered across my face as I watch Sharon struggle.

"Let me out of here! Right now!" she screeches. "You think you're so clever, stabbing me and knocking me out. You think you can keep me confined in this?" She looks down with a huff,

her eyes widening in disbelief. "Am I wrapped in duct tape?" She fights against her bindings unsuccessfully and eventually stops moving. I chuckle at her futile attempt.

I slam my hand against the table, startling her. "*You* are the stupid one. Why would you tie me to a chair when you had this perfectly good table?" I tap the wood with my knuckles. "Why wouldn't you check my body for anything I could use to escape? Why would you go up against a serial killer?"

Her eyes widen, but she quickly schools her features, scoffing as her eyes trail over me with venom. "Killing two people doesn't make you a serial killer."

"You're right, but killing five does."

"F-five," she stutters, her face paling.

"Yes, Sharon, *five* and you're about to make six. Having a serial killer as your boyfriend means you learn a few things."

"Aster takes after his parents?" She asks in awe as she shimmies her arms, her eyes showing a fear that wasn't there before. My breaths grow heavy, the anticipation thrumming through me. *The tables are turned, you stupid old bitch.*

"No use in trying to escape, I took away everything before I secured you." I motion toward her body with my chin, knowing her skin is sticking painfully to the tape. "And to answer your question, yes; he is the Morbid Monet."

Her eyebrows disappear into her hairline. "So, the news reports, the rumors that the serial killer going after serial killers being the Morbid Monet are true? And you, of all people, are his sidekick?"

"I'm his *partner*; we are equals," I grit out, taking a deep breath so I don't strangle her.

Sharon closes her eyes, thinking everything over. "No wonder Cynthia wants you dead. You changed her son completely. You *ruined* him."

"You're wrong. We are both who we were always destined to become. Partners in crime, the fox and his vixen, taking out one killer at a time." I wish Aster was here to see me turn Sharon into nothing. If I know him, and I do, he is on his way here right now. Biting my lip, I glance towards the door. *I should wait.*

The tape groans, the table squeaking as Sharon continues to struggle. I look down at the woman trying to put on a brave face, but the sweat glistening on her forehead shows me she's anything but brave. She's just a scared girl who isn't ready to die. *Too bad; she should have thought twice about trying to end me.*

Picking up the needle she was going to use on me, I stick it in the air and press some liquid out. "Is this what you used to make my mother deteriorate? To kill her slowly?"

She turns her head, ignoring my question. I balk at her audacity as I scoff, my nails digging into my palm around the syringe. *You'll regret that.*

"You didn't bring any other weapon besides this needle. You didn't want to see me bleed?" I ask, cocking my head to the side.

Sharon's lip curls. "Blood is messy; I prefer a long, painful death, not something quick."

I slowly slide out the blade, the edge already coated in blood. "Unlucky for you, I love watching my victims bleed."

Her body trembles as I bring my box cutter to her face, tapping the point against her forehead as I decide where to start. Slicing into the top of her eyebrow, I slowly slice under her eye. Her screams echo as my hand digs deeper, her eye popping under the pressure. The two sounds blending together bring me a sense of calm, washing over my anger and covering it in retribution. *This is for Mom.* I leave the other eye alone, wanting to see her fear as I slice her up.

"As much as I'd love to cut your whole body, I can only carve the exposed parts and cutting any other piece would free you." I glide the blade along her wrists. "How long would it take for you to die if I slit your wrists? Shall I start draining you?" Sharon flinches away, the flat end of the blade staying pressed to her.

I bring the box cutter up to her bicep, carving deep into her skin, the word 'alone' and adding a broken heart beneath it. I drag the blade across her chest as I walk to the other side, a small red line appearing as the blood slowly drips down. On the other arm, I carve 'forever' and a little lotus, my brand forever marking her.

Stepping back, I admire my work. "How many injections did you give my mother?"

Her silence has me grinding my teeth together as I jam the small blade into the eye I already cut, pulling out her eyeball while she shrieks. "I'm only going to ask one more time. How. Many. Times?"

"Ten!" she sobs. "I gave her ten."

"Perfect, you have just enough."

"Wha-"

Grabbing her hand, I flatten it against the table and start with her pinky, slicing through her skin. Once I get to the bone, I have to really push, not having the right tools for a clean cut. I slice harder, the irritation in me growing at not having my own tools to cause more damage. *Guess this will do.*

One by one I cut each finger off, her wails becoming almost soothing background noise as I concentrate. When I finish, I wipe the sweat with the back of my gloved hand, admiring what remains of Sharon's hands.

Tears, snot, and blood coat Sharon's face, the three liquids making her uglier than her black soul.

"As much as I love hearing you scream, I think I'll kill you the way you intended to kill my mother." I read the label in the needle, slowly pronouncing the name. "Xylazine. If I injected all of what you brought, would it kill you? Shall we test that theory?"

Slowly injecting the needle into the side of her neck like Aster taught me, I watch the the liquid disappear beneath her skin. After the first one is drained, I quickly repeat the steps. After the third one, her body spasms, foam flowing from her mouth as her one eye rolls to the back of her head.

After what feels like forever, her body stops moving, the breath in her body ceasing.

She's dead. My shoulders finally relax, the syringe falls to the floor as my head falls back and my eyes close to savor this moment. I feel like I've avenged my mother, freeing my father from a life spent with the one who stole his one true love from him.

Admiring my handiwork, I decide it isn't enough. This woman who destroyed my childhood, stole years of my life from me. *She deserves utter annihilation.*

I leave the room I'm in, wandering around the barren home attached to Sharon's kill room. I search but find nothing, huffing an annoyed breath I leave the house and step onto the porch to see a barn. I don't try to squash the hope filling my chest. *There has to be something in there.*

The closer I get to the towering building, the louder the sounds of pigs become. When I open the door, I see a pen full of huge hogs. The perfect place to dispose of her body. *I wonder if this is where she took Jessica.*

The smell is putrid, one that would take a lifetime to get used to. Gagging, and not in the fun way, I cover my face, which does nothing to hinder the stench. Looking around quickly, I find exactly what I'm looking for.

A hand saw, perfect for cutting up a body, gleams in the low light. Gleefully, I grab my weapon and head back into the house, ready to prepare the body to feed to the pigs. *I hope the medicine doesn't affect them.*

CRIME SCENE - DO NOT CROSS
BLACK LOTUS
EXCLUSIVE
ASTER
SOLITUDE
SOLITUDE
CROSS
DO NOT CROSS

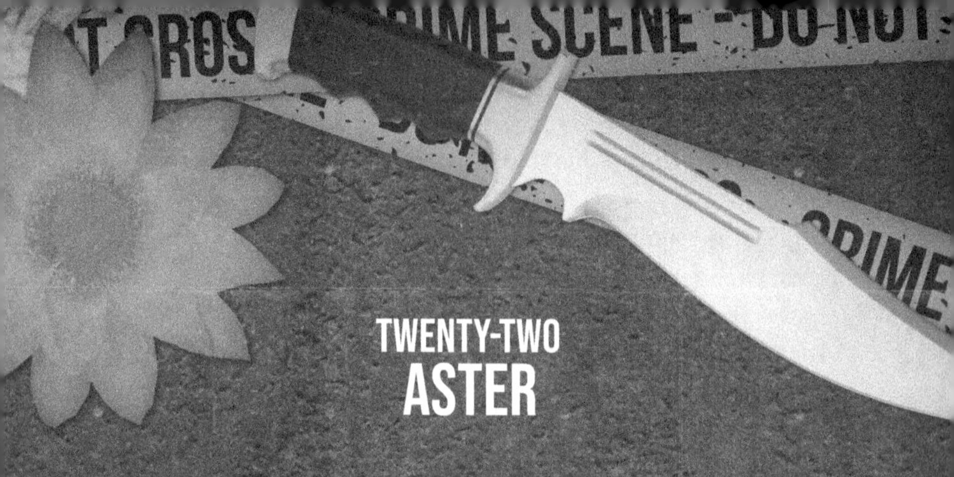

TWENTY-TWO
ASTER

Skidding to a stop in front of a farmhouse, I rush out of the car unsure if I should go into the house or the barn where I hear what sounds like angry pig grunts. *What the hell?* Trusting my instincts, I run into the house, pausing to listen for screams. Nothing greets my ears except a quiet hum I follow that gets louder. Each step through the house has my shoulders relaxing and my breaths coming easier.

She's alive. My vixen is alive.

The lyrics to *Fool and The Beggar* by Melrose Avenue pierces through the empty home. Stepping through the open door, I see my girl swaying back and forth as she saws Sharon's body. It's gruesome, something better fit for *Saw* or *Hostel*. Most would turn and empty their stomach, but I'm not most people. And watching Serena, realizing she turned the tables and became the predator when she was supposed to be the prey, has my cock growing by the minute.

"You are a sight to behold," I muse, leaning against the door frame with my hands crossed over my chest.

Serena's head jerks and her eyes light up. "Aster! I knew you'd find me." She drops the saw, the sound of metal hitting the table creating a low thud. She runs into my arms with her whole body covered in blood and I catch her to savor this moment.

She pushes off me. "Oh my god; I'm so sorry! Now you're a mess too."

Despite her efforts, I pull her back into me. "A little blood would never keep me from you. I would take this over never holding you again."

She wraps her arms around me looking up with a red stained face. "Did you think you would never see me again?"

I squeeze her harder, scared that if I let go she might disappear again. "I didn't know what to think. All I knew was that I had to get to you. That if you didn't kill her before I found you, I would."

"Thanks to Lena," she says, holding up her arm, the little box cutter still hanging from her wrist. "I had a means to escape, and with all our training, waited for the perfect moment to strike."

"Thank you, Lena," I breathe, dropping my forehead against hers.

"I only had this and the chair I was tied to." She walks out of my arms, heading back to Sharon. "I took this drug," she holds up the needle proudly, "stabbed it right into her neck, and she fell into my arms. I lowered her to the floor and went and grabbed this table."

Walking back to the table with her, I listen to her excitedly tell me step-by-step how she took down Sharon. Her eyes light up when she mentions finding the pig farm, thinking out loud about if this is where Jessica ended up and how perfect it is that the place that has ended so many lives is the one that destroys hers.

She picks up the saw and resumes cutting. "You know, cutting up a body is hard work, but what was even harder was lugging her unconscious ass onto this table. At that moment, I really wished you we-"

Placing my hands over hers, I rest my head on her shoulder and press down, helping her slice back and forth. We look like some bloody version of that couple in *Ghost* during the pottery scene. *Instead of clay it's a dead body.* I chuckle at the thought.

"What's so funny?" Serena asks, turning her head to look at me with one eyebrow raised.

"I was just thinking how we look like some fucked up version of *Ghost.*"

She looks down at our hands, then at Sharon, and busts out laughing, her joy infectious and I'm powerless, joining in instantly.

After the last piece of her is cut, and what I assume is the right size for the pigs to eat quickly, we place the saw down. I tuck a strand of hair behind Serena's ear and glance down at her lips, the erection in my pants tightening against the fabric, begging to be set free. *Would she be opposed to fucking next to a dead body?*

As if our minds are one, her hands grab the back of my head and my lips crash against hers, our hands frantically tugging off each other's clothes. Her hands fiddle with the belt buckle of my pants, but her fingers are too slick with blood. With one hand, I undo it, taking it off with a growl. She gawks at me, her eyes full of lust as she jumps into my arms without a second thought.

"Before I remembered the box cutter, I was hoping you'd save me," she pants.

Kissing her hard, I calm the panic threatening to overtake me. "I will always come for you." Kissing her neck, the dry blood cracking when she stretches it for me, I savor the feel of her under my hands. "But I knew you never needed saving. You're my vixen; when danger comes at you-" I stop, looking her right in her eyes and repeat the words she once said to me, "-You look them in their eyes, say 'time to die' and slit their throat or something."

She smacks my chest, her infectious laugh surrounding us as she gets down on her knees, her plump lips hovering inches from my cock, teasing it with her breath. "And to think I was going to suck your dick as a thank you for coming for me." She releases it as she tries to stand, but I twist my hand in her hair, her tongue darting out to lick her lips.

"How about I paint your body in my cum instead?"

Her eyes widen as her lips slowly wrap around my cock, my head falling back as she bobs around my length. "Fuck, Serena, I will never grow tired of your mouth." Her tongue flicks the tip, forcing my head down to watch as her spit combines with my precum. "Or your tongue."

Faster she goes, bringing me to the peak of my orgasm, my moans echoing around us. I push further down her throat, tears springing to her eyes as she gags around me. Her hands grip my ass, pushing me further into her, and I explode, my hot cum, shooting down her throat as I roar my release.

She looks up at me with a playful smile, and I wipe my cum from the corner of her lips, sticking my finger into her mouth. She wraps her tongue around it, her lashes fluttering closed as her moan vibrates around me. My dick rising from the action, more than ready to feel her sweet heat.

Ready to go again, I pull her up and roughly turn her around, slamming her front on the table, her face inches from the dead body parts.

"Who would have thought a dead body and a blow job would turn you feral," she teases.

I slam into her mercilessly, making her scream in ecstasy. "I am always feral for you." The sound of our skin slapping together and mixing with our moans is a sound I want to capture forever. The way our bloodied bodies make love next to a dead one is something I wish to capture on a canvas.

Her hand reaches for something to grab, something for her fingers to curl around, and I smirk. *You can't hide from this pain, vixen.* I grip her head and drag her up, her back meeting my chest, my length fucking her deeper and harder.

"Aster!" she screams, her back arching as her hands wrap around my neck.

"Scream my name, let everyone hear who you belong to."

"No one is here. Just the dead," she grunts.

"Then scream loud enough the Grim Reaper will want to stop and listen before taking her soul to the pits of hell."

At my command she does just that, shrieking loud enough my ears will be ringing for days, her explosion matching my own. The walls shake, my head spins, and it's all I can do to ride through our passion as I close my eyes.

Her legs buckle and I catch her in my arms, lowering us to the ground and wrapping my arms around her, setting her in my lap while we catch our breaths.

"How did you find me?" she asks.

I scratch the back of my head, nervous to tell her I called her father for help. Will she be upset I pulled him into our mess? Grateful? Will she be pissed? "Actually… I called your dad."

She sits up straight, turning to face me. "You called my *dad*? As in Sharon's fiancée?" She scrambles out of my arms, looking around at the chaos around her. "Is he on his way here?" I nod, my lips thinning. "Oh my god! He can't see what I did. He's going to kill me for killing her!" She motions to the pile of flesh on the table.

She paces the room, biting her nails. I need to calm her mind, she needs to understand that the only way I could have found her was through her dad. Standing, I grip her shoulders, stopping her panic and forcing her to look me in the eye. "He told me to kill her if you haven't already. He told me to promise to save you."

Her eyebrows dip in confusion. "He told you to kill Sharon?"

"He did."

She lets out a breath of relief, her knees nearly buckling again. "We should still clean up and get those pigs fed before he gets here." She walks over to the table, throwing a leg over her shoulder. "I doubt he'd want to see what I did to her."

Agreeing, I walk over and grab her torso and arms, tucking them under mine as, piece by piece, we get rid of any evidence. When her head is the final piece left, we both stand there, naked, thinking the same thing. *Can a pig digest human hair and teeth?* She asks and I shrug, knowing that wasn't the disposal method my parents or I preferred. "I display or burn bodies, never thought to feed one to pigs. I will say, it is clever though."

"Should we chance it?" she asks, answering her own question. "Otherwise, I think I saw an incinerator in the barn."

"Let's burn it, just in case."

We burn the last of Sharon, watching the flames melt her and our bloodied clothing. It isn't until we hear Serena's father calling her name out that we are shaken from the trance we're in.

I pull her behind me, hiding her from her father's view as he walks in and abruptly turns around, clearing his throat. "I have towels and clothes for you both in the car." He closes his eyes as we walk past, ready to clean our bodies off with the hose and get dressed.

CRIME SCENE - DO NOT CROSS
CRIME SCENE - DO NOT CROSS
THE BLACK LOTUS
SPECIAL EDITION
Daily O...
...RDELLA
10 APRIL 2025
A DARK ROMANCE
VOL. 10, NO. 5
THE BLACK LOTUS
EXCLUSIVE
EXCLUSIVE
EXCLUSIVE
CRIME SCENE - DO NOT CROSS
SOLITUDE
SOLITU
SOLITUDE

CRIME SCENE - DO NOT

THE BLACK LOTUS

EXCLUSIVE
EXCLUSIVE
EXCLUSIVE

Regular solitude fosters deeper self-discovery
and personal growth. In these quiet moments
you build resilience, gain new
and strengthen your inner
solitude as a tool for
body, and soul
and purpose

SERENA

SOLITUDE *

CROSS

CRIME

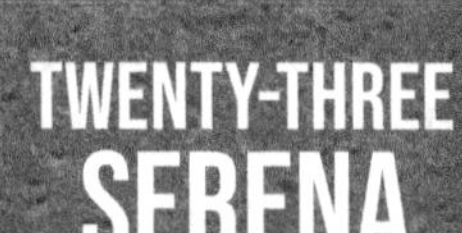

TWENTY-THREE
SERENA

My dad, the person I grew up loving and admiring, then hating and forgiving, is standing at the incinerator watching his fiancée's head burn, and I'm the reason for it. *How could we ever come back from this? What have I done?* In the moment all I felt was pure unadulterated anger towards Sharon, and it was within my grasp to take it out on her. He's already protected and forgave me for Mom and Jessica. *Can he do the same for Sharon?*

I play with the edges of the shirt Dad brought to help some of the growing anxiety to stay at bay. The smooth fabric feels comforting as I drag my feet back into the barn. The air in here feels like a vacuum sucked it all out, the edges of my vision growing fuzzy since I can't take a deep breath. The only sound is the buzzing in my ears from trying to explain why she was fed to the pigs, their excited squeals finally dying down as their mouths and some parts of their body are caked and bloody from tearing her apart. Even though Aster told me what he said, I don't think he's okay seeing it.

"She killed Mom," I whisper, the only thing I can manage to get out as I chew on my bottom lip, looking at the ground and feeling like a little kid waiting to be scolded. When he doesn't even flinch from my words, the words spill out of me like a waterfall. "She was going to kill me. I'm sorry, Dad. When she told me she wanted you to herself, I understood, because after the truth was finally revealed and I found out that you are actually the best father in the world, I wanted you to myself, too. I wanted to get to know the man you've been hiding from me and let you into my life. I want us to grow closer, being a daddy and daughter duo that others are jealous of." I pick at the cuticles on my nails, nervous to tell him the next part. The truth of how she killed his soulmate. "When she told me she was the reason Mom never got better, that she was poisoning her, making her worse and watching as she slowly died; I snapped. I was raging inside, but I kept my calm, just like Aster taught me, waiting for the right moment to, well, to make *her* the victim…"

I trail off as he turns around, my heart in my throat until he wraps his arms around me so tight I can hardly breathe. His embrace doesn't feel angry. It doesn't feel sad. Tears burn my eyes. All I feel is relief in his trembling body. "Dad?" I look up at him, concern twisting my features.

"I'm so sorry, Serena."

He's sorry? Why is he sorry? He didn't know his psycho fiancée killed his wife then planned to kidnap his daughter. *Did he?*

Stepping out of his arms, feeling like I'm on a rollercoaster waiting for the impending drop, I stare at him, waiting in fear for him to continue. I look back and see Aster staring down my father, eyes blazing like he could rip out his throat at any minute. *Does he know something I don't?* The anxiety that died when my dad hugged me, comes back full force as I glance back and forth between the two men, my stomach in knots as the silence wears on.

I force myself to turn back around. "Why are you sorry? Dad?"

He rakes his fingers through his hair, stepping closer as I take a tentative step back, inching closer to the safety of my killer's arms. If Dad is about to tell me something I'm not ready to hear, I need to be next to the one person who can catch me when I fall. "I didn't know she was poisoning your mom," his voice breaks, "we can talk more about that later. But... but I knew she was trying to keep us apart. Granted, I never assumed she would go to such lengths. I should have known she would because of where she came from. I am so sorry, Serena." He stays right in front of the pig pen, the grunts quieting as the pigs fall asleep, happy, bloody, and full.

Should we spray them off with a hose or will the blood eventually mix with the mud?

Aster's hand gently, but protectively, grips my shoulder, distracting me from my thoughts and calming my rage. I look up at him with a reassuring smile, placing my hand on top of his.

Narrowing my gaze at my father, I ask, "Tell me, *Dad*, where did Sharon come from? How did you know she wanted me gone?"

"Can we get out of here and drive as far away as possible from this place first? Then I will tell you everything."

Me and Aster share a look, nodding in unison. I get in Aster's car, my father looking disappointed that I'm not going with him. I give him a sad smile wanting to comfort him, but with what he just told me, I need the comfort Aster brings me, but I don't want to hurt him anymore than I already have.

"We will follow you." Aster states, leaving no room for argument.

My father's face falls, but he relents, getting into his car and driving away.

"Thank you," I whisper, picking at a sticker on Aster's middle console.

Aster's hand clasps mine, ceasing my nervous picking. "Talk to me. What's going on in that beautiful head of yours?"

I look up at him, a small smile lifting my lips. "You know, you're really sweet for a serial killer."

He chuckles, bringing my knuckles to his mouth and kissing

them. "I wear a mask for everyone except you. You're the only one who will ever see all sides of me."

"And accept them," I finish, staring at his profile as we bounce along the road.

His thumb brushes against my knuckles. "Now will you tell me what's bothering you? Do you regret killing Sharon?"

"No!" I hurry to answer, pulling my hand from his. "She deserved the death she got. It's just… I worry about my dad. He's alone again. He's alone again because of me…"

"He has us. And I think he knows more than we think."

Tilting my head to the side, my eyebrows dip as I stare at him, waiting for him to elaborate. *Does he know why Sharon tried to kill me? Did he know she was coming for me? Was he hiding the truth of her nefarious plans to eliminate me?* The way his hands tighten on the wheel, his jaw ticking, tells me it's something else entirely. I chew on my bottom lip, wondering what about my father could have Aster so rattled.

"What do you mean?" I finally ask. He wouldn't be so rattled from anything that has to do with my dad. The only thing that would rattle him like this would have to do with me, but Dad can't possibly know about the hit on my head. *Right?*

"He made a comment about me not getting caught if I killed Sharon."

My brain turns to mush, my thoughts racing and jumbling together like a giant ball of yarn that can't be untangled. *He can't know Aster is the Morbid Monet. Even the killers coming after me don't know that.* My chest rises and falls, my vision blurring. *Surely, if my dad knew that he would make me break up with him.* Not that he could or that he has any room to talk considering the woman he fell for was behind Mom's downfall and my kidnapping and almost death.

"I don't think he knows I'm the Morbid Monet, but he knows something. When you talk to him this time, I'm not leaving your side. We will find out the truth."

CRIME SCENE - DO NOT CROSS
CRIME SCENE - DO NO
THE BLACK LOTUS
SPECIAL EDITION
Daily
A DARK ROMANCE
10 APRIL 2025
VOL. 10, NO. 5
THE BLACK LOTUS
EXCLUSIVE
EXCLUSIVE
EXCLUSIVE
CRIME SCENE - DO
DO NOT CRO
SOLITUDE
SOLITUDE

CRIME SCENE - DO NOT
THE BLACK LOTUS
EXCLUSIVE
SERENA
T. CROSS
CRIME

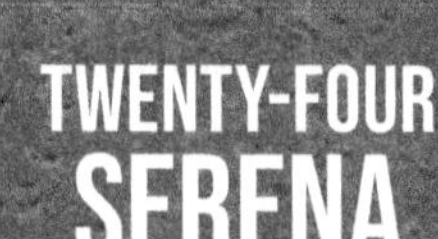

TWENTY-FOUR
SERENA

Dad's house doesn't feel as welcoming as it did when I was here last; granted, I never really felt warm here after Mom died. The house lost its love and brightness, the joy replaced with a constant fog I could never escape. One that ultimately made me leave. I couldn't shake the depression that clung to me; not even the fake Jessica could break me from myself. Once I got a place of my own and became truly independent, I was no longer tied to the lie of my old self. I was finally able to see my truth and breathe in the happiness I was deprived of. Although, the self I found was a mask. The person I am now is the woman I can proudly look at in the mirror and say, 'I love you'. It's crazy to think I was once a scared, insecure girl, when I was always meant to be a strong, independent killer.

"Serena." My dad's voice breaks through my thoughts, as he offers me a hot mug of tea.

I shake my head. "I don't like hot drinks this late."

"Sorry. Would you like water? Or a soda? I could add ice to the tea." Watching him fumbling to make me more comfortable in a place I don't think I ever could be makes me soften as I relax into the couch.

"Water would be nice."

He retreats into the kitchen, coming back with two waters, one for me and one for Aster. Taking the bottle from my dad, Aster's arm tightens around me, pulling me into him. My dad's eyes flash with something I don't dare put a name to, collapsing into a chair opposite and spreading his legs wide as he leans forward.

His fingers twist between his thighs, his body nearly vibrating with tension as he takes a deep breath. "Sharon comes, *came*, from a…" His thumbs dance as he finds the right words to say, silence filling the room with a heavy weight. Aster and I impatiently wait; my leg bounces while his fingers tap along my shoulder, sending goosebumps skittering along my back and down my arms.

Dad looks up at us as he breaks the silence. "Her family is complicated. Where she came from. How she grew up."

"What, was she in some kind of cult?" I scoff.

"The family she was a part of came from a lot of money. Old money. She grew up saying yes sir and ma'am and if she stepped out of line she was punished."

I sit up straighter, scooting towards the edge of the cushion. "Is her family tied to something dangerous? Like the kind of danger I should be scared of?" He says nothing, just stares at me as if his eyes are answering my question. *Holy fuck.* Will we be punished for killing her? Another problem to deal with on top of everything else? Aster must be thinking the same thing because he's intently listening to my father as he leans forward with his leg slightly bouncing.

"Her family was heavily involved, but she left when she was of age. She could never perform the sacrifice they require of all their members."

"Will they come for me since I killed a family member of whatever her family was a part of?"

"No. I won't let that happen. I know her family. They weren't fond of her rejection, but they also can't know she is dead. I promise I will take care of it."

"So they will come for me?" I lean back, gripping my water bottle in my lap as Aster places his bottle on the side table and wraps his arm around me, holding me close. Fear wraps around me like the claws of a bird capturing their prey. Not only do I have Aster's mother and other serial killers to worry about, now I have Sharon's family with their endless money and power.

I'm dead.

"Serena." I look up at my dad, my eyes blurring from unshed tears, Aster's hands steadying my shaking ones. "There are no cameras on that property, and you got rid of all evidence of you being there. I will go back and do a deep clean and scrub the place of everything. I'll send a message to her family telling them she went missing after leaving me a message ending our relationship. Yes, they will look into it and me, but I'm sure, with your boyfriend's help, we can get away without any consequences. No one else's blood will be shed." He levels his gaze at Aster.

I trust my father's words, something is telling me we will get away with it, that they will find nothing linking us to Sharon's disappearance. But another part, a small voice in the back of my mind is telling me that *this* is not over. That what I did cannot be hidden and we all will pay the price for my actions. Taking a sip of my water, I let the cool liquid wash away the rest of my worries, hoping that little voice is a liar.

"Back at the farm you said she killed your mother; what do you mean?" His eyes bounce back and forth between mine, searching for the truth I know will shatter him.

Breaking my father's heart is not something I ever wanted to do. Old Serena would have shredded it, but New Serena is dreading it. I cap the water bottle and place it on the coffee table between us, stalling. I don't want to tell him the real reason why the love of his life withered away slowly.

"You know how every villain loves to tell you their wicked plans and the reason behind them when they think they're getting rid of their nemesis?" He nods, his hands clasped in front of his mouth, his arms digging into his knees. "Sharon was no exception."

I bite my bottom lip and look my father in his eyes. "She said she was Mom's nurse, and when Mom started getting better, she injected her with a drug that made sure she was dying slowly and painfully." My eyes water, my voice cracking as I acknowledge the truth. "So, the doctor was right. Mom *was* beating the cancer, but Sharon didn't like that." My dad's fingers dig into the back of his palms, his jaw clenching as he listens. "She said she didn't want to share you. She needed to get rid of Mom to make that happen and when it was taking too long for her to die, when Mom was fighting to stay alive, she started poisoning her." I look away, not wanting to see the look in my father's eyes. "Then Mom begged me to kill her, and I did. So, while Sharon didn't deliver the final blow, she was the reason Mom never got better."

My dad gets up calmly and walks away, my heart aching in my chest. I sob, and try to chase after him, but Aster grabs my wrist, shaking his head and stopping me from moving. I reluctantly sit back and flinch when I hear glass after glass shatter. I don't know what my father is destroying, but it sounds endless. He starts to yell, his words incoherent, but just as soon the breaking started, the sound stops, his quiet sobs filling the sudden silence.

Aster and I sit in silence waiting for my father to return, and when he does, his clothes are wrinkled and his normally styled hair falls over his face. He falls back into his seat acting as though he never left, running his fingers through the black strands in an attempt to put it back in place.

"Thank you for telling me."

His voice sounds dead. Broken. Unlike anything I've heard before.

"Are you okay, Daddy?" I ask, nervous to set him off further.

His head whips up. "You called me Daddy," he whispers in

awe. "I-I just needed a minute, but yes, Daddy is okay." He forces a tired smile.

I return a sympathetic smile as my lip quivers. "I killed her the same way she tried to kill Mom." The words leave me before I have a chance to stop myself.

His mouth drops open, then he laughs. A full blown belly laugh, one I haven't heard since I was a child. Swiping the tears from his cheeks, he says, "My daughter, the karma of justice is impressive. Delivering the same treatment to that witch? You are your mother's daughter."

Standing up, I walk around the coffee table, dropping to my knees and hugging my father, the two of us crying.

"Your mother would be so proud of you." He swipes the tears from my lashes, cradling my face in his hands.

Sniffling and looking up at him, I summon the courage for one final question. "Aster told me something that I've wanted to ask you about."

"Go ahead, I will be honest."

"You said Aster wouldn't get caught if he were the one to kill Sharon. What did you mean by that?"

He glances at Aster over my head, and I hear the fabric of the couch shift behind me. I know he's just as curious as me. *Are we ready for the new truth?* Looking back down, he answers, "After you told us about Aster, Sharon did some digging, and even though she couldn't find who he really is, she found a video of him crushing some guy's hand you were next to, then that guy and his brother later went missing. It's not hard to put two and two together. Even if the police are too stupid to figure it out, we are not. He obviously killed them both."

"Why do you think that?"

"I could tell in the video Aster was protecting you. So, you have nothing to worry about; his secret is safe with me. The only other person that knew is dead." He looks to Aster, a small smile lifting his lips. "Thank you for looking after my daughter." I turn around to look at Aster, he doesn't answer, just dips his head in acknowledgment.

After that, we sit and make plans on what to say if anyone comes knocking, and I go into details about what I did back at the farm because he asked. Then we say our goodbyes and leave.

Aster and I both let out a collective sigh when we sit down in the privacy of the car, relieved my dad doesn't know he is the Morbid Monet. I don't know how he would process that bomb or knowing I was meant to be his next victim. Any sane father would kill Aster, but my father isn't sane. Something I am more grateful for every time he needs to clean up one of my messes.

We all have our secrets. I just hope he never sees the truth behind the masks we parade in.

CRIME SCENE - DO NOT CROSS
CRIME SCENE - DO NOT CROSS
THE BLACK LOTUS
SPECIAL EDITION
Daily
ARDELLA
10 APRIL 2025
A DARK ROMANCE
VOL. 10, NO. 5
THE BLACK LOTUS
EXCLUSIVE
EXCLUSIVE
EXCLUSIVE
EXCLUSIVE
EXCLUSIVE
EXCLUSIVE
SOLITUDE
SOLITUDE
SOLITUDE
CRIME SCENE - DO
DO NOT CROSS

CRIME SCENE - DO NOT
THE BLACK LOTUS
EXCLUSIVE
EXCLUSIVE
EXCLUSIVE
SERENA
SOLITUDE
T. CROSS
CRIME

TWENTY-FIVE
SERENA

Aster still hasn't told me where he's taking me on our date. He said to dress nice, but not fancy. He wants to take my mind off everything and give us a night to breathe, to date, to be normal. I snort, glancing at myself in the mirror. *Well, whatever normal is for two serial killers.*

After his shower, Aster left me alone in our bathroom to get ready. As much as we've been in here, I haven't really looked at the massive space. We're usually distracted with one another's bodies. *Not that I'm complaining.* It's bigger than mine, boasting a huge shower that could easily fit five Asters in it, with charcoal walls and grey tiled floors. *Definitely a man's bathroom, but I do love how dark it is.* The toilet is in a separate room right off to the side of the huge tub we frequently bathe in. Past the double sink is a huge closet that I have since added my clothes into, and his home is slowly becoming ours. I just need to find a dedicated place to do my art. I haven't picked up a brush since Zephira broke into our lives, and I miss the feeling of creating.

I swipe red across my lips, a sad smile looking back at me as I think about the last time I was at my vanity like this. Jessica was behind me, doing my hair and getting ready with me. *But it was*

all in my head. That was the Jessica I wished she had been, not her true self. *That bitch was a cunt.*

Smacking my lips, I stick barbed red heart earrings in each ear and whisper to myself, "No outfit is complete without earrings."

"You look ravishing," Aster says, leaning against the door-frame, his eyes darkening as he takes in my outfit for the night.

Blushing, I take his hand as I do a twirl, my black dress flying up. "These leggings are in my way," he growls into my ear, pulling my back flush to his chest.

"Got to make you work for it," I taunt, arching my back and feeling his length pressing into me.

"You'll regret saying that later when these are shredded on the floor."

I spin around to face him, my eyes wide with false rage. "I swear on everything, Aster, if you destroy *anymore* of my clothes I will-"

"You'll what?" he taunts, his hand slipping beneath my waist-band as his fingers rub up and down slowly over the fabric of my panties.

My face smooshes into his chest as I collapse into him and moan, "I'll.." I swallow hard. "I'll, uhm. *Fuck.* Right there."

His hand slips out just as I was finding a good rhythm, and I look up at him, my spiteful eyes meeting his playful ones. "Can't have you falling apart and missing our reservations." He takes my hand in his and walks us down the stairs, stopping at the bottom to look back at me. "I want no time restraints on what I have planned later." A shiver of excitement races down my spine as he locks the door.

WE PARK DOWNTOWN IN A PARKING GARAGE. "IS THERE NO PARKING where you're taking me?

"There is, but then you'd see where we're going."

I eye him skeptically, grateful I opted to wear my boots instead of the heels I was debating on. *Always better to be prepared.* Heels would have made running painful and me falling face first onto the ground a matter of *when,* not if.

Aster gets out and opens my door, interlocking our fingers as we walk down Salem's busy streets. The moon is high in the sky, but the stars are hidden from all the bright lights of the city. A cool breeze makes my dress flare, my hair blowing all around us as goosebumps pebble my flesh.

We slow when we get closer to a building I've only driven past. Aster pulls open the door as a smile stretches across my face. I bounce on my heels when Aster tells the lady at the front his name and she leads us into a room full of canvases and talking, excited people wrapping aprons around themselves.

We get handed aprons and sit down in front of our own canvases as I look around the room taking everything in. Layered across the walls are art pieces I assume the instructors painted themselves and hung as examples and pictures of smiling groups holding up their completed works.

"Guess I chose right," Aster says, smiling sweetly. "I know neither of us has painted in far too long, and I thought this could be a nice chance to." Before I can object, he adds, "the tattoo doesn't count."

"Thank you," I whisper, tears threatening to fall, but I blink them back so I don't ruin my makeup.

"When we get back home, we can turn a guest room into an art studio so we can both start painting again."

I lean in close, whispering low so no one can hear. "Just canvases? No little lambs?" I ask.

He sits up and looks at me with a familiar longing look in his eyes. "As much as I miss painting my lambs-" He stops, searching for the right words and grabbing my hands. "The

Monet is dead; the lambs are no more. The Fatal Floral Killers live and will be Salem's most notorious duo," he whispers, bringing my knuckles to his lips.

"Better than the Patchwork Killers?" I murmur.

"The best."

Our conversation is interrupted when the instructor begins talking, our brushes begin swiping. *To think he doesn't want to be the Morbid Monet anymore...* My brushstrokes slow as I glance over at him. *Does he really mean it? Or is he saying it for my benefit?* Aster is changing who he is for me. He hasn't even had a chance to kill anyone. He just sits back and watches me. *Is he okay with that?* The thought of being a certain way for so long and then having to change on a whim, would feel like whiplash to me. He was raised with the teachings of who he was supposed to grow up to be and now since meeting me he's lost that part of himself. *I hate to admit it, but... Maybe Cynthia is right.* Aster has changed and it is all because of me.

I look over at Aster concentrated on his work, a regretful feeling washing over me making it hard to keep painting. I know he said he's fine with never having another lamb but.... *All his victims looked similar to me.* I get why he would want to change, but he's been the Monet for so long. *People don't just change.*

Aster's breath tickles the back of my ear, his hand wrapping around mine to glide the paintbrush through the paint. "Killing beside you is better than killing by myself," he whispers.

My eyebrows shoot to my hairline, my mouth parting with a silent gasp. *How did he know what I was thinking?*

He spins me around so I'm trapped between his legs, and taps his finger against my forehead. "Get out of that beautiful head of yours. I wouldn't change a thing."

A tentative smile crosses my features, my chin dropping in understanding. He may say he's okay with it, but I know he has to miss it. *After all of this is over, we can talk about how we can both continue to kill.* I have a knack for it, and my hunger for spilled blood is growing with each kill.

His lips lightly press against mine. "I'll be right back; I'm just going for a smoke." I want to tell him to stay, to not leave my side. I want to scold him for smoking, since he knows how much I despise it. But I don't. I know he needs a minute to just breathe in the toxic fumes. To slip back into who he was for just a moment, before he has to come back to the present. "There are too many people in this room for anyone to try anything. Do *not* move until I come back."

"I promise."

He kisses the top of my head and walks out the door. I turn back to my painting, listening to what the instructor is saying, but turning it into my own style because what she is walking us through is boring. I look over at Aster's painting and see he hasn't listened to anything the instructor said either, choosing to freehand his own beautiful masterpiece instead. I glide my fingers along the wet paint, getting some of the red on my fingers. Rubbing my fingers together, I watch as the paint blends into a color matching the blood Sharon spilled. It's drying the same way her red crimson did, even getting stuck under my nails. I hope Dad cleaned every speck left of her in her kill room. Any trace of her DNA could lead her family to believe she didn't run away, but was killed and I don't even want to think about that.

I shake away the thoughts, rubbing my hands down my apron as I turn back to my canvas and decide if Aster went off script, so will I. Letting my hand flow, colors splash in harsh lines the faster and more into it I get, releasing every emotion into my art. The voices in the room quiet as I enter my own space.

Once I finish, I stand to admire the piece I created, coos of *oohs* and *ahhs* echoing behind me. The brush drops from my hand as I spin around to find everyone gathered around and looking at our paintings. *How long have they been standing there?* My cheeks tint red as I offer the crowd a bashful smile.

The last time I felt this kind of admiration was at the flea market, another place I miss. I wonder if Alice has been wondering where I am? I wonder how they're doing. I'm sure when I see them again she would show me a picture of where she hung my painting and take me through another memory. I could just imagine how she would react to meeting Aster, she would drool all over him and Jerry would grumble, but eventually warm up to Aster as well.

Wait… Where is Aster? My eyes scan the room as I search for him, my head darting around, but no sandy hair or green eyes meet mine. No familiar smell of sandalwood or mint either. Just everyone else around me, snapping pictures of our work.

Everyone, except Aster.

Pushing people out of the way, I search the room and building and even the men's bathroom for him. He's been gone an hour when he should have come back in ten minutes. How could I let myself get lost in my own world, only to find it shattered when I returned. Why wasn't I watching the clock waiting for his return? *How could I miss his absence?*

My breathing accelerates, my chest rising and falling with panic as I stumble out the front door screaming his name. No one has noticed my freak out since they're too absorbed in capturing what isn't theirs. Not even the host noticed me run out of the building since she was a part of the crowd as well.

I run down the alley, knowing it would've been the spot he'd choose to be alone to smoke. I see a half-smoked bud lying on the ground, surrounded by fresh scuff marks. I kneel to the ground, grazing my fingers against the pavement and pick up the cigarette. Closing my eyes, I inhale the bud, my senses instantly picking up a faint hint of sandalwood and mint. *Aster.* I stare into the dark void, a scream of agony interrupting the otherwise silent night for anyone to hear. Bending forward with the cigarette clutched to my chest, I rock back and forth as the feeling of numbness covers me with its suffocating embrace.

He's gone.

CRIME SCENE - DO NOT CROSS
CRIME SCENE - DO NO
THE BLACK LOTUS
SPECIAL EDITION
Daily O...
...RDELLA
10 APRIL 2025
A DARK ROMANCE
VOL. 10, NO. 5
THE BLACK LOTUS
EXCLUSIVE
EXCLUSIVE
EXCLUSIVE
CRIME SCENE - B
DO NOT CR
SOLITUDE
SOLITUDE

CRIME SCENE - DO NOT

THE BLACK LOTUS

EXCLUSIVE
EXCLUSIVE
EXCLUSIVE

SERENA

CROSS

CRIME

TWENTY-SIX
SERENA

I've searched everywhere, I even went back inside and asked if anyone saw him. In my heart, I know he was taken but I don't want to believe it. Luckily, he left the car keys, so I grabbed our art then sped home. I know he won't be there, but I also know someone who is always watching that I hope will help. If I had her number I would have called her, but with her hacker skills I'm sure she's always watching us through our cameras.

"Zephira!" I yell, bursting through the door on the verge of a complete breakdown. "Zephira, if you're listening, I need your help. *Please!* Your brother was taken, and I don't know how to find him or where to even begin looking." I spin around the living room, yelling at the empty space, desperately hoping she's watching. "We were on a date, then he went for a smoke and never came back. I went searching for him and saw signs of a struggle." I fall to my knees, begging as the tears fall. "Please, Zephira. I know you care for him. I can't… I can't lose him." Curling in on myself, I cry, whispering the word *please* over and over.

Why would anyone take Aster? Is it to get to me? Is this my fault? Sorrow fills my heart thinking about all the why's, my lower lip

trembling as I hold my knees to my chest, rocking back and forth. All that matters is finding Aster, killing whoever took him, and getting him back. My hand covers my heart, my fingers digging into my chest from the ache I am feeling, my eyes burning from my mascara. *I probably look like a crazed raccoon.*

After an hour of waiting and still no word from Zephira, or sign she's heard me, the numbness returns and nearly strangles me. I stand and trudge up the stairs like a zombie. If she were to come knowing I was alone, she could kill me or send someone else after me and I don't feel the strength I need to fight back. *This is the perfect time to strike,* but, *Aster needs me.* Aster didn't fall in love with a weak girl, he fell for a strong woman. *I can't back down. I can't give up.* I need to stay vigilant, but I *need* to find Aster.

I grab my laptop, my phone, my charger, my knife and head to the attic. Clicking the button behind the picture on the wall, I go up and lock myself inside. *I should talk to Aster about getting a remote with a button for this room.* If anyone comes for me, they'll have to find me first. I glance back at the door. *There is only one way in and out.* I sit in the corner opposite the mirror, placing the knife beside the laptop, and open the document we labeled 'Hunters', seeing the list of serial killers who could come after me.

There are two files, one that says 'Still Hunting' and one that makes a sob bubble up into a laugh. 'Hunters Slain By The Vixen.' *When did he even do this?* I swipe my nose clicking to see the rather extensive list of potentials.

We don't know who Cynthia has sent or if every single one of these names will soon make our list, but it's better to be safe than sorry. Scrolling through, my brow furrows as I squint at the screen. No one on this list stands out. No one who would cross Cynthia to get to me. Surely, if Cynthia knew one of her killers took her son, she would find a way to get him back and have that person taken out.

Biting my thumbnail, I search her name and find *her*. My

finger hovers over the button, the face of the woman who wants me dead staring back at me. The photo was from the day she was arrested; she looks exactly like Zephira. *I wonder what she looks like now?* Has age been kind to her? Does Zephira still resemble her? Or does she look like a completely different woman? Clicking the tab to enlarge her photo, a bunch of extra information pops up with it.

Name: Cynthia Balcom aka Patchwork Killer
> **Age: 55**
> **DOB: November 5, 1970**
> **Number of Victims: 45**
> **Date of Incarceration: November 13, 2002**
> **Spouse: Adam Balcom**
> **Dependents: 0**

I zoom in to make sure I'm reading the information right, my heart racing. Her file says she has no children, but Aster and Zephira are living proof she has two. *Who covered up the truth and why can't anyone know?* Curiosity getting the better of me, I click on newspaper articles from the day she was arrested, scanning all of the pictures taken, but all traces of Aster have been erased. Unease settles low in my gut, the little voice in the back of my mind screaming at me; there is more to this.

"Serena!" a singsong voice calls out, one I recognize instantly. My head shoots up, eyes widening as hope reignites within me, making me forget all about Cynthia. I click out of everything, close the laptop and answer Zephira.

"In the attic," I call out through the stairs I left open, trying not to sound too excited that she heard my plea as I wrap my hand around my knife in case she tries anything. She may be a flirt, but I can't trust her to not kill me.

The floors squeak as she slowly walks up the stairs, her bright blonde hair coming into my view before the rest of her does. She's wearing a long sleeve, skin tight black shirt and black jeans with black boots. *Is black the only color she wears?*

"You sure my brother was taken and this isn't some type of training test for you?" she asks, walking towards me.

Hiding the knife behind my back, I stand to be eye level with her, getting myself in the right position to take her down. "Didn't you hear me call out to you?"

She shrugs. "Yeah, I heard when you said he was taken and you begged for my help, I turned off the feed and headed here." *I knew she was watching.* "I'm not going to hurt you Serena, so you can put that little knife you have there away."

Eying her suspiciously, I slip the knife into my boot and sit back down at my laptop, irritation thickening my voice. "He was taken. This isn't a test. He wouldn't leave me." I whisper the last part, biting the inside of my cheek.

She plops down next to me, taking my laptop and typing as she glances at me hungrily. "No, you're right. My brother has literally killed for you. No way he'd change his mind. *Ever.*" Her nails click against the keyboard harder, her frustration with her brother having stolen my heart obvious. "Mom knows that, too. It's why she wants you dead."

I stare open mouthed as she continues digging. She knows more than she has let on; *maybe I can see why she's being her mother's puppet.* I need to gain her trust first. I need to see if there is any crack in the mother-daughter relationship she has with Cynthia and break it apart without being too obvious. I glance at her face, her tongue is sticking out slightly in concentration with her brows dipped. She's younger than me, but she is smart, smarter than me so I don't know how impressionable she is. This could take some time, time I don't have. I'll try to create a bond later, right now I don't want to interrupt her, but I also can't sit still.

While Zephira tracks down who took Aster, I start going through the drawers of the dresser that holds the tattoo supplies to feel like I'm doing something, even if it isn't important. Coming across a black book, I flip through it, finding page after page of sketches. Some are the tattoos he has, while others are random things. Images of animals, scenery, some gothic drawings as well as some abstract images that make you stop and think about what they mean. What secret is hidden inside the art?

A tear slips free when I get to a page with a lamb holding a blue rose in its mouth. The next page is a ticket from Graves with the knife he used to fuck me in the background. I flip through a couple more until I get to the last page. *Serena's first tattoo? This isn't the one he tattooed on me;* it's something more beautiful than I could have ever come up with.

"He thought of tattooing me before I brought it up..." I whisper, gently touching the anatomical heart, a knife stabbed through it and blue roses and black lotuses bursting from the veins, scared if I rub too hard it will disappear. *Even when he had this prepared, he still tattooed my art on me.* When we find him, and we will, I promise I'm going to have him tattoo this on my arm as a reminder of my hope that everything will work out.

I close the book, putting it back where I found it and leave the attic to let Zephira do her work. Hoping she is too absorbed in her work to notice my disappearance. Who am I kidding, she's probably watching me walk to the stairs.

"I'm going to lock you up here until I get back."

She looks up from the laptop, shakes her head and returns to it. "I won't leave or do anything while you're gone." Her tone changes to one of sarcasm, "but if I have to pee, don't be surprised when I treat this room like my bathroom."

I gape at her, my head dipping slightly. "Zephira-"

She holds her hand up to silence me. "Chill, Serena, I'm joking. Go do your detective work and tell me what you find. I'll be good."

Cautiously, I walk down the stairs and lock her in, hoping she doesn't violate our space with her urine.

With a new determination firing up inside me, I leave the house to go back to the scene of the crime to look for any clues I may have missed.

I will find you, Aster.

THE BLACK LOTUS
CRIME SCENE - DO NOT CROSS

SPECIAL EDITION   Daily   ...RDELLA
10 APRIL 2025
A DARK ROMANCE
VOL. 10, NO. 5
THE BLACK LOTUS

EXCLUSIVE
EXCLUSIVE
EXCLUSIVE

In these quiet moments, you reflect on your
thoughts and emotions, gaining clarity on your
true desires and values. Embracing solitude helps
you recharge, enhances mental clarity, and
fosters emotional well-being. This introspection
nurtures personal growth and cultivates a more
balanced and fulfilling life.

SOLITUDE

CRIME SCENE - DO NOT CROSS · CRIME SCENE

BLACK LOTUS

EXCLUSIVE

ASTER

SOLITUDE * SOLITUDE

SOLITUDE * SOLITUDE

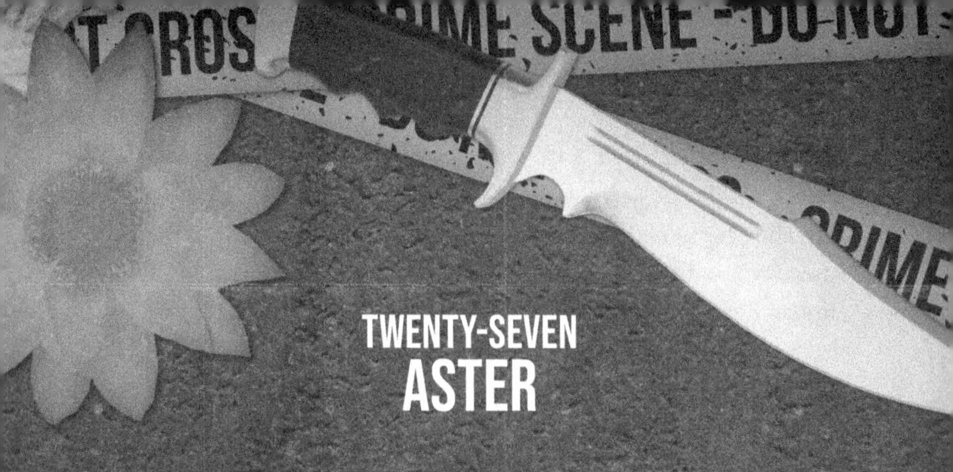

TWENTY-SEVEN
ASTER

This is fucking bullshit. Rage simmers beneath my skin, my flesh feeling tighter than my bindings. *How could I let anyone take me? How could I let my guard down?* I was so worried about keeping Serena safe, about being on alert for her, that I never thought anyone would dare to come for me. *Who is stupid enough to incur my mother's wrath and face my blade?* Not that I have my blade to use, but I'll improvise. I'm nothing if not creative with my kills.

My legs are numb from sitting in this chair for so long, rope bites against my skin with every little movement I make. I stretch my neck side to side, forcing my muscles to relax, for my body to remain calm. Focused. Ready. The room is so dark it's hard to make out anything, and the person who has taken me has yet to reveal themselves. *If they're not showing their cards, I'm not playing mine.*

Even with no one in the room, the hairs on the back of my neck raise, alerting me someone is watching. Waiting. Calculating my moves, planning for the right moment to strike. Calming my breathing, I focus on everything I can see and hear around me, but the room remains silent, my shallow breathing the only sound. *Now I know how my victims felt.* It's unnerving, but this killer picked the wrong one to catch.

They took me to get to Serena. To try and lure her out to save me. My jaw ticks. I know how Serena is; she will most definitely find where I am and try to save the day. *I have to get out of here before she finds me.* I can't let anything happen to her.

My eyes spring open when I hear footsteps approaching, the steps sounding as if they are coming from a woman, given how quiet they are. My back straightens at the opportunity to kill a woman again. A woman who deserves it.

I look up and see light after light turn on as the figure strides closer and closer. Squinting, I'm unable to make out who the person is until the tip of a katana touches my chest. I tip my head towards the blade as my caged beast rattles the bars begging to be set free. "If you don't move your weapon from my chest." My eyes collide with shrouded ones filled with hatred. "You'll find it embedded in yours." She doesn't respond to my threat, just assesses me instead.

Breaking her stare, I study my captor, looking for any hint of who was ballsy enough to kidnap me. She has long, straight, black hair, dark brown eyes, and a tiny build, but if she got me here without any help, she has some muscle hiding beneath her kimono. Seeing her weapon and the way she dresses, I know exactly who this woman is. I grit my teeth, irritation bubbling to the surface, begging to be snuffed out by the rage wanting to consume me.

"Hello, Aster."

"Dishonored Bushi."

A wicked smile curves her lips. "Ah, you've heard of me. That's good." She lifts her sword, forcing me to lift my chin. "But I prefer my victims to call me by my true name since it is the last one they'll ever learn."

I scoff. "If you think you will get me to kill myself, you're wrong."

She tsks and shakes her head slowly. "Oh. No, *you* are the one who is wrong. You won't die in the way my other victims have. I have special plans for you."

I hiss as her blade slices my chest, blood seeping into the dark fabric. My arms strain against my bindings, my heart racing as pain courses through me. Based on all the information I've gathered, which isn't much, all her victims are only marked once with a deep and jagged cut by the blade she has them end their lives with. She has never once cut them like she's cutting me now. Tugging against my restraints, a new sense of urgency to get out courses through me, but I can't show her any semblance of fear. She can't see me shaken, which is what I assume she wants. *Relax Aster.*

"Watching you bleed is the satisfaction I've been craving for a long time," she muses.

Has she been waiting all this time for a victim she could bleed? One she could hurt? Am I just a guinea pig for what she has planned for Serena?

A deranged laugh escapes me. "If you think hurting me will help you get Serena, it won't. Taking me will only end in your death, but I'll let you choose from my hands or hers."

Now she's the one laughing as she sheaths her sword. "You think I took you to get to her?" Her finger taps her lower lip as she mumbles, "Though, I can see why you would think that." She braces both her hands on the side of my chair, whispering words that send chills up my arms. "I don't care about your mother's bounty on your little girlfriend. You were the one I've always wanted."

My eyebrows shoot into my hairline, but I quickly school my features when she stands back up. *Finally something I can work with.* If this little kidnapping is like the premise from Mercy, then I can just flirt my way to freedom. If she wants to be a little lamb, then let the games begin.

In society's eyes, she is beautiful with her striking eyes, thin face and body, a sharp jawline and high cheekbones. I press my skin harder against my chair, trying to create more distance between us. *She will never have me in the way she's been waiting for, but I can play the part.*

My gaze travels across her body looking for any kind of weakness. It was easier with Kelsey since she was in love with me and I knew how to get her to let her guard down, but I don't know anything about this woman. I don't know what would make her fall to her knees or how to get her swooning, but the more we talk, the quicker I can figure her out.

"What is your nam-" I stop when I see her nose scrunch in disgust, her lips curled and baring her teeth. *Guess she isn't in love with me.* Relief floods me like a dam breaking as my shoulders relax. *New plan, release the beast and find a way out of here.*

Despite looking absolutely repulsed, she answers my unfinished question. "Kara." She steps away, swinging the sword so fast it isn't until I feel the warm blood fall down my face that I realize she sliced my eye. I pinch it closed, grateful I can open and close it as the sting from the cut begins to register. *I can still see.*

"Don't look at me like that again. I don't want you in the way you're thinking. The only thing I want is your life." Stopping in the door she came from, she looks over her shoulder. "I want you to hurt before I end your life. For now you can bleed."

The door shuts before I can reply, leaving me in darkness strapped to a chair with pain setting my nerves on fire. *At this rate, if I don't find a way out I'll either die from blood loss or her wrath.*

CRIME SCENE - DO NOT CROSS
THE BLACK LOTUS
A DARK ROMANCE
SPECIAL EDITION
Daily
ARDELLA
10 APRIL 2025
VOL. 10, NO. 5
THE BLACK LOTUS
EXCLUSIVE
EXCLUSIVE
EXCLUSIVE
SOLITUDE

THE BLACK LOTUS

SERENA

CROSS

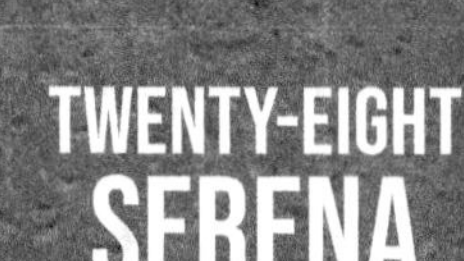

It's been three days since Aster was taken. Zephira has been trying her best to find him, but no matter what she does, she comes up empty. Everytime I ask her for updates and she shakes her head with a sympathetic smile I deflate a little more. *The person who took him definitely knows how to cover their tracks.* When I went back to the studio, I found fucking nothing. Even the scuff marks seemed to have disappeared like there was no crime committed.

Zephira and I have been growing closer, *as close as someone who is helping her mother kill me can get to a person.* I'm staying cautious with everything she does, eyeing her skeptically when she does it. She has been rather motherly, making sure I eat, stay hydrated, and reassuring me Aster will make it out of this.

She's trying to comfort me during this time of duress and honestly, it's a little unnerving. Crazy, flirty Zephira who loves to tease and taunt is the girl I'm used to and have gotten comfortable with. But this version of her, this personality switch up will take some time to get used to.

I hope this isn't some kind of trick to get me to lower my guard for someone else to strike so she could have a front row seat to my execution. That thought alone has me keeping her at an arm's length.

I walk into the room and Zephira scrunches her nose. "You need a shower," she grumbles, eyes glued to her laptop.

Lifting my arm, I sniff my armpit and flinch. "Maybe you're right." I can't remember the last time I bathed myself. I haven't even thought of stepping under a hot stream of water, for fear of spiraling in the one place I can be alone. Being Zephira's helper has been the only thing keeping me grounded, but maybe a quick wash wouldn't hurt.

She rolls her eyes. "I ordered us some food, so make it quick. And..." she glances at me before focusing on her screen. "I have some news you're not going to like."

My heart drops, my hopes of finding him dimming, her words making me queasy. I nod once and make my way to the bathroom.

After my shower, I find Zephira placing pineapple pizza on paper plates, the box left open on the couch. A sad laugh bubbles up as she looks up with a tilted head.

"What's so funny? And are you crying?" She sits down and pats the spot next to her.

"Nothing; it's just... that's our favorite pizza, and the last time we had it, well..." My cheeks heat, my breaths shallow as I swear I can feel Aster thrusting deep inside me.

She puts her hand up, not wanting to hear anymore. "I don't want to hear about my brother's sex life, no offense." She hands me a plate with two slices, her eyes unfocused. "It's my favorite, too." She forces a smile, whispering around a mouthful of food so quietly I barely made out the words. "I wonder what else I have in common with my brother."

Even though Cynthia has her claws embedded deep in Zephira, I can tell she wants to be close to her brother. I push back the urge to place my hand on top of hers as I busy my hands, slowly chewing my pizza. There is no way to form the relationship she wants when she is helping their mom keep tabs on me. Sure, she may not be *actually* attempting to kill me, but that's beside the point.

"So… how did you and my brother meet?"

I look up at her, eyebrows raised. *Is she trying to make small talk?*

I swallow my bite before answering. "We met at a bar called Boozy Books. But you know that already, don't you? Haven't you been watching us this whole time?"

"Nope," she answers, popping the p. "Only after I bought the painting from you at the market."

That's surprising. I thought she'd been keeping tabs on him and feeding Cynthia information since she'd made contact with her. *If she isn't the one who is the informer, I wonder who is?*

Zephira's blonde hair falls around her shoulders as she sits back on the couch, her back pressed up against the cushion to eat the rest of her food. "Are you going to tell me, or will I have to force it out of you?"

"Surprised you haven't already." I tease, a small smile lifting my lips. "He approached me at the bar, we flirted, then exchanged numbers, and I didn't hear from him for two weeks."

"It took him two weeks to text you?"

I laugh. "No, it took him two weeks to stalk me on a date and crush the guy's hand for trying to kiss me."

She covers her stomach, laughing as she says, "He killed him after I bet."

"Actually, yeah; he did." That makes her laugh harder, and I find myself joining in. Surprised by how easily we can fall into comfortable and 'normal' conversations, I relax and enjoy the moment, hopeful there will be more.

"My brother must really love you to kill a guy for you."

I place the empty plate down beside me. "I really love him too. Plus, I killed that guy's brother, so it evened out."

She stares at me wide eyed, her mouth dropping open. "*You* killed him? I'm impressed you have a dark side, too."

"If only you knew how dark I can be."

She cocks an eyebrow. "Why don't you tell me?"

I bite my lip. *Can I trust her with the truth of my beast?* Will she keep my secrets, or will she run straight to her mother and tell her everything? Maybe if she tells Cynthia that might get her to cancel the hit and accept me. Or it could just make her more mad and come for me herself.

"He wasn't my first victim," I whisper, my heart in my throat.

She whirls toward me, grabbing my hands, excitement shining in her eyes. "You've killed before? You *have* to tell me your serial killer journey!"

I nibble my bottom lip before telling her everything from my first kill to Sharon.

"I would have killed Jessica in high school, made her fear me the way she made you cower from her." She places her hands behind her head as she lets her head fall back to look at the ceiling. "You had the patience of a saint."

I nod my head, letting that be a good enough answer. *I wish I knew Zephira back then; I feel like we would have been amazing friends.* She probably would have helped me kill Jessica. *If I'd had a friend like her, maybe I wouldn't have been as broken as I was.*

I shake that thought away. The person I am today, the reason Aster fell in love with me, is because of my past. As lonely as I was back then, I don't regret a single moment. Without the hell I went through I wouldn't be the killer I am.

We fall into a comfortable silence, both of us reminiscing about our kills, before I remember what distracted me into forgetting. "Zephira…What's going to upset me?"

She scratches the back of her head, her hesitancy making me nervous as I stare at her, waiting for her to answer. "I… can't find Aster."

My breath catches in my throat, my world crashing around on me. My heart is beating out of my chest as the oxygen is stolen from me. *If Zephira can't find him, who can?* It's already been three days. I don't think either of us can go much longer without getting him home.

"Don't panic, but… I know how we can find out who took him."

I look at her with a blank stare. "How?" I whisper, my lip trembling.

"This is the part you're really not going to like…" She hesitates, twisting a strand of hair around her finger. "My mom."

The world spins as her words crash through me like a wrecking ball. My body sways as I blink several times to come to terms with the only solution. *She's right.* I don't like it, but if it means finding Aster then I will swallow my pride and let her ask Cynthia.

"Do it." I say, getting up and walking up to our room.

The urge to do something, anything, overwhelms me as I pace the room, chewing on my fingernails and biting them off. I find myself walking to our dresser, pulling out all the newspaper clippings of Aster's kills.

Before I can stop myself, I begin taping them to walls until every inch is completely covered. With my chest rising and falling, I glare at the worn paper. *It needs more.*

I rummage under the bed until I find the supplies I haven't touched in so long; my paints. Some semblance of familiarity relaxes my body as I pull them out. "I've missed you," I whisper, gliding my fingers over the bottles as I pick up a paintbrush, a sad smile crossing my features..

Newspapers aren't the best kind of canvas to paint over, but I find myself lost in the movement and dance of it all. Creating nothing and everything all at once, I let all my feelings and emotions come to life on the wall.

Chest rising and falling, the paint dries slowly as I stare at it, still not satisfied with the result. *It's missing something.* Tapping the end of the paintbrush against my lips, my mind whirls as I contemplate what to add.

I drop the brush and fall to my knees scrambling for a pencil. *I know exactly what's missing.* Standing back up. I begin doodling all the weapons the killers have used against us.

A light knock taps against the door, and Zephira pops her head in. "I know who has Aster," she says. I whip my head in her direction, my eyes lighting up as my hope for finding him reignites.

CRIME SCENE - DO NOT CROSS
CRIME SCENE - DO NO
THE BLACK LOTUS
SPECIAL EDITION
Daily
...RDELLA
A DARK ROMANCE
VOL. 10, NO. 5
10 APRIL 2025
THE BLACK LOTUS
EXCLUSIVE
EXCLUSIVE
EXCLUSIVE
S
SOLITUDE
CRIME SCENE - DO
CRIME SCENE - DO NOT CR
SOLITUDE

CRIME SCENE - DO NOT CROSS   CRIME SCEN

BLACK LOTUS

EXCLUSIVE
EXCLUSIVE
EXCLUSIVE

ASTER

SOLITUDE   *   SOLITUDE

SOLITUDE   *   SOLITUDE

CROSS

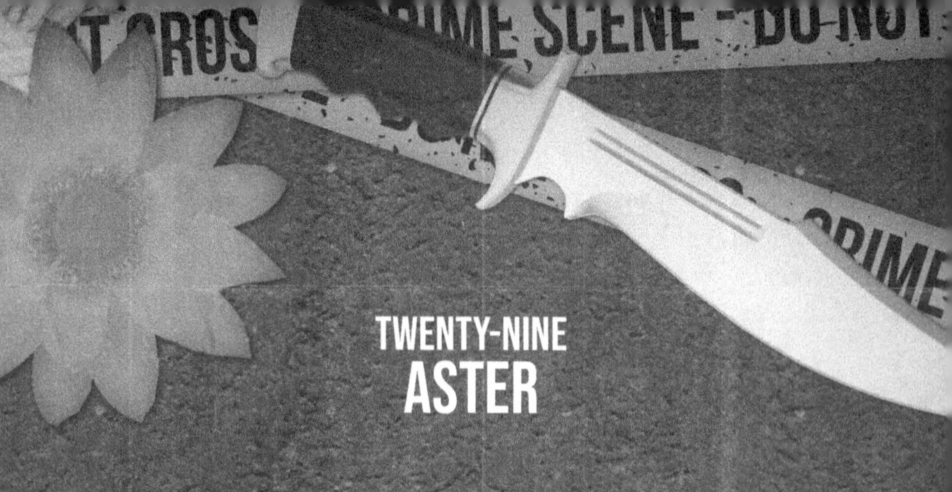

TWENTY-NINE
ASTER

It's been days since I was taken, but I can't tell how many. The room stays dark, and Kara has kept me starved, dehydrated, and in pain. My lips are chapped. My body is weak. Dry blood coats my skin, and I'm finding it hard to stay awake.

This kind of torture weakens not only the body, but the mind as well. *This must be how she gets into her victim's heads*, getting them to lower their guard and kill themselves. The only change is the physical torture, she likes to come in once a day and cover me in more scars. Her strikes are ones of someone who has been scorned and hurts me like I've wronged her somehow, but I've never met her. Her blade slices like each one is filled with her revenge. If I die not knowing why she's torturing me, I'll haunt her for the answers I desperately need to know. The amount of blood my body has lost isn't enough to kill me, but it is enough to weaken me. The only thing she has done which I find odd, was clean the cut on my eye and bandaged it for a day, then came and took it away the next. The only explanation I can think of is that she doesn't want me to die from an infection. At least, that would be *my* reasoning.

My lambs should be grateful I never gave them this kind of torture.

Their suffering, their fear is over quickly and it's more psychological torture than anything. *I'm generous that way.* Laughter bubbles within me, but I swallow it down. I can't reveal my hand yet. *When I get out of this, I'm going to treat Kara like one of my lambs.* I miss the kill, the paint, the displaying. I miss being the Morbid Monet.

I shake the thought away when Serena's smiling face comes into my mind. Monet is dead. Fatal Floral Killers live. *Maybe Serena could watch me like I watch her.* She was a fan before she was mine. *Maybe we could turn it into our special brand of foreplay.* My cock twitches thinking of the last time our bodies blended in a puddle of blood.

The door creaks open, my eyes squinting against the only light this dreadful room receives as Kara makes her way in. She's wearing a new kimono and has her katana in her hand. *Another day of pain with no answers seems to await me.* I don't even look at her as she comes in, I just slump over with my head down to await today's torture. My body has gotten used to the feel of the steel slicing against my skin. I feel numb to it, the pain doesn't even register anymore.

Day in and day out, she slices my skin with her blade, dragging it through my flesh with surgeon-like precision. She pulls up a chair and places it in front of me, sitting down with her legs spread around the back of the chair.

"I've decided to tell you my story today."

My head lifts, a sense of anticipation rushing through me as I strain to sit up straighter, my muscles screaming at me from the small movement. Once I find out why she wants me, I can use her truth against her, find her weakness and exploit it.

"Last time we talked, I told you that you were always my target." She places her hands over the back of the chair, leaning her chin on them. "You can blame your parents for your current situation."

I scoff, rolling my eyes. "I'll add it to the list of reasons why they're dead to me."

"You and I both know they aren't dead to you or else you would have found a way to truly end them."

Her words make me laugh. *Is this her way of getting in my head?* I roll my eyes, move my neck side to side to show how unbothered I am by her. If she thinks my parents are my weakness, then she clearly didn't do her research.

"You laugh, but you know it's true."

I stretch my neck towards her. "They're locked behind bars. I couldn't get in to visit them when I was eighteen, no way I'm breaking in to kill them now." I lick my chapped lips.

"After I kill you, I'll get them. Your entire bloodline will be wiped out in an instant."

She thinks she's going to break into two high security prisons, kill my parents, and get away with it? I don't bother hiding my disbelief. She has a death wish. Even my blood lust for my parents isn't that strong.

She pulls her sword from her back where she keeps it and points the tip of her blade at my chest. "You have always been my one true target. Everyone who came before was simply practice for *you*."

"You like to repeat yourself, don't you?" I groan, flexing against my bonds once more. "Are you going to tell me why my parents are the reason I'm your *one true target*, or are you going to keep talking in circles?"

She places the sword on her shoulder, staring into my eyes, trying to assert her dominance. If she thinks I'm going to look away from this stupid staring contest, she's wrong. *I'm not one to lose.* She looks away, gritting her teeth and I smirk. *I won.*

She gets up, sheathing her blade and starts walking around the room in front of me. "I may not look it, but I am twenty years older than you. Before you were born, or before you were even thought of, *I* was going to be your parents' successor." She looks up at the ceiling, her eyes glowing at the memory. "I wanted to be a serial killer, to be feared like them. But I didn't know the first thing about death. I had the urge to kill, but I never followed through."

My gaze follows her strides, risking glances around my cage, looking for any means of escape. *She's been so careful until now.* Every time she's come in before, was to inflict pain, the lights only on long enough for me to bleed.

"I didn't know the true identity of the Patchwork Killers, but I knew how they worked and how they scouted their victims. So I did what not even the police or FBI could. I stalked prime loca-tions, ones where I knew they would strike, and waited. Several couples were at every venue, but only one stood out to me." She places her arms behind her back reliving the memory.

How could she find out who my parents were when not even the best profilers in the country could? If she can get helpless victims to kill themselves, finding my parents shouldn't surprise me.

"I stalked them. For months and, well, they caught on." She turns towards me, her eyes shining from talking about her role models. "Turns out they knew I was watching the very first day."

Listening to her story drag on, having to listen to her voice longer than I've already had to is making my hands twitch with the need to be wrapped around her throat. I'm not surprised my parents knew she was watching. They outsmarted the Feds for years, how they got caught still is a mystery to me.

"When they approached me, I was a ball of nerves and excite-ment. I couldn't believe my idols were talking to me. Was I going to be their next victim? I didn't know, but I wanted to find out, so when they asked me to come home with them, I did."

Is she fucking stupid? Why would she want to be their victim? Her becoming one was a huge possibility, especially since they had absolutely no preference in their kills. There was no true profile for anyone to track to find out who was next. *That's why they were so successful. That's why they should've never been caught.*

"They took me back to the house, the one you currently live at with your girlfriend." My jaw tenses when she talks about

Serena, but she's been watching and waiting for so long I'm not surprised she knows we live together. "You really should upgrade, you know." She scoffs, watching my muscles flex beneath my skin. "We sat in the living room and the first thing your mother said to me was," she changes her voice to sound more like my mom, although Kara isn't very good at it, "We know you know who we are. So either you're with the police, or you're stupid."

She sits back down in front of me, a dreamy, faraway look on her face. "I wanted to be like them, and they told me they would think about it and be in touch." Her eyes darken, her lips pursing as her hands shake.

The chair falls in front of me as she abruptly stands causing me to flinch from her sudden outburst. "After months of not hearing anything, I went back to their house only to be turned away because of *you*." She points at me accusingly and spits. "Your mother was pregnant with you! They said you were going to be their prodigy and shut the door in my face!"

Her chest rises and falls as she gasps for breath. She unsheaths her sword so fast, I blinked and missed the movement. She swipes the air closer and closer to my face. *She's already cut my eye; I can't let her cut any other part.* It's Serena's favorite thing about me, minus my dick. I can't show fear. I can't look away.

She slices the blade swiftly and quickly, stepping back just as suddenly as she attacked. I feel my shirt fall away in pieces, leaving me bare, but no blood flows down. My eyes widen at the sight, my mouth parted slightly at her skill. How did she shred my shirt without cutting me? *She is scarily precise.* I swallow down the panic threatening to claw its way up.

Her voice shatters my rising panic. "I bided my time. I watched. Waited. I learned when you would have your first kill. I couldn't let that happen, so *I* was the one to turn your parents into the Feds, ensuring *you* never got your first kill."

I clench my bound hands into fists, my teeth grinding as the truth sinks in. *She* is the reason I lost my parents. *She* is the reason my first kill was taken from me. She is the reason I lost everything. All because my parents wouldn't train her to become like them. I glare at her, my teeth grinding so hard I feel as though they will crack from the pressure as anger crashes through me like a wave, building the longer I stare at her.

She will die. I will show her fear like no other, I will drag her own blade through her flesh, but first I need to get out of here.

She turns around, a satisfied smile playing on her lips, the lights fading as she walks away without marking my skin, until I'm left in the dark. Left to plan my escape. Left to plan my revenge.

CRIME SCENE - DO NOT CROSS
CRIME SCENE - DO NOT
THE BLACK LOTUS
SPECIAL EDITION
Daily O...
A DARK ROMANCE
VOL. 10, NO. 5
10 APRIL 2025
THE BLACK LOTUS
EXCLUSIVE
EXCLUSIVE
EXCLUSIVE
CRIME SCENE - DO
DO NOT CR...
SOLITUDE
SOLITUDE

CRIME SCENE - DO NO
THE BLACK LOTUS
EXCLUSIVE
SERENA
CROSS
CRIME

THIRTY
SERENA

Cynthia was oh so gracious to tell us who was behind Aster's kidnapping, but not where or how to find him. It seems that even the great Patchwork Killers can't track down the one person whose name gives me chills. *The Dishonored Bushi.* When Aster gave his lesson about her, I remember chills running down my spine and thinking that she is the one I would be terrified to go up against. Knowing she has Aster makes my stomach churn.

I toss back and forth, pulling the covers up to my nose to comfort myself in Aster's smell. Tears prick at the corners of my eyes, my hope dwindling on finding him and bringing him home. I feel utterly worthless. If the roles were reversed, Aster would be tearing down every door to find me.

I throw back the covers to go find Zephira. *I can't give up.* Cynthia told Zephira The Dishonored Bushi's real name is Kara and what she looked like twenty years ago, but no last name. Even with that little information, Zephira is determined to find her big brother.

Sticking my head into the guest room I find it empty. *Where is Zephira?* She is nowhere to be seen, not even in the connected bathroom. With her living here, it feels like we are roommates

who are getting used to one another's presence. I can tell she wants to get to know me better, with her subtle glances and awkward silence, but she is keeping a wall up and not getting too close. I know she's hiding something her mother said to her on the phone. It was a longer call than I was expecting and Cynthia calls everyday. Zephira claims it's to check the progress on finding Aster, but she locks herself in the room away from my ear shot, so I don't believe her. *Do the guards not check her cell?* Maybe I should call and leave an anonymous tip that she has a phone.

As sure as Cynthia is in my demise, I'm hopeful that I can defeat anyone she throws my way. With Aster. My heart falls at the thought of not being partners in crime with my fox. Placing my hand on the wall to keep from falling, I shove away the dark thoughts, my desperation in finding him pushing forward.

I walk slowly downstairs, taking a breath on each step so as to not lose my balance.

I find Zephira sitting at the island in the kitchen, hard at work on her laptop, half a blueberry bagel hanging from her mouth while the other half sits forgotten on a small plate next to her.

"Coffee?" I ask, walking to the cupboard and taking out all the stuff needed to make mine, including my Chucky and Tiffany glass.

"Nah, I'm good," she mumbles around a mouthful.

Grabbing a stool next to her, I look at her computer. I bite my cheek, squinting at the screen. Several windows are open and running, data flashing by faster than I can understand. "What is all this?"

She looks at me like she's deciding if she should tell me or not. It should annoy me that she still hasn't let her walls fall, but she's stuck in between a rock and a hard place with obeying Cynthia and wanting to get closer to me. I can't blame her for the hesitation.

Swallowing her last bite she answers, pointing to each one,

"This one is looking for any Kara's in Massachusetts. This one is pinpointing women with the features my mom gave me. This one analyzes The Dishonored Bushi, looking at where she strikes and what her victim profile is. This one is going over every single second of camera footage from the attacks and where the bodies were found. This last one puts all the information the others are searching for into finding a name."

I stare slack jawed at the screen, utterly impressed with the woman in front of me. She may be young, but she is a genius when it comes to hacking. *This is the kind of technology seen in movies that you think can't possibly be real, but it is.* Zephira is living proof of it. *I wonder if this is how she chooses her victims.* Seeing her sitting next to me, eating a damn bagel and tapping away at her computer, makes me forget she's Salem's Man-Eater.

"We will find him, Serena," she promises, eyes focused on her screen as concentration dips her eyebrows.

"You said that already and we still have nothing."

Her jaw ticks. "We have more than what we started with. Do you doubt my skills?"

I give her a sheepish smile. "After seeing you in action, I don't doubt your skills. I actually think anyone who makes your list should be terrified."

A wolfish grin spreads across her face. "You're right about that."

"I'm glad I'm not on your list," I mumble, rubbing my arms and trying to erase the goosebumps running along them.

"Who says you're not?" she teases, leaning in to inhale my scent like a predator.

"Am I?" I turn towards her, our faces inches away. Her eyes glance at my lips and I move my head away from hers. *She's not Aster.* She giggles, sitting and turning back to her laptop.

"I only hunt men."

I chew on the inside of my cheek, debating on asking the question I've been dying to know since meeting her.

"You're going to bleed if you keep gnawing at your mouth

like that." She pushes her laptop away, turning toward me. "Let me guess, you want to know why I only hunt men."

"No, but yes. That wasn't my question, but now I am curious."

"No?" she cocks an eyebrow. "What do you want to know then?"

"Well, now I want to know why you only go after men. But my first question is not that."

She says nothing as she places her plate into the sink.

I tilt my head. Is she going to answer my questions or are her walls going to stand strong? Will she stop us from getting closer or will she let me in? The only time she seems to answer anything is when Aster is around. My lips thin. *I think she flirts and reveals her truths to get under his skin.*

She stands and walks to the couch, tapping the spot beside her. *Play it cool, Serena; if you get too excited, it could spook her.* I suck in a sharp breath, getting up to sit next to her on the couch.

"What do you want to know?" she asks, letting the silence build between us.

"Will you answer both questions if I ask?"

She shrugs, sitting back to get comfortable. "Depends on what you want to know."

"Are you only into girls or men too, and why only hunt men?" I blurt out before I lose the courage.

"That's it? Seriously?" she scoffs, sucking her teeth. "That was the question that made you a nervous ball of energy?"

Was I really putting off that much nervous energy? Shifting uncomfortably, I jam my hands under my thighs to hide their shaking. *I thought I was holding myself together better.* My nerves are from wondering if we will find Aster in time, but she doesn't like when I doubt her. She covers it up with jokes and heavy flirting, but I can tell she's just as worried.

I nod as she lets me sit in the deafening silence. She swallows, blowing a raspberry and looking up at the ceiling "I like both, but I prefer girls. There has only been one boy and one girl who I have ever been interested in, but *no one* is privy to that information." She levels me with a glare that says 'don't ask, because I'm not telling'. So, I don't. I motion, zipping my lips closed and pretend to hand her the key as she takes it gratefully, tucking it in her bra and patting it, which makes me chuckle.

She takes a deep breath. "As for the other question…" She nibbles on her bottom lip, her hands balled into fists. "I grew up similar to Aster, except I was placed in a foster care where a bad man did bad things to me. He's dead now, but him and his sons are the reason why I bathe in men's blood."

"What do you mean you bathe in their blood?" I ask, with wide eyes as my mouth hangs open, my body frozen by this new information. *The more I learn about her, the more amazed I am.* I shake my head and blink a couple of times, excited to learn more about not only Zephira, but the Man-Eater.

"After I make my newest victim eat my previous one, I drain them of all their blood and bathe in it. Makes me feel powerful. Godlike. No longer the helpless girl I once was. I reclaim a little of what I lost with each kill." She thrusts her arms in front of me. "Plus, look at my skin; I'm *always* glowing like the goddess I was born to be."

My face falls, wanting to know more but knowing I shouldn't press. I need to let her open up to me when she is ready. *Baby steps.* Getting to learn about her rituals is making me excited, but what happened to her, the horror that made her who she is makes my heart ache. I place my hand on my heart as the two emotions battle inside me. As much as I want to learn more about her rituals and past, I need to keep my mouth shut.

She holds her hand up, her face hardening. "Don't. Don't give me that face or feel sorry for me. My past made me who I am today. And I like being the bloodthirsty Man Eater."

"Wait… you drink their blood?" I ask, trying not to make a what-the-fuck face.

"Sometimes," she shrugs, "but I'm not fond of the taste of iron."

"Then why do it?"

"Why do anything? Because I can and I want to; simple as that."

Something tells me it isn't as simple as that, but we all have our secrets, and I'll let Zephira keep hers. *For now.*

CRIME SCENE - DO NOT CROSS
CRIME SCENE - DO NO
THE BLACK LOTUS
SPECIAL EDITION
Daily
ARDELLA
10 APRIL 2025
A DARK ROMANCE
VOL. 10, NO. 5
THE BLACK LOTUS
EXCLUSIVE
EXCLUSIVE
EXCLUSIVE
CRIME SCENE - DO
DO NOT CROSS
SOLITUDE
SOLITUDE

CRIME SCENE - DO NOT CROSS - CRIME SCENE

BLACK LOTUS

EXCLUSIVE
EXCLUSIVE
EXCLUSIVE

ASTER

SOLITUDE * SOLITUDE

SOLITUDE * SOLITUDE

CROSS

CRIME SCENE - DO NOT CROSS

<h1 style="text-align:center">THIRTY-ONE
ASTER</h1>

I need to figure out a way out of here. There is nothing sharp for me to rub my restraints on. Nothing I can grab to cut them. Even the stupid chair is bolted to the ground. *If I don't get out soon, I will die. I'll never get to see Serena again.* I pull against my restraints as a new sense of urgency hits me from fear of never getting to hear her laugh again. Never getting to feel her touch. Never getting to see her beautiful face. *My last resort. The only thing I can do.*

Before I can put my plan into action, the familiar creak of the door breaks the silence, the lights flickering on as Kara walks into the room. My fingers twitch against my restraints as irritation thrums through me. *Of course she comes in right when I was about to escape.*

Instead of taking a seat, she stands in yet another kimono with two katanas strapped to her back. *She always has one, why would she bring two?* My chest tightens, my breath catching in my lungs. *Is she planning on decapitating me?* That would be a way to go out, but she doesn't seem like she would make my death quick.

"I did some research on your little girlfriend." My body locks at her words. "I've decided that after I'm finished with you. I'm going to pay her a little visit and send her to hell right after you. Can't have the lovers being separated."

I clench my jaw, my teeth nearly cracking from the pressure. "If you so much as touch a single hair on her head, I'll kill you."

She tilts her head with a crazed look in her eyes. "How will you do that when you're dead?"

If she would just leave, I can get one hand out and free myself. Distracting her won't be enough.

"Has she always been a killer like you? Actually, don't answer that." *Does she not want to know?* My eyebrows scrunch together, her indecisiveness confusing me. "Let me take a wild guess; she has and, based on the locked files I found, she had a hand in her friend's disappearance. Right?"

I stay silent, not giving anything away. She's going to think what she wants regardless of what I tell her. From how she's watching me, I fear she could spot a lie a mile away.

"She killed her, didn't she?" She peers at me, her eyes flashing. "I knew it. You know the night you met her, the night you planned to make her your next victim? I watched her, too. She was talking to herself, but as I got closer, I realized she was talking to someone who wasn't there."

A dry cough leaves me as an invisible noose chokes me. *How the fuck does she know so much?* The way she watches and observes and figures things out is unnerving. I didn't even realize Serena was crazy when we first met. I'd assumed her mumblings were just drunken ramblings. But her crazy is something I admire most about her; it's what made me fall for her.

"Finding out she was not only crazy, but also a killer," she claps her hands together, a manic grin twisting her face, "Wow! You really know how to pick them."

"Shut your fucking mouth," I warn with the threat of a deep menacing sound rumbling from my throat.

"I don't think I will." She bends over, her eyes level with mine. "Do you ever think that if she'd never met you, she'd be none the wiser to her truth? That she never would've been a serial killer? Have you even asked her if she likes killing or did you just assume that she did and then throw her into it?"

My face falls as a twinge in my chest has me aching to cover it. Sure, Serena has killed before, and seeing her in her element when she killed Bradley to protect me was fucking priceless, but she's right, I never asked her if she wanted to. She was thrown into the life of murder because of my mother and her connection to me.. *Does she… does she even* want *to?*

"Ah! I see I've struck a nerve." She walks behind me, her fingers dancing along my shoulders, making me shiver at her touch as she bends to whisper in my ear. "Are you the reason for the bloodlust she now seems to carry?"

"It's my mother's fault. She has to kill or else she would be dead," I grind out as she steps in front of me. I'm not the reason she is being forced to fight for her life. She isn't being given a choice.

Kara places her finger on her lip, tapping it with an exaggerated huff. "Are you sure about that?" she asks, looking at me. "Or would you have made her your partner even without her life on the line? Would you have forced her to become a monster like you?"

I shake my head, not letting her words get to me. If it was anything else, I wouldn't care, but because it's about Serena I don't know what to think. *Would I have forced her to kill alongside me? What if she said no? Would I have let her go or would she have become a lamb?* The thought of hurting Serena forces me to swallow down the vomit threatening to rise. No matter what her answer would have been, no matter what her choice was, I would have stuck by her side.

I know if she was given a choice, I wouldn't get in the way of anything she wanted. If she didn't want to be my partner in crime, it would gut me, but I wouldn't force anything on her. If all she wanted was to paint all day I would buy the biggest gallery to display her art and watch her thrive. But that isn't who Serena is. Serena is *my vixen* and I know without a shadow of a doubt that if she was given a choice, she would choose to be my Fatal Floral Killer.

"She is who she was always meant to be."

"Or did you make her that way?"

"*No*. Her choices are her own. Even if she doesn't want to be a killer, I would respect her decisions."

"And kill her," she states, no question in her voice.

I lock my eyes with hers, straining against the rope as I lean forward. "Never."

"Could you stop killing if she asked or would you do it behind her back, breaking her trust forever?"

Killing is in my bones, it's my very reason for living. The rush of the hunt. The high of the execution. *I could never give that up.* But Serena is my new purpose, and I know she'd never ask me to give up the one thing that makes me, me.

"She would never ask me to," I grind out in irritation.

"Are you sure about that?"

"She fell in love with the monster inside; she wouldn't cage my beast. She relishes my darkness swirling around hers."

Talking about Serena makes me more desperate to get back to her. My legs shake, the need to bounce them being restricted from the bindings. To ask her these questions and see if I really am the only reason she is tangled in my shadows. *I need Kara to go away.* The only way to make her leave is to turn the tables against her. To play the same mind games she's attempting with me. *It's time to let the Morbid Monet out.*

A cruel smile stretches my face as Kara's head twitches back. "No matter how hard you try, no matter what you do, my parents will *never* see you as anything more than an annoyance," I say, causing her lips to purse as her eyes harden. "Even if I wasn't born, they never took you seriously. They never would have trained you. You are nothing. You would just be in their way, and when Mom finds out you're the reason for their capture," I let out a low whistle, "You're going to live up to your name, so be honorable and kill yourself."

She screams, lunging for me as her tiny hands wrap around my throat. I laugh as she chokes me, dots forming around my vision. A frustrated huff fills the air as she gets up and pushes her hair back into place.

"I'll be back." She quickly strides back through the door, slamming it behind her.

Coughing, I stretch my neck, trying to ease the bruises I know are going to appear. I rattled the Bushi. She wasn't expecting her psychological mindfuck to be turned back onto her, but there is one thing she failed to remember. I'm the Morbid Monet, and mind games are my favorite.

CRIME SCENE - DO NOT CROSS   CRIME SCENE

BLACK LOTUS

EXCLUSIVE

ASTER

SOLITUDE   SOLITUDE

SOLITUDE

THIRTY-TWO
ASTER

I wait a couple of minutes before biting the inside of my cheek, closing my eyes and popping my thumb out of place. I shouldn't have waited so long to do this, but I thought Serena would have found me by now, and when Kara started talking about killing her, I knew I was out of time. I needed to act now.

The pain shoots up my arm, my head dizzy even with my eyes closed. The first and only time I had to do this was when Crumbwell forgot me in the basement and I needed to free myself. The taste of copper fills my mouth as I strain against the rope, my eyes watering as I pull my hand free. *Fuck, that hurt.* With my hand limp and painful, I lean down to free my feet and other hand from the rope. *For someone so smart, she is really stupid with how she keeps her victims tied.*

Grabbing some discarded cloth from my shirt, bite down hard and pop the joint back into place, wrapping my hand in the scrap of fabric.

Standing up too quickly, my vision blurs as my body sways. I catch myself on the chair, staring without seeing as the world slowly settles around me. I may be free, but I'm still weak. I slam my fist into the chair, my frustration from how weak I am slipping out of me.

"Took you long enough."

My head snaps up at the sound of Kara's voice. *When did she walk in? How did I not hear the loud creak of the door?*

"What do you mean?" I groan, my knuckles white against the warm wood. I slowly stand, turning to face her.

"You really didn't think I was stupid enough to tie you down with such an easy way of escaping did you?"

"You wanted me to escape." I shake my head, not believing her.

She walks into the room, one of her swords skidding across the floor and stopping at my feet. "I wanted to see how long it would take for you to be desperate enough to try." She draws her sword, staying where she is. "Turns out all I had to do was threaten Serena."

"Don't say her name." I growl, fisting my hands.

A wicked smile flashes in the low light. "Se-re-na," she says slowly, taunting me with every syllable.

She points her sword toward mine, motioning for me to pick it. I keep my gaze on her as I lean down to retrieve my weapon.

"Let's see how well you can fight in your condition."

She lunges, her sword clashing against mine, the sound of metal on metal echoing around us. My arm shakes against her attack, my teeth cracking with the effort I need to hold her back. *For someone so tiny her strength is impressive.*

We go blow for blow, back and forth, sparks flying around us. The sweat on my head and chest drips, my blade loose in my grip as my eyes burn. I want to swipe it away, but that would give her an opening and the look in her eyes tells me this is a fight to the death. I'm worried this is one fight I might lose, but I know if I want to see Serena again I *can't* lose. No matter what.

I position my feet as she jabs and flinch out of the way before her sword can pierce my ribs. Slicing in response, she spins out my way, her kimono swirling as her katana glints in the air around her.

Her sword flashes through the air, grazing my arm, a thin red line appearing. Adrenaline swirls through me, and I swing like my life depends on it. I've never fought with a sword before, but I'm finding I'm a natural when it means life or death.

I land a shot on her leg, the slice doing nothing to the momentum she has. I stagger as I blink, my hazy vision giving her an opening to slice my arm again. I don't have time to react, so I shake my head and press forward. She brings her blade up and I block her strike, crossing my arms above my head. Her sword slices my other arm, but before she can cut through my flesh I swipe my foot under hers, sending her crashing to the ground.

My chest rises and falls erratically as I step over her and I can see the panic swirling in her eyes. She swipes the air as I smack her sword away with mine, her grip loosening as it goes skittering across the room and I pin my sword to her chest.

"Any last words?" I ask, pressing the blade deeper, blood seeping into her kimono.

She looks up at me with half her face covered by her hair. "Did you know Serena is alone with your sister right now?"

"You're lying," I grit out as my grip on my sword tightens.

"I'm not. I've been watching them. They have teamed up trying to locate you."

I scoff. "If that was true, Zephira would have found me by now."

Her head lolls as an evil chuckle slips past her lips. "The Man-Eater. The woman who matches me in my hacking skills. Well, I thought she did. Until she had to ask your mother who took you."

Her tongue glides across her lip as if she was tasting my fear. My hand twitches, the grip on my katana loosening. *She did what?* I search Kara's eyes for any lies, but find none.

"No," I breathe out, stumbling backwards.

"Yes!" she cackles, getting to her knees as she stands. "She told her my name. But lucky for me she never knew my *true* name." Her eyes go wild as her hands fly through the air. "Without that information, no one can find me. No one can save you."

I slam my hand to her chest, pushing her up against the wall and angle the sword to her throat. "If that's true then why hasn't she used my kidnapping to her advantage? Why hasn't Zephira tried to kill Serena?"

She wraps both hands around the blade as blood drips down her arms. "She isn't allowed to." I press the blade deeper, the tip of the sword disappearing into her flesh. "Your mother has plans for Serena. Plans I won't tell you no matter what you do to me," she chokes out.

I pull the sword away from her neck, her hands falling at her sides as she laughs at me. *What does my mother have planned?* I step away from Kara as negative thoughts plague my mind of what else my mother is capable of that she hasn't done already.

Kara uses the distraction to her advantage as she runs towards me with no weapons, shrieking. I quickly lift my blade and silence her scream by piercing her stomach, the steel sliding smoothly through her flesh. She wheezes, spitting up blood. "I knew you'd be the one to kill me one day," she coughs with a sad smile, "Tell your mother to go to hell."

I push the blade all the way through, watching her eyes flutter before she falls over. I bring two fingers to her neck, needing to check that her pulse has truly stopped.

"She will meet you there," I tell her dead body before looking around for anything to clean my DNA from this room.

Limping to the door, I find a room full of screens. *She wasn't lying.* This place wasn't random; it's her lair. One screen has my breath hitching when I see Serena and Zephira sitting at a laptop in the living room looking like they're bonding.

I touch her face, the image distorting under the pressure. "I'll be home soon," I whisper.

Serena looks up, like she heard me and I gasp. The other screen shows the room I was in. *She really was always watching me.*

I find a cloth and gloves and walk back into my cage to wipe my fingerprints off everything and place Kara's hands around the katana piercing her stomach, making it look as if she'd taken herself out. I pick up every piece of shredded clothing I can find, then find a broom to clean up anything I missed. Looking at the blood stains on the ground, I walk back into the room, searching for any type of cleaning supplies.

After what feels like forever, I find a small bottle of bleach. Thanking whichever god is listening, I go back and scrub away all of the evidence, taking small breaks in between to catch my breath. My body is exhausted and I need rest, but I also need to push through.

Once I'm satisfied with my work, I look for an exit but find none. *If she's anything like me, there must be a secret doorway.* I start clicking buttons, moving things around but find nothing.

I plop into the chair as exhaustion begins taking over me, placing my elbows on my knees to rest my head on my hands and catch my breath. *No, I need to find a way out.* Getting up once more on shaky legs, I look at the ground and notice scuff marks by a bookshelf. Wrapping my one good hand around the frame, I pull as hard as I can, watching with relief as the shelf slowly drags open revealing an opening. I stumble through, a living room greeting me. *This is a house, her secret location was in her own house. She really wanted to be like my parents.* I pass a long hallway with several doors I don't care to go into, heading straight for the kitchen.

Relief floods me as I open the fridge with my gloved hands and find a shelf full of water. It could be poisoned, but with how thirsty I am, I twist the cap and down three bottles back-to-back.

Once I'm satisfied, I look for keys. My legs wobble the more I search, my body on its last leg. *I can't rest. I can't give up. I need to make it home.*

Stumbling to the front door, I see a little hanger full of keys.

Should've looked here first. I grab the set that has a little fob and click the unlock button, listening for the sound of a car. I hear it further into the house which tells me the car is in the garage.

Slowly, I make my way back down the long hall, clicking the button again and noticing a door I failed to see the last time. Relief floods me as I swing it open to find the garage and Kara's car.

Getting in, I slam the door and look at the GPS to see where I am. I don't recognize the name of the city I'm in, but, according to her home address, I'm still in Massachusetts.

Instead of punching in my address, which the cops could trace, I type the address of somewhere I know I can get home to by heart.

The little voice tells me my estimated time of arrival is two hours. I smack both of my cheeks to shake away the drowsiness begging to pull me under as I grip the steering wheel and pull out of the garage and speed onto the empty road.

Hang on, Serena, I'm coming.

CRIME SCENE - DO NOT CROSS
CRIME SCENE - DO NO
THE BLACK LOTUS
SPECIAL EDITION
Daily
ARDELLA
10 APRIL 2025
A DARK ROMANCE
VOL. 10, NO. 5
THE BLACK LOTUS
EXCLUSIVE
EXCLUSIVE
EXCLUSIVE
CRIME SCENE - DO
DO NOT CR
SOLITUDE
SOLITUDE

CRIME SCENE - DO NOT
THE BLACK LOTUS
EXCLUSIVE
EXCLUSIVE
EXCLUSIVE
SERENA
SOLITUDE
T. CROSS
CRIME

THIRTY-THREE
SERENA

K nowing who took Aster and finding her are two completely different things. One was only possible because of Cynthia, and the other is impossible. I feel defeated, everytime we think we're close to any kind of answer, a giant wall; and I mean a literal wall on Zephira's program, it covers her computer and then we're back to square one. She said she is close to figuring out how to work around the virus, but it's been five days, and we aren't any closer to locating him than when we started.

I have locked myself in our room while Zephira continues to run her programs. She was trying to talk more, opening up and offering the friendship I was desperate for, but I can't be around anyone right now. *Not until Aster is home.*

I lay on my back, staring up at the ceiling and creating shapes out of nothing. I look over to where Aster sleeps as my hand glides across the bedding, my fingers squeezing around the black fabric and wrinkling the otherwise pristine surface. "I miss you," I whisper.

"I've missed you, too," I hear his voice say back to me, my lower lip quivering as a sad smile covers my face.

Great; now I'm hearing him in my head. Soon I'll be seeing him and imagining he's there when he's not.

I feel the bed dip, and my heart accelerates as I whip around to see a very bruised, very cut up Aster in front of me. *Is this real?*

Springing up, my hands cup his face as tears flood to my eyes. "Are you real?"

His hand cradles around my own. "I'm really here, little vixen," he softly says.

A sob bursts free as I wrap my arms around him and cry into his shoulders. My body relaxes in his hold, the chains that were constricting me breaking free, and I feel like I can breathe for the first time since he was taken. The weight that has been heavy on my heart from not being able to do anything finally falls free. *He's here. He's home.*

I extend my arms to get a good look at him, searching his features. *What is this?* My brow furrows as I slowly bring my hand up to touch the new scar on his eye. He winces and my face falls.

"Hey," he whispers, bringing my sad gaze to his concerned one. His features soften watching me watch him. "I'm okay."

"I'm sorry we couldn't find you." I grab his hands, a hiss escaping his lips. Releasing his hands quickly, I'm scared I've injured him further. "What happened?" I whisper, my body shaking as I realize how badly he's been treated.

He holds up his hand. "I had to dislocate it to escape."

My mouth falls open. We took too long. We couldn't find him. *If Zephira's programs just ran faster, we could have saved him.* Maybe... maybe he wouldn't be so broken. He looks skinnier than usual, and his complexion is paler. He has healing cuts along his arms and abdomen, fading bruises. *She really did a number on him.*

He grabs my hand, his thumb rubbing gently back and forth. "Hey. Come back to me. I'm here. I'm alive; that's all that matters."

I shake my head looking down. "If we'd just found you sooner, then you wouldn't be so…"

"Broken." he finishes for me.

I snap my head up, a wave of sadness washing over me for what he thinks of himself. "You are *not* broken."

"I let my guard down. I got caught, tortured, and barely escaped with my life. That isn't very Morbid Monet of me." He laughs sadly, a faraway look in his eyes.

Looking at him, seeing a side of Aster I've never seen before only makes me want to bring back the person he fears he lost. The one he always was. *He doesn't look like the killer I fell in love with.* He looks like a shell of himself, and my soul is shattering. *Can the broken parts of him be put back together?* Can I be the one to rearrange the puzzle pieces and bring back the man everyone cowers from with just a stare?

Sitting on my knees in front of him, I straighten my back and place my hands on his legs. "You're home now, and you came back stronger than when you left. Yeah, you lost some weight and you have some new scars." I cup his face, forcing his eyes to meet mine. "But they're a part of you now. You went through something terrible, but if I've learned anything, what doesn't kill us makes us stronger." His eyes burn into mine, the same look of defeat I had when he was missing. *He needs tough love right now, not soft.* "Plus, that just means *I* get to train *you*. And I won't go easy on you just because you're injured." I crawl off the bed, reaching my hand out to his. "I'm going to make you swea–"

My words are cut off, his hand gripping my wrist and pulling me onto the bed. He lays me on the bed as he crawls over me, my cheeks heating from the sexual tension. His cock presses against my aching cunt, my hips move to create some kind of friction we both desperately need. "I can think of other ways to make you sweat," he teases.

I watch his arms tremble as he struggles to hold himself up. All thoughts of making love evaporate as I give him a sympathetic smile and lean up to kiss the lips I've missed so much, feeling their dry and chapped texture. They're not the soft smooth ones I remember, but that doesn't deter me from consuming him.

When our lips part, his eyes glaze over and I slip out from under him. As much as I would love to be devoured, he is too injured to do anything.

"You need to heal," I say, standing at the end of the bed.

"I can heal later," he counters, sitting up so he can wrap his arms around my waist, pulling me into him.

I push against his chest, shaking my head. "As much as I would love to feel your cock deep inside me," I groan, my core clenching around nothing, "We can't. You look like you have been starved of everything and, as your vixen, I am going to make you a hearty meal and get you some electrolytes." I sniff the air around him, my nose curling. "And a nice bath because you smell like death."

He chuckles. "That's what being locked up and killing someone smells like."

I step out of his embrace and walk us to the bathroom.

"I'll shower, but only if you wash me."

I shake my head, pushing him into the bathroom. "Nu-uh mister, I know as soon as we get under that water you will shove your dick in me and that is the opposite of healing." His hand braces the top of the door as I try to close it. *Even weakened, he's still stronger than me.*

Standing on my tiptoes, I give him one last kiss. "Please bathe and get some rest; I'll wake you when the food is done."

He grunts but relents, releasing his grip on the door and closing it softly behind him.

I hear the water turn on and it takes everything in me not to turn around, to not run back into his arms and give into the temptation of *him.*

Zephira is standing outside the door when I walk out, causing me to nearly fall over, my hand pressed against the wall to hold me up. "Holy shit, Zephira! Warn a girl next time you're stalking around."

She reaches her hand out to mine and I gratefully take it. "Sorry. I just wanted to make sure big bro was okay."

I smile. *She's worried about her brother.* Spent days searching for him only to come up with nothing. She has to feel like she failed. I know I do.

"He's taking a shower right now, and I told him to rest after. I'm going to make him something to have for when he wakes up. How did he get past you without you noticing?"

"I was in my room with the door shut."

"What about the alarms? The cameras?" I ask, with my head tilted to the side.

"With all the programs I have running, I only set up the alarms to my phone and that was… away from me."

My back stiffens, her confession causing a knot of anxiety to form in my stomach. Anything could have happened. Anyone could have come in unnoticed. I had my phone on silent because I wanted to wallow in my misery and I thought Zephira was keeping an eye out for anyone. But, I should have known better, she is working for Cynthia after all.

I lift my head, my anger bubbling up, but stop when I see her. She nibbles her bottom lip, her arms behind her back. She looks more her age than she ever has before. *It's kind of cute to see her all bashful like this.*

"Is there anything I can do?"

I brace my hand on her shoulder and all feelings of irritation are gone. "Can you go to the store and get some ointment, antibiotics, bandages, and some drinks with electrolytes?."

She nods, her eyes lighting at my request. "Yes. I'll be right back."

She runs to grab her keys, and I head downstairs to prepare Aster's meal.

Her footsteps come bounding down as she bolts into the kitchen to hug me, her embrace throwing me off guard, my body stiffening against hers. I'm not used to this kind of affection, especially from her, but maybe since Aster is home, she's putting on an act of the loving sister-in-law? Granted Aster isn't around, so maybe this is real.

I turn around to wrap my arms around her, returning the hug. *She smells nice, too.* I inhale her scent of honey and lavender, a soft cloud around me. She pulls away from me as quickly as she came in, and before she can walk out the door, I ask one last thing.

"Hey, Zephira?"

"Hmm?" she asks, turning to look at me.

"Why didn't anyone attack when I was left unguarded?"

"I can't tell you."

She leaves before I can ask anything more. If she knows, does that mean Cynthia has called it all off? *Is she finally done with me?* Can I breathe without having to look behind my shoulder every second?

My stomach churns, the cracking on the stove forcing me back into reality. Something tells me the worst is yet to come.

CRIME SCENE - DO NOT CROSS
CRIME SCENE - DO NOT CROSS

THE BLACK LOTUS

SPECIAL EDITION
Daily O...   ARDELLA
10 APRIL 2025
A DARK
ROMANCE
VOL. 10, NO. 5

THE BLACK LOTUS

EXCLUSIVE
EXCLUSIVE
EXCLUSIVE

S

In these quiet moments, you reconnect with your thoughts and emotions, gaining clarity on your true desires and values. Embracing solitude helps you recharge, enhances mental clarity, and fosters emotional well-being. This introspection nurtures personal growth and cultivates a more balanced and fulfilling life.

Finding peace in solitude is not about isolation but creating a personal space where you can deeply connect to your own needs and aspirations. It is in this way and you can...
more fulfilling

SOLITUDE

CRIME SCENE - DO NOT
THE BLACK LOTUS
EXCLUSIVE
EXCLUSIVE
EXCLUSIVE
SERENA
SOLITUDE
CROSS
CRIME

THIRTY-FOUR
SERENA

Keeping my hands off Aster and his grabby ones off me is way harder than I thought it would be. When two people who have been deprived of one another for longer than they are used to, finally get in reach of the other *and* are denied the one craving they need, things become… tense. Let's just say after a couple days of making sure her brother was healing properly, Zephira got out of our house because she was tired of both our snappiness.

It's been *five days*, and I personally have had enough. It's been almost two weeks since he was taken and he is healed enough. *It's time.* He doesn't know it yet, but I am in a playful mood, so when those grabby hands become forceful, I am going to give in.

I'm currently whipping up an assortment of food for break-fast, one that will not only satiate our appetite, but will be payback for that time he teased me with pizza. *Let's see how he feels when the roles are reversed.*

Walking up the stairs in nothing but an apron, I hold a tray of waffles, whip cream, strawberries, and chocolate syrup. *Things are about to get messy.*

After everything we've been through, this is a moment we

both need. A moment to breathe and be with one another with no distractions or looming threats from Cynthia.

Aster's already sitting up in bed, most likely checking the camera feed for anything out of place. His paranoia has been on high alert since the incident, causing my anxiety to rise along with his. He can't help but feel this is not the end. That inkling grows stronger each day in me, as well.

As soon as I shut the door, I see a feral Aster staring at me, his hungry, darkened gaze has me weak in the knees.

"You've brought me breakfast."

I walk towards him, placing my food on the side table and the tray of his on the bed. "I have. It's all your favorite sweets." My voice squeaks when his hand grips my ass, his fingers digging into my plump flesh, the food nearly spilling over before I let go.

"You know that's not what I'm talking about."

I swat his arm, stepping out of his hold. "You need to eat."

"If you expect me to eat anything except your dripping cunt when I've been starved from it for so long, you're more delusional than I thought."

I mindlessly lick my bottom lip. "If you eat your breakfast, I might let you have me for dessert."

Without another word, he grabs the plate in front of him and scarfs down the food, not leaving a single crumb. I watch, amazed and turned on by the way his throat bobs up and down with each swallow.

The plate clatters back on the tray. "Done. Now come here," he demands.

I pick up the plate, giving him a playful smile, acting clueless as I fork a piece of waffle. "You may be done, but I haven't even started on mine." I sit down, the apron rising up and revealing my exposed pussy.

He growls a warning, his fingers bunching around the sheets as he tries to contain himself. It is quite amusing watching him impatiently wait; I was hoping he'd throw a tantrum or feed me himself, but watching him struggle is even better.

I slowly eat, taking my time savoring each bite and licking my lips when a little chocolate and whip cream falls. A big dollop of cream plops directly on my chest, and I take my finger, swiping it off. Before I can bring the white sweetness to my mouth, Aster's lips wrap around it and we both moan.

Once our heated eyes meet, all bets are off. The predator lurking beneath his eyes, the one that is done waiting for his prey to finish, tenses with lethal grace, every single muscle straining against his skin. Before he can pin me down, I grab the can of whip cream, holding it out in front of me.

"You think a little sugar is going to stop me from taking what is mine?"

"I think if you move one inch off that bed you'll find out."

A wolfish grin spreads across his face. "Is that a threat, little vixen?"

"It's a promise."

I spray the can in his face as he leaps towards me. It hits his chest, and I run, not ready to be eaten, enjoying the game too much. He lunges forward, but I jump out of his reach and land onto the bed, legs spread and readying myself to run.

He stands with his head cocked, an amused gleam in his eyes as he watches for what I'll do next.

"Nowhere to run, Serena. Why don't you just give up and give me what I want?"

"Never," I breathe.

"If you run, I will catch you, and when I do, I will shove that can so far up your cunt you'll be begging for mercy." His next words come out as more of a promise than a threat, sending shivers down my spine. "Unlucky for you, that's one thing I will never grant you."

He wouldn't actually do that. I jump down on the other side of the bed and sprint towards the door. If I can just make it down the stairs, I'll have a fair chance at escaping and prolonging our game of cat and mouse.

Just as my hand wraps around the handle, I'm pulled back, and my back collides with his chest. His arm wrapped around my waist, keeping me trapped. "Now you'll be filled with another kind of cream."

He tosses me over his shoulder, untying the back of my apron and throws me onto the mess of our bed. I kick and punch and try everything I can to break free, but he has me in a strong grip.

He crawls over me, taking his shirt off and dropping to the floor. He bends down to lift my apron over my head and I let him, finally giving in to what we both want, as he grabs each hand securing them to the restraints connected to our bed. Once my hands are bound above my head, he scoots down my body, his hands massaging my breast. I let out a pleasurable hiss as he pinches each nipple, hard.

"Aster!" I moan, my head falling back as my eyes close.

He dips his head to trace circles around the sensitive peak, kissing and nipping his way down my stomach to my needy, aching cunt.

"Has your pussy missed me?" He dips his head, his mouth hovering over me.

"Yes," I breathe, my body bowing off the bed.

"Do you deserve to be eaten?"

"Please," I whisper.

His tongue swipes over my clit, a whispered moan leaving my lips as his lips latch on to my pulsing center. I want to tangle my hands into his hair, push him deeper into me, but being confined, he's stolen any chance I have.

A whimper falls out of me as his tongue stops the magic it was performing. "As much as I want to devour you. You need to be punished." *He better not do what I think he is.*

My body tenses as he gets off the bed, taking his pants off as my eyes trace the movement. He tosses them to the floor and retrieves the can of whip cream. *Fuck.*

"You've made quite the mess with this. I should have you lick every inch of me clean." He gets back on the bed, straddling me and spraying a dollop over my breast as he leans down to lick it off, his eyes never leaving mine. "But first I'm going to show you what happens to little vixens who don't listen to their fox."

He grabs a strawberry from the plate behind him and sprays a dollop onto the fruit. "Open," he demands. I wrap my mouth around his offering, his eyes darkening as sweetness coats my tongue, my tastebuds dancing at the combination.

He bends down to lick the whip cream off my lips, my chewing stopping as his mouth demands mine. Our lips dance with a hunger of being apart for too long, our tongues tangling as sugar drips down my chin.

My eyes spring open, my pussy clenching when I feel cool metal parting my entrance. "Aster, what are you-?"

"Shhhh," his finger covers my lips. "I told you I was going to punish you." He drops the can on the bed and a relieved sigh leaves me.

I know he told me that, but I didn't *actually* believe he would torture me with it. The girth is intimidating as hell and no sane person would ever insert it into themselves let alone have someone else do it.

"Aster, please. It won't fit." For the first time since meeting him I am scared. Sweat beads at my forehead as I slowly swallow down the fear.

He scoots down, spreading and bending my legs with an iron grip on each ankle. In a threatening tone, he says. "Don't move or there will be more pain than pleasure."

I gulp in a shuddering breath, doing as he says and keeping my feet planted as he gets off the bed and straps them open. So even if I want to, I can't move.

He positions himself between my legs, retrieving the can and spraying it on my wet and traitorous cunt. No matter how scared

I am that the can will rip me in two, my body eagerly awaits the intrusion with how I'm dripping.

The cold cream covers my pussy as the can slowly enters me. The pain is excruciating; my eyes pinching closed as my breath catches in my lungs. I can't enjoy whatever pleasure this could bring because the only thing I'm worried about is if this will give me a UTI or some other kind of infection. *This isn't my idea of foreplay.*

"Breathe, Serena," Aster says, and I take in a huge breath of air as the can slides a little deeper, ripping a scream from my throat.

"I can't." Tears prick my eyes, the stretching becoming unbearable.

"You thought you couldn't handle me, yet you did."

"Your dick isn't as big as this can!"

I heave a sigh of relief as he takes the can out of me, my body jerking from the relief. "Shall we compare?"

He places the white covered metal next to his cock as I strain to lift my head to look. "See? Pretty close."

Pretty close my ass! That can almost ripped me apart to the point where I wouldn't be able to have sex for months if he went any deeper.

He chucks the can onto the floor, and I close my eyes, thanking whoever is listening that the punishment was over quickly.

"You look relieved."

My eyes spring open. "I am."

"Don't be. I'm not done with you yet." I wiggle my body from instinct, but fail as the restraints dig into my flesh.

Fuck me.

THE BLACK LOTUS

SPECIAL EDITION   * Daily O...   ARDELLA

10 APRIL 2025

A DARK ROMANCE

VOL. 10, NO. 5

EXCLUSIVE
EXCLUSIVE
EXCLUSIVE

In these quiet moments, you confront your thoughts and emotions, gaining clarity on your true desires and values. Embracing solitude helps you reconnect, enhances mental clarity, and fosters emotional well-being. This introspection nurtures personal growth and cultivates a more balanced and fulfilling life.

SOLITUDE   *   SOLITUDE

SCENE - DO NOT CROSS   CRIME SCENE

VOL. 10, NO.

BLACK LOTUS

EXCLUSIVE
EXCLUSIVE
EXCLUSIVE

ASTER

SOLITUDE   *   SOLITUDE

SOLITUDE   *   SOLITUDE

CROSS

DO NOT CROSS

THIRTY-FIVE
ASTER

The fear I see and smell coming from Serena's sweaty pores is enough to make me want to retrieve the can and shove it back into her just to hear her scream again. I do love her screams, both of pleasure and pain. A feral grin twists my face. *I haven't decided which is my favorite yet.*

I unlock the restraints holding Serena bound to the bed and watch as she massages her wrists. *Guess I made them tighter than I thought.* She glares at me with pursed lips, and I'm helpless, leaning in and trapping them between my teeth.

Instead of pushing me away like I thought she would, she moans as we kiss, returning the bite, her teeth piercing into my flesh. She pulls back, taking the skin with her, releasing only when my skin doesn't give anymore.

I grip her waist with a bruising force as she straddles me, her hands tangling in my hair, tugging when she wants more.

She is as addicting as the kills I miss performing. I haven't had a moment to think about everything Kara said. If I'm being honest to myself, she did get in my head about Serena not having a choice in anything. As much as I keep trying to convince myself, a little part of me does miss being the Morbid Monet. Killing Kara wasn't enough; I need more. I miss the feeling I get when a lamb is laying on my table. I miss the satisfying ripping of skin as my knife slices through their flesh. I miss the questions of why and their screams begging me to stop. But most of all I miss turning them into a Jane Doe. I miss being the only one to know who they were before. All the killing we've done, we have revealed their true identity, so everyone knows who they were before and after death.

My kissing slows as my grip on her loosens, making her pull back from our kiss, her face concerned. "Hey, where'd you go?"

"Just thinking about the Morbid Monet." *Way to ruin the moment, Aster.*

Her face falls and my pulse quickens with the fear I've said something I shouldn't. "Not that I'm not happy-"

"It's okay," she interrupts, looking away from me. "You were the Monet for so long, of course you miss it. I'm… I'm sorry I've taken you away from that path."

"You didn't," I rush to get out, desperate to reassure her. "Yes, I miss having little lambs. Yes, I miss the rush of the hunt and the finality of a kill, but I love being half of the Fatal Floral Killers with you. It's just…" Frustration of my inability to stop going back and forth over my feelings is making me fumble for the words I desperately want to say.

"Half of who you are is being shadowed by me," she finishes, her words more of a statement than a question.

I lift her chin, forcefully bringing her eyes to mine, making my intent clear. "I am not your shadow, and you are not mine. We are two halves that make a fucked up whole. But Kara… she got in my head."

"The Dishonored Bushi?" she asks, taking my hands in hers.

I nod.

"What did she say?"

"She said…" I sigh, phantom ropes and blades digging into my skin. "She said that just because you killed before, doesn't mean you were a killer. That I never asked if you wanted to be like me, I just assumed and you were thrown into it because of your connection to me. It's… it's been eating at me." I drop my hands from her face, dipping my head too embarrassed to look at her.

She lets go of one hand and lifts my chin to look at her. No empathy or sympathy shines, just determination with a swirl of anger. Anger for me or at me I'm not sure, but I know she won't lie to me. She will speak her truth and no matter what it is, I will accept it.

"You think you turned me into who I am? That you never gave me a choice in everything that happened?" Her face tightens, her eyes focusing with clear intent as she says her next words. "I was asleep for so long, Aster. Your darkness wrapped around mine and destroyed the pieces that were keeping me blind. Once the truth of what I did became clear, I didn't feel remorse. I didn't feel guilt. I felt empowered. I had the urge to spill more blood to those deserving of it."

Her words have every thought and doubt vanishing as though it was never there. I open my mouth to respond, but she squeezes my cheeks with one hand, her eyes fierce. My cock jumps between us, my vixen setting me aflame unlike anyone I've ever met.

"My obsession with true crime became a reality. Imagine my delight when *I* was the one behind it standing next to the man I was obsessed with. Yes, you did wake the killer inside me, but you did not force me into becoming one. You have done nothing but help me embrace my true self, and I never want you to doubt who *we* are." She pushes against my chest, my back hitting our bed as she straddles my waist with a ferocity that surprises us both. "We are the Fatal Floral Killers." She grabs my erect cock, stroking it a few times before lining it up to her cunt. "If you *ever* doubt yourself again," the tip barely passes through her lips, "you won't get sex for a month."

Losing my patience, I grip her waist and slam her down onto my cock, our moans filling the air.

"You could never go that long without me inside you."

"Do you want to find out just how stubborn I can be?" she gasps, grinding down on me.

I thrust into her and her hands slam down onto my chest. "You look delicious covered in whip cream, but I prefer you covered in me instead."

She bounces harder and faster, the sounds of her ass slapping against my balls sending shockwaves of pleasure into me. "I'd rather your release be inside me than on me."

"That can be arranged."

Her nails scrape down my chest, leaving scratch marks, next to the scars of Kara's blade. Teaching Serena to channel her pain into pleasure was helpful, necessary more than either of us thought possible, but I wish I took part in that training myself. I love when she bites, scratches, and even cuts me, but her marks don't leave scars, they just make me bleed. Kara left lasting scars that will always be a reminder to never let my guard down again.

"Aster," Serena moans, quickening her pace as her pussy clenches around my cock.

"That's it, Serena, coat my cock in your cum."

Thrusting deeply into her, we explode at the same time, my balls constricting as her pussy clenches around me. "Fuck," I grind out.

She collapses onto me, her breathing heavy as she draws circles around the tattoo on my chest. I wrap my arms around her, pulling her to the side and kissing the top of her head. "I'll be right back."

She hums as I go to the bathroom to get a washcloth. When I return, she's half awake. I wipe the cum dripping down her legs, then all the sugar off her body. Gathering all the food from the bed, I place it on the side table before cleaning myself and crawling into bed next to her. Wrapping my arm around her, I throw the blanket around us, my body relaxing for the first time in weeks.

CRIME SCENE - DO NOT CROSS
CRIME SCENE - DO NOT
THE BLACK LOTUS
EXCLUSIVE
EXCLUSIVE
EXCLUSIVE
SPECIAL EDITION
Daily
BARDELLA
10 APRIL 2025
A DARK ROMANCE
VOL. 10, NO. 5
THE BLACK LOTUS
EXCLUSIVE
EXCLUSIVE
EXCLUSIVE
SOLITUDE
SOLITUDE
CRIME SCENE - DO
DO NOT CRO

THE BLACK LOTUS

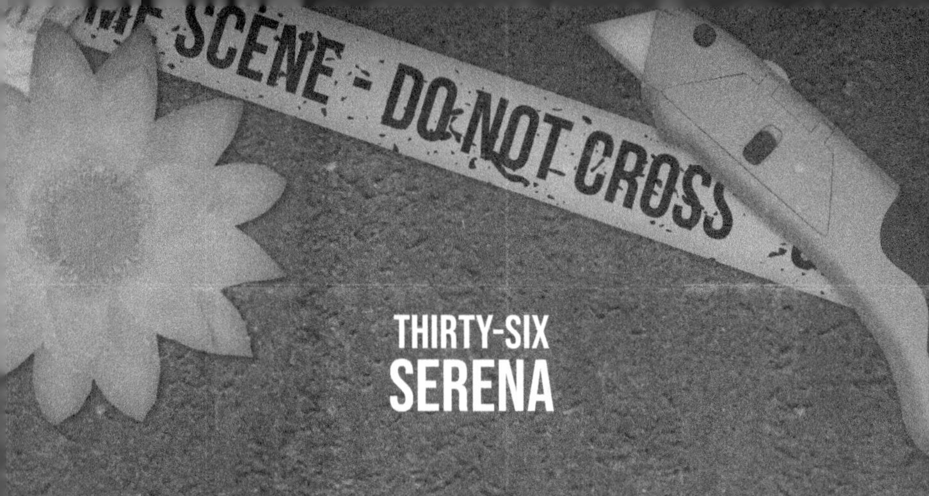

<h1 style="text-align:center">THIRTY-SIX
SERENA</h1>

The weather outside has been gloomy, and according to the weather app on my phone, there is a warning of an incoming thunderstorm. Which means it's the perfect weather to sit in my cozy chaise and read. I can't remember the last time I opened up a book and really lost myself in one.

Slowly and as quietly as I possibly can, I leave Aster's embrace as I glance back to see if he is still asleep. He's on his back, one arm rests beside him the other over his face, leaving only his lips in view. A soft smile lifts my own. I want to lean down and give him a soft kiss, but I know that would definitely wake him and I want to let him sleep.

With a soundless, defeated sigh I walk away, throwing on a pair of leggings and an oversized t-shirt. I already know which book I want to read; it's a new release about a serial killer couple by my favorite author. *I wonder how right she got it.* I creep towards the door, but my body locks when I hear Aster's deep, raspy, morning voice. "Where do you think you're going?"

I turn slowly on my heels to find Aster sitting up in bed, his chest exposed as he lifts a questioning brow. I thought I was being stealthy enough, we both need rest especially after yester-

day, him more than me. But I should have known he'd sense me sneaking away.

"I was going to go make some coffee, then read in my library."

He gracefully crawls out of bed, and my eyes travel down his body landing at his exposed and very erect cock. *This man is insatiable.* My traitorous cunt clenches around nothing as I mindlessly lick my bottom lip.

His gaze darkens. "I can think of something else much more appetizing than coffee and a book."

I slowly walk backwards towards the door, my hand searching the knob behind me. "As much as I wish that were true, your dick can't fill me up."

He pulls on a pair of grey sweats, the ones he knows make me feral.

"Last I checked, my dick fills you more than anything else."

With a slow swallow, I trap my lip between my teeth as my hand finds the knob. Hoping he won't notice, but knowing he will, I take a deep breath and unlatch the door.

"Not the way food can." I fling the door open just as he lunges, wrapping his arms around my waist. He is quicker and stronger than me, pulling me back and slamming the door shut as I collide with his chest. One arm bands tightly around me, keeping me trapped, while the other braces above the door. *It's last night all over again.* No matter how much I wiggle and punch and kick, I can't escape, so I do the only thing I can think of and elbow him in the chest.

His surprise gives me the opening I need to duck, spin, and run. I sprint towards our bathroom, the only place left with a lock since he is still blocking the hallway. I quickly shut and lock the door, sliding down and keeping my back pressed firmly against it.

A bang makes me flinch. "I just want to play, little vixen, I won't hurt you," Aster taunts.

I press my back to the flexing wood, my chest rising and falling as I look around for anything that can help me escape the beast trying to break in. I know he won't hurt me, but I know I will be punished. All I wanted was to drink my coffee and read, but now I'm hiding in the bathroom from the man who wants to fuck me and ruin my plans. I mean, a little dick in the morning isn't a bad thing, and seeing Aster back to himself is making me want to have him work for it a little, but a girl also needs some time with her book boyfriends.

The knob rattles as I cover my mouth, stifling my squeak. Will he win and claim my pussy, or will I escape and get a day with my books? It's going to be fun to find out. I press my thighs together, rubbing them to create some friction to ease the building ache in my core.

"Serena, if you come out, I promise I won't punish you! We can go downstairs, and you can have your coffee."

"I don't believe you!" I yell, bending my legs, keeping my feet planted on the ground as I push harder against the flimsy barrier.

He pounds his fist once more before silence blankets us. Then a low, menacing chuckle shatters our standoff. "I'm going to count to three, vixen, and if you don't come out by then," he scoffs, the sound harsh, "well, you better move."

I slowly turn my head towards where he stands between our barrier as goosebumps skitter up my arms. *What does he mean by that?*

"One."

I stand up, scrambling as I look all around the bathroom for a place to hide.

"Two."

He's going to pick the lock and get me. I run and dive into the closet, searching for a good spot I can hide. I know trying to escape my fox is futile, but I still have to try.

"Three."

A loud bang echoes around the bathroom, my body jumping

and as a tiny yelp slips past my lips. *Did he just kick the door down?!* I cover my mouth to quiet my breathing, making myself as small as possible, pushing my back flat against the wall in the back of the closet.

"Serena. Come out, come out, wherever you are," he sings in a haunting tone.

I shake my head as a silent answer to his request. Looking around, I find a pair of shoes. *The perfect weapon to escape.*

"There is nowhere to run. The longer you hide, the more you'll be punished."

That's what he thinks.

The sounds of cabinets opening and closing become louder the closer he gets. I don't hear when he enters through the left open closet, but his shadow envelopes the space, blocking the light from the bathroom.

"Are you in here, little vixen?"

I clutch the shoe in my hand, ready to throw it when the time is right. Moving my head a little to see what he's doing, I see the strength of his back, the sounds of moving hangers making me tense. I crawl out of my spot as he slowly turns, a wicked smile splitting his cheeks. Without thinking, I throw the first shoe, watching it smack him in the chest.

"What the fuck?" he balks as I run past him, shutting the door behind me. Not a second later is it thrown open, slamming against the wall, and I chuck the second shoe, aiming for his head, but he catches it.

My mouth drops open but I don't have time to gawk, I just run, and dart across our room. I swing the door open and dash down the stairs. The sound of angry footsteps thunders behind me, my heart pounding as they get louder and louder. I can't outrun him, but if I can get to the kitchen, I can go behind the island and force him to take longer to get me.

I make the mistake of turning around to see where he's at. Aster stands at the top, holding the boot I threw at him, a crazed look in his eyes.

"Did you throw a boot at my head, Serena?"

My eyes widen. "Nope. Wasn't me."

"Oh, really?" He takes one step down, and I want to run but his looming presence keeps me rooted to the spot. *Run, Serena. Move your feet!* "It sure looked like you." Another step, slow and calculating. "But my vixen would never dare do something so childish."

"Never," I whisper, fighting a smile.

Two more steps and he inches closer, my feet still refusing to move from where they're glued. I feel like a deer caught in head-lights and Aster is the light I fear will be the reason I meet my maker. Maybe, I can't move because I want to get caught. Maybe, I want to be punished and this is my body's way of telling me. Maybe, I do want to be fucked into oblivion, again.

A few more steps and he's standing right in front of me, his gaze one of a predator daring their prey, and even as every bone in my body screams at me to run I can't. My chest rises and falls as my breath catches in my throat, his energy sucking all the oxygen out of the room as I wait to see if my body will listen to my brain and run.

"Do you know what happens to vixens who hurt their foxes?" he asks with a daring smirk.

I nod, knowing the answer, but not wanting to say it.

"Use your voice and tell me."

I swallow, lifting my chin with a confidence I don't feel. "They're punished."

"That they are. Do you know *how* they're punished."

"Yes," I breathe.

Aster steps even closer. "Are you sure about that?"

I bite my lip, forcing myself to stay in the power of this orbit. The first time it was anal, which I've come to enjoy, and the last time was something I never want to go through again. I have no idea what he has in store.

One word leaves his lips. *"Run."*

Obeying immediately, I turn and run towards the front door,

swinging it open, only to run square into a hard chest and fall backwards onto my ass.

When I look up, I see Aster stands in front of me, the muscles in his back more tense than they've ever been, and the face I've seen on tv too many times stands ominously at our door.

Deputy Wiley.

CRIME SCENE - DO NOT CROSS
CRIME SCENE - DO NOT CROSS
CRIME SCENE - DO NOT CROSS
THE BLACK LOTUS
SPECIAL EDITION
Daily
10 APRIL 2025
A DARK ROMANCE
VOL. 10, NO. 5
THE BLACK LOTUS
EXCLUSIVE
EXCLUSIVE
EXCLUSIVE
SOLITUDE
SOLITUDE

CRIME SCENE — DO NOT
CRIME SCENE
THE BLACK LOTUS
EXCLUSIVE
EXCLUSIVE
EXCLUSIVE
SERENA
SOLITUDE
SOLITUDE
T. CROSS
CRIME

THIRTY-SEVEN
SERENA

What is Deputy Wiley doing here? Aster offers me his hand, and I easily rise to stand next to him as I place my trembling hands behind my back.

"Afternoon. Ms. Raven, can we speak in private please?"

Aster places his arm across me in a protective stance, his body taut and his senses on high. "What is this regarding?" Aster asks, not happy to have a cop at our home.

Deputy Wiley glances at me as if asking permission. "This is regarding the disappearance of Tyler and Bradley."

I stop breathing, the blood draining from my face before I'm able to regain my composure as to not give anything away. *Was there more evidence pointing to me as the killer?*

"Anything you have to ask can be said in front of Aster." I state plainly interlocking my fingers with his. "Please, come in." Aster tenses beside me, clearly not keen on the invitation.

He dips his head not giving anything away as he walks past us into the living room. Aster squeezes my hand in reassurance as we follow behind him. My heart races a mile a minute and my hands so sweaty I'm worried I'm going to slip out of Aster's hold. *I need to do something to get rid of this nervous energy,* but showing any sign of distress can give me away, so I sit next to Aster and wait for the deputy to start talking.

"We have found new evidence which points to you," he looks at me, "since you were the last person to be seen with Bradley."

What do I say in this situation? Yes, I was the last person, then I took him back here to have Aster watch me kill him before we made love under the stars covered in his blood. *I can't say that,* but if they have evidence or a witness, then I can't lie.

"I was," I say, keeping my voice neutral as Aster tenses beside me. *I hope I didn't just mess everything up.*

"Can you tell me what happened?"

Sucking in a deep breath, I hold the air in my lungs before slowly breathing out my nose. *Already threw myself under the bus, might as well tell half the truth.* Deputy Wiley gets out his note and paper, ready to jot down everything I tell him.

"I was having coffee at a shop I frequent, and he found out where I was because I posted it on social media, which I have stopped doing because of that."

Deputy Wiley freezes. "You're saying he stalked you? Why would he do that?"

"He said he knew I was the last person who went on a date with his brother. He claimed he saw the footage of Aster at the end of our date and wanted answers." I lick my lips, my nerves getting the better of me, and Aster places his hand on my lap, steadying me. "I told him I didn't know anything since I left with Aster after their confrontation. Bradley didn't like my answer and got threatening."

The deputy looks up from his notes, the pen stopping mid sentence. "He threatened you?"

I nod and he begins writing again the anger coming off of Aster in waves. "The shop owner defused the situation, and I left but he chased after me. I managed to calm him down, somehow, before I gave him a hug and my apologies, then we went our separate ways. That is the last time I saw him." Aster stays still as a stone taking in all of the information.

"Thank you." He closes the pad and stands. "But I'm going to have to ask you to come down to the station for further questioning." He looks at Aster. "Alone."

Aster jumps to his feet, making Deputy Wiley step back from the look in his eyes. I stand, touching his arm and lightly shaking my head, mouthing, 'it's okay', but Aster doesn't relent, my anxiety growing with each tug of his arm.

"Why does she need to be questioned further when she answered all your ridiculous accusations?"

"I'm not accusing her of anything, Mr. Graves. I simply need to take her down to get every detail. The more information we have, the higher the possibility of finding the two brothers."

"Fine. I'm coming with." Aster states, grabbing my hand and turning towards the door.

"That isn't necessary; we only need to question Ms. Raven for the time being."

Aster steps towards the Deputy, hovering over him as if daring him to question his judgement. *I need to defuse this situation.* The worst thing that could happen right now is Aster getting arrested for putting his hands on a cop. Plus, if they had any actual evidence, they would arrest me already.

I wrap my fingers around Aster's bicep and he whips around, fire blazing in his eyes. A tense silence passes between us, his rage meeting my calm, defusing the longer he looks at me.

"It's okay," I whisper, my thumb brushing against his skin. My eyes flinch towards Deputy Wiley. "Okay, I'll come with you."

He walks to the door with a stern nod, waiting for me as I stand on my tiptoes to whisper in Aster's ear, "I'll be okay; he's a cop. They have nothing, right? Like you always say, 'no body, no crime'." I kiss him quickly, stopping at the doorway to give Aster a reassuring smile. "I'll be back."

He stands in our living room, his body as stiff as stone unable to do anything as he watches me walk to the deputy's unmarked cop car. He opens the back door for me, I hesitate before getting in and thanking him. He gives me a stiff smile and gets in the driver's side to start the car.

I look out the window and watch as Aster steps out onto the porch to watch me drive away. Even though I know I'm safe, something in the back of my mind screams at me not to trust the man I'm sitting behind.

"Deputy Wiley…" I start.

"Jason," he interrupts. "You can call me Jason."

"Jason. You were the cop that first questioned us about Bradley's disappearance. right?"

"I was." He glances at the rearview mirror.

I knew he looked familiar and not only because of his screen time on TV.

Even though I already know the answer, I murmur, "Can I ask what new evidence has surfaced on Tyler and Bradley's disappearance?"

Silence greets me, and I take that as my answer until. "You really made this too easy. You're too trusting of the law."

All the color drains from my face, and I reach for the handle, pressing my back against the seat. "What do you mean? Where are you taking me?

He glances at me, his knuckles white against the steering wheel. "You can't escape. I'm the only one who can open your door. So sit back and get comfy until we get to our destination."

We pass the police station, driving out of the town towards the unknown, every hair on my arm standing on edge. "Where are you taking me?" I yell, banging against the iron gate that separates us as I look for my phone before remembering I left it in our room. *That's why we didn't know anyone entered the property.*

I lay down and point my legs towards the window attempting to kick it, but before I can even try he pulls his gun out and points it at me, his finger resting on the trigger. "I wouldn't try that if I were you. I was ordered to bring you in; I wasn't told you needed to be unharmed." I glare at him and sit back, scared for my life for the first time. "That's better. Now sit there and be quiet, we will be there soon."

Not wanting to risk getting shot, I stay silent thinking of all the training Aster has given me as I desperately plan my escape.

CRIME SCENE - DO NOT CROSS · CRIME SCENE

BLACK LOTUS

EXCLUSIVE

ASTER

SOLITUDE

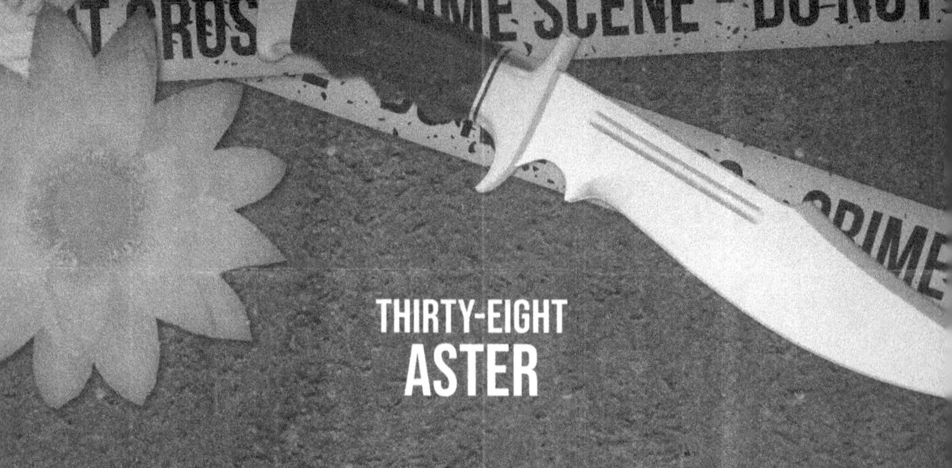

THIRTY-EIGHT
ASTER

Something is wrong. My bones ache, and there's a nagging in the back of my head, a voice screaming that I need to act before it's too late. *I should trust in my instincts.* Especially since every unanswered text is just another distraction as my anxiety rises. The stupid emotion won't seem to leave me alone, like a gnat you just want to swat away and kill, but can't seem to. *I hope, after all of this is over, I can go back to the psychopath empathy-free killer I am.*

I check my texts, *again*, my phone trembling as I send another one, hoping this is the one she will answer.

ASTER

Hey, how is it going?

Serena? Is everything okay?

Answer me. Your silence is driving me crazy.

Okay. I'm worried now. Answer me. Please

It's been over an hour since you left; are you still at the police station? What's taking so long?

Call me when you see these messages or so help me vixen, I will come down there and drag you out myself.

"Fuck!" I yell, throwing my phone and dragging my hands through my hair. I watch numbly as the useless piece of plastic bounces off of the couch and clatters onto the floor.

She's safe. I keep trying to convince myself as I pace the living room, glancing at the clock and watching the dial tick slowly by. *Has the clock always moved so slow?*

Jason Wiley, my fingers curl into fists so tight my knuckles go white, he always made snide comments about me looking familiar and was a part of every investigation that pointed in my direction. He is a cop. He is the *good* guy. Serena is safe at the police station, and if they arrest her for anything, I will just bail her out and find a way to clear her of all charges. *If I can't do that we'll just flee the country.*

Sitting around and doing nothing isn't doing me any favors. Sighing heavily to breath out some of the tension does nothing, so I grab my phone and walk up to our room. "Fuck," I mutter as I walk in and see Serena's phone sitting on the bed. *No wonder she hasn't answered me.*

I search for the station number to see how much longer it will be. If her questioning takes any longer, I'm going to drive down there, give her phone to her, explain they can continue tomorrow, and take her home.

The line rings a couple times as I pace the room before an automatic woman on the other end talks. "Salem Police Station, if this is an emergency, hang up and dial 911; if not, please press one to be connected to a member of our staff."

I press one, my fingers tightening around my phone as I wait. "Hello, this is Claire. How may I help you today?"

"My girlfriend Serena Raven, was taken in for questioning by Deputy Wiley a little over an hour ago and she forgot her phone here. I was wondering how much longer she will be there and if I should bring her her phone."

"Hold please." I hear her nails click against the keyboard as her mouth smacks what I can only assume is gum. She said hold, but hearing her and muffled voices on the other end isn't really putting me on hold; *where is the music or the silence?* My jaw clenches as I wait listening to the annoying sounds.

"Shit." I hear her whisper before the line switches to the annoying music I was waiting for. *I guess she finally realized that she never actually put me on hold.* I collapse on the bed, the spring squeaking as I lay there, staring at the ceiling and wait for her annoying voice to come back on the line.

"Hello, sir?" her voice interrupts the shitty music.

"Yes, I'm here," I say, sitting up.

"I'm sorry, but Deputy Wiley wasn't scheduled to work today. I checked with the other officers, and he never brought anyone in. Are you sure you were told the correct information? Maybe someone else brought your girlfriend to a different police station?"

The pit in my stomach grows and drops all at once, my voice sounding like a robot as to not give anything away. "Thank you. I was probably given the wrong information."

Hanging up, a deep guttural roar rips from my throat as I throw the phone, watching it smash into pieces on the floor. *She was taken.* She was taken because we were both foolish and thought a cop could never hurt her. Of course, Cynthia has a cop on that damn list of hers.

Any cop could go dirty if offered enough money, and with everyone else dead, he will get the most money if he succeeds.

I don't think, I just act, ripping the bedding off of the bed, and smashing the side tables to pieces, tossing the dresser, and breaking everything in my line of sight.

My chest rises and falls in deep breaths as I look at the aftermath of my rage. At the result of my stupidity, my *stubbornness* at refusing to listen to my gut and going with her.

He drove a personal car. I didn't even think it was strange. Most police officers drive unmarked vehicles now. If he's smart, which it seems like he is, he would have made it untraceable.

I fall to my knees, retrieving the laptop to find out any clues and praying it was spared from my wrath. I may not be a genius hacker like Zephira- My breath catches. "Zephira," I whisper.

"Yes, brother?"

I clutch my chest, the laptop falling off my lap. "Fuck! Where did you come from?"

"I heard you whisper my name," she muses, crossing her arms as she stands by the door, looking at me with a knowing smirk. "Does this mean Serena is fair game now?"

She fucking knows. I spring off the floor, striding towards her and wrapping my hand around her throat as I slam her against the wall. My grip tightens with each word. "Where. Is. She?"

She struggles to breathe, her answer gargled. "Who?"

"You know who," I growl, watching her face turn blue.

She claws at my hands, silently begging for release, I toss her to the ground, my body begging for her blood. But I won't kill my sister, not until I have answers. I don't want to kill her, if I'm being honest, but if anything happens to Serena, I will end her.

She coughs, as she looks up at me and laughs. *Is she fucking kidding me? She has the balls to laugh in my face right now?* I kick her stomach, smirking as she grunts.

"I'm not fucking around, Zephira! Tell me where she is!"

She looks up at me, wiping the spit from her mouth with a crazed, unbelieving look in her eyes. "You kicked me," she says more as a statement than a question. "You kicked your little sister. Not even Serena-"

I lift her by her shirt, her feet dangling helplessly in the air. "Don't. Say. Her fucking. Name."

Taunting me like the little girl she is, her lips start to form Serena's name. My vision goes red and before she can utter a word, I slam my fist into her gut.

"If you don't want me to throw you down those stairs, you better start talking."

She looks over her shoulder at the stairs that may not kill her but will do some damage and presses her lips into a thin line.

"Speak!" I demand, my face twisting into a ruthless snarl, my muscles tight as I bare my teeth.

I feel no remorse hurting her like this. I would do worse if I had the time to bleed the answers out of her, but I don't know what that dirty deputy has done or where he has taken her, so brute force is my only tool.

"Ask nicely," she rasps.

Is she fucking with me right now? I hold her body over the staircase like a ragdoll, showing how serious I am, but no ounce of fear shines in her eyes as she waits for what I'll do next. My head flinches back at her brazen personality as I start to see how much we are alike, our similarities really starting to shine in the face of danger.

I growl as I bring my hand over my face. "Will you *please* tell me where Serena was taken?" I grind out, annoyed with our little game. But if this is the only way to gain any answers, then I will play. *I would do anything to find Serena.*

"See? Was that so hard?" My hand tightens in her shirt, and I wish it was her throat I was squeezing. "Put me down so we can have a nice discussion like adults."

"There is nothing to discuss! Just tell me where she is!" I scream, spit flying into her face.

"Uh huh." She shakes her head at me, an impossible smirk on her face. "I'll only tell you if you're nice. And big brother," she smacks my cheek a couple times and my muscles strain with my desire to chuck her down the stairs, "you're not being nice."

"Fine." I place her down as nicely as I can, watching her fight to regain her balance.

"Say sorry."

I stare at her, my mouth open and my fists clenched, refraining myself from killing her. "I'm... I'm sorry."

"For?" She prolongs the word.

I'm sorry I'm growing tired of this stupid game and am about to murder you is what I want to say, but instead I relent and apologize. "For throwing. Kicking. And… Punching you," I mutter.

She turns her back and walks down the stairs. "All your questions will be answered soon."

I should have just snapped her neck. I asked nicely and that's all she is going to tell me? I stomp down the stairs after her, gripping her arm and forcing her to stop. "That wasn't the answer to what I asked."

She shrugs. "That's the answer you're getting. Be patient and you can see her again."

Her fingers peel back mine and she walks to the kitchen acting like she owns my house, grabbing something from the fridge. I slam the door closed as she pulls out a water, my hand resting above her head as I look down at her. "I don't have time. Serena doesn't have time." She glances away, swallowing slowly. *I knew she cared.* "Now, if you know where she is, *tell me*, otherwise, I will be the last person you ever see."

"We both know without me you'll never get to her. You can't kill me, Aster, and that's killing you." She ducks under my arm and plops down on the couch, patting the spot next to her. "Come sit. I don't want to miss the look on your face when you get invited to the show."

The show? What the hell is she talking about? What ticket? Will there be others watching? *I will kill anyone in my way if this show has anything to do with hurting Serena.* Spilling the blood of everyone in my way as I slash through body after body to get to my vixen.

Reluctantly, I sit beside my sister and wait. Zephira holds all the cards, and she and I both know it.

"Let's watch some TV." She grabs the remote and flips through until she lands on the station she was searching for.

What I see on the screen has all the blood draining from my

face. *No!* I jump to my feet, taking a step towards the TV. *No, no, no; it can't be. This has to be another trick. A lie. This can't be true.*

"That's the face I was talking about." She takes out her phone and snaps a picture. "Your ticket should be here soon."

The doorbell rings and I don't hesitate, rushing to answer it. All that greets me is a sleek black box. *How did the messenger get past my cameras?* I look back at Zephira as she holds up her phone showing my system on it and smiles. *Of course she deactivated it.* With shaking hands, I reach down and open the latch, seeing a ticket to Graves. All thoughts dissipate as I drop the box, turning around to grab my keys.

"Oh look! It's your ticket. Now you have your answer." She walks down the steps, looking back over her shoulder. "Are you coming? I thought you wanted to get the girl."

CRIME SCENE - DO NOT

THE BLACK LOTUS

EXCLUSIVE
EXCLUSIVE
EXCLUSIVE

SERENA

SOLITUDE

CROSS

CRIME

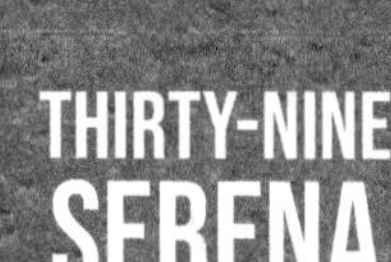

THIRTY-NINE

SERENA

W ho would have thought the person supposed to serve and protect would be the one to kill me and finish the job? Irritation boils in my veins as I struggle against my restraints, trying to piece together a plan to escape, run, anything besides staying an obedient little captive. When he came to get me from the back seat, I was ready to head-butt him right in the gut, but he snatched me by my hair and dragged me out. I wanted to fight but the moment his gun pressed against my back I froze as he quickly secured my wrists with zip ties. *I'm shocked he didn't blindfold me and let me see where he took me.* When I got out of the car, I didn't know where I was at first since only seeing an empty dirt parking lot, lights off to an entrance of some sort. It wasn't lit up and nothing was fully done, but once we got to the entrance, I saw the big sign for Graves Haunted House and my heart soared.

I wanted to say a snide comment about taking me to Aster's place, that he would surely find me and cut off his balls for being stupid enough to bring me to his sanctuary, but I thought better of it, Jason's cold steel was still digging into my spine.

Best to stay quiet in a situation where you don't know your oppo-

nent. Heading deeper into the grounds, all thirteen houses are bare. With everything we've been dealing with, he hasn't had time to think about what the houses will be this year. He told me once this was all over, we would sit down and design everything together. I feel tears threatening to spill over at the thought that our vision won't come true. That this *pig* will be the one to succeed and take me away from Aster.

We walk through the forest, through each abandoned house, finally stopping at the last one. There are old chains hanging from the ceiling, ones that were forgotten or maybe ones to be used again. *Who knows; maybe Dirty Cop was the one to hang them.* An attempt to give his little lair a creepier feel to it.

I snicker at the thought.

"Is something funny to you?" Jason asks, ramming his gun into me harder.

"Just your futile attempt to make Aster's haunted houses creepy, it is laughable. You know you really should have done your research. I happen to love horro-"

The last word vanishes from my chest as he smacks the back of my head with the barrel of his gun, my knees buckling as I collapse onto the dusty floor, almost face planting as my head spins.

"Keep up that smart ass mouth of yours and I'll show you how scary I can be."

I must have had some kind of stupidity juice this morning because, even though I scream at myself to shut up and stay quiet, I laugh in his face and say, "You don't scare me, *deputy.* If anything, you intrigue me."

He doesn't say anything, but his eyebrows dip in confusion as he holsters his gun.

Why would he pocket his weapon if he was planning on killing or torturing me. I glance around the room, noting there is no other weapon in my line of sight. Not one he could use on me or me use on him. *Guess the chains will be my way out of this mess. If I* know anything about Aster, one if not several of the dangling silver is real, I just need to pinpoint which one I can wrap around his neck. I wiggle my arms as I rub my wrists together, tugging them apart in front of me, but feel nothing except resistance as my shoulders drop. *I will find a way out of this.*

I shake the thought away as I run my mouth again. "Allow me to elaborate. I'm intrigued to find out what faces and sounds you'll make when the roles are reversed. When I get out of here and get-" I ponder the right word, sucking my teeth as a shiver of desire works through me, "-creative with the many ways *I will torture you.*" *I really must have a death wish.*

He kneels down, sitting on his heels and looming over me. "You say you like horror? Will you like it when you're the star of your very own movie?" He smirks as he stands up and walks to the corner of the room, dragging a chair I didn't notice before back to the middle. "Have you ever seen the movie *Jeepers Creepers?*"

Now I'm the one staring at him like he has two heads, but I'm curious to see where he's going with this. "Of course I have. It's a classic."

He pulls me up by my hair, a hiss dying to escape, but I keep my pained feeling locked behind my lips, not wanting to give him any kind of satisfaction. His nostrils flare as he pulls harder, throwing me onto the chair, my head finally getting relief as I almost topple over from the force.

"The screams you hear at the end of that movie won't compare to the ones I plan on ripping from you," he threatens, bracing his arms on the armrests and boxing me in.

He doesn't have his gun on me anymore, and he's in the perfect position. *He may have been smart enough to catch me, but he's too stupid to keep me.* I keep my eyes pinned on him, not giving anything away as I kick out, hitting him right where it hurts.

He curls over me with a yelp of pain, and I headbutt him,

shouldering him onto the floor and rushing towards the exit. *This is my only chance.* My heart pounds as I sprint through the chains. *I need to get free before he can stay true to his threat.*

Stepping into the dark hallway, my body slams into the ground, my head cracking against the floor as Deputy Wiley tackles me. Our bodies spin as we fight for control and, even with all the training Aster gave me, I'm no match for a trained deputy.

I thrash under his weight, kicking my feet up, punching my restrained arms at his face, and just as I'm about to land a hit, he pulls his damn gun stopping all movements. "I suggest," he gasps, his eyes wild, "you be a good little girl and do as you're told, or this will be over rather quickly."

I turn my head, submitting to his threat and laying limp in the dirt.

Grinding my teeth, I'm angry at myself for not being strong enough to take him. My nose burns, begging me to keep fighting. To not give up. *If I had use of my hands, I might have stood a chance.*

He wraps his fingers around my wrist, digging them into my flesh, not bothering to make me stand as he drags me across the floor back to the chair. My legs scrape against the cold concrete, leaving a tiny trail of blood as he tosses me onto the ground just below the spot I fear might be my end.

Pointing the gun at me, he motions towards the chair. "Try that again and I'll put a bullet in your leg. Now, get up," he demands.

Without a sound, I crawl onto the chair, trying to pinpoint the real metal from the decorations, but this room is so poorly lit, bathed in a dull orange I can't tell real from fake. Scanning the walls for a loose nail, I drop my head in defeat, seeing nothing aside for the already bloody and peeling wallpaper, which is no help. There isn't anything around except this chair I'm in. There is not even a shelf I could throw down to slow him down.

"Spread your legs." My head shoots up, eyes widening as I stare at him.

"Excuse me?" I ask, baffled at his demand.

"Spread your fucking legs before I lose my patience."

Is he about to rape me? Sweat beads on my forehead. *That would be far worse than any torture he could do to me.* Him forcing himself on me would break me.

"Please, don't," I breathe as I slam my legs shut.

He grips each calf, digging his nails in to make his point. "Good to know you fear my dick more than my gun." Throwing them open, he secures them in place against the leg chairs. "I'm no rapist," he spits, tying my bonds tighter than necessary. "Even if I was, I prefer my women older and," his lip curls in disgust as his beady eyes trace my body, making me feel exposed, "smaller." I press my lips together to keep from spitting in his face.

Not only is he a dirty cop, but he also shames women for their weight. *Makes me want to cut off his tiny dick and shove it down his stupid throat.* I stare daggers as he tells me not to try anything while he cuts my arms free. *Where did that knife come from?* I glance at the sharp blade and weigh my odds. Could I take the weapon and use it on him before he has a chance to react? I nibble my lip, even though I want to, I know if I do, he would shoot me without a second thought, so I let him wrap my arms behind the chair and trap me in place.

"Oh, look, you *can* follow directions."

I so badly want to carve his skin, my fingers aching for the moment I can retrieve the blade I know Aster keeps in the first house and drag it through his flesh. Glancing towards the darkened hallway, I'm thankful Wiley set up shop here. *He doesn't know all the houses are connected.* I fight a smile. *He doesn't realize how close to his death I am.*

He turns his back and walks away, looking over his shoulder as he says, "Don't go anywhere. I'll be right back." He laughs, his face twisting. "Not that you could."

Is this what Aster had to go through? Will I get the same chance to escape as he did? He told me she wanted him to escape and fight to the death, but Jason doesn't look like he has any plans for me to try anything.

He doesn't want a fair fight; he wants me dead.

THE BLACK LOTUS
SPECIAL EDITION
Daily O...
A DARK ROMANCE
VOL. 10, NO. 5
10 APRIL 2025
EXCLUSIVE
EXCLUSIVE
EXCLUSIVE
Solitude
In these quiet moments, you connect with your thoughts and emotions, gaining insight into your true desires and values. Embracing solitude helps you recharge, enhances mental clarity, and fosters emotional well-being. This introspection nurtures personal growth and cultivates a more balanced and fulfilling life.
CRIME SCENE - DO NOT CROSS
SOLITUDE

CRIME SCENE - DO NOT
THE BLACK LOTUS
EXCLUSIVE
SERENA
SOLIT
SOLITUDE
CROSS
CRIME

FORTY
SERENA

"Wake up!"

Cold water cascades over me, jolting me awake as it drips down my hair and soaks into my clothes. *When did I fall asleep? How did I fall asleep?* I slowly lift my head, looking up at him through my wet hair as I grin. *Guess Jason isn't as much of a threat as my exhausted mind thought he was.*

"What are you smiling about? You're trapped here; you're going to die here," he sneers, looking at me like I've lost my mind.

I shrug, sucking my teeth. "I fell asleep."

His eyebrows pinch together. "Why is that funny?"

"Because…It means you really aren't a threat."

His features morph, confusion twisting into anger, his eyes wide as he slaps me across the face. I don't register the abuse at first, but it has enough force, my head snaps to the side.

I must want to greet death quickly. "You slap like a bitch," I spit, tasting iron on my tongue as I spit at his feet.

Stupidity and bravery go hand in hand, my words making me question my sanity. By the look on his face, I've said the wrong thing, but I can't bring myself to regret it. Laughter fills the room, mine or his I'm unsure, maybe both? As he pummels his fist into every inch of me he can reach, not relenting until my body slumps against my restraints, silence blanketing us as the room spins and copper fills my mouth.

I close my eyes, trying to make him think he knocked me out. I can hear his heavy breathing and feel him standing over me, waiting for me to flinch, to groan. Waiting for proof he didn't go too far. *Waiting to go again.* I keep my head down, not in the mood to be punched any more. Aster taught me the pain of a blade, not fists; he never expected someone to be so blunt in their attack. My body screams for any type of relief as I feel bruises beginning to form. The need to taunt him more, to see how far I can push his control, battles with the need to stay quiet and wait for him to walk away.

Slowly cracking my eyes open, I see his feet still in front of me, so I stay still, forcing my body to remain limp and lifeless. I want to groan, the need to make some type of noise because it feels like he might have cracked a rib. *I guess the bitch was holding back.*

I contemplate talking again, but gaining his attention in any way could lead to more harm. Still, I am curious as to what he's going to do. Aster knows he was the last person I was with, surely he isn't stupid enough to think he wouldn't come looking for me.

Fuck it.

"Hey," I croak when I see his footsteps receding. Looking up, I gather what little saliva I have left in my mouth and say it louder. "Hey!"

He flinches, turning slowly on his heels. "You're still conscious after that?" he asks in disbelief as he stalks back over.

"I have a question for you," I say quietly, swallowing back the blood pooling in my mouth, satiating some of the burn.

He crouches in front of me. Making sure we're face to face. " Oh yeah? What's that?"

"You're not scared?"

His head jerks back, his eyes narrowing in surprise.

"Scared?" he scoffs, "Scared of what? A little girl tied to a chair in a place she can't escape?"

A bloody smile lifts my cheeks as I shake my head. "Not of me, not yet." He barks a laugh, and I wait for him to shut the fuck up. "Aster," I breathe his name, wishing so badly I was whispering it for another reason. Wanting him here punishing this cop and freeing me so we can make him scream together. I pull against my restraints, hoping to instill the fear he has been desperately trying to make me have.

He stands, placing his hands on his knees and crowding me against the chair as he tips his head to the side. "I'm not scared of the Morbid Monet."

Everything else he says fades to the background as all the air in the room is sucked out. *He knows Aster is the Monet?* If he knows his true identity, then why hasn't he locked him up? Aster was never questioned by the cops until he met me. He was safe until he started breaking his rules for me. *Am I the reason this little bitch figured out who he was?*

Tears slip free from my swollen eyes as a sob bubbles up, begging to be heard. He snaps his fingers in my face, his lip curling, aware I stopped listening. "Why are you crying?" he asks, annoyed.

"Am I the reason you know?" I sniffle.

His face scrunches. "You?" His harsh laugh bounces around the cement cell. "You think you're the reason I know who Aster is? You're not as bright as we thought if you still haven't figured it out."

"We?"

Tension bleeds from my muscles. *I'm not the reason.* He didn't get caught because of me. Not that he is caught, unless this is an elaborate setup to get Aster to come here and kill a cop while the other officers are waiting to come in and arrest us both. *Then why would a whole police force let one bitch cop torture a potential accomplice? And if they had the evidence, why wouldn't they just arrest him?*

No, that isn't it.

"Think, you *stupid* girl."

My breath catches, my ribs aching in protest. "You have a partner."

"And what else? Come on, think."

My eyebrows scrunch as I replay the events that lead to this moment. The moment I met Aster. The moment he killed me and vice versa. The moment Zephira coming into our lives and everything after.

"You're almost there. I can see your brain searching for the answer. Come on, Serena, think harder," he encourages, which confuses me even more.

The desperation in his voice makes me even more determined to figure out everything, but the pain slows my brain, my thoughts sluggish and jumbled.

"Who is the one common denominator in all of this? The one connecting everyone to you," he whispers, his eyes taking on a crazy look.

My eyes widen. "Cynthia."

"Ding, ding, ding! We have ourselves a winner!"

His partner is Aster's mom. Cynthia, the woman who set the hit and wants me dead, has been pulling the strings from the very beginning? No wonder he hasn't turned Aster in; he is working for the very woman who would do anything for her son. How did she get a police officer into her clutches? It can't only be for the money, there has to be more to it.

"Do you want to know how I, Jason Wiley, became partners with the one and only Cynthia Balcom?"

I nod quickly, finding out that was the wrong answer as his fist collides with my mouth again, my teeth cracking from the blow. "Use your words! I refuse to deal with your silence any longer."

"Yes," I quietly say.

With a satisfied smile, he sneers one word. "No."

No? No! After all of that, all the taunting and beatings, he isn't going to tell me? Why ask the stupid question in the first place if he wasn't going to give me anything?

"I think it's best explained coming from the woman herself."

My head snaps up as fear consumes me crawling up my throat, my body going cold with dread. Not when Sharon had me. Not when Aster was taken. None of that compares to hearing the door creak open as heels clack against the floor, becoming louder and louder the closer she gets.

I look away, not wanting to look at the woman. I need to swallow my fear down before she makes me look at her. *How the hell did she escape? How is she here?* Of course, she is the one who will kill me.

Sharp nails dig into my cheeks, tears burning in my eyes as she adds to my bruises. "Look at me, Serena."

Her voice sounds like a succubus, one who truly is evil inside and out. She presses harder and I obey, opening my eyes and I'm met with a woman who looks like an older version of Zephira with Aster's eyes. *Definitely a succubus.* She is truly beautiful, but her black soul makes her so ugly not even her beauty can hide the darkness her energy produces.

"So this is the one who has bewitched my darling little fox."

THE BLACK LOTUS

Finding peace in solitude is not about isolation but about creating a sacred personal space where you can reconnect with your own needs and aspirations...

Regular solitude fosters deeper self-discovery and personal growth. In these quiet moments you build resilience, gain new perspective, and strengthen your inner self... solitude as a tool for... body, and soul... and purpose...

FORTY-ONE
SERENA

Her fox? Her fox! Is she delusional? Aster hasn't been hers since she abandoned him when Kara turned them in. I suck in a sharp breath, trying desperately to conceal my rage. Her breath, which is surprisingly minty fresh, wafts over my face as she lifts a strand of my wet hair and examines it before dropping it and wiping her fingers on her pants.

"You did quite the number on her." She glances at him over her shoulder, her frustration obvious, then looks back down at me, her eyes scanning every part of my broken and bruised body as her lip curls in disgust. "I truly don't know what my son sees in you. Jason!" she snaps her fingers, "Get me my knife."

"Are you flirting with me?" I say, her head whipping around as I look up at her.

Jason scrambles to retrieve what she's asked for while Cynthia stares through me. "Jason did say you had a smart mouth on you, but I didn't think you were stupid enough to use it against me."

"Guess I have a death wish."

"You certainly do. Jason!" she screeches, crossing her arms over her chest and tapping her nails along her arms. "Useless man," she mumbles.

She doesn't have much patience for someone who has waited a long time to be free. Jason had to have helped her escape, unless she has other cops in her clutches, maybe even the warden of the prison she was held at. Chilled to the bone at the thought. *How else would she have escaped? Did they help Aster's dad escape too?*

Jason stumbles back into the room, tripping over himself as he runs to get back to Cynthia. She snatches her knife out of his hand, nicking him in the process as he cradles it to his chest and bows his head at her, stepping out of her space like she's some kind of queen. *What is she feeding this man for him to worship and cower away from her at the same time?*

She points the tip of the blade towards me, the edge gleaming as it catches the light. "Now, you're probably wondering what I will do with this, right?" She brings her wrist to her forehead, dropping the knife to her side as she dramatically speaks in a different voice. "Will she kill me? Will I get out of here alive? Can I escape her evil clutches?" She tips her head back and pretends to cry. "What can I do?"

She really loves being the center of attention. I roll my eyes at her dramatics as she uses a voice she thinks sounds like mine, putting on a show. *She must've been alone for too long in that cell of hers.*

"Is that supposed to be me?" I ask.

She swings her head up, pointing the knife at me again as she looks at me with crazy eyes that make me shiver. Not from fear, but from the heebie-jeebies as I shift uncomfortably in my seat. She's like a woman out of one of my favorite movies, utterly demented and possessed. The ones you see standing in a hall wearing a nightgown and a smile too stiff to be real.

"What? You didn't like my performance? You wound me, Serena." She waves the knife towards me. "Enough of that nonsense. Shall I tell you why I started this whole thing?" She motions around the room with her last words.

I roll my eyes and she's in my face in an instant, the tip of her blade sliding into my neck as a small drop of blood forms and drips down. "Don't be so rude, my dear. You don't have a choice in the matter. I am going to tell you my story, and you are going to sit there and listen like a good little lamb. Then, when I ask you a question, you are going to answer without a smart ass remark or there will be consequences." She grabs my cheeks again, forcing me to look her in the eye. "Am I making myself clear?"

"Yes," I grind out.

"Yes, *what*?" she asks, the knife digging more into my flesh.

"Yes, Cynthia."

She removes the blade from my neck and smacks my cheek with the flat side. "Good girl."

My skin crawls. *That is not the kind of praise I want to hear coming out of her mouth.* If I get out of here. If by some miracle I am found in time, and when the tables are turned on her, I will spit those same words back in her face to see how she likes it.

"Now, where was I? Oh yes! Why am I doing all of this?" she throws her arms wide, encompassing the bullshit that's taken over my life. "It's simple really; no one is good enough for my boy. Especially a girl who was meant to be his lamb."

I chuckle, lifting an eyebrow at her as I shake my head. "Too bad for you, I am his *vixen*."

I bite my lip, copper filling my mouth as fire explodes through my leg. *Now I know how Jessica felt.* She leaves her blade there, her grip around the handle turning her knuckles white.

"Didn't I tell you not to back talk or sass me?"

I don't say anything, fearing that if I open my mouth a scream would rip through and the last thing I want is her satisfaction from my pain.

"Answer me, or I'll dig this knife further into your leg." She wiggles it a little, my teeth cracking as I hold back my tears. "Or maybe I'll drag it down and slice you open."

"Yes," I grit through my teeth.

"Yes *what*?"

Not this shit again. I don't take my eyes off of Cynthia as I try to concentrate on anything except the pain. Breathing in slowly through my nose, parting my lips slightly as I blow out, not letting her see the small act. If she didn't hold all the power, I wouldn't be backing down so easily. If the roles were reversed, I'd tie the cop up like the pig he is and take inspiration from Zephira, cooking him until his flesh bubbles and burns. Then I'd force Cynthia to eat him and kill her after, but how to kill her…

The knife is ripped from my leg, my mouth parting as an agonizing scream echoes around the room. My leg shakes uncontrollably from the pain, a satisfied smirk lifting her cheeks as my blood drips down her blade. She swipes her finger through it and smears it across my lips, the crimson liquid slipping through the cracks even though I keep my mouth pressed closed in a firm line.

"Now, where was I before you so rudely interrupted? Ah yes, you not being good enough for Aster. You see, I worked so hard to fix his brain as a little boy. He watched and learned as we bonded over horror movies." She paces slowly in front of me, the blade mimicking her movements. While Jason stands creepily in the corner watching her like the world begins and ends with her.

Someone please take me out of this misery.

She turns, asking a question, I know she doesn't want an answer to. "I was a good mother, right?" She shakes her head, mumbling to herself, "Yes, yes I was. I was the best mother he could've ever had."

Cynthia twirls the blade through her fingers, her comfort and practice obvious. "He would never kill an animal, did you know that? The start of every serial killer's journey and he wouldn't do it. That worried me. If he couldn't kill a helpless beast, how was he going to kill a human? Take the life owed to his greatness and skill?" She begins watching me again, standing eerily still as if she just remembered I was in the room. Hearing he refused to end the life of an innocent animal proves he isn't the monster she desperately wants him to be. I imagine a small Aster being told to kill a small animal and how his refusal made Cynthia mad enough that steam came out of her ears. I smile with pride knowing my Fox has lines he still won't cross. "I thought he was defective, because no son of mine would be too weak to kill."

Closing my eyes, I will my tears away, my heart aching at the thought of what Aster had to go through before he was thrown into that hell of an orphanage. *She's a monster.* Could he tell his mother didn't like him? That she wanted him to be something he wasn't? I picture a small Aster again, this time him wanting to be loved and willing to do anything to gain his mother's attention. That hurts more than any cut from the beast that birthed him.

Her hands brace either side of my chair, her teeth glinting under the light. "But all was not lost. I saw the way his eyes lit up when someone was killed in a movie. I knew there was hope, a chance to turn him into what he was born to be." She pushes herself back up as she places the tip of the knife to her lips, my drying blood touching her skin. *She can't stand to touch me, but has no problem with my blood?* "So I did what worked with every child; told them they couldn't do something, which obviously made him want to do it more."

There are a lot of evil people in this world, but Cynthia is at the top of that list right alongside pedophiles. I sneer at the woman in front of me, who seems to think she is untouchable. I'll show her just how delusional she is, as soon as I get out of these bindings. I tug against the zip ties, irritation rising with small movement my body can handle. *Why didn't I think of asking Aster to teach me how to escape these damn things.* There has to be a way.

How could she want her own child to kill with her? Did her husband feel the same? He had to since they were partners. Both of them make me sick. I need to figure out a way out of here, but the blood is still pooling against my jeans, my body is becoming weaker with every passing second. *I could take one of them, but I couldn't take both.* Not now. Especially since Jason has a gun.

"One night, I told Aster that Daddy and I were taking our friend to the barn and he couldn't come." She laughs with a sigh.

"You should have seen him. He wanted to listen so badly, but he was curious. I'm sure even someone like you knows curiosity gets the best of us all. And my Aster was such a good boy, until he wasn't. One night he decided to follow us. I heard him coming before he peeked through the hole; he wasn't as stealthy as he is now." She stops walking, taking her heels off one at a time. "My feet are killing me; I don't know how some women wear these. Jason!" she snaps, and he comes running to her side.

"Yes, Cynthia?"

She sits on the dirty floor, spreading her legs as she stabs the knife into the floor beside her. "My feet are killing me."

She doesn't even have to ask, in an instant he's on his knees, pulling her leg over his lap, and massaging her bare feet. My lip curls in disgust as I look away, setting my attention on the chains as I look for a real one again. I smile when I see the glint from a real one swaying right above Cynthia. *Bingo.* I look back down unable to contain my grin as Jason rubs up her leg. *He really is a little bitch; guess the name suited him perfectly.*

"What are you smiling about?" Cyhthia moans, tipping her head back as she side eyes me.

Shit. I quickly mask my features. "Nothing."

"I know you're lying, but I don't care at the moment. Lie to me again, though, and I'll make you bleed more. Aster wasn't as stealthy as he thought."

Oh, great, she's back to talking. I thought I'd get some time to plot an escape somehow, but the cunt apparently loves to hear her own voice.

"When I knew he was watching, I made the kills extra… bloody. He would come out every time and watch until I had to scold him one night, tell him no more watching. Of course, I knew he wouldn't listen, but that led to him finally asking why we killed and shyly saying he wanted to try." She kicks her feet and Jason drops them, scurrying back to his corner as she stands, keeping her heels off. "I was so excited. This was the moment I was waiting for! I wanted to hand him a victim right then and there, but his *father*," she says with a sour tone, "said we had to wait until his tenth birthday. Unfortunately, that fight between Adam and I ended in him winning." My eyebrows dip slightly in confusion. *Is Aster's dad not all that bad?*

Something resembling regret crosses her features, but she quickly masks it, picking up the knife and twirling it once more. "I'm sure Aster told you what happened; how I was blindsided when that stupid girl, Kara, teamed up with my husband to entrap us both."

My mouth falls open. *I'm sorry, what?* Her *husband* helped Kara send them both away? *Why would he want to be locked up forever?* They were the best killing duo of all time, and Aster's father-

"I didn't know at first, that my dear Adam was behind our capture, but once I found out, I set my plans in motion." She slices the blade across her finger and watches with a blank expression as the blood drips down her finger. "Adam claimed he didn't want our son like us, that he didn't even know Aster was watching us work. He only found out when Aster asked, and the only reason he agreed to ten was so he had time to try and fix him." She sticks her finger in her mouth, popping it out as her knuckles turn white around the handle.

"My husband went behind my back and tried to get Aster to understand that what we were doing wasn't good, that we were bad people, but my sweet fox was too far gone. There was nothing the dead weight attached to us could do to turn him back." She raises her hand to the light, staring at the spot her wedding ring used to be. "We didn't speak after we were arrested. Not until I found out I was pregnant and I knew that would get him back on my side. Back to obeying me. I told him and to no one's surprise he was a sobbing mess, begging for my forgiveness, which I gave. When Zephira was born, I knew I'd never get to see her again, I knew I couldn't give her the same upbringing I gave Aster, and that made me angry at Adam all over again."

Everyone assumed Adam was the mastermind, the one forcing his wife to do unspeakable crimes, but just like a lion, the lioness was the one who was truly in charge. My hand twitches wanting to reach up to cover my aching heart. He was her cover up, but he made sure she couldn't hurt Aster any more than she had.

Adam is a good dad; he was just poisoned by his evil wife.

"I was devastated, and during my horrible depression, sweet, young, innocent Jason found me." She looks at her personal servant, his eyes lighting up like a puppy. "He may not look like it," she walks over and pinches his cheek, "this handsome fella is a lot older than he looks. He has been so good to me despite everything we've been through." His cheek pulls out as she drags him, letting go and leaving him by the door when she walks back towards me. "He helped me from the beginning, keeping tabs on Aster and my sweet Zephira. With what that poor girl went through, there was no need for me to push her to be evil. The ones taking care of her were doing that for me."

"What happened to Zephira?"

Her gaze locks mine as she stalks towards me with lethal intent. "Did I say you could speak?"

"No."

"Then why did you?" She drags her blade slowly across my cheek, drawing a line of blood. "You're lucky I was going to ask if you wanted to know or else this would be worse." She licks the blood from my cheek, and I have to swallow the vomit threatening to spill as her slimy tongue touches my skin.

"My sweet Zephira was tortured, raped, beaten, chained, and so much more I don't have time to go into all the glorious details. But I let it all happen. I needed it to because when she was old enough, she killed them all and the Man Eater was born."

"You knew your daughter was getting raped and you just let it happen?" Disgust fills me as my lip curls.

"Some sacrifices had to be made." She shrugs, playing with her blade like her daughter's innocence never mattered.

"If Zephira knew this, she'd hate you."

"Too bad she will never believe you over her dear sweet mother."

"There is nothing sweet about you. Even your husband knew that."

"Well, he's dead, so his opinion doesn't matter either."

"Dead?" I whisper in disbelief.

"Oops! Guess the cats out of the bag. Yes, I had Jason kill Adam once he found out I was trying to puppeteer our children's life again. He wanted his son to be happy with *you*, and, well, I didn't."

I struggle against my binds, my body pushing forward as I scream, "They will never forgive you!" How could she take away the one person who actually cared about them and wanted them happy? *They need to know.*

She motions for Jason with her finger and he obeys instantly. She walks behind him, whispering and looking at him. "Why would they need to forgive me? I didn't kill him. Jason did."

"Under your order!"

"Yes, but they'll never know that. All they'll know is that their dear, darling mommy killed daddy's killer." Jason's eyes widen as she plunges her knife into his neck and drops him like a sack of potatoes.

This was her plan all along; get a cop who could somehow get her free, to kill her husband, then pin all of it on him as she rides off into the sunset after she kills me. Aster would never forgive her, she has to know that. *She would lose both of her children if they found out the truth.* They're not dumb; they'll find out. They have to-

Stepping over him, she stops in front of me, leaning over me once more. "Finally, we are alone."

CRIME SCENE - DO NOT CROSS

BLACK LOTUS

EXCLUSIVE

ASTER

SOLITUDE

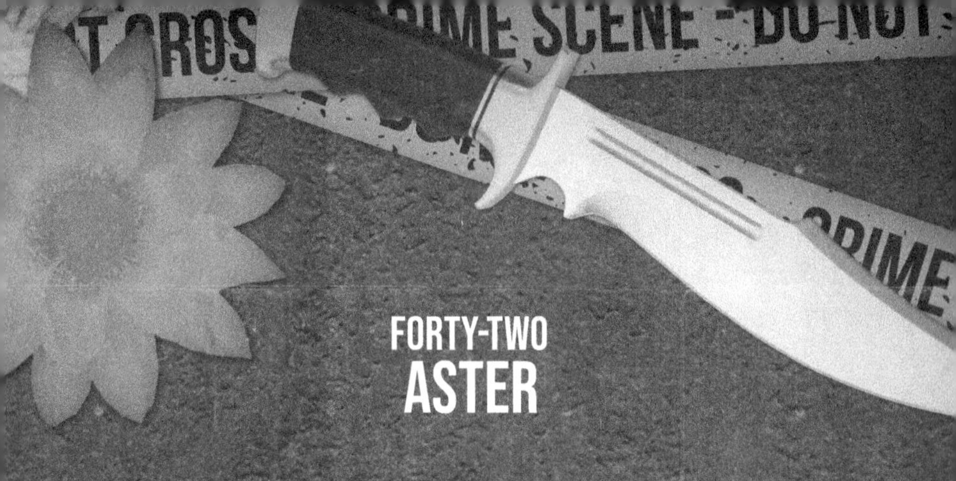

FORTY-TWO
ASTER

Zephira is crumbling, her body trembling as her hands cover her mouth and her eyes fill with unshed tears. Cynthia signed her own execution; there's no coming back. If Zephira was her puppet, those strings are permanently cut after hearing the awful things she let happen to her. If I was Zephira, I'd let my silence be my answer enough for all the revenge I would plot. We are flesh and blood. I look down at my little sister with the sudden urge to shield her from what is unraveling, but I don't. She needs to be on our side. *This is the only way.* I feel bad having to use Zephira's pain to my advantage, but I'll do whatever it takes to save Serena.

As much as I want to barge in, I keep my feet planted, no matter how badly my body fights to push forward. I know that would be the wrong choice. We're dealing with Cynthia and she's smart, smarter than either of us realized. The only way any of us will get out of this alive is by working together. I just hope Zephira will snap out of the state she's in and help me help Serena.

I know she just killed Jason, which means she's alone with Serena.

I don't have much time.

I grip Zephira's shoulders. "Look at me," I whisper, dragging us out of earshot. "You heard all of that, right? Cynthia doesn't care about us. She let those terrible things happen to us to create the monsters she was unable to." Her lip trembles, tears streaking down her cheeks. "I need your help, Sister."

Her glassy eyes look at mine, surprise drawing her brows together. Her eyes clear as I tell her my plan, determination straightening her posture. I squeeze her shoulders, making my intent clear. "Can I rely on you? Will you help me save Serena?"

She nods, and I sink into the shadows, leaving her to play my part in this mission.

I step through the door, holding up my ticket between two fingers and forcing myself to walk further into the room despite seeing Serena tied, bleeding, and beaten behind Cynthia. Every instinct in my body screams at me to run to my vixen's side, to wrap her in my arms and get this over with, but I know that is what Cynthia is expecting. I *need to stay calm. I need to follow through with the plan.*

"Wanting to reunite at the place I've made my own, with my girlfriend's head on the line? You have a lot of audacity, *Mother*."

Cynthia spins around, her bloody knife streaking through the air, looking like she hasn't aged a day while locked away. It's unnerving considering all the years that have gone by. *Seriously, was she getting injections of youth in prison?* She looks exactly the same as the last time I saw her minus the small crinkles around her eyes and a few strands of grey hair.

"My little fox, you came!"

"What did you do to Serena?" I ask, not taking my eyes off the predator challenging me.

She looks over her shoulder, then back at me. "Your little girlfriend has quite the mouth on her; she needed to be taught not to talk back and only speak when spoken to." She twists her blade, her eyes softening at the glittering red hue. "It took a couple of punishments, but she eventually learned to keep her mouth shut."

Don't look at her. Don't look at her. My hands ball into fists at my sides, my fingernails piercing my palms as I grit my teeth, and watch my mother's every move. If she sees I care about Serena as much as I do, things will get worse for her. The quick glance I got at her when I came in showed me she isn't in too bad of a shape. The wound on her leg looks like the worst of what Cynthia has done to her. *I hope she hasn't lost too much blood.*

"That's not the way to get her to listen." My eyes darken as the memories of making Serena submit to me play through my mind.

"I am your mother, Aster; I don't need to be hearing about your sex life with one of your little lambs." She walks behind Serena, placing the tip of the blade against her neck and my body twitches forward. "Do you fuck all your lambs? Take after Mommy and Daddy with that, too? That was my favorite part, besides the kill, of course. Getting to fu-"

"No. I don't fuck any of my victims. Never have. Never will."

She picks up a strand of Serena's hair matted in her blood. "But you did. She is living proof." A cheshire grin lifts her cheeks as she inhales her scent.

"She was never meant to be a lamb." I grit out, my fingers twitching with the need to snatch that knife and plunge it into Cynthia. "Serena has been, and always will be, my vixen. She will never fall to the same fate as the others. Not by my hands or yours." I steal a glance at Serena, her eyes shining with love and unshed tears.

"That, my dear son, is where you are *wrong*." She steps away from Serena and walks closer to me, my body bracing for the moment her hand lays gently across my cheek. The little boy who wanted this from his mother for so long wants to lean into her touch, but the man I became when I was abandoned, overpowers that boy and instead moves away.

She frowns, but steps back, allowing me my space. "Serena was always meant to die by your hands. She brainwashed you, my little fox. You were perfect until you met her." She steps behind me, whispering across the back of my neck, "Think about it."

I do. I think about the moment I first laid eyes on Serena. The moment we shared our first kiss. Our first touch. Our first fuck. The moment my heart started to beat and I felt more alive than I ever have before. I think about every single moment, good and bad, spent with the woman who shows me every day what it means to be loved. Loved in our dark, twisted, fucked up way. *There isn't a thing I would want to change.*

"You started to change when you met her. You started breaking your rules."

She knew I didn't fuck my lambs yet asked me anyway just to try to get under my skin. *Calculating woman.*

"You let her into your home, tainting it, changing it. Changing you."

She stands in front of me, her back to Serena. *The moment I've been waiting for, the distraction I needed.* I knew she would want my full attention while she tried to sway me with her words. Which gives Zephira the moment she needs to enact her side of our plan. *I just hope she does.*

"Serena helped form me into the man I was destined to become. Helped steer me away from the killer you wanted me to be." Cynthia's brows crease as her lips purse. "You want me to kill the woman I love. You want me to be alone again. Do you know what your rejection did to me?" I slam my hand against my chest, the ache growing as I let out the words I've been dying to tell her for so long. "Do you know how long I waited to see you and Dad only to be turned away? Told my parents didn't want to see me? Is that true? Did Dad turn me away, or was it all you?"

"It was us both."

"I don't believe you." I sneer hovering over her until our chests touch. "Now because of you," I spit, "I'll never get the chance to ask him."

Her eyes widen for a fraction of a second before her calculated mask smooths her features. "I killed the man responsible for your father's death." She glances at the dead body behind me. "Jason killed your father, he was desperate to have me all to himself, and when I found that out, I had to get revenge."

"Cut the shit. I heard your confession. I know you told him to kill Dad. I know Dad didn't want me to be a killer, so he teamed up with Kara to set the trap that took you both down. I know he wanted me to be happy with Serena."

Cynthia sighs and places her hand under her elbow, her chin resting delicately in the other. "And yet, even after your father helped Kara, she went after you. Why? And you're here, which means she must be dead. Now neither of us will ever know."

"I don't care about that! What I care about is *her*. Ending this bullshit once and for all. Why did you want your children to become killers? Did you even love us?" The last part makes my voice crack. Part of me wants to know the truth, the other part wants to stay oblivious. Her actions have always spoken louder than the lies she covered and I am not some impressionable little boy she can manipulate anymore. I need to hear the words leave her lips. I need her to hammer the final nail into her coffin. I need to kill her.

"Love?" she laughs, wiping a tear from her eye. "Oh, my dear, sweet boy. That is where we differ. True sociopaths don't know what it means to love. Lust and deception? Pretending to love? That is what I am. Where I shine. And as your mother, I wanted so badly for you to be the same. You *and* your sister. I was hoping with your training and her trauma, I'd killed every trace of that incessant emotion, but it seems a little flicker remained, and your *lamb* reignited it completely. That's why-"

The words get lost on her tongue as she turns around and sees Serena free and leaning against Zephira.

CRIME SCENE - DO NOT CROSS
CRIME SCEN
BLACK LOTUS
EXCLUSIVE
EXCLUSIVE
EXCLUSIVE
ASTER
SOLITUDE
SOLITUDE
SOLITUDE
SOLITUDE
CROSS
CRIME SCENE - DO NOT CROSS

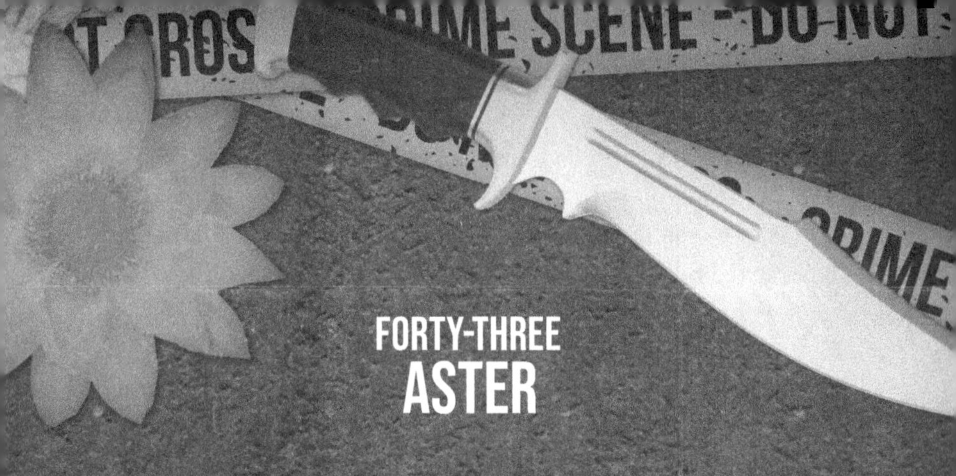

"What is this?" Cynthia looks back at me utterly dumbfounded as she turns back around, glaring at Serena sitting back down in her chair, free. She looks at Zephira, lifting her hand and reaching towards her. "Zephira, honey, what are you doing? Why would you let Serena go when we worked so hard to catch her?"

Zephira stands with her arms wide, shielding Serena from our mother, not that I would let her get any closer to either of them.

"I heard everything. Why did you kill Daddy? I was just getting closer to him! He was finally letting me visit." Tears stream down her face as she swipes her nose with the back of her hand. "Daddy tried to tell me your intentions weren't good. He said getting Serena out of the way to be a family was a lie. He told me Serena was *good* for Aster, for me, but..." She looks down sniffling, her next words a quiet whisper, "I didn't listen."

I wish she would have listened. I wish she would have told me she existed before Cynthia got her claws into her. I'm glad she is finally seeing the truth that she'd been denied for so long, but I fear what's to come might be too much for her. She just lost our dad, a man who I wish I could speak to again after learning the truth. A sad smile tips my lips as I think about Zephira, Serena, and I visiting my father in prison. Telling him everything about my life he was denied the privilege to learn. I know he would have loved Serena as much as I do. I know the moment he saw us together he would feel the peace he never got to feel. I wish he would have given me a chance to get to know him.

Cynthia takes a step forward. "Zephira, your father didn't see your potential." Zephira steps away from Serena as Cynthia's body relaxes and mine locks. *Please don't fall for her words*, I silently beg my sister.

"He couldn't see the vision I had for-" Cynthia's words are cut off when Zephira punches her in the face.

I choke out a laugh, but quickly recover from my shock and take that moment to reach up and grab one of the real chains dangling from the ceiling. I wrap it around Cynthia as she stumbles back from the blow and I slam her into my chest, growling into her ear, "Don't you dare go near them," my protectiveness, not only for Serena, but for Zephira taking over. *Weird.* I didn't think I would care about anyone except Serena, but my little sister is starting to grow on me.

"Your father was blinded with love for his children. He couldn't–*wouldn't* see the potential I saw in you both. Without me, neither of you would be the notorious killers everyone fears. Without me, no one would know your names!"

My grip on her tightens as she wiggles against the chain. Zephira screams, flailing her arms around her. "No! Without you, we would have never been traumatized. Without you, Aster wouldn't have had to grow up in an orphanage that tortured him. Without you, I wouldn't have had to grow up locked in a room where the only light I saw was when that man came in and raped me!" Her lip trembles, her pain filling the air. "Without you, we wouldn't be so fucked up and broken," she whispers, her chest heaving. Serena meets my eyes, lifting her chin slightly, as she slowly gets up on wobbly legs, reaching out. Zephira flinches at first, glancing back at Serena, but lets her hold her hand, gripping it so tight the bones protrude.

Cynthia thrashes in my grip, the girls backing up as she tries to break free, but the chains restrict her movements, her scream and gasps echoing around us. I kick the back of her legs, forcing her to crumple to the floor, her blonde hair falling over her face.

"You would have been caught without me," she grunts, her voice barely loud enough to be heard. "The mistakes you both made as you figured out your signatures, and you," she looks up at me, "you made so many mistakes after meeting *her*. I was the one who had Jason cover them all up for you, erase them from existence, and throw the police off your trail. Without me, you'd both be rotting alongside me and your father."

A muscle in my jaw flutters. She may have been the one to keep us from being caught, but she is the reason we crave the kill, the reason we relish in taking a life. *Her protection is just a cover to keep tabs on us.* Locked away, we'd be out of her reach. If we were locked up, she couldn't control everything. With us free she was able to keep tabs on our lives and treat us like a chess piece, moving her pawns to make her stay in control.

The way I kill is because of her. The way Zephira kills is because of her.

We've never been free to make a choice ourselve-

"Don't speak about him after you had him killed!" Zephira yells.

A maniacal cackle fills the stillness. "I should have killed you all before you were born! I should have killed your father sooner." She laughs sadly, shaking her head as false tears drip down her cheeks. "Why are my children so ungrateful?" She groans as her head sways back and forth. "Was I not a good mother? Was I not considerate to keep you both free?"

"No." I wrap my arms around her neck, squeezing until her head lolls to the side, "You weren't."

"Is she dead?" Zephira whispers, taking a cautious step forward as I drop Cynthia to the ground.

"She will be."

I take my syringe out of my pocket and roughly stab the needle into Cynthia's neck. *Can't be too careful with anyone, especially her.* I just want to grab the knife she was using on Serena and plunge that into her instead, but I know I can't be selfish. I need to let the girls join in killing her if they want.

She may have passed out from my hold but waking anytime soon is not an option. I grab some zip ties out of Jason's pocket, pushing his lifeless body out of the way to wrap them around her wrists and ankles.

Even if she wakes before I want her to, she won't be able to move.

I rush to Serena and pull her into my arms as she lets go of Zephira's hand. Inhaling her, I force myself to hold her at arm's length, cupping her cheek, my thumb brushing over the cut on it. She embraces me, nearly falling over from exhaustion, and I lift her, studying her.

She's safe. She's alive. She's here.

Neither of us say anything as she nuzzles into my chest. No words can be said for what happened. I could apologize, but she'd tell me it isn't my fault, and I know she won't want to hear that. It would turn into us consoling one another and the silence says more than words ever could. I brush my hand down her head, my fingers getting stuck in the bloody knotted parts. She doesn't wince away from the pull even though I quickly remove my hand from fear of causing any other kind of pain. She needs a bath and I will be the one to wash her, restraining myself from doing anything else. I kiss the top of her head, her breathing finally evening out as her body relaxes fully into my hold and her eyes fight to stay open.

"Hate to break up the sweet moment, but what are we going to do about Mom?" Zephira asks, pointing her thumb behind her at the unconscious body on the floor.

"Kill her," I state plainly, refusing to let Serena go as I bury my head in her neck and her lips part with a dry giggle. *She needs water and to be bandaged.* It's my turn to take care of her after we take care of Cynthia. I hope her recovery ends with another food sexcapade.

"Obviously, but I don't see anything here we could use to do that besides the knife she brought, and I don't know about you, but after learning the truth, I want her to feel pain."

I look down at Serena, and with a shared look, we both answer at the same time. "Home."

ASTER

SOLITUDE * SOLITUDE

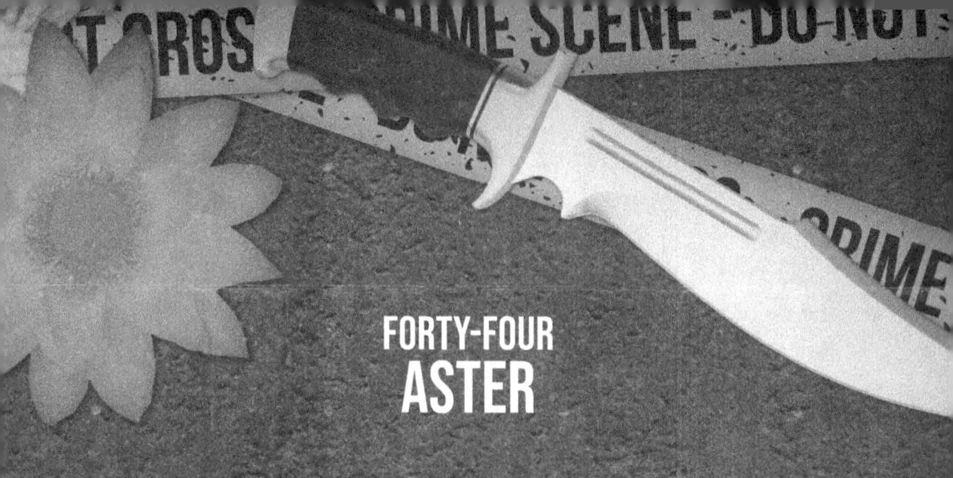

FORTY-FOUR
ASTER

The sky is clear, the moon shining bright as stars twinkle and tease the darkness, the moment of peace we have been working towards finally within reach. We all decided Cynthia would die in my kill space as my final lamb and Zephira's first. Since she has never killed a woman before, I'm going to have her go before me, let her experience the difference.

Luckily, I had a first aid kit under the seat of my car, thanks to my smart and thoughtful vixen, so I was able to clean and patch Serena's wounds before we left. Cynthia lays strapped to my table still sleeping as I help Serena put up the final pieces of plastic over the walls before handing her and Zephira both a brown leather apron.

Setting up my shop and putting the apron on feels nostalgic. It's time I say goodbye to the man I once was, and killing him alongside my mother feels like the perfect end. *She wants me to be the Morbid Monet?* I don't bother hiding the twisted smirk darkening my features. *It's about time she met him.*

With my two girls by my side, I prepare everything like I would for my lambs. Getting out my paints and my rose, I finally open the drawers for us all to select a weapon of choice, one we can pour our hatred into.

She's still fully clothed, because I don't want nor need to see my mother naked, so instead of painting her body, I'll just paint her face.

Finally, I get out the red lipstick my mother hated and swipe the color against her lips. Stirring, she presses her lips together like she knows what's happening.

When her eyes finally open and sees me holding the red tube, she sneers. "How dare you mark your mother's lips like a whore."

"I mark all of my lamb's with the color you despise," I say, capping the lid and handing it to Serena to throw in the incinerator.

She looks around, realizing all three of us stand over her. She rolls her eyes, laying perfectly still, like this doesn't faze her, like she could still escape. But she should know there is no escaping the Monet once he catches you.

"I'm not one of your little lambs."

I pick up the knife behind me, looking at my reflection in it as I speak to her. "Wasn't it you who said I lost who I was?" My gaze meets her own. "Didn't you say I haven't had a lamb since meeting Serena?" I slam the knife down next to her head, making her flinch. "It's time to meet the monster you created." I step to the side, grabbing Serena's hand to help her fill the space between us. "But first, his other half will have some fun with you."

She scoffs. "I'm not scared of your failed kill."

Serena tilts her head and smirks, my cock hardening at the sight. "You're not scared of me, Cynthia?"

Later I will show her how my body reacts to her bloodlust, but now my girl is about to make my worthless mother bleed. I refuse to be distracted by my carnal needs.

"You may have everyone else fooled, but I know how weak you truly are."

"You were the only one I was fooling." Serena lifts her choice of weapon, the flame on the kerosene torch blazing to life. "Do you know what burning flesh on a living corpse smells like?"

Cynthia's eyes widen as she tries to move away from the heat from the flame, the brave face she has been holding on to this entire time slipping when the roles reverse. I stifle the laugh so as to not interrupt Serena's moments as I watch Cynthia try to cower away from the flame. Serena loves to play with fire, and when my vixen is in the zone, there is no stopping her. She knows she can't go too far though, she knows we all get a turn ripping screams from Cynthia's throat.

The first of many screams comes, as if on cue, when the flame licks the flesh on her thigh. Serena holds it there until her skin bubbles and melts, her eyes captivated by the scene, the smell not bothering her one bit as she holds herself up with her other hand braced on the table. Zephira and I have to cover our noses with our shirts to escape some of it.

"Are you scared of me yet?" Serena asks, slowly moving around the table.

No words leave Cynthia's lips, her shrill shrieking making my heart race, and when the flame dies down, so do the screams.

"That was fun, but it was over too quickly. I do wish I had more time to make you regret ever doubting my power, but my time is up." Serena slowly turns, placing the canister down with a pout. "Who's next?"

Zephira steps up, looking down with a snarl. "Me."

We knew the order of who would torture her before we started, but watching my mom fear for what's to come, who is next to make her bleed is what we wanted. We wanted to see fear for who is next.

Zephira's weapon is a twelve inch carving knife; she didn't say what she planned to do with it, but knowing how the Man Eater operates, I have my ideas. To see her eyes so full of hatred at the burnt pile of trash on the table brings me a sense of pride as a small smile lifts my cheeks. She is shining as brightly as Serena did, and the fire in her gaze doesn't show an ounce of regret. I'm grateful to have them both by my side, laying waste to the woman who made all our lives a living hell.

"Mother, it didn't have to be like this. We could have been the family Daddy desperately wanted, but you ruined it." Zephira grips Cynthia's face with a bruising force. "Do you know why they call me Salem's Man Eater?"

"Zephira, baby girl, don't do this; I'm your mother. I love you." Cynthia sobs real tears, not the fake shit we've been greeted with before. *She's finally broken. She knows the end is coming.* Her tears make my fingers twitch, desperate for it to be my turn.

"I make my victims eat the man I killed before them, but I don't have anyone for you to eat," she pouts, tapping the flat of her blade against her cheek, "So, I'll have to settle for you eating yourself."

"Zephi-" Cynthia's pleas are replaced by screams as Zephira carves into her. The skin on her arm curls up like a piece of dried mango, blood pooling off the table and splashing onto the ground, hitting all of our feet. I stand watching with my arms crossed, impatiently waiting for my turn and hoping the blood loss doesn't kill her before I get the chance to.

"Open wide, Mommy." She takes the piece of cut flesh and tries to shove it into her mouth, but Cynthia clamps her mouth shut and turns her head away. Serena steps in, holding her head still as Zephira plugs Cynthia's nose, the two of them working together perfectly without saying a word. As soon as she opens her mouth to greedily suck in oxygen, she shoves her bloody snack down her throat.

"You better eat it all, or I'll cut more while Serena burns you again."

Cynthia slowly starts chewing, blanching at the taste, her cheeks puffing out like she wants to throw up.

"Swallow," Zephira demands, her knife poised and ready to fillet the pathetic excuse for life on my table.

Cynthia listens and swallows, ire in her gaze as she glares at her daughter.

"Now you're a cannibal like me. Granted, I don't partake in it often and I never eat it uncooked; that's just gross." Cynthia goes to say something but Zephira holds up her knife. "Uh, uh, uh, you're not allowed to speak anymore." She looks at me as Cynthia stays quiet, pulling weakly against her restraints. "It's your turn, Big Brother."

Finally. The moment I've been waiting for is finally here. The moment has come to make Cynthia my final lamb. I lick my lips as I grab my choice of weapon, standing up straight as I stride towards the table to have Cynthia meet her maker.

Zephira and Serena step away as I take my place, the knife my father gifted me in my hand. "Do you remember this?" I ask, more rhetorically than not, as Cynthia's eyes flutter, her consciousness starting to fail her. "This is the knife Dad gave me on my tenth birthday. Did he really mean what he said, or did you make him say those words to me?"

"Your father meant every word he said," she stutters, drool pooling in the corner of her mouth as she gives into the darkness threatening to take her.

"Don't lie to me!" I yell, losing my patience.

Her eyes snap open, her breath catching as she gives me a bloody smile. "I made him."

"That's what I thought. And for finally telling me the truth, I'll make this hurt."

This is the last time I will use this knife on anyone. A part of me forever being locked away with it. I don't feel sad or regret, I feel hopeful for what is to come, for the new chapter of our life together. I am one half of the Fatal Floral Killers, and I refuse to be used anymore. I won't be making her proud by killing innocent women.

She will be my last little lamb.

She will be the death of the Morbid Monet.

"Goodbye, Mother." I slam the knife into her heart, her body lifting as her eyes roll to the back of her head and her body becomes lifeless. I dip my brush in the red paint and begin painting her into the monster she has always been.

Finally, it's over. All the stress she has caused, not only me, but Serena is lifted off our shoulders. I feel like we can breathe. We can live our lives without having to watch our backs. We can be comfortable in our home, without the worry of anyone coming on our property uninvited. I can let go of everything. All the questions that ate away at me have released their hold and they will burn right alongside her. She's gone and she can't hurt us anymore.

"Can I drain her?" Zephira steps forwards holding her hand in the air. "I don't want her blood to go to waste."

Me and Serena look at one another, but she shakes her head, mouthing 'you don't want to know', and she is right. I don't want to know how she will use Cynthia's blood.

I step to the side after dropping my brush back in its bucket and hold my arms out. "She's all yours."

Her eyes light up as she runs and grabs three buckets, placing one under each arm and the third under her head. Slicing Cynthia's wrists and her throat, Zephira watches as the blood collects in the buckets below.

I motion with my head for Serena to follow me, wanting to give Zephira her privacy, and we're greeted by the fresh breeze of the oncoming summer air.

"It's finally over." Serena breathes a sigh of relief, wrapping her arms around her waist. *We really do think the same.*

She stands in front of me, and I wrap my arms around her waist, kissing the top of her head as we enjoy the serene night. "It is."

"What will we do now? With no one coming after us, who will we kill?" She looks up at me, her head resting against my shoulder.

I look down at her and say in a playful tone, "Little vixen, do you enjoy killing?"

"I mean, I enjoy killing the bad guys." She blushes as she smiles, looking away.

I slowly spin her around, mindful of her injuries as I lift her chin, desperate to have her look in my eyes. "Then the bad guys we will kill. After all, we are the Fatal Floral Killers."

Her eyes light up, matching the night sky. "Do you mean it?" she braces herself on my chest, "How will we do it? Will we hunt down the true monsters of the world. The ones who hurt children and innocent people. The ones who cause the bad to fester and grow. The ones who deserve to be put down for their crimes. I think we should do that."

She rambles on, talking about all the ways we can catch them and how Zephira can help us track them down. Getting justice for the ones who deserve it.

Capturing her lips in mine, I silence all the ideas I will grant her. I pull away, both of us breathless. "Anything you want, it's yours."

"Right now, I just want my fox." She wraps her arms around my neck, kissing me under the stars.

CRIME SCENE – DO NOT
CRIME SCENE
THE BLACK LOTUS
EXCLUSIVE
EXCLUSIVE
EXCLUSIVE

Regular solitude fosters deeper self-discovery
and personal growth. In these quiet moments
you build resilience, gain new perspectives,
and strengthen your inner self. Embracing
solitude as a tool for nurturing the mind,
body, and soul.

SERENA
SOLITUDE
SOLITUDE

CROSS
CRIME

EPILOGUE
SERENA

1 MONTH LATER

After leaving Cynthia's body with Zephira, she left and we haven't heard from her since. She put on a brave face, but something broke in her that night. With her already so damaged, I worry. I hope she isn't falling into the darkness that almost consumed me. I know it's different, but we both killed our mothers. Her out of hate and mine out of love, but it changes you. I just hope she reaches out soon, if not I will somehow find out where she lives and drag her back into the light. Aster and I both agreed she needed time to process everything. In the moment, filled with rage, it's easy to kill anyone, but that was their mother. Her silence is proof that she's taking it harder than we thought.

Aster won't admit it, but I can tell it affected him. It's in the way he spaces out sometimes, claiming nothing's wrong when I ask. It's the way he disappears for hours at a time. Honestly, I'm beginning to get worried, and if he shuts me down one more time, I know ways to get him to talk. I'm not opposed to using my womanly charm on him. But I have one more thing up my

sleeve, a surprise for him that I hope will break this spell he's been put under.

The sun is sitting high in the sky, the heat a blazing inferno keeping me plastered to the couch. I have my feet draped over Aster, tucked under a blanket despite the AC being on full blast as we watch a new crime documentary on Netflix.

I'm grateful Aster is like me and treats the sun like the plague, avoiding it unless we need to go shopping for anything. The world will see us again once the fall begins, and that is when we will begin hunting. I'm grateful for the break we're getting after everything our bodies have been put through, this time a full recovery is just what the doctor ordered. And by doctor, I mean Aster. He said we needed to lay low and prepare. Reluctantly, after some persuasion on his end, I conceded.

Aster pauses the show and lulls his head toward me. "What were you thinking for lunch?"

I'm about to answer by telling him that I'm not hungry, that we need to leave soon, but my stomach betrays me. Aster chuckles and gets out his phone, scrolling through takeout options. He still has all the cameras up and running, along with the sensors, but since Cynthia is dead, the hit has been called off. Zephira triple checked and split the money into offshore accounts for us before she disappeared. The amount of money that we were given made my eyes bulge, let's just say our future generations are going to be set for life. But we don't want to live like we're part of the one percent. We will still live as we always have just adding a few extra things here and there. Like a new section to our house for an art studio, a room big enough for us both. With the threat gone, Aster has been more relaxed, letting strangers come bring us food, although it isn't often.

"I'm craving Chinese food. How does that sound?" He hands me his phone and I laugh, shaking my head as I scroll. *Chinese it is.* I scroll until I find what I want, adding my items to the order.

Handing him back his phone, he goes over it one more time before adding payment and relaxing back into the couch. "Food will be here in twenty minutes." I nod, getting back into my comfy position with my hands pressed together and my cheek resting on them as Aster presses play.

Not even ten minutes go by when the phones go off and me and Aster share the same look. He takes out his phone and tenses, making me immediately sit up. "What's wrong?" I ask, the hairs on my arms standing up.

"That's not the delivery driver." He zooms in on the video and grabs the knife we keep in the drawer of the coffee table. "Stay here."

"What do you mean 'stay here'? I'm not going to let you die on your own," I whisper harshly. *This man is always putting himself in harm's way.* Even after I told him not to and he agreed that if anyone ever comes after us again, we'd never leave the other alone.

I throw the blanket off myself and grab my knife from the coat rack by the door. Having hidden weapons in multiple places in our home has come in quite handy. He looks at me out of the corner of his eye, giving me a 'I'm going to punish you for not listening' look and I roll my eyes, pointing at the door.

Aster presses the voice button on his phone. "Who is it? What do you want?"

The young and startled man looks around, finally finding the camera, and holds up a box. "I have a package for Aster Graves."

His body tenses as his grip around the knife tightens. "Who is it from?"

The kid reads the label on the box and his eyebrows lift. "S-salem State Prison." Every bone in my body locks up, until I remind myself that Cynthia is dead and not to freak out. I just hope it isn't some kind of last ditch effort to take me out. I could see her doing that, but then again, she was too vain to even think she would lose. I take a deep breath, shaking that thought from my head. *We are safe.*

"Leave it on the porch," Aster demands as he watches the camera and waits for the kid to leave.

The prison. The same one his parents were at. The news has been reporting non-stop about finding the escaped convict, Cynthia Balcom, and the death of her husband, Adam Balcom. Authorities speculate she left the country after killing Jason, but we know the truth. We know where she'll rot for all eternity.

We went back the next night to get Jason's body and dumped it somewhere else for the police to find. It took them a few days, which meant he was barely recognizable, but we didn't care. He was a dirty cop that helped Cynthia escape; he deserved far worse than he got. The service for him only held his family, all of the other officers turned up their noses, wanting nothing to do with him, and I don't blame them.

When the car is off the property and Aster checks every other camera, he snatches the box on the porch and stiltedly walks back to the couch. He places the box on the table, and we just stare at it.

"What do you think it is?" I ask, anxiously tapping my fingers as I wait for Aster to open it.

"I'm not sure," he mumbles, his fingers twitching like he wants to tear into it, but isn't ready to see what's inside. *Should I nudge the box towards him or leave it be?* Like he was reading my mind, Aster slides the box onto his lap and slowly opens the lid.

His brows crease as he lifts a single piece of paper. Unable to stop my curiosity, I lean over to read it over his shoulder.

"What does 'hide and seek' mean? Is it the game?"

Aster places the note back in the box, and without saying a word gets up and leaves the room. *What the fuck?* I pick up the note and examine it for any hidden meaning but find none. It has to be something only he knows that no one else would catch on to or be suspicious of, *but a note by itself from a mass murderer in prison is suspicious regardless.*

Aster bounds back down the stairs holding a little black book and hands it to me with tight lips, his grip loosening as my fingers wrap around it.

"What does hide and seek mean?" I ask, placing the book in my lap.

Aster looks up at the ceiling as if he's reliving the memory. "When I was little and Dad wanted to give me something to keep hidden from Cynthia, he would use the code word hide and seek." He clasps his hands in his laps, looking down at his fingers. "I hid so much stuff in that spot over the years, and honestly, I forgot about it." He points to the notebook. "This was the last item we ever played the game with. He hid it in our spot and when he used the code word again, then I could seek it out to see what it was." A sad laugh slips past his lips as he shakes his head in disbelief. "Even after death, he made sure to get this message to me. Like he knew what Cynthia was planning," he whispers the last part, "I wish I could ask him."

I place my hand over his and give him a sympathetic smile. "Isn't this last gift meant for you? Why give it to me?"

"It's all the victims my parents had. I looked over it upstairs, and… there is something you should see."

Reading through the dates and names, I drop the book when I see someone I had forgotten, the faceless woman in my dream coming to the forefront of my mind as tears fall down my cheeks. Aster wraps me in his arms, cradling the back of my head.

"Tina Raven," I whisper, "she… she was my aunt."

All the questions my parents had with no answers, the very reason we moved to Salem in the first place after she disappeared when I was six.

She was killed by Aster's parents.

She was the reason I have a love for art. She was the person I looked up to most, and her disappearance crushed me. I remember it all; every holiday, every moment spent with her, the pain when my parents stopped bringing her up. Soon after, she was a forgotten memory.

I sniffle and look up at Aster. "She was my dad's sister. They were inseparable, and I... I forgot her."

He places his hand on my cheek, pressing his lips to my forehead. "It's okay; you remember her now. Are you going to tell your dad?"

I nibble my lip. I want to, but if I tell him who killed his sister, he will want to know how I found out and opening that can of worms is something I'd rather not deal with. "No." I shake my head.

"You can if you want. You can tell him I'm the son of the Patchwork Killers and what was sent to me from my dad and what I found. He deserves closure after everything he's been through."

"You're right, but not today." I lean into his chest and close my eyes, enjoying the memory of Aunty Tina. She was a light that was stolen too soon, and now that I remember her, I will never forget.

"Do you think she could be the reason you dreamt about me from a young age?" he asks, rubbing circles on my back.

I look up at him as I place my hand on his chest. "It would be just like her to somehow connect us. Maybe we have her to thank for bringing us together." I quietly laugh, my chest warming at the thought.

"Thank you, Aunt Tina." Aster says, pulling me onto his lap, I wrap my arms around his neck and kiss him as the doorbell rings again, this time for our food.

After we finish our food with the heaviness seeping through the air, I get up and reach my hand out to Aster. "Come on, I have a surprise for us." He cocks an eyebrow, a tent already growing in his jeans, making me laugh, "Not that kind of surprise." He frowns. "Yet."

He grabs my hand, quickly standing. "Where to, my vixen?"

I step in front of him, and drag us out the door, towards my reading room, excitement buzzing in my veins as we quickly walk through the grass. Before I even bring out the surprise I stashed, we are going to have a heart to heart and if he doesn't open up, I'll just have to persuade him to talk. I am tired of this bottling your feelings bullshit. *We don't do that.*

"The surprise is in your reading room?" He looks around the room as we walk in, looking under stuff, on the top shelf he hid my surprise. Finding nothing he starts to pull the three books to open the kill space and I run in front of him, stretching out my arms. "My surprise is in here, then." He tries to push me out of the way, but I cover the books he needs to pull.

"Yes, but you can't have it, not until we talk." His movements stop, looking down at me as I stare back at him. "Please," I whisper.

He lets out a deep breath, but steps away from the bookshelf with his hands raised in the air. "I knew this was coming."

I walk over to the chaise and pat the seat beside me, the butterflies in my stomach flying at full speed. "Does that mean you're ready to talk?"

"Not being given much of a choice," he mumbles as he sits next to me.

I grab his face with both hands, pushing his cheeks together. "You always have a choice. I think it's time though." I release his face and look away. "I don't like this wall that has been built between us, since… everything."

"Okay. Let's talk."

My head snaps up to meet his gentle eyes. "Really? You're serious?"

He cradles my hands in his. "Very. And I'm sorry I built the wall after we promised to never shut the other out. I just… needed time to process before I put this weight on you too."

"Your problems are my problems, Aster. Your burdens are mine. You are never alone, and I need you to get that in your thick skull." I tap his head a few times to get my point across. He flinches, rubbing the spot on his head, but smiles. "I love you. Don't shut me out."

"I love you, too." His lips lightly brush mine. "I was

mourning my dad, but never felt that emotion before, so... I shut down." I sit back and listen as he talks, not wanting to break his courage. "There have been so many new emotions that I have been experiencing, and I don't know how to cope with most of them." He rakes his fingers through his hair. "For so long I painted my father as the villain, when he was trying to be a dark knight and save me from Cynthia." A sad laugh slips past his lips as he frowns. "After learning the truth, all I wanted was to see my father's face. Talk to him one last time. Ask him so many questions to help me see things from his perspective, but... Now, I'll never get the chance." I grab his hand and squeeze it, he brings our joined hands to his lips and kisses the back of mine. "I miss him, and I'm jealous that Zephira got to speak to him and connect with him in a way I dreamed of for so long."

He goes silent after that, his head dropping. I pull him into my chest, cradling his head as I rub his back. "We all deal with grief differently, some shut down, some act like it never happened, while others block it out completely." He looks up at me, so much love filled in his gaze. "Most are alone. Feel like no one can understand the emotions swirling inside, but that isn't true. When a hand reaches out to help you instead of shutting down, grab on and let them help keep you afloat." I cup his cheek. "Yes, no one can ever truly understand, but letting that person in a little can make a difference between sinking into the darkness and floating above it." I wrap my arms around his neck, our mouths inches apart. "You are not alone, Aster. Let me be your liferaft, like you are mine. If you don't, you go down, and I'm going down with you."

Our foreheads rest against the others, his eyes closing as he whispers, "Thank you, Serena."

This is what we needed. We needed a moment to come back down from all the chaos that interrupted our lives. Lives we barely got to build together. Now that the waters are calm, we can *finally* have a chance to get to be together. Finally have a chance to connect in the way we were denied.

I slowly get off the chaise after pecking Aster on the lips, ready to give him his surprise.

"Is it time for my surprise?" he asks, scooting to the edge of the chaise.

"It is. I'll be right back, close your eyes. And no peeking."

He closes his eyes and I open my kill space retrieving the items and walk back into the library, laying it all at his feet. My hands shake as I lay the final item in the middle. I take a deep breath, sitting on my knees. "Okay. Open your eyes."

His eyes slowly flutter open, looking at me then the items, a wicked grin splitting his cheeks. "Is this for me or for you?"

I blush. "Both?"

He tackles me, my back smacking against the floor as his hand cups the back of my head. "When did you find that?" He hovers over me, his arms brace on either side of me.

"When you were kidnapped. I was looking through your things and found it. Ever since I saw the drawing, I knew I wanted your art tattooed on me."

He leans down, his lips pressing firmly against mine, his growing erection rubbing up against me. "Like last time?" he whispers in my ear.

My beast purrs at the thought, and I let out a breathy moan. "Yes."

He helps me to my feet, collecting everything off the floor as we walk into my kill space. The air feels lighter, the weight that was dragging us down has been tossed, and we are ready for the next step of life.

Starting it with a needle, ink, and spilling blood.

EPILOGUE 2
ZEPHIRA

Killing my own mother was harder than I thought it would be. Not the act itself and not even forcing her to eat her own flesh, but everything else. I did what I do after every kill and bathed in my victim's blood. I steal their essence, their soul, and rub it all over my body, soaking in the last piece of them. Usually I relish in the feeling, but something about Mom's blood made me feel gross, and I washed it down the drain the moment I stepped into it. It was a zap of instant rejection, and since then, I've felt numb.

After a month of sulking, I am starting to feel better, and I called my brother to meet up with him and Serena. *I miss them.* I'm not the kind of girl to allow anyone into my life, but being around them so much, teasing them, my walls slowly dropped without even realizing it. I like the feeling of belonging some-where after being lost for so long. I thought I was supposed to be with my Mom and Dad, but it was the biggest lie I refused to see. I want to create my new normal, get to know my brother and Serena better, and now I can finally do that since I'm not helping threaten Serena's life. The one thing I wish I'd never agreed to. I don't regret meeting Serena, but I regret being my mother's little spy for her.

I'm tapping along to the music on my steering wheel as I pull into the diner, some place called Sinister Beans. Aster said it was Serena's favorite and that they have the best coffee, and when I heard that I couldn't say no.

I may flirt with Serena and tease my brother about wanting to bang his girlfriend, but I would never cross that line, nor do I want to. That's how I talk, and I know I can get Aster to lighten up when I do. Plus, it's just fun.

The little bell on the door jingles as I walk in, and Serena excitedly jumps to her feet, her black dress flowing around her as she waves at me.

"Zephira! Over here!"

I place the sunglasses over my head and walk to their table as every eye locks on my movements. I'm used to people staring at me wherever I go, but this is ridiculous. Still, I like the attention, so I keep my head high as I stride to the table. *Have they never seen a hot blonde before?*

Serena squeezes me tightly, and I inhale her scent, returning her hug. *Lavender and chamomile.* The muscles in my shoulders start to relax. *A scent I can get used to.*

"Didn't know you were a hugger," I laugh, turning to Aster. "Brother." He surprises me with a hug as well and I lean into it. *Sandalwood and mint.* Another smell I can get used to. I take a seat across from them and pick up a menu, feeling their eyes pinned to me. "What?" I ask, looking over the coffee choices. *Hannibal sounds good.* I chuckle at the irony.

Serena's soft voice breaks my concentration. "Are you okay?"

I shrug, not wanting to get into my feelings, nor never having that question asked to me. I rather keep them locked up tight and take it out on my victims. "I'll be okay."

They both eye me skeptically, but before Serena can question it, a voluptuous waitress walks up to our table and instantly gains my attention. She's wearing short, cut up jean shorts, a tight, little, black shirt with the shop's logo on it, and her red hair swings back and forth in a high ponytail.

Reminding me of the red hair I crave to run my fingers through again.

When our eyes lock, I give her a flirty smile and run my fingers along her arm when I tell her my order. She blushes and gets Aster and Serena's, her eyes glancing at me the entire time. When she walks away, I cock my head watching her ass sway side to side. *Damn.*

"You should get her number," Serena says with a playful smirk on her face.

I reach my hand towards her, getting ready to flirt, but Aster ruins my fun with one word. "Don't."

I pull back, crossing my arms. "You're no fun."

"He's just territorial," Serena says, kissing him on the cheek.

My nose curls as jealousy rages through me. *They're disgustingly cute. You would never know they kill people in their free time. Speaking of...* "So, what will you two do now?"

Serena tucks a strand of hair behind her ear and nibbles her lip. "We wanted to ask you something, and you can totally say no."

"Ask away." I lean back in my chair, my curiosity peaked.

"We still want to do our thing, but," she drops her voice to a whisper, "only the bad ones, and we want you to join us. Not in the act itself, unless you want to, but in the computer stuff. Tracking down their actual identity."

I sit back in my seat, letting the question sit in the air. I definitely want to, but watching Serena move her little butt in her seat as she nervously waits for my answer makes me want to watch her squirm more.

The waitress returns with our orders, interrupting my fun, and I take a sip of the best coffee I've ever had before answering. "Yes. I would love to be a part of the team." I lean forward, obviously checking Serena out. *She does look amazing.* "Does that mean-"

"Don't even ask what you're about to ask or that coffee won't go in your stomach," Aster warns as he takes a sip of his drink.

"I don't mind the smell of coffee." I wink at Serena, and she just shakes her head. *Guess my womanly charm wore off; that's too bad.* "Fine. I'll behave. For now."

Aster rolls his eyes and starts eating as Serena surprises me with her next question, "I know you're interested in the waitress, but do you want to find anyone?"

I spin the straw in my cup, looking back at the cute redhead who can't seem to take her eyes off me. "No. They're only good for sexual reasons."

"You don't think you've found anyone you could see yourself being with?" she asks, taking a bite of her eggs.

I place my hand on my cheek as I look out the window, picturing the smiling faces of the two I long for. I think about them every day, and I fear I'll never see them again. The boy and girl I grew up with in foster care. My only comfort in that wretched place. My teeth grit. *People I can't seem to find no matter what programs I use.*

I look down at my plate, moving food around with the fork, having lost my appetite. "I was in love with two people, a guy and a girl; we were all supposed to escape from the foster care we were in." I swallow back the tears threatening to spill over at the memory. *Don't cry, Zephira. They wouldn't want that.* "They got out. I got caught. I told them to run, so they did. I haven't seen them since, despite trying to find them."

Serena's hand covers mine in the comforting way she knows that grounds me and I smile at her before I move away shaking my head. One day I will see them again. I feel it in my bones.

"Maybe *they'll* find you," she says.

"Yeah. Maybe."

The waitress returns with the check and Aster takes care of it, the two of us stepping outside while Serena chats with the owner.

"Are you really okay?" Aster asks, blocking the sun from my view.

"I already told you I will be."

"Zephira." He gives me a 'don't bullshit me' kind of look. "I have a lot of brotherly duties to catch up on and I may not be the best at consoling, but I was there with you. I helped take care of her, too."

"Then I should be asking if you're okay."

"She was dead to me long before I killed her."

I nod. He got to grow up being manipulated by her every day, whereas I grew up not knowing where I came from. *But I'm glad I found out.* I watch Aster stick a piece of gum in his mouth, pocketing the wrapper. I can tell he wants a smoke, and I'm tempted to give him one, but I know Serena would kill us both, so I keep my pack in my purse.

I glance into the street, my breath catching as I see a wave of red hair and mussed mop of brown. My feet move before I can stop myself, chasing after the two people as if my life depended on it. *It can't be. Could it?* I hear Aster shouting my name, but I ignore it as I grab the couple walking, both of them turning at the same time.

I can't believe it. My hands cover my mouth as the tears I fought back for years finally fall. "Calliope. Ryland." I whisper, scared they're just a figment of my imagination.

"Hey Zee," they say at the same time, watching as I crumple to my knees.

They're here.

They're alive.

They're alive.

The End...

ACKNOWLEDGMENTS

First and foremost, I need to thank my husband, Nick. From the first book to this one he has been in my corner cheering me on. He isn't much of a reader, so he reads a chapter at a time or I read to him, but it means everything to me that he wants to hear my words in some way. Without his constant support and always pursuing me to go after my dreams, no matter what they are; either book would not be possible. Thank you for always taking over parenting duties no matter how tired you were when you got home so I could write or edit. Going to Every signing to help set up, take pictures, and just being there with me, means more than you'll ever know. To the love of my life and light in my eyes, thank you.

Casey, my amazing editor. I can't believe we finished two books! This is crazy. I seriously would have never made either book as amazing as they are without you. You always help me think outside the box, always push me to give you and my readers more. Our brainstorming sessions where our ideas play off the others and grow are my favorite. You helped me come full circle in Black Lotus, you are the absolute best at naming some of my serial killers. You know the ones. I am so unbelievably grateful to have you not only as an editor, but a friend. I don't want to work with anyone else except you, you are the best always treating my book babies like your own. I will forever send everyone who asks for an editor your way because they all deserve the best. Thank you Casey.

Mallory, my phenomenal PA, I don't know how I survived without you for so long. I am so grateful Amber introduced us and I took the chance on even getting a PA. Not only did I gain someone so amazing at what she does, but I gained a lifelong friend. I love you so much and now you are stuck with me for life. You have made my life so much easier, taking care of all the graphics, making the best stickers and bookmark design for this book, handling all the forms, and also being an alpha reader on top of it all. You have given me the time I needed to complete this book in the timeline I gave myself and helped tremendously in taking the weight of marketing off of my shoulders, because let's be honest marketing is hard. I want to thank you for making the signing events a breeze too, while I was dying in the bathroom you and Nick both set up the booth and made sure I was okay. I can't wait for all the fun we will get into in the future and to make more memories with you.

My Alpha readers, Alyssa, Brianna, Megan, Rebecca, and Naomi you all have helped tremendously in this book. You helped me fill in the spots that were lacking in some, telling me where you wanted more and getting me out of my head. Catching the grammar errors and everything else, to get it ready for my betas. I especially want to thank Becca and Bri. I was struggling with Serena's epilogue, hating the way the first one ended, hated how I ended the second and you could see it in my writing. I voiced to you both that I wanted them to have their moment to be together after all the chaos, and told you how I wasn't loving the ending. You both were honest with me that the first two endings were not good, but helped steer me to where we ended. That you both were hoping it would end where it began and the surprise could be what it is now. So thank you for helping me give my characters, my babies the ending they both deserve. It's perfect.

My Beta readers, Alex, Ashley, Brenna, Carlee, Katie, Rebecca, and Natasha, y'all have been truly amazing. You have caught all the last minute errors, helped fix some sentences that were incomplete in a way, and felt lacking. You have all given me so many loving words of encouragement and some of y'alls comments crack me up, so keep them coming. Thank you, truly for wanting to be a part of this journey with me.

My amazing cover designer and formatter. You have done it again, created a beautiful cover that not only tells a story, but is beautiful. Readers want to give my book a chance because of what you have created. I love the way your brain works and thinks out of the box. Thank you for working with me again and being patient with me until we got everything perfect. Without you the cover and the inside would have been utter shit, because creating masterpieces like that is not in my wheelhouse. Until you decide to stop making covers and formatting, I will be coming to you for every book I write, because I know you can bring it to life in a way no one else can.

Finally, to you the readers, none of this would be possible without you. Thank you from the bottom of my heart for loving my twisted little world and characters. They have been living in my head for so long and putting my work out into the world for you to read, has been everything. It still amazes me that you all love my work. Whenever you write reviews, give reaction videos, make little graphics it makes my little heart explode with happiness from each one.

ABOUT THE AUTHOR

Katelynn is a stay at home mom, who spends her day playing with her son and five dogs. When she isn't working on her next book, she spends her time reading all things smut, watching tv with her family, and making the best memories. She has a small business making satin ribbon roses as well, and loves making them for customers. She loves all things spooky, especially Pennywise. She loves Disney, anime, and Elvis. She is an Aquarius, who was born and raised in sunny California, but has made a life with her family in North Carolina. She has always dreamed of being an author, but her passion died off long ago, but was reignited through trauma; and in the darkness beauty was created.